CORAL A. WARD

A SLICE OF *You*

A Slice of You

1

One Too Many - Part One

I slotted the final pizza board into the rack of Mon Amour's sardine-sized kitchen, then let out a sigh. You'd think Mon Amour would be a French restaurant, considering the name, but no. It was, in fact, a Moroccan one. Daniel, the owner, was adamant the name would attract a high turnover, and he wasn't wrong. Tonight's shift was a prime example of how we were run off our feet. But I think the reason for busyness was more to do with the food than the name.

'Naomi, you ready, chicka?' Deb asked me. 'Come on. Everyone is waiting for you.'

'Sure am.' I grinned over my shoulder and caught sight of her sleek auburn hair, all fresh from yesterday's hairdressing appointment. Sandy at Colour n Cuts foiled my thick hair blonder, and Deb got a recoat of auburn and a trim.

Deb's ebony eyes observed my stripey apron. 'Naomi, have you seen your apron?' She let out a chuckle.

I looked down at the flour-covered cotton, shook my head, and laughed. I'd been too busy to notice the state my clothing was in.

'You look like you've been rolling in flour.' Her mischievous eyes glinted.

'I kind of have.' I shook off the flour into the bin behind my workstation and noticed some landed on the floor. So I quickly crouched and was about to grab the dustpan and brush to hide any traces of mess, but two black, shiny shoes appeared in front of me. My heart began to race, and I took a deep swallow as I lifted my head to see Daniel standing there with crossed arms. His wide hazel eyes glared into mine – making my stomach curdle. He was dressed in his usual all-black ensemble consisting of a shirt tucked into his fitted pants and a thick belt. *Geez, how tight does he want his shirt? He must love the nipples-on-display look, and why are his nipples so hard all the time? Bizarre.*

'What's this mess on the floor, Naomi?' he asked in that condescending tone of his.

'Oh, I-I was just shaking my apron into the bin. I'm sorry.'

'Well, you have *clearly* failed that task.' He eyed the small sprinkle of flour on the freshly mopped floor.

'I'm sorry, Daniel. I was about to—'

'I didn't realise it was such a hard task to clean flour off the floor. Isn't cleaning supposed to be the *one* task women excel at?' His slicked-back grey hair caught the fluorescent light.

I looked at Deb for moral support, but she was staring at her iPhone screen and tapping away on it.

My face went red-hot and my cheeks burned as I dug my toes into my boots. I couldn't help but think about all the times he'd lazed around on his shifts, getting waitresses to clean up the coffee-bean granules that he regularly spilt. On quieter days, he would scrutinise their cleaning skills with a keen eye, using his forensic vision to detect any traces of mess. If they missed a spot, he wouldn't let it go until the floor was spotless, making sure they heard about it until every corner was clean. I pushed down my thoughts, and instead of expressing my disgust at his conniving behaviour, I apologised to him once more. *He's your boss, Naomi. He's always right ... Don't argue back ... Best to smile and play along. Bastard.*

He grabbed the dustpan and brush and dropped them on the floor for me to fetch.

'Clean it. I will not have my restaurant in this state.'

I nodded and swept the flour into the bin, then checked it over so many times I lost count. My hands and knees remained on the floor until I was positive the floor was spotless.

After Deb and I had clocked our hours on our timesheets, we left the restaurant through the back door and followed the narrow pathway to the car park. It was instinctual to head straight to my Mazda hatchback, but the only car in sight was Daniel's brand-new Mercedes Benz. Mine was at home in the garage.

'Daniel's Mercedes would've cost a fortune,' Deb said as she eyed his four-wheel drive. 'Dad was looking at buying one of those, but he said there was no way in hell he'd pay over one hundred grand for a car.'

I let out a laugh and looked around to see if Daniel was anywhere to be seen. The last thing I wanted was to be caught talking about his car in the car park. To my relief, he wasn't. We continued walking and took a left turn as we made our way along Gympie Terrace AKA Noosa River. It was a long street that went for nearly two kilometres and boasted expansive river views and eateries galore. Our destination was only four restaurants down from Mon Amour.

'I'm so glad you said yes to drinking tonight, chick. Honestly, everyone was super shocked when I told them you'd come for drinks,' Deb said as she turned her head to me. We were walking side by side as our hands swung back and forth.

My response was delayed while I watched a group of women dressed in flamboyant, flowy frocks strut across the path towards a restaurant. The pitch of their giggles and pace of their quipping suggested that many beverages had already been drunk.

Charged with a sudden spike of enthusiasm and a desire to feel as giggly as those women, I replied, 'About time I put my cooking books down and joined you all for a drink.' I laughed, suddenly unsure if I was making the right decision or if I was in the wrong mindset and should've stayed home reading or watching another Netflix movie.

'I can't even remember the last time you had a drink. How long has it been?' Deb glanced at me, then back at the pathway ahead illuminated by the streetlamp.

'Not since...' My throat tightened, and my eyes welled up. I cleared my throat, pushing the memory aside. 'Not for a while. I think seven months ago.'

'Well, I'm just glad you've *finally* given in.' She ran her hand up and down my back, giving it a warm rub. Her auburn hair blew in the September night's breeze.

'My God, my feet are sore. Well, especially the left one,' I said as an ache tore through the arch of my foot. 'Do your feet ache?' I halted for a moment and attempted to stretch out my foot as best as I could, but it didn't help much. My only chance of relief was to take my boot off in the middle of the footpath (and I'd more than likely fall into a bush during the process because I was so tired and hadn't sat down for hours).

'All the bloody time. But that's what you get when you do a ten-hour shift and are on your feet all day.' She kept walking and didn't look back.

'Tell me about it.' I continued walking and tried the 'mind over matter' method as I focused on the footpath ahead.

When we arrived at the trendy restaurant, we were greeted by the smell of herbed fries and aioli – the common after-nine-o'clock snack – and upbeat jazz music playing through the speakers. Deb walked over to the high table in the left corner of the room where everyone was chatting and pulled out a stool next to Victor, the underweight, near-thirty French waiter from work. The screech of the stool legs dragging across the floor brought Victor's conversation to a halt. Deb took a seat while I scoped out the layout for a spare spot for myself.

'How's my favourite French boy doing?' Deb kissed him on the cheek as the light bathed the hollows of his collarbones.

'*Bonsoir*, Deb. Have you ordered a wine yet?' He turned his pasty face to her with raised eyebrows and flashed his chip-toothed smile, which quickly turned into a frown as he looked at his empty glass. 'As you see, mine is empty.'

'No, Vic, I haven't, but I'll be sure to shout my favourite French boy a wine.' She beamed. 'A sauv blanc?'

He nodded. '*Oui.*'

'Time for a beverage, then.' She winked as she hopped off her stool and walked over to the bar, too eager to get her drinks to bother waiting for table service.

I sat on the stool on the end next to Deb's and said hello to Kelly, the female sous chef from Mon Amour, who was opposite me and one seat down, leaving an empty chair in front of mine.

'Hey, chicken,' Kelly, said giving me her usual masculine nod. Every time I looked at her, I got distracted by the Madonna piercing above her naturally pigmented red lips. You couldn't miss her – without a doubt, she stood out in any room. Well, her blue hair and orange foundation did, anyway. She was lucky she didn't have green hair or she'd pass as an Oompa Loompa for sure.

'Hello, Pi— I mean, Naomi,' Martin, who was beside her, interjected with a sly grin.

He was a lanky, flat-haired man in his late twenties who happened to be the other sous chef of our kitchen.

'Hello to you again, Martin.' I nodded, glad he stopped himself from saying what he was about to.

Kelly and Martin had finished off a bottle of sauvignon blanc already, and they returned to their previous conversation about meat cuts.

I rested my chin on my palm and half-listened as the conversation murmured. My eyes watered and a yawn stretched across my face as I tried to ignore the aches and cramps tearing through both of my feet. *Oh goodie. What's better than one ache? Two aches!*

Deb returned with two glasses of wine. She perched herself back on the seat beside me and slid one glass to Victor.

Minutes later, Kelly waved the waiter to the table so she could get another bottle, and I ordered a vodka and lemonade. Deb took advantage of the waiter being there and upgraded her glass of wine to two bottles of pinot grigio.

The drinks came out, quicker than expected, and just as I was about to check my iPhone for any messages, I caught a whiff of a familiar scent: a woodsy, musky cologne. Sebastian, the man I was about to text, pulled out the stool directly in front of me, his denim jacket slung over his shoulder, half-grinning as he got comfortable.

Sebastian's curly hair was gelled back, and his eyes looked lighter than the usual russet brown. He was my definition of sun-bronzed skin and pearl-white teeth.

Deb nudged me as she caught sight of Sebastian, flashing me a sassy smile while raising her eyebrows. She turned back to Victor, and her sleek auburn hair bounced as she laughed at her own jokes.

Sebastian greeted me with a cheeky grin. 'Well, hello, gorgeous,' he said with his eyes fixed on my face.

I gave him a pained smile and tried to ignore my aching feet. 'Hey, Seb. I was just about to text you.'

'Well, lucky I'm here now.' His eager eyes gleamed under the warm glow of the lights above. 'Have you been missing me, you cute little twenty-five-year-old?'

'Maybe.' My cheeks bloomed red. 'And hey, twenty-five isn't little.' I shot up a playful but defensive brow.

He chuckled. 'Fuck, you're cute. And, fuck, I love what you've done to your hair.' His gaze lingered on my fresh blonde hair styled in a low bun.

I laughed and looked around the room at the other diners, who were snacking on calamari, cheese platters, and pizza. The drink of the night seemed to be either a Cosmopolitan cocktail or a glass of wine.

'You're not bad yourself, Seb.' I winked and swallowed a mouthful of vodka lemonade.

'You weren't that blonde two weeks ago, I swear. Has my little snow angel been in the sun?'

I shook my head. 'Nope, all artificial, sadly, and as you can see, I'm still as white as milk.' *Okay, wow, these boots seriously need to come off.*

'So that's what you get up to on your days off when I'm not around, eh? Pamper days at the salon?' He raised one of his perfectly arched brows.

'Tuesdays, I tend to indulge, and you can't say I'm the only one who goes to the salon. Surely you get your eyebrows done somewhere?' I stared at his brows, holding back a playful laugh.

He held his arms up in surrender. 'You caught me. Nah, funny story. Billy's mum does them for me.' Smiling, he stroked two fingers across his brows as if to pull any stray hairs into place. 'Cute, hey?'

'That's nice of her. They're very well done. Actually, Deb was hoping Billy was on tonight so we could get a ride home with him, considering I didn't drive.'

'Yeah, he is Ubering. I'll give him a call later to pick us up.' He nodded his head as if to say 'no big deal'.

I nodded back, then turned to Deb and tapped on her shoulder, interrupting her 'hilarious' story about spilling wine on a customer during service. She seemed to get extra loud and showy when she was down a few wines, which meant she was probably on her second, or maybe third, depending on if she was sculling them or not.

'Where's the bathroom?' I asked.

'Back of the restaurant, then turn right,' she replied and turned away.

The second I stood up, I regretted it. *Far out.* My feet were painfully sore. *If this wasn't a restaurant, I'd go barefoot.* Half-limping, I passed the crowded tables, heading towards the back of the building. I turned right and pushed open the door with the ladies' restroom sign.

Inside were three cubicles. The two on the left were occupied, so I went into the vacant one. I usually inspected toilets before deciding, but this one would have to do as I couldn't walk any further. My feet throbbed in pain with each step. I stepped into the confined space, locked the door, sat down, and felt instant relief as I took the weight off my feet.

After I finished, I washed and dried my hands, then painfully made my way back over to the table. Seb was gone. I looked around the room and couldn't see him anywhere. *I wonder where he is?* My sore feet won the battle, so I surrendered my boots to the floor and stood in my mismatched socks – one blue and the other purple.

'Naomi,' a familiar voice called from behind me.

I turned around to find Seb holding an overflowing glass of beer. His grin was complacent as he raised his eyebrows and cleared his throat before pointing to the back of my pants. *Oh no.*

I held my breath as I brushed my hand against my bottom and felt a piece of toilet paper hanging down my pants. Blood rushed to my face as my throat began to burn. I yanked the toilet paper off and sprinted shoeless across the wooden floorboards back to the bathroom, flushed it, and then sat down for a moment to catch my breath as my face burned with humiliation. A minute passed before I could open the cubicle door and face my reflection in the mirror.

Now, do I go home overcome with embarrassment or get drunk and forget about it all? After some quick musing, I decided to stay. After all, one more drink can't hurt, right?

I walked back to the table, sat on my stool, and avoided eye contact with Seb. How many people saw the toilet paper dangling from my pants? That, I'd never know, but just the thought made my skin burn some more.

I took a moment to recompose myself before facing Seb. *What does he think of me now? Will he pay me out?* I'd seen the way he carried on with his best friend, Billy, whenever one of them made a kook of themselves. Their banter resembled a ping-pong match with constant back-and-forth quips. *I can't believe the one night I go out with all my work friends, and in a restaurant of all places, this happens. If I were an emoji, I'd be the girl who facepalms her forehead right now.*

'I've seen worse, gorgeous. Don't stress,' Seb said in his carefree tone.

As soon as he said those words, I felt a bit better. No payouts for me. *Phew.*

I cleared my throat. 'I'm just glad the whole restaurant didn't laugh at me.'

'Don't sweat it,' he said, obviously still trying to put me at ease. 'I doubt anyone else saw it but me.'

I laughed it off, but inside, I knew I'd be internally embarrassed for life.

Seb looked at my tall glass. 'Your drink is empty. Do you want another one?' His eyes widened as he waited for my response.

I took a moment to think about whether I truly wanted another drink, as images of my dad drinking shiraz entered my mind. My pulse quickened and my fingers gripped the edge of the table as I envisioned Dad's glass being filled to the brim with ruby liquid. His pupils enlarged from each sip, and the more drinks that went down his hatch, the more he raised his voice and fought with Mum. Suddenly it felt like I was swallowing gravel each time I took a sip as the thoughts of him and what happened raced through my mind. My eyes began to well, and I tried with all my might to hold back the tears as my shattered heart couldn't face the pain.

After a few shaky breaths, I redirected my thoughts towards enjoying the evening with my colleagues. It took effort, but I managed to steady my emotions and dismiss the image of the real reason I had abstained from drinking for seven months ...

'Mmm, okay, just one more drink.' I held up my index finger.

Seb hailed over the waiter and ordered one beer and another vodka lemonade.

'So, what's been happening in the two weeks I've been gone, gorgeous?' he asked as he peered down into his wallet brimming with one-hundred-dollar notes. Straight away, I knew where that money came from: pokies. That's where he would've been before he arrived here.

'It's September school holidays, so I've been working a lot.' Reminding myself of my long day made a yawn escape from my lips as my eyes watered.

'That's a change. Weren't you only getting three shifts a week a few weeks back?' He placed his wallet back into his pocket.

All the moisture in my mouth evaporated, and my hands began to sweat. I tried to swallow but couldn't. The waiter appeared at the most convenient of times and placed our drinks down on the table. I grabbed my drink, placed my lips on the straw, and took a huge swig until it was half-empty.

'Naomi, are you thirsty tonight or what?' Seb's eyes were alight with surprise.

'Apparently.' I shrugged and put on another smile as I tried my best not to think of anything that would ruin my night.

'In the whole three months we've been hanging out, this is the first time I've ever seen you touch alcohol ... You must be really stressed about your job, I guess?'

I gave a laugh that came out more like a squeak and diverted my gaze outside the window, hoping he would change the subject so I didn't have to think about Daniel and the lean times that were bound to reoccur.

Deb butted into the conversation and slung her arm around my neck. 'What's going on here, aye?' She waggled her eyebrows. 'Everyone is leaving like weaklings. You two kids keen to keep drinking up like champs?'

'Alright, I'll have one more.' I looked at Seb's impressed face. 'What about you?'

'For sure.' He held his drink against mine, and our glasses clinked.

Deb grinned. 'Hell, yes. Great choice, Naomi.' She raised her free palm, and I gave her a high-five. 'I'll walk everyone out, then we'll get this party started.'

Oh my, was I seriously going to drink more? How will I work tomorrow? With the hangover from hell, I'm sure.

2

One Too Many – Part Two

As the night went on, the drinks kept flowing, and Seb didn't shy away from saying what he was thinking.

'So, are you going to let me stay tonight, or should I count on Billy to drop me home?' he asked with that intense gaze – it was his way of 'peacocking'.

'Sure. You can crash on the couch if Deb doesn't beat you to it.' I flashed a cheeky smile.

God, he's cute, I mused as I studied his physique. His strong build resembled that of a football player – broad shoulders, a well-defined chest, muscular arms, and narrow hips. Despite his arrogance, there was an undeniable allure to his face and physique that drew me in.

'Is that right?' He lifted his manicured brows. 'So even though we've cuddled heaps of times in your bed, you *still* won't let me sleep in there?' His voice was heavy with frustration.

'Oh relax. I'm just kidding,' I said, swatting his hand and laughing.

'You're one challenging woman, you know that?' He leaned over the table, and I caught a whiff of his beer breath as he whispered, 'Will you ever let me taste you?'

Seb reached his hand under the table and placed his warm palm on my thigh.

My eyes widened at his words, and my immediate reaction was to push his hand off, but I decided to place my hand on his and pat it like you would in an awkward hug situation.

I swallowed hard before answering. 'Seb, I'm not ready for anything sexual just yet.'

He moved his arm from my leg and folded both of his hands across the table. 'Sorry, Naomi. That was wrong of me. Your blonde hair just turns me on.'

My face flushed crimson, and I glanced around to see if anyone had overheard, but there were only a few patrons left in the restaurant. Deb stood outside, deeply engrossed in conversation with Victor and taking intermittent puffs from her cigarette.

'Yeah, I like it too.' I smoothed my hair down and smiled, hoping for a change in subject.

'I wish I didn't have to work away for two weeks. The mines pay bloody great money, but not seeing you for that long ... It's tough, Naomi, and I know how hard it's been for you with your new job.' He looked deep into my eyes with a vulnerable look on his face.

I wanted to cry at the continual mention of my work situation, but I fought off the sensation and instead decided I'd definitely be having a third drink.

'Yes, it was tough losing my previous job, but they closed, and there was nothing I could do about it.'

The effects of the vodka were in full swing, and avoiding talking about work was a losing battle as the stark reality of my job situation sunk in.

'Do you know what's even tougher? Never being a full-time employee. Every job I've had, it's been as a casual. I put so much effort into the kitchen, like you would not believe. I've read countless books, and everything I know, I owe to my dad – he taught me all the fundamentals. But do you know what hurts the most? People always branding me as just a "cook" and treating me as if I'm less simply because I'm not a "qualified chef".'

I shook my head at the thought, feeling the insides of my stomach burn. Employers always seemed fixated on labels when it came to me securing a job.

Those labels were like an instant golden ticket to earn respect, propelling you above the others in the mountain of resumes. Skill only seemed to matter if it was backed by a certificate.

Seb's eyes lit up with surprise. 'Babe, you really need another drink. It will help relax you.'

I gave a half-smile. 'Mmm, maybe I do.'

Seb waved over the waiter, and 'one more drink' turned into three, and, *oh God*, that is where it ended – my spinning head and churning stomach couldn't take anymore.

Pretty soon after the final round of drinks, Seb, Deb, and I piled into the Jeep of our Uber driver, Billy. Throughout the entire drive home, I kept my head out the window, letting the breeze rush against my face, its violent hiss echoing through my ears. My sandpaper-like throat scolded me for not sticking to soda water.

'Naomi, are you okay?' Deb asked, doing her signature move by pinching my left cheek with her thumb and pointer finger.

'I'm okay. Feel tipsy and need water.' I pictured the fizz of soda water as a lime wedge splashed into the glass.

'Boringgggg,' Deb said. 'It's so fun when you drink. Let's get rowdy, chick.'

I didn't respond. The thought of the heat in the kitchen and my freshly brewed hangover was enough to make me chuck—

Aaaaand there it was, right down the side of the car.

'Billy! Pull over. Naomi is sick,' Deb called out.

'Jesus-fuck! You couldn't hold it in?' Billy asked.

Unable to speak, I grimaced and watched as he indicated left to pull over into the row of empty car spaces along the Noosa River. Dim light drifted from the shop windows. We were stationed across from the newsagency and a flamboyant women's boutique.

Billy hopped out of the car and then inspected the side of my door for damage. He was wearing a white Hawaiian-style shirt with sleeves folded just above his elbow. A tattoo of a palm tree was inked down his left forearm. He fit the category of a 1970s surfer boy perfectly.

'Oh, it's just a tiny bit of liquid. All good.' He smiled at me. 'Last time a friend did this to my car, it was chunks. Not pretty, that's for sure, and definitely not fun to clean up.'

'I'm so sorry. This vodka is having a bad effect on me. I'm not even that drunk.'

'All good, Non. It's legit just a splash.' His reassuring eyes matched his tone.

'Non?' I squinted at him in confusion.

'Yeah, Noni.'

'My dad used to call me that.' I took a deep breath and squeezed my thighs with my hands to steady my emotions.

Billy swallowed hard and looked down at the road. 'It's a good nickname.' He nodded.

'It is,' I agreed.

Billy reached into his pocket and pinched a Winnie blue between his lips. He lit it and sucked in a long drag. Deb smelt the smoke and gave me a gentle push out of the Jeep.

'Shove, love.'

Deb slipped out, and her enormous boobs jiggled as she landed on her feet. She had trouble hiding them. No matter what she wore, they would always come out to say 'hello'. It didn't help that she was wearing a low-cut, black T-shirt. Her shirt was paired with her usual black capri pants and ballet flats. She held her weight liable for her enormous boobs. Still, I begged to differ, considering I'd seen curvaceous women with mosquito bites.

She untwisted the clasp on her purse, pulled out a ciggie, and lit it with her sparkly midnight-blue zippo lighter. It was satisfying watching her put the flame out with the cap. I saw her give Billy the eye as she stood a few inches away from him. He remained casual and focused on sucking down his cigarette while she cried in laughter as she told him about the time she drunk-drove and hit a pole in her first car.

Seb stayed seated, his phone illuminating his face as he scrolled through Facebook. He seemed unfazed about my accident.

'Non, you do realise there is cold water in the boot?' Billy stubbed his cigarette out with one of his black Vans.

I let out an awkward laugh and hopped out, suddenly feeling very dizzy. 'I hadn't even thought to ask.' The road swayed for a moment as Billy popped open the boot and passed me water from the esky.

Seb helped himself to a mint in the side compartment of his door, and Deb slid back into the car.

Billy shut the boot and walked back to his seat. 'Noni, if you feel like you're going to be sick, just yell out, and I'll pull over.'

'Okay, thanks,' I said and hopped in.

I took a much-needed gulp of water and kept drinking until there was just a splash at the bottom of the bottle; the plastic crunched in my hand, and I felt the dizziness slowly start to dissipate. Deb was playing DJ with Billy's phone, which he had attached to an aux cord. Indie music, of course.

The drive home was bearable. Well, just. My stomach and head settled during the six-minute trip. Thank God for water.

Billy pulled into our driveway.

There was an awkward pause.

'I feel like I should pay after spewing down the side of the car?' I asked Deb and Seb.

'No, I'll cover it,' Seb replied. 'Special rates for your best mate. Isn't that right, Billy boy?'

Billy looked over his shoulder with a grin. 'Haha. Just shout me a beer or two tomorrow, and we're even.'

'Deal.' They shook hands to seal the agreement.

The headlights shone on the grey-panelled garage door, and I couldn't have been more relieved to be back at our modern suburban home. I was more than done with embarrassing myself for the night.

'Thanks for the lift, Billy,' I said. 'I appreciate it.' I gave him a smile and patted him on the shoulder.

'No worries, Noni. Any friend of Seb's is a friend of mine.' He winked.

I listened as Seb and Deb both thanked Billy.

'You coming in for a beverage, hon?' Deb asked as she raised her eyebrows at him.

'Nah, I'll pass, lovey, but next time, hey.' Billy ran his hand through his sun-bleached hair, then tapped it against his thigh to the soft music humming from his car speakers.

Once we farewelled Billy, I pushed aside my damp, stripey apron in my handbag and rummaged through it for the keys as we walked up the sleek, grey driveway to the main entrance. The sensor lights came on, revealing the snow-white exterior of the house and grey gable roof. As soon as we were inside, Deb jumped straight onto the red leather couch in the lounge room and kicked off her flats. I flicked on the lights and bent down to pull off my boots.

'Seb, hang out with Deb for a moment. I need a shower,' I said and quivered at the thought of what I must smell like.

'Don't leave me hanging too long, baby.' He took a seat on the zebra-patterned armchair opposite Deb.

I grabbed a bottle of water from the fridge, twisted off the cap, and then sculled it down. Once the water was devoured, I walked to the bathroom, flicked the light on, and closed the door. And as I caught sight of my reflection, I shook my head at the smudged mascara under my eyes and the frizz on my previously smooth salon-hair.

I sighed and peeled off my uniform, catching a glimpse of my reflection in a matching black bra and undies. A wave of nausea churned in my throat as I flashed back to the awkward toilet paper incident. *Could I be any more embarrassing, seriously?* I reached for my toothbrush and squeezed a drop of minty paste onto the bristles, then undressed and stepped into the shower. After I turned on the water, steam rose up, and within seconds, the glass was foggy.

Feeling refreshed from the shower, I grabbed my paddle brush and embarked on the challenging mission of taming my mane of curls. Long strokes through my hair hit a snag halfway through. *Ouch.* Brushing your hair shouldn't be such a laborious task and should make your hair smoother, not frizzier, right?

Ten minutes later, after I made my hair somewhat presentable, I reached for my black cotton nightie hanging on the towel rail and got dressed. The finishing touch was my berry-tinted lip balm.

'Naomi? What's taking so long? Have you fallen and cracked your skull or are you crying again?' Deb called out.

'No, I'm not crying. I'm coming now,' I replied, opening the door and making my way to the lounge room. As I entered, I noticed Deb was lying down and engrossed in texting, while Seb was also occupied on his phone.

'Hey, she's back.' Deb smiled and reached to pull me down next to her. 'How are ya?' She put her phone face down on her stomach and didn't react to the dinging of incoming messages.

'I'm feeling okay. The shower helped, but, my God, I'm ravenous.' My stomach let out a loud growl, prompting giggles from me and Deb.

'Better make a sandwich; bread is super good for lining your stomach.'

'Good idea. Does anyone want anything?' I glanced at Deb, then turned to Seb.

Together, they chimed in, 'I'm good.'

As I made my way into the kitchen, I caught sight of Scott's ribbed tumbler sitting on the sink. A sudden pang hit my heart, and my stomach churned in response.

'Deb, can you come here for a sec?' I called with urgency.

'Yep. What is it?' She appeared behind me almost instantly, and the faint scent of her patchouli perfume wafted past.

'Why is Scott's glass on the sink ...?' I trailed off, my voice wavering at the end of the sentence.

'Oh, I used it this morning for an ashtray.' Her voice was as casual as when you'd tell someone you were going for a stroll in the park.

A laugh of relief escaped my lips. 'My God, that freaked me out because I had it shoved in the back of the cupboard and didn't expect to see it.'

She patted me on the cheek. 'I'd never let that fucker over here. Don't worry.'

I nodded, and once I caught sight of the Vegemite jar and butter in the fridge, my worries dissipated. After lathering the spreads onto a piece of rye bread, I took a big bite. Each bite tasted heavenly, so heavenly that I closed my eyes, while my stomach grumbled as it greeted what it had longed for all day.

'Anyway, chickie, I'm going to bed. I'm super spent.' Deb leaned in and kissed me on the cheek, then whispered in my ear, 'Have fun, tiger.' She gave my arse a quick slap.

I let out a laugh and then diverted the topic away from her comment. 'What time do you start tomorrow?'

'Same as you, pretty sure.'

'So, eleven?' I raised my brows.

'Yeah, so I'll come with you.' She smiled. 'Oh, by the way, thank you for helping me out with my phone bill the other day. I'd be screwed without you.'

'All good, sugar.' I nodded.

'Night, chick.' Deb blew me a kiss. 'Oh, and don't mind me if you hear me moaning in my sleep. I'll be dreaming of Patrick Vitello.' She let out a mischievous laugh and walked towards her room.

I laughed too and didn't think twice about the name. Instead, I put the food away and gave the bench a wipe-down.

'When are you coming into the lounge room?' Seb called.

'Now,' I replied as I threw the sponge into the sink.

As I walked in, he just stared at me, grinning, with his jacket draped over the back of the chair.

'Looks like the couch is free.' I winked and gestured to the three-seater.

'Oh, is that right?' He stood and walked so close to me that I felt his breath tickle my neck.

'Mmm-hmm.'

'You cheeky bitch.' He shook his head while smiling at me.

He flopped onto the couch and tugged my arm, signalling for me to sit beside him. As I sat, he began rubbing his foot on mine, and I laughed, then flinched as his toes tickled my feet. I politely moved my foot away and smiled. He flashed his ridiculously good grin again and looked into my eyes. I wanted to look elsewhere – his stare was so intense – but I didn't. He gave off a lustful, tired-of-waiting-three-months-and-only-getting-kisses-and-cuddles vibe.

Is three months too long to make a guy wait before having sex? And if I make him wait longer, will he just look for it somewhere else?

'Anyway, why do you look so sexy for bed?' he asked as he eyed me from head to toe in admiration. 'I love how your lips are so full of colour. So plump. Mmm, and don't even get me started on your blue eyes; they should be illegal. *You* should be illegal.'

I let out an embarrassing chortle. *God, he's funny. My eyes should be illegal. They aren't that blue, are they?* I always thought of them as greyish.

'So now can I have a kiss? I've missed those lips.' He leant in and tucked a loose strand of hair behind my ear.

As I leaned in for a kiss, an unwanted memory interrupted. Images of Scott's lean, muscly back and his pineapple-and-coconut scent flooded my mind. His divine smell and tanned skin, along with his sparkling turquoise eyes, had a way of weakening and enticing me. I banished the thought and quickly pecked Seb.

'Naomi? What's going on? That kiss felt lifeless.' He snarled his lip in annoyance.

'Oh, nothing. It's stupid.' I attempted to dismiss it with a laugh, avoiding eye contact as I focused on the shaggy, grey rug.

'There always seems to be something on your mind. If it's not your Dad, it's your work. Why is it whenever we try to get close, you pull away? Always a bloody restriction.' He shook his head.

'I mean it. It was nothing.' My voice was stern as I eyed him.

'I'd do anything for you, bloody anything.' He let out a breath of frustration and folded his arms. His eyes were now the ones fixed on the shaggy, grey rug.

I leant in closer, unable to think straight over the buzz of my drunken brain, but something in my gut had always cautioned me to take things slow with Seb.

'Seb. Thank you. I appreciate your kind words.'

He softly tapped his finger on the side of my head. 'I honestly wish I could work out that mind of yours.'

I sucked in a deep breath and contemplated whether I should tell him why our kiss felt 'lifeless'. *Might as well.*

'Seb, the reason our kiss was so pathetic just then is because I was reminded of my ex tonight.' I glimpsed at his low but broad cheekbones.

His eyes widened as his forehead creased. 'Has he been messaging you?' A large vein I never noticed before emerged on his forehead.

I shook my head. 'No, we haven't spoken in months, and I plan to never speak to him again. I was reminded of him tonight when I saw his old whiskey glass sitting on the kitchen sink. Deb had used it for an ashtray, so don't worry – he hasn't been here or anything.'

'And you still love him?' His eyes widened with curiosity, a flicker of jealousy crossing his expression.

'No, I don't, but he hurt me bad.' I sighed.

'Oh, I get it now. You think I'm going to hurt you, don't you? That's what this is all about, isn't it? This is why you won't sleep with me.'

I gave a pained face. 'Partly. But there is no rush, Seb. We're still getting to know each other. Let's save that for a night when we're both ready.'

'Naomi, are you a virgin?' He eyed me curiously.

I shot up a defensive brow and folded my arms. 'No, I'm not.'

Seb exhaled. 'Man. I can't figure you out, no matter how hard I try. I always seem to miss the mark.'

I couldn't help but chuckle at his statement. 'We've only known each other a few months, Seb. It's not a big deal. Let's just be patient and see what comes of us.'

'My fly-in, fly-out situation makes me impatient. Not seeing you for two weeks is hard, and all I want to do is make love to you. But I know that's not what you want, and I'm happy to take it slow, for you. If it were anyone else, I would've lost interest by now – just know that.'

I nodded and placed my hands on his cheeks, and we kissed once more.

After our kiss, I said, 'I've got work tomorrow. I should probably hit the hay. I think I've done enough damage to my body for the evening.'

'Can I come with you to your room, or do you want me to stay out here?'

I reached my arms out for a stretch. 'You can come to my bedroom.'

I switched off the lights and navigated the way into my room with my phone light. Anxiety struck me as I thought about the possibility of Seb hurting me. *What if when we do have sex, he stops talking to me, like Scott did?* I walked around to the left side of the bed, reached for my charger, plugged my phone in, and switched on my bedside lamp.

Seb climbed onto the other side, slipped under my lilac bedsheets, and grinned at me.

'What time do you have to be up tomorrow?' he asked as the amber glow of my lamp shone on his face.

'Ten-ish.'

'That's a sexy little sleep-in. I'll be long gone before then. Billy and I are going for a surf early morning.' He stretched his arms as he looked up at the ceiling.

'Cool. Sounds fun.' I stared at his smooth skin and thought about the sun browning it an even darker olive.

'I'm hoping we can cuddle lots before I go.' He moved in closer to me and let his arms fall back into place.

I nodded and smiled. *That sounds nice.*

My phone buzzed – the wallpaper of Dad and me covered in flour and sharing a giggle flashed on the screen. A sudden pang hit my stomach, accompanied by an urge to cry, as that familiar burning sensation arose in my throat. Determined to hold back the tears, I focused on Deb's goodnight message, trying to anchor myself in the present.

3

A Kitchen Shift

With one bleary eye, I reached for the digital clock on my nightstand and checked the time: 6:23am. Less than four hours until I had to get dressed for work. I squeezed my eyes shut again, and just as I was about to drift off, I heard my iPhone buzz. *Who is texting me soooo early?*

I opened the text.

Deb: *Morning Chick, sorry if I woke you, I know you hate early mornings. But I need your advice. Were you lying when you said my hair looks good this short? No one complimented me and it just made me think I looked crap.*

Me: *Deb, you looked great last night, you always do & no one probably said anything because you only got a trim. It's not that big of a difference lol.*

Deb: *Yeah, you're right, but the auburn looks better brighter don't you think? Like no one even mentioned the colour ...*

Me: *I promise you looked great. Now I better get some sleep or I'll be grumpy all shift xx*

Deb: *Haha you're not wrong about that. You know ... the quickest way to re-energise is sex ... just remember that. See your tired arse later.*

A quiet chuckle escaped my lips as I placed my phone back on the nightstand. I turned my attention to Seb and observed his face while he slept. His eyes were twitching, and his mouth was slightly open. The lilac blanket covered the bottom half of his body, from his hips down, baring the dark hair on his chest and the snail trail down his belly. His arms were the smoothest part of his body, with minimal hair. He must have felt me staring because he opened his eyes, smiled, then wrapped his arm around me. An unsuspected warmth ran through my body as we cuddled for a few minutes, silently, and I found myself staring into his eyes. The ceiling fan whooshed above our heads in an attempt to keep us cool in the late-September heat. My room felt like Mon Amour's kitchen as beads of sweat trickled down my forehead, and to top off my discomfort, a sharp pang sliced through my stomach, reminding me of the abuse it copped from last night's vodka.

It felt nice, Seb being in my bed. I never had men in my bed at Mum's. It was too awkward to bring someone home. *What if it failed?* I hated the thought of introducing someone to Mum and my younger brother, Carlos, and within months, they're gone. Right now, stability was what my family needed more than anything.

Seb yawned and stretched his arms out wide, then did snow angel-like movements with his legs as he flexed his feet.

'Good morning, gorgeous.' He leant in and pecked me on the cheek.

'Morning,' I croaked as I glanced at his russet eyes. The gel that slicked his hair back had softened, and his small curls dangled.

'How was your beauty sleep?' He looked at my sleepy face with a smile.

'Deprived. Wish I was still sleeping, to be honest.' I fluffed up my pillow, sank my head back on it, and sighed.

Seb laughed and slid his arm under my neck to pull me to his chest so that our faces were only inches apart. 'You're such a cutie, you know that?'

I let out a chuckle. *Gorgeous. Cutie.* He sure liked his pet names.

'Billy is picking me up at seven. Do you know the time?' His carefree demeanour disappeared, and his voice was raised with sudden urgency.

'Last time I checked, it was nearly six-thirty.' I let out a yawn and closed my eyes for a few seconds.

'Looks like I'll have to love you and leave you sooner than I realised, but before then, toilet duties call.' Seb rolled out of bed and landed on his feet before creeping out of my room and taking a right turn.

There was no point trying to get sleep now, when Seb was about to leave, so I grabbed my phone and tapped on the Instagram app. The first photo on my newsfeed was Deb posing with her eyes squinted shut and her tongue poking out while Victor squished his face to hers, flashing his goofy chipped-tooth grin. It was captioned as *'Shameless selfies with my favourite Frenchie'*. I hearted the photo, then scrolled through photos of food, cosmetics and the odd selfie of a friend or celebrity.

Seb returned with a grin as he slid back into my bed and placed his head on the pillow. I couldn't stop staring at his mangled hair, the texture wiry and greasy.

'Naomi ... I ... uh ... hope me staying over can be a regular thing.' He cleared his throat.

'Well, I must admit that you not paying me out after I made a fool out of myself last night did leave quite a good impression.' I nodded, pleased.

'Sounds promising.' He winked.

'I am never drinking on an empty stomach again, though, and that's a promise. I don't know what I was thinking, drinking vodka like that.' I patted my belly and internally said sorry to it for making it sick.

'We should get takeaway next time, and we'll pass a bottle of Jack Daniel's around.' His face was alight with hope.

I shook my head. 'No, thanks. Me drinking last night was a *one-off*.'

'Aw. No fun.' His forehead creased with disappointment. 'How's that hangover treating you?'

'It's doing okay, but I've got copious amounts of water to thank for that.' I glanced at the almost-empty bottle on my nightstand, but as I moved, another pang ripped through my gut.

'Nothing worse than working with a grim hangover, eh? Greasy hash browns and an egg-and-bacon burger are my cure.' He eyed me propped up on my pillows as I stared down at him.

'Yes, nothing worse indeed. Not the wisest of choices to get drunk and work the following day during school holidays … I really hope to God the dishy is on tonight. Juggling pizzas, desserts, and dishes all at once is not ideal.' I sighed.

'You'll smash it, baby. Billy and I might get one of your pizzas tonight.' His brows raised in excitement.

'Let me guess. A takeaway ham-and-pineapple with extra ham and cheese?' I arched my brow and tried to hide my disapproval.

'You know it, baby.' He laughed.

'I don't understand the fuss with ham-and-pineapple pizza. Everyone seems to order it, and it's boring. Moroccan chicken is the best.' I twirled a stray strand of hair around my index finger, then tucked it behind my ear.

'That's biased as fuck because you designed that pizza with the head chef.' He squinted his eyes in defence.

I let out a laugh. 'Mmm. Maybe you're right.'

Seb looked around my spacious, high-ceilinged bedroom. 'This house must cost you and Deb the whole of your wages to rent, surely? How do you two afford it?'

'Deb's parents own this house.' I sank my back further into the pillows.

'Really?' His eyes widened in surprise.

'Yes.' I nodded, looking at him.

'They must earn a shitload.'

'Seems to be the case for most property developers.'

Two years ago, Deb lived in Brisbane, and we barely talked. Her excuse was she was 'too busy with work', yet she still wrote daily Facebook updates and posted photos at trendy bars and restaurants with her new besties. I was lucky to hear from her once a fortnight, and that was when she was having a self-conscious breakdown, and once revived, she'd be gone again. My God, I missed her and how it was when we used to do everything together. Things returned to normal when she came back in July last year, and then we moved in together.

'Least she knows she can't get kicked out then,' Seb said, grabbing my attention again.

'Yeah, she uses that to her advantage.' I shook my head while smiling.

'Well, aren't you both *lucky* girls!'

'I'm very grateful and feel secure here. Her parents said we can live here for however long we want as long as the bills are paid, which I seem to pay more of, but I get it – it's Deb's house.'

'Sounds like a solid arrangement. Is this furniture yours or her parents'? Including this bed?' Seb patted his hand on the mattress.

'The house came fully furnished, and her parents had it as a rental until she persuaded them to rent it to us.'

'Yeah, nice. How old is Deb? She's older than you, isn't she?' His face looked so certain, I was sad to burst his bubble.

'Actually, I'm the older one, but only by a year.' I held up one finger to confirm.

'Bullshit. Seriously? I thought she was easily twenty-eight.' His mouth dropped a little as his eyebrows raised.

'It's funny you say that because a lot of people think she is older than she is. Personally, I don't see it, but that might be because I've known her for so long. She's like the sister I never had.' I smiled before continuing. 'We've been best friends since I was in grade nine at school ... She was one grade below me. Her parents used to live in the same street as me, and that's how we met. We would walk home from the bus stop together.'

'Bit like Billy and me. We've been best mates since grade eight.' He smiled and nodded.

'I still can't believe Deb's only twenty-four, though.' Seb's face was saturated in disbelief.

'Actually, she's twenty-three, turning twenty-four. Her birthday is next month.' I let out a laugh at his facial expression – he was truly surprised.

'Wow.' He shook his head in amazement.

'I think it's her mannerisms and confidence that make her appear older.' I lifted up my palms and shrugged.

We chatted until Billy picked him up, and then I crawled back into bed and shut my eyes, almost instantly falling asleep.

At precisely 10.20am, I was woken by my vibrating iPhone and its wind chime ringtone. *Why do alarms go off when you're dead asleep and having peaceful dreams? Annoying.*

Once I was showered and my makeup was done, I threw on my work clothes and darted to the front of the house to pull on my boots before knocking on Deb's door.

'Just a minute,' she called out over the top of her Indie music playing; I didn't recognise the song, but it was nothing cool like Radiohead or Vampire Weekend.

'Alright.' I clicked the side button of my phone: 10.40am. 'Deb, I don't want to be late, and I sure as hell don't need any reason for Daniel to have a go at me.'

'I know,' Deb said as she swung open her door. 'I was just doing the finishing touches, you know.' She rubbed her sheer-red lips together and made a popping sound with her mouth.

'You scrub up well after a big night.' I looked her up and down and gave her the *damn-you-look-good stare.*

She laughed, then said, 'Look at yourself, you hot stuff. I'd kill for your tiny pins.'

'I try.' I curtseyed in my checked pants that came to my ankles, feeling far from attractive. And if I was going to be ultra self-loathing, these pants did nothing for my legs. They made my calves look like chubby tree stumps.

***

The drive to work took the usual six to ten minutes, due to minimal traffic, which was odd for a Thursday during school holidays. I was more than thankful there was one space left in the small six-space car park behind the restaurant. My Mazda hatchback squeezed nicely in between Daniel's four-wheel drive and someone else's. Deb hopped out of the car as soon as I pulled on the handbrake and grabbed a ciggie from her clutch.

With a click on my keys, my doors were locked. I walked straight into the kitchen through the back door and hoped to God Daniel was in a good mood but thankfully didn't see him as I passed the coffee machine. The kitchen was a confined, rectangular space, much smaller than others I had worked in. It didn't even have a cold room, just lots of fridges, but despite that, it did the job, and everyone made do with its confined vibe.

'Hey, Pinky,' Martin said with his usual smirk, his lanky body towering over me while he pulled the kosher salt from the shelf above. I caught a gush of his Lynx deodorant, and it made me want to sneeze. My nose tingled, but I fought off the sensation.

'Martin, I really wish you'd stop with that nickname.' I rolled my eyes and thought of the *one time* I wore pink frilly undies in the kitchen. *Never again.*

'Lighten up, sweetheart. What's the matter?' He swivelled around and placed the container of salt on the main workbench. The green-and-white tea towel flapped in his back pocket from the swift movement.

'Nothing. I'm just sick to death of that name.' I gave him the *don't-piss-me-off* stare.

'What's with the dagger eyes? You're the one who bent over wearing pink frillies to work.' His annoying flat hair looked extra flat and annoying at that moment.

'That happened *once*, Martin.' *Why does he feel the need to bang on about this joke every shift?*

'Okay, okay.' And to my relief, he held his hands up in surrender and backed off. 'By the way, Tyren called in sick. He's got a stomach bug.'

'Aww, poor thing. Is he okay? Please send him my love when you text him later.' I gave him a concerned look.

'Will do.'

Tyren hardly ever pulled a sickie. He was our dedicated apprentice, and his hard work really made the kitchen better. The kid had good knife skills.

'Is Joel on?' I asked as I walked over to the handwashing sink in the far-left corner of the room and cleaned my hands, hoping I'd hear a yes.

'Not tonight. Daniel said he's trying to save money, so looks like you and Kelly will do the dishes.' He smirked.

'Oh, goodie.' I raised my brows and exhaled a breath of frustration. *Typical.*

We stopped talking as Martin concentrated on filling a smaller container with the salt for his section.

I put my hat and apron on, chucked my bag under the sink, and then walked over to my station.

''Sup, chicken,' Kelly said, giving me her nod. Her blue hair was slicked into a bun, and her usual orange foundation was pale and oily.

'Hey, Kel. Busy morning?'

'You bet. I just want to go home already.' She wiped the sweat from her forehead with the back of her hand and let out a long sigh.

'Where's Daniel?' I whispered, then looked around to make sure he wasn't standing behind me.

'He stepped out to get more milk.' She scraped her chef clog on the edge of the lined bin.

She smelt like sweat, cigarettes, and the slightest bit of cheap, strawberry deodorant.

'Are you on tonight?' I asked while I watched her put her clog back on.

Her neck muscles tensed as they always did when she was annoyed by a question. 'Naomi, is that even a legit question? Of course, I am. Daniel loves getting his money's worth – you know this.' Her feisty eyes widened.

I felt some relief at being a casual employee. Kelly was on a fixed wage and could work up to eighty hours in a week and still be paid the same. She was always exhausted, but the upside was she got sick and holiday leave, and I didn't.

Unsure of what to say, I nodded, hoping I appeared sympathetic.

At 2:50pm, after our lunch rush, Paul, our head chef, walked in looking relaxed and sipping fresh coffee. Daniel would have made it for him. He always made Paul's cappuccinos. Paul had on his tall, traditional chef hat, signalling his authority, while everyone else's sat flat on their heads. His fluffy, walnut-coloured hair was tucked behind his ears, the shade nearly identical to his eyes. As usual, his white, buttoned jacket hung loosely over his black pants. Everyone else wore checked pants in our kitchen.

'Well, don't you all look like a bunch of zombies. Kel, take your hour break,' Paul said while looking at her pale face. He paused. 'Are you okay?'

'Yeah, I'm fine,' she let out in a rush of annoyance.

'Uh-huh.' Paul cocked his thick eyebrow at Kelly as she gathered her things and left the kitchen.

'Martin, start the prep. And, Naomi, you can go on a ten-minute break,' Paul said in a fast, authoritative tone that got the momentum going.

'Yes, chef,' Martin replied.

I nodded in relief. 'Thanks, Paul.'

I listened as they chopped away, and just as I was about to turn left to leave the restaurant, Daniel appeared and stopped me with his hand. This time, his pants were as tight as his shirt and he had an oval-studded belt wrapped around his hips, with pointed black shiny shoes to complete his outfit.

'Where are you going, Naomi?' he asked while munching on a mouthful of something potent with garlic. I looked at his slicked-back hair, which, so I had been told, had been grey since his late twenties, then at his thin lips as he swallowed.

'Paul gave me a ten-minute break.' I glanced at the dark specks of colour in his hazel eyes while trying not to inhale his breath.

'Is that right?' He gave me his usual patronising stare that made me feel guilty for nothing.

'Yes.' I nodded and took a step back.

'And how many hours have you worked?' His large eyes widened.

I wanted to say, 'Enough for you to give me a pay rise,' but what I ended up saying was, 'I got in at eleven this morning.'

'Oh, right. I see.' He looked down at his golden, oversized watch. 'See you in eight minutes, then.' He sneered.

'Uh-huh.' I held a neutral face as I looked at him.

He turned around, and as soon as he did, relief flooded every inch of my body, but then suddenly, he spun back to face me. 'Oh, and, Naomi, empty the kitchen bin while you're at it,' he said in his condescending tone.

I sneered too but only inwardly. 'Okay.' I walked into the kitchen and grabbed the bin bag, which had a few takeaway coffee cups and a banana peel in there. Paul stopped cutting and gave me a strange look.

'What are you doing, Naomi?' Paul asked, his knife mid-air.

'Daniel asked me to empty the bin.'

'There is hardly anything in there.' He placed his knife down on the chopping board and shook his head. 'What a waste.'

I shrugged. *Yep, I know.*

Daniel appeared and looked over my shoulder with one hand on his hip, watching my every move.

'Come on, woman.' Daniel clapped his hands in my face. 'You've got to be fast in a kitchen.'

I tied up the bin bag, and just as I was about to walk outside, Daniel stopped me in my tracks again.

'Squash these boxes while you're at it,' he said as he piled ten cardboard boxes on top of my arms, all the way up to my chin.

I used my chin to balance the boxes and let them fall to the ground when I reached the bin area. The time it took to walk out the back, chuck the rubbish, and flatten the boxes left me a measly four minutes to spare. I didn't see the point in sitting down, so I headed back into the kitchen. *You won, Daniel, yet again.*

When I returned to my station, there was a latte in a glass sitting on the bench. I looked down at the artwork – a heart patterned on the froth. The intense aroma filled my nose, making my mouth water. *Oh, Deb, your coffees are to die for.* I smiled, then took a sip as the heat warmed my clammy hands. Vanilla latte. *Mmm.* A mix of sweet and bitter hit my tongue, and I swear that drink was the highlight of my day. It was delicious.

'Did you enjoy your coffee?' Daniel asked as he stood in the doorway.

'Yes, it was perfect. Tell Deb I said thanks.' I wiped the froth from my lips with a napkin.

He raised his brows. 'Deb?' He laughed. 'Oh, I see. You think Deb made you that coffee. Well, no, it was me actually.' He crossed his arms, back in serious mode.

'Top job.' I smiled.

This man is so confusing – one minute he's being a complete arsehole, and the next, he's making me coffee with hearts? It was a love-hate relationship at its finest, with a tad more hate than love.

As soon as 6pm hit, we were flat-out. The waitstaff paced in and out and hung docket after docket in the kitchen. I had five takeaway orders to create and ten pizzas for dine-ins. The stress was building, and the more I panicked, the faster I moved and the more damp with sweat my back became.

Once I'd rolled out the dough balls into bases, I placed them on round, wooden pizza boards, which were already sprinkled with semolina. God knows who named a food 'semolina' when a sickness was called 'salmonella'.

Within minutes, twenty pizza bases were ready to go. *Okay, I got this. I can do this.* I took a deep breath and clapped the excess flour from my hands into the bin.

We got slammed. I must have made over one hundred pizzas on my own; Kelly had to take over desserts and dishes solo, while Martin took care of the grill and fryer, and Paul did the tricky stuff.

By 9.30pm, the restaurant was dead, and it was finally closing time. Paul was out the door ten minutes later, leaving us to clean the kitchen.

Martin reluctantly cleaned out the dishwasher while Kelly finished wiping the benches. I cleaned the floor (which, to be honest, I'd always kind of enjoyed – there was something satisfying about a squeegee mop). Martin gave Kelly and me a scornful stare every chance he got, like it was our fault Daniel was trying to save money and didn't want Joel on. Ugh. God, he could be such a child. He felt superior being sous chef, and even though Kelly was too, cleaning a dishwasher was beneath him. I bet he was just pissed about me not wanting to be called 'Pinky'. That was Martin for you – he would let his anger develop over the course of several hours and then death-stare you when he was pissed off. Not much of a verbal abuser, at least.

Once we finished cleaning, everyone clocked their hours. I wrote *'11am to 10:15pm'* on my timesheet.

I said farewell to everyone, the mood in the kitchen finally a little lighter as everyone was done for the night, then left and hopped into my car, waiting for Deb to come out of the bathroom. Five minutes later, she strolled out with a lit cigarette in her mouth. Behind her was Victor. I heard a muffle of laughter exchange between them and watched through my rear-view mirror as they hugged. Victor kissed Deb on the cheek and waved to me, then jumped onto his Vespa.

Deb stomped out her cigarette, then plopped into the car and stretched her arms as she yawned. She smelt like a sweaty ashtray with a smidge of patchouli perfume.

'Come on. Let's hit the road. I'm completely wrecked.' She fanned her breasts with her shirt while her forehead dripped with beads of sweat. Her under-eyes were flecked with mascara.

'Me too. What should we get for dinner?' I asked as I started the car so the air con could blast.

'You should have made us one of your pizzas.'

'I've had enough of pizza for the night.' I laughed.

She laughed too. 'No wonder your legs are so great.' She eyed my pins. 'Maybe if I worked as fast as you, my thighs would be half their size.' She let out a sigh as she looked down at her thick legs. 'Hey, I got an idea. Why don't you cook us crispy salmon with your peppery butter sauce?'

We were lucky that my younger brother kept us stocked up on seafood from the fish market he worked at, which came in handy when all the shops were closed.

'Sure. I think I've got some salmon already defrosted in the fridge.' I turned on the lights and reversed out of the car park.

I half-turned to Deb while watching the road. 'Daniel was acting extra-ar-sehole today. I was on a ten-minute break, and he was like, *"Oh, Naomi, can you take out the bin?"* When the bin wasn't even full! And he gave me a stack of boxes to flatten. Like, who does that? Seriously. He does not appreciate his staff.' I flicked my indicator and veered left.

Deb didn't say anything, not even looking up from her phone.

'Deb?' I took another left turn and as we passed the restaurants on the block. I winced as I caught sight of last night's restaurant and dismissed the thought of the toilet paper incident.

'Yeah?'

'Did you hear me?'

'Oh, sort of.' She laughed. 'Yeah, Daniel can be a bit silly sometimes.'

Really? That is her response? A bit silly? What happened to her not being able to stand him? Odd.

'So, are you excited for the function tomorrow?' I asked, hoping for a proper response.

'Yes, it's going to be massive. I can't believe we're catering Patrick Vitello's house.'

'Where's his house again?'

'Noosa Sound. His backyard is actually the *river*.' Her tone was packed with excitement.

'Lucky man. What does he do again?' I asked as I concentrated on the road ahead.

Deb scoffed. 'Oh my God, how do you not know this? He owns three of the top restaurants in Australia. We tried his food a few months ago. Don't you remember? You know, the one in Hastings Street?'

'That insanely gorgeous Italian food? The place we had to book two weeks in advance. That's his?' I raised my brows and felt a surge of anxiety zoom its way into my heart.

'Yep! It's so fancy – heaps of celebrities and socialites go there.'

'Was he even in the restaurant that night? All I remember are those exotic-looking waitresses.' I quickly glanced at her, but not long enough to catch her facial expression.

'Yeah, he was there. He was on the phone a lot. He is seriously so hot.' Deb's voice went sensual as she lusted over him.

When we got home, I made my crispy salmon specialty with lemon, pepper, and butter sauce, and we ate at the dinner table until nothing was left on our plates. Deb went as far as licking her plate clean.

After the dishes were done by me, we slumped on the couch in our pyjamas while Deb googled photos of Patrick on her iPad. She scrolled her finger down the photo-covered screen. Most of the photos were of his mouth-watering food and the interior of his restaurants, but there was the occasional headshot as well. He was enthralling, with deep-olive skin and a model-like sculptured face, complemented by ridiculously green eyes. I was a sucker for green eyes; I once read that green was the rarest eye colour in the world, and *oh God,* his were as fine as apple pie.

Deb's eyes were glued to the screen as she stared at Patrick's face. She took a sip of pinot grigio from her glass while I gulped down water from my bottle. The fan above us was going full bore.

'That man's jaw structure would make any car crash,' Deb said as she perved at his face.

I burst out in laughter.

Why was Mon Amour, a small Moroccan-inspired restaurant, cooking for someone so renowned? I was in awe but also incredibly nervous. *What if he didn't like my pizzas?* I'd only tasted his food once, but the pictures and reviews suggested mine might not measure up. *Why would he want our food when his was phenomenal? Perhaps he sought variety?*

4

The Function

The sound of pounding on my bedroom door and the twisting of my doorknob awoke me from my deep sleep. I grabbed my phone and gasped: 10:58am. *Noooo!*

'Naomi, are you seriously still sleeping?' Deb called through the door.

My stomach sank, and I lay glued to the bed, my mouth dry as paper.

'Deb, I am so stupid. I forgot to set my alarm.' I pressed my hand to my forehead and sighed.

'Let me in.' My doorknob twisted again.

The blood in my head rushed and the room swayed as I stood up too fast. My heart pounded, and all I could think was, *Seriously, Naomi, you're going to be late for such an important work function? Come on, girl. Get your shit together.*

Just as I was about to open the door, my phone buzzed and *'Daniel (Boss)'* flashed on the screen. My fingers worked faster than my brain, and before I knew it, Daniel was yelling on the phone.

'Naomi, hello? Earth to Naomi. Where the fuck are you, woman?' The loudness of his voice pierced through my eardrum.

Before I could reply, he was at it again.

'Do you take this job seriously at all?'

I swallowed hard. 'I'm so sorry, Daniel.'

'Just fucking get here, okay?' He hung up before I got my 'okay' out of my mouth.

My hands shook, and I fought hard not to cry. I'd been mentally preparing for this function for weeks, and now Daniel was furious at me again, and for an *actual* reason this time.

I unlocked the door, and Deb gave me that concerned look she does when I'm in a dilemma, then wrapped her arms around me. Her usual jasmine and patchouli perfume comforted me as I cried on her shoulder, overwhelmed with emotion.

'You can do this, Naomi. Daniel is counting on you. Remember that,' she whispered into my ear.

I sniffed. 'And Paul.'

Deb took a step back to look at me. 'Oh, didn't you hear? The only thing Paul is cooking for the function is the duck spring rolls. The rest of the menu got pulled.'

'What? So just spring rolls on the menu?' My eyes widened with surprise.

'Yep, and the pizzas and salmon filo cups.'

'Why did the other food get pulled?' I raised a worried brow and tilted my head in curiosity.

'Because Patrick said he has enough food. Daniel told me Patrick came in last night and tried the pizza and duck spring rolls. He didn't bother trying the salmon filo because *who can stuff up that?* His words, not mine.'

'Oh my God, he tried my pizza last night?' The blood rushed from my face again, and my neck turned hot. 'What did he say?'

Deb's response was interrupted by another buzz from my phone. This time it was a text message:

Daniel (Boss): *Naomi, you're never late, so I will try to be understanding in this matter. Can you and Debra be in by noon? Dan.*

Me: *Thank you so much. See you then.*

'Daniel just said we can start at twelve.' My words came out in a rush.

Deb's face lit up. 'That's awesome.'

'I can't believe it, to be honest.' I sucked in a deep breath, then slowly let it out. 'So, back to what we were talking about. What did Patrick say?'

'He said he was blown away by the pizza and that whoever made it could work in his kitchen any day.'

I burst out laughing and gave Deb that *are-you-kidding-me* look.

'Stop laughing. I'm dead serious.'

'Wow. Okay. I am stunned.' I couldn't help but grin that Patrick had said those words about my pizza. It made my stomach melt like warm honey.

'Daniel told me not to tell you, but you know I can't keep anything from you. Plus, you're just really damn good at pizza. You definitely take after your dad when it comes to cooking.'

'That really means a lot, Deb. Thanks.' I smiled again but this time with a shaky lip.

I closed my eyes, and for a moment, I was a kid again, sitting on a stool kneading dough with my tiny fists, next to Dad. His hands smell like herbs from the garden as he chops them chiffonade-style on the stone board. His crinkly eyes smile at me as he watches my knuckles indent the dough. The late-afternoon sun is pouring in, and his face is all golden and full of laughter and life.

Deb snapped her fingers in front of my face. 'Hey, wake up. You better get moving.'

I snapped back to the present. 'Oh God, I have to shower and do my make-up.'

'And hair,' she added, smirking at my puffy, unbrushed hair.

'Haha,' I replied, grimacing as I ran my fingers through the tangled mop on top of my head. Rapunzel hair had its perks at times, but I sure wasn't looking forward to raking through those curls this morning.

In the shower, I thought of the night ahead. This was the first time I'd be serving food at an event as a waitress. I was a behind-the-scenes kind of girl, happy to not interact with customers and just focus on the task at hand. Deb had talked Daniel into letting me join her; she had a knack for talking herself up and dragging me into things. She said it would be a great experience. *We'll see about that.*

The dress code was very specific: black halter-neck dress just above the knee (Patrick had mailed them to us Express Post last week wrapped in rose-scented tissue paper), black wedges, hair in a high bun.

After my shower, I did my skincare and makeup (natural with a sheer crimson lip), brushed my hair, and twirled it into a high bun. Then I got dressed in my usual work clothes and placed my folded dress into a duffle bag along with my wedges, a spare black bra, underwear, and a cosmetic bag for touch-ups. *I want to look damn good tonight.*

We arrived to work at 11:45am, and I smiled warily at Daniel as I walked into the kitchen to place my things under the sink.

'You girls are here, finally,' Daniel said with an unusually warm smile. 'So, normal lunch service today, then you both have to be ready and be at Patrick's house by five. Okay?'

'Yep, got it,' I said.

'No, worries, chief,' Debra added with a huge smile.

'Good stuff, ladies.' He rubbed his hands together and grinned again.

***

Lunch service was surprisingly quiet for a Friday, but I wasn't complaining – it gave me time to finish the pre-made pastry cups for the salmon filos and weigh and divide the pizza dough (which I'd made during last night's shift). Tyren, our apprentice, would fill in for me and take over pizzas that night.

Four o'clock hit, which meant time to make the pizzas for the function. Five Moroccan chicken, five pulled pork, five Moroccan lamb, and two eggplant. The task was more daunting than ever. As the pressure began to mount, I tried to shake off the stress – it was just pizza I had made hundreds of times before – but my inner voice kept repeating his name: *Patrick Vitello.* I was making pizza for Patrick frickin' Vitello. *Oh my God, they have to be perfect.*

I drew in a deep breath and covered the pizza bases in their sauces, applied the toppings evenly, then sprinkled the herbs. It was all about balance. Too much sauce equalled a soggy pizza, and not enough toppings equalled a bland pizza.

While I waited for the pizzas to cook, I began filling the crispy filo cups with the mixture of cream cheese, chives, dill, capers, red onion, and salmon curls.

After preparing the salmon filo cups and cutting and packaging the pizzas, the final task was to cook the eggplant pizzas. Once I had assembled them and placed them in the oven, my forehead perspired from the heat as I waited for them to bake. I took a sip of water from my cup and noticed all the ice had melted. *Of course, it has. It's a frickin' sauna in here.*

When it was time to take the pizzas out, I grabbed the lifter, slid the pizza onto it, and carefully walked over to the boxes. I tilted the lifter and waited for the pizza to slide into the box, but it missed and landed upside-down on the ground. Sauce and stringy cheese smeared over the floor. My heart raced, and I looked around to see if Daniel had witnessed this catastrophe. He wasn't in sight. Thank God. After I cleaned the pizza murder scene off the floor, I slid the other pizza from the oven and (even more carefully this time) placed it into the box. It didn't slip. *Phew.*

Paul returned from his brief break. 'You're doing great, Naomi.'

'Thanks, Paul. I am sooo nervous.'

'You'll be fine.'

Paul's reassurance made me feel a little better as I moved on to the final pizza, and when I slid it out of the oven, sliced it, and placed it in the box, I felt nothing but victorious.

Once the food was packaged in heat bags and placed in Daniel's car, Deb and I hurried to the bathrooms, touched up our makeup, and changed into our outfits. I wore everything besides my wedges because safety comes first when driving. Deb smelt under her arms and made a face before spraying deodorant and topping up her perfume. I did the same, then we ran to the car. Small stones jabbed my bare feet – *ouch* – while Deb did a small ankle twist in her wedge but carried on before opening the passenger door and climbing in. She gave her ankle a quick rub while I got ready to set off.

It was a short drive, just over five minutes, and my heart pounded the whole way as my phone GPS navigated us to our destination. As we entered the mansion-filled street, we could see it was already lined with fancy cars. Mercedes, Porsches, Bentleys, Audis – you name it.

'The street is completely full. Where do I park?' I asked Deb as my clammy palms clutched the steering wheel.

'Over there.' She pointed to the last vacant spot in front of a park layered with green springy grass and overlooking the sparkling river.

I sighed with relief and reverse-paralleled in between a Porsche and a Bentley, holding my breath as I did so.

Deb hopped out first, lit her cigarette, and waited for me to put on my wedges. I hadn't worn high heels in forever and hoped I wouldn't fall over while wearing them. Fortunately, I had practised strolling up and down the hallway in front of Deb while she cracked up laughing at my incompetent walking skills.

As Deb squished her cigarette with her wedge, I peered down at her apple-red painted toes that matched her fingers. My toes were painted a sparkly silver, but my fingernails were bare due to work regulations. She crouched and looked into my side mirror while she pulled her hair tie tighter. Bits of auburn hair stuck up and the hairstyle just wasn't working, so she unravelled her thin hair and slicked it into a ponytail.

She straightened up and turned to me. 'Come on, chicka. We got this.'

I gulped. 'Yep. I'm ready.'

Deb took the lead, and I followed closely behind her as my heart thrashed like a drummer going hardcore during his solo. There were no signs of the fancy guests on the street, so I assumed that meant they were already inside. As Patrick's cobblestone driveway came into view, we noticed Daniel's four-wheel drive parked in front of the gate with the boot open. He was dressed in a black tuxedo and, surprisingly, didn't look bad at all.

'Just on time, ladies,' he said, glancing at his oversized, golden G-Shock watch.

'What should we do first?' Deb asked with a confident expression plastered on her face.

'Walk around with platters and serve all of Patrick's guests.'

'Where's the food?' I asked.

'Already inside.' Daniel shut his boot and hopped into the driver's seat. The scent of new leather came wafting our way. 'I'm going to find a park. I'll be back shortly. Go inside. Patrick is expecting you.' He dismissed us with a flick of his hand.

As soon as Daniel said those words, my throat tightened and I could barely swallow. *Why am I so damn nervous?*

Deb took one look at my face and could tell I was freaking out. She'd known me way too long.

'Naomi, what's going on? I haven't seen you this nervous in ages. Come on. It will be fine. It's just a function at some insanely rich person's house.'

I nodded, took a deep breath, and braced myself. Deb strode over to the gated entry and punched in the pin code. The gates slid open, revealing a gigantic mansion that was bigger than all the others on the street. The house was encased in stonework the colour of pizza dough. As we walked up the driveway, the sound of cascading water caught our attention. On the right side, just before the front entrance, was a lion's head water fountain, like something you would see in Italy.

We walked to the ornate, glass-panelled double doors. Deb pressed the doorbell, and while we waited for someone to answer, I smoothed my dress down repeatedly.

Moments later, a stunning, Italian-looking woman opened the door. She had pale olive skin, brown almond eyes, plump red lips, and supermodel legs. I stared in awe at her outfit: a black, short-sleeved mini dress with white lace up the sides, paired with white, classic, studded Valentino pumps. *Is this Patrick's girlfriend? Holy smokes.*

'You must be the caterers. Come this way,' the woman said in a welcoming tone. Her voice was peppered with an Italian accent.

Her golden-brown ponytail swished from side to side as she walked us across the plush, red Persian rug. Underneath the rug was a white marble floor. As we entered the gigantic kitchen, an expansive view of the glistening Noosa canals greeted us through the glass doors. Above the main kitchen counter was a long skylight, brightening the space with the remainder of the late-afternoon sun. For a moment, I wished I was a guest so that I could admire the intricate furnishings that looked imported from overseas and the view. *Wow.*

'Here are the trays.' She pointed to the polished wooden trays on top of the marble benchtop. 'Which one of you did the cooking?' She observed our faces, awaiting our answers.

'Me,' I answered, my voice rasping. 'I did the pizzas and the salmon filos.' I cleared my throat with an awkward 'hem' sound.

'Fabulous work. Mastering pizza crust and pastry is an art,' she said with an impressed smile.

I smiled in return, not sure of what to say. Patrick's girlfriend knew her food, and I was glad she approved of mine.

'Well, I'm going to attend to the guests. Daniel should be back shortly. So, prepare the trays, and let me know if you need to know anything.'

'Okay, thanks.' Deb nodded.

We arranged the trays with salmon filos on one plate and pizza on the other.

A few minutes later, Daniel walked in and gestured for us to move the trays aside. 'Come on. Start serving. We don't want the food getting cold. I'll plate up the spring rolls and sauce.'

We carefully carried the trays into the lounge room, where all the guests were socialising. Patrick's house was packed with people all dressed glamorously, and I couldn't have felt more out of place if I tried. I was the Mazda in a room full of Bentleys. He even had a pianist playing classical music on a white grand piano in the corner of the room. Fancy, alright. There were at least one hundred guests stylishly chatting away.

We moved around the room, offering our food to guests. From the speed at which the trays emptied, and the looks on their faces, we were a hit. I felt myself calming down a bit and even began to enjoy myself. Maybe waitressing for fancy people wasn't so bad after all.

My eyes scanned the room for Patrick, but I couldn't see him.

Hmm. I wonder where he is.

Just as I was making my way through the throng back to the kitchen to top up the trays with Deb, a man caught my eye. *Oh my God. It was him ... Patrick Vitello ...* My heart skipped a beat as he approached us. He wore a plain red jacket paired with a white shirt underneath and matching red pants. The first two buttons were undone, which allowed his smooth olive chest to peep through. His eyes were even greener in person, and I noticed he had both ears pierced. Two gold hoops hung from his earlobes and glinted as they caught the light. His eyes alone were enough to send goosebumps all over anyone's skin. *Jesus Christ, how does such a beautiful creature exist?*

He gave us a nod and flashed his white teeth as he turned towards the crowded room. A trail of cologne wafted past: a warm, spicy, leathery scent. It was intoxicating.

A lady who looked to be in her early sixties, dressed in a flowing, peacock-blue kaftan, stopped Patrick in his tracks. Her gold-rimmed spectacles complemented her heart-shaped face. Everything about her exuded a cultivated vibe, including her backcombed bun, which was evidently done by a team of professionals.

She looked him up and down with pursed lips, then said in a faint Italian accent, 'Patrizio, why do I bother hiring a tailor to style you for your birthday when you can't even wear what he suggests?' She shook her head before continuing. 'Where is your silk bowtie?'

Before he got the chance to speak, she was at him again. 'This outfit is incomplete.' The short woman reached up and did up his two top buttons. 'Remember you're a *Vitello*.'

'I know, Mama, but I like it as is.' He had the most alluring, melodic, and calming Italian accent I had ever heard.

'Come, now.' She waved him over and lowered her voice. 'Please don't embarrass me in front of *our* guests.' She walked upstairs, and he shook his head before following.

Deb turned to me and gave me that look she does whenever she sees a hot guy.

'I'd do bad things to that man,' she whispered in my ear.

I laughed, and in my mind, I couldn't help but imagine what it would be like to kiss his perfect lips. His eyes were the kind you'd have trouble not staring into, and *don't even get me started on his eyelashes,* so dark and long. I bet he's been offered countless modelling jobs.

By six o'clock, everyone was livelier and laughing and had moved outside onto the spacious terrace. Festoon lights were strung along the roof, adding a magical glow to the setting. There was a crisp-linen-covered table set, where a barman poured a champagne tower. It was satisfying watching the top glass fill and spill into the bottom ones. I noticed the champagne he was using said *'Vitello'* on it. Could that be another one of Patrick's businesses?

On the table beside the champagne was an Instagram-worthy feast of fresh produce, Italian meats, crackers, olives, and countless amounts of cheeses. My God, there was a lot of food. It was the biggest grazing table I'd ever seen.

Once our duties were done, we cleaned the trays in the kitchen, and as slowly as possible so we could spend more time in his house. I secretly wanted to gawk at his face one more time before we left.

Just as we were about to leave, I felt a tap on my shoulder, and I spun around to see Patrick standing there with a champagne glass in his hand. I noticed he was wearing a square-cut ruby ring set in gold on his pinky. His dark, tousled hair sat effortlessly above his shoulders. *Okay, that was unexpected. Wow.*

'You must be the famous Naomi?' His melt-worthy smile spread across his face.

I tried not to blush. 'Famous? I think you've got me confused with someone else.'

'No. I'm ninety-nine percent sure you're the Naomi who works at Mon Amour. Am I right?'

'Oh. Yes, I am, but I'm not famous.' *Famous? What? That's ridiculous.*

He laughed, then said, 'Everyone loved the food and service tonight. Why don't you both stay for a bit and relax? Enjoy yourselves. We're about to have cake.'

'Oh, I don't want to intrude,' I said modestly.

Deb appeared in front of me, blocking my view of Patrick. 'I'd love to,' she interjected, elbowing my boob. 'Naomi?'

'Okay, I'm in.' *Ow*.

'Excellent! I'll see you both outside, then.'

Patrick strolled outside, and a swarm of people instantly surrounded him like moths to a light. God, he was magnetic.

We walked out on the terrace and sat on two vacant chairs away from the main crowd and watched as a waiter rolled out a table with a gigantic triple-layered white-chocolate cake with sparklers on top.

'I'm craving a smoke so bad,' Deb said.

I ignored her, my mouth watering looking at the sight of that cake. As I scanned the rest of the area, I noticed Daniel was nowhere to be seen.

'Hey, did you see where Daniel went? He disappeared.'

'Since when do you care about Daniel?' She shot up a brow.

My reply was interrupted by the stunning lady who had let us in earlier. The crowd quietened down and gave her their full attention as she began to speak.

'I want to thank everyone for coming here tonight to celebrate Patrick's thirty-fifth birthday. As all of you know, our papa passed away three years ago. I know he would have loved to be here with you all and spend time with friends and family. Patrick, he would be so proud of you. Truly, you're incredible. Few people could do the things you do. Happy birthday, brother.' She held up her glass to salute him.

He raised his glass in return.

A tear formed in my eye and I smiled at her speech as I tried to fight a resurfacing memory. *Be happy, Naomi. It's a birthday party, for crying out loud. No tears. Not here, not now.*

The crowd sang 'Happy Birthday' to Patrick, with Deb and I joining in as we watched Patrick cut into the cake. Huge slabs of cake were handed out on golden-rimmed plates.

***

We left the party once it got too awkward with no one to talk to but Daniel. We found him red-faced and yelling at someone on the phone. It was nine o'clock when we arrived home, and as the car lights illuminated the garage door, I noticed Seb was there, back against the wall and eyes glued to his phone.

Minutes later, Deb passed out on the couch with her red polka-dot knickers on view for Seb and me.

'Told you she steals the couch,' I said as casually as possible, but my mind was flooding with pain as I tried with all my might to resist the suppressed sorrow I'd been trying to manage.

'Yeah, she's sure out to it.'

I put the zebra cushion on her crotch and left her to snore away.

'I didn't expect you to be waiting out the front for me. How long were you there for?' I raised a curious brow as I leant against the dining-room table.

'I was missing you really bad. How come you dress so sexy for work now?' He eyed me up and down as he walked closer.

'I was at a function, and this was the dress code.' I pointed to my dress.

'Nice. You look sexy.' He gave my arm a quick tickle. 'So, can I stay the night again?' He stared into my eyes and waited for my response.

'Yes, that's fine,' I replied in a fragile voice as that familiar burning feeling arose in my throat and tears began to well. I couldn't get Patrick's sister's speech about their dad passing away out of my head.

He moved in close and kissed me and tried to put his tongue to mine, but I pulled away.

'Not now, Seb. I just need some alone time for a minute.'

'You all good, gorgeous?'

I nodded and went straight to the bathroom and locked myself in. The tears came rushing as soon as I was alone. All the pain flooded back into my mind as I thought of the police coming to Mum's house and them telling her that Dad had passed. It was so sudden and out of the blue. He didn't stand a chance against that heart attack, and my heart didn't stand a chance against the pain that it would endure, forever. A million memories flickered in my mind as if a projector was flashing photographs. Suddenly it became impossible to breathe, and I slid down onto the smooth tiles and just let the tears gush.

A few knocks followed by a few twists on the doorknob disrupted my crying session.

'Yes?' I called out with a sniffle.

'It's me, Seb. Everything alright?'

'I'm okay. I just miss my *dad* so much.' My voice broke as I said the word 'dad', and a sharp feeling pierced through my heart.

He didn't say anything. That was the usual response. What could you say to someone who was grieving?

A few minutes later, I stripped and hopped straight into the shower. The running water poured down my head as I closed my eyes and held my breath. I turned away from the water and faced the shower door and practised deep breathing. My pain would always be there and at times would resurface, but I always managed to find the strength to carry on, and hot showers seemed to soothe me.

On my return, I jumped straight into bed and pulled the lilac sheets to my chest. I rolled around until I was cocooned in them, then fluffed my pillow. Seb walked into my room and lay beside me.

'Sorry about your dad, Naomi.' He kissed my damp cheek.

'Seven months have passed, and it feels like just yesterday he was alive.'

'Stay strong, babe. It will be alright.'

He leant in and tried to French-kiss me, but I moved my head back.

'I'm exhausted. Can we just go to sleep?' I asked in a brittle, tired voice.

Disappointment filled his face, and he slowly exhaled. 'Yep. Fine.'

I set the alarm on my phone and, this time, double-checked it was on.

As soon as I switched off the lights, I took some deep breaths and tried to distract myself from my grief. An image of Patrick and his ridiculously green eyes entered my mind as I replayed the whole evening like a movie from beginning to end. It ended up being one of my favourite work nights, and I wanted to redo it all over again, except for the cake. It was delicious but too rich, and I had a bigger slice than I should've, which resulted in a bloated, rumbling gut.

I'll try to make up for the overindulgence with healthy food tomorrow.

5

Leaving So Soon?

I could've sworn I was trapped in some kind of Groundhog Day, being awake far earlier than was to my liking, again. Seb was to blame for this ... If it weren't for my deep sleep during the night, I'd be highly annoyed. Him staying over had grown on me, though, or I would've tossed and turned and not slept at all, like I'd done in the past. One time, Deb wanted to sleep in my bed at Mum's house, and I tossed and turned countless times and lay awake staring at the ceiling fan the whole night. It was weird. I just couldn't get comfortable with her next to me, and so whenever we had sleepovers as adolescents, one of us would sleep on a blow-up mattress on the floor. Seb tried to French-kiss me again before bed, but eventually settled for cuddles and fell asleep with his arm wrapped around me.

'Let's go to brekkie, gorgeous?' Seb asked with his chin propped on his palm as his elbow dug into the pillow. He had an excited-schoolboy expression etched on his sunlit face.

'I want to show you off.'

'I hate to burst your bubble, but I'm not a breakfast person.' I looked down at my tummy and noticed the bloat had left. Thank God.

'Not even for me, baby?' He put on a sulky voice and stuck out his bottom lip.

Is he serious? *Not even for me, baby.* I mimicked his words back in my head and let out a laugh. Maybe I am in a viler mood than I thought.

'Uh. I guess we can, but let's go somewhere *really* good, and I mean *good*.'

I hope I'm not coming across as a bitch, but if we're going to work out, he better learn that I'm the queen of sleep-ins.

'Too easy, baby.'

It better be good, Sebastian.

We went to a breakfast café along Noosa River just a few minutes' walk from Mon Amour. It was modern with wicker chairs and round, smooth tables. Soft chatter surrounded us as the other diners clinked their cutlery against porcelain plates. Noosa River was known as a prime spot for foodies and coffee snobs, and there were plenty of places to choose from, considering nearly every building was an eatery, but this one seemed like today's flavour.

I sipped on freshly juiced pineapple with muddled mint leaves while Seb drank his cappuccino with five sugars. Our table overlooked the street and was under a white umbrella, which shielded us from the early-morning glare. As I turned my attention away from the busy street and back onto Seb, I couldn't help but be distracted by him wearing the same outfit as last night. The thought of old clothes made my skin itch. He was wearing a black shirt with a wave print, his denim jacket slung over his shoulder, faded denim knee-length shorts, and, of course, his Vans shoes.

The vibe got weird as Seb began to avoid eye contact with me and kept his eyes fixed on his coffee instead. He swallowed hard repeatedly, and his head grew more damp with sweat by the second. Judging by the look on his face, he was in deep thought, and I couldn't understand why he didn't tell me what was wrong before breakfast because it was rather distracting. He looked up at me for a brief moment, then swallowed hard once more.

What on earth? What is going on with him?

Finally, the silence and weirdness were broken, and he made proper eye contact. It was a stare full of nerves and questions, which made me curious to know what was going through his head. There was nothing I hated more than people acting out of character.

'You look exhausted. Did you get much sleep?' Seb asked.

So not even a deep sleep can wipe my tiredness away? Ah, the joys of hospitality.

'I think these long shifts are draining all of my energy. I'm so worn out and have no idea how I'll make it through today.' *Please just tell me what you're hiding already. Why do you look so nervous?*

'Yeah, I know how you feel. I struggle to do my twelve-hour shifts and can't wait until teatime.' He nodded to himself and cast his eyes out onto the road.

'So, when do you go back to work again?' I asked as I shifted in my chair and crossed my ankles, waiting for him to spill what he was concealing.

'I fly out Wednesday.' He turned his gaze back to me, and I noticed his eyes were a deeper russet.

'Wait. I thought you had two weeks off. Not one. That means you leave in four days.' My forehead creased as I processed the information.

I can't believe he's leaving so soon, and just when we're getting close, and you know what they say: absence makes the heart grow fonder.

He nodded, assuming his usual carefree demeanour. 'Yeah, I got called in. One of the crew is sick.'

'Oh, okay. Are you okay with that?' I eyed him over the top of my pineapple juice as I took another sip.

'Yeah, all good. I need the extra cash.'

'Fair enough. As long as you're okay with it, that's all that matters.' I gave him a smile and placed my glass back down.

'Which brings me to the real reason I brought you to brekkie, Naomi.' His tone was laced with nerves as he swallowed hard again.

My stomach sank. *God, this is it – the moment he reveals what's making him nervous.*

'And what's that reason?' I said, trying to appear as unflustered as possible while my mantra of *'play it cool, play it cool'* repeated in my head.

'You're sexy, Naomi, really damn sexy. Just thought you should know that.' He flashed his smile as he eyed my face.

'Thanks.' I laughed and raised my brows, wondering why something he usually said freely was making him nervous.

'I mean it, Naomi. You drive me bloody crazy. I don't even know what it is about you, but I really like you.' His stare was intense again.

I was the one swallowing hard this time and could already tell what he was going to say next.

'So ... Would you say *we're* together *like* boyfriend and girlfriend?' He raised his perfectly arched brows while his eyes remained on mine.

I took a moment to respond and looked at him while twirling a straw around my half-empty drink. 'We're seeing each other, but we're not exclusive. I like to take things slow.'

'Yeah, but it's been, like, three months. I think you should know now whether you like me or not.' His eyes squinted in curiosity as his lip snarled a little.

He's right. I should be sure of my feelings after three months, but it's not like I see him every day. He does FIFO. Two weeks on, and two weeks off, so in actuality, we've been hanging out around six weeks or so. Still quite some time, but I'm scared of committing and him playing with my heart, and I sure as hell don't want to be hurt again.

'I do like you, Seb. I like you a lot. I just don't want to commit to anything just yet. That doesn't mean I don't like you, and I'm definitely not seeing anyone else if that's what you're worried about,' I said in a reassuring tone as I looked into his hurt eyes.

'I didn't think that. I'm not used to this whole waiting so long. Most women date me pretty quickly. And I don't get what's stopping you. I've got the looks, the money, and the personality you're after.' He crossed his arms and looked out onto the street banked up with traffic.

Our conversation paused as the waiter brought our food to the table.

Just as I was beginning to trust Seb and see his soft side, he had to ruin things by throwing in an egotistical line that made me question whether his feelings were genuine and whether I was special or not. *Was I just another woman, but one that 'challenged' him?* There were genuine feelings for him, and I wanted to explore 'us', *but why did a part of me feel so unsure?* I wanted him in my life, and I sure didn't want to lose him, but there were doubts on my mind – that was certain. To say I was confused was an understatement, and I knew more than anything, life could take someone away in a heartbeat, just like my dad. My heart was too fragile, and the last thing I needed was to trust and have my heart trampled on, again.

Despite my doubts, I did admire Seb's good looks and his charming efforts, and I appreciated his commitment to proving to me that he was genuine, even though certain things he said grated on my nerves. At least he showed he was dedicated with unexpected visits and the unwavering attention he gave me. *Also, as much as I hate getting out of bed early, it is nice being here with him.*

'Well, I'm not like most women and don't want to be categorised as if we're all the same.' I knitted my hands together and leant my chin on them as I stared at him. The table was warm under my elbows.

He swallowed hard again and gave me a look full of exasperation.

'You are the most difficult woman I've ever met, Naomi.' He shook his head and let out a laugh.

'I am what I am.' I twirled one of my curls, then tucked it behind my ear while smiling playfully.

'It makes me want you more. You keep me on my toes and make me go crazy. There's no need for us to play the cat-and-mouse chase game, baby. I'm done chasing. I've got my eyes on the prize.' He pointed in my direction. 'You're the only mousey I want ... and this big cat just wants you all to himself without the games.' He winked.

A chuckle escaped my lips. 'You seriously make me laugh, Seb. Thank you, though. You're sweet.' My walls came down at the realisation that being my complete self still made him want me.

His features softened, and he gave me a huge, impressed smile.

His feelings are genuine, aren't they? Maybe I'm overthinking things. Just because one fool broke my heart doesn't mean Seb will too.

'I'm glad I got my feelings off my chest, and this food's bloody good. This has got to be my favourite brekkie place on the Coast,' Seb said while munching on his toast lathered in egg and salmon.

I cut into my poached egg and nodded my agreement as the yolk oozed across my toast.

'So, I forgot. What's your favourite colours again?' Seb asked. It felt like the question came out of nowhere.

My brows pulled together in thought. 'Oh, that's hard. Umm ... Usually anything pastel, so, like, lilac, baby pink or aqua.'

'Oh, cool. Good to know.' He grinned.

What is he up to? I ground salt and pepper onto my eggs as I watched him across the table, searching his face for clues.

The food was, in fact, well worth getting out of bed for, I mused as we finished our breakfast. A deal-breaker for me would've been hard eggs and soggy toast, but those eggs were perfectly cooked, and the toast was light, crispy, and had just enough butter, and the mushrooms were nicely sautéed with thyme and garlic.

As we went over to the register to pay, Sebastian beat me to it, pulling out his wallet first, but that didn't stop me from pulling out mine too.

'I've got this, baby. Put your purse back.' He shooed my wallet away with his hand.

'No, I'll pay. It's fine,' I insisted.

'Naomi, put your purse away, okay? I'm paying.' He smiled at the lady and looked into his wallet stacked with fifty-dollar notes. He turned to me with a grin and said, 'I had a huge pokie win with Billy last night. Don't sweat it.'

He grinned at the lady again and watched as her eyes ogled the cash. Jesus, there would have been at least a few thousand in there.

'How about I pay for myself and you pay for you?' I raised my brows.

'Naomi, I've got my money out right now, and *I'm* paying. Okay?' he snapped with squinted eyes. They were so squinted you could barely see the colour.

I allowed him to pay because I didn't want to cause a scene, and it was becoming awkward; plus, we were holding up other people in the line.

We walked over to my car as my cheeks burned with embarrassment. My intention wasn't to bicker over who paid. I just wanted to pay for myself. I didn't see the harm in that.

'I *am* paying next time,' I said as I jumped into the driver's seat and slipped on my black, cat-eyed sunglasses.

'No, Naomi. I *like* treating you. You're money-better-spent than most of the other crap I blow my pay on,' he asserted.

'Uh ... that's nice and all, Seb, but I feel uncomfortable when you insist on paying for things.' I looked at him over the top of my sunnies. 'I have my own money, you know.'

He shifted in his seat and exhaled. 'Naomi, I only see you every two weeks because of this job. I enjoy paying, and you earn nothing close to what I earn. Don't worry about it. Once I've saved up enough, you won't have to work at all.'

As he finished his sentence, it felt as though a missile pierced through my chest. Suddenly my head started to spin with thoughts about the instability of my job, but I didn't want to focus on that. My job was the best I could do for now, and as long as I had some form of wage coming in, that was good enough.

'Naomi, look at you. You're fucking gorgeous and could be a curve model with your figure, with that mermaid hair and milky skin. Girls like you shouldn't have to work. Leave that to the ugly women who can't find a man to pay for them.' His voice was filled with surprising passion.

I lost count of how many times I blinked at him, and then I stopped and stared, unable to speak. *Does he realise how insulting his compliment was? Women working has nothing to do with looks. If anything, it is empowering to support yourself without the need for a man.*

I thought hard about whether my inner feminist was going to strike at him, but I decided, no, being calm and understanding were the better options. In his mind, he was complimenting me, but he was degrading women who weren't his idea of beauty in the process.

'Seb, I can see our opinions differ on certain things, and that's normal. No one agrees on absolutely everything, but if you want to compliment me, there's no need to degrade other women. It doesn't make your compliment any better.' I gave him a half-smile.

Seb scoffed. 'Sorry, baby.'

I knew if I were to go on further about how I felt, it wouldn't register in his mind, so I decided a change of topic was my best choice.

'Do you know the time?' I pulled off my Doc Marten boots and chucked them on the back seat.

'Half-past eight,' he said while looking at his phone.

'Alright. Would you like a lift home? Because I'm going straight to mine and most probably having a nap before work.' I let out a laugh, and my heart warmed at the thought of diving back into my cosy bed.

'No. I'll get Billy to pick me up from yours because I want to go for another surf. I checked Coastal Watch and the waves were pumping earlier.' His eyes were wide with thrill and adrenaline.

I nodded my *okay* and turned up the volume on my CD player. Def Leppard came pumping through the speakers. Seb played air guitar with his hands, and I sang along with the lyrics as I pulled out of the car park and flicked the right indicator. As I entered the roundabout, I glanced at the people in activewear who walked briskly along the footpaths with small pooches on leads in one hand and takeaway coffee in the other. The river glistened and matched the colour of the blue sky. It was a picture-perfect Saturday morning, and judging by the amount of people posing on the river with selfie sticks in hand, Instagram fanatics felt the same.

The traffic was banked up, with everyone after their dose of weekend sun, so the trip home took around fifteen minutes.

Seb stayed until Billy picked him up at nine o'clock, and as he was leaving, he asked, 'Can I see you again tonight, you gorgeous thing?'

'Yes, I should be home by ten.' I gave a small nod.

Work, without a doubt, always thieved my energy, but despite Seb's random sleazy comments, a part of me wanted to give him a fair chance.

'Cool. See you then, gorgeous.' He pecked me on the cheek, then walked out of my room.

'Bye, Seb.'

6

Would You Like Hair With That?

From the moment I stepped into work, just before eleven o'clock, I knew it was going to be a tough shift. Kelly's blue hair was limp, and her orange foundation was streaked like lightning bolts down her cheeks from crying. She looked so overworked, to the point she nearly walked out of breakfast service and kept chucking frypans into the sink and barging past waitstaff who were in her way.

She gave me her quick, masculine nod. 'Hey, chicken. Wish this stupid brekkie shift would end already.' She exhaled. 'Can you believe Daniel made me do all this on my own?' She chucked another frypan into the sink, and it clattered as it hit the bottom. Then she zoomed back to a frypan on the gas stove and stirred the scrambled eggs.

I knew it wasn't the time for a conversation, so I got myself ready for the shift by placing my work gear under the sink and washing my hands.

Martin was preparing his section by folding a tea towel and placing it under his chopping board so it didn't slip. He didn't look up when I walked past, which was always a giveaway that he wasn't feeling his usual flirty self, so when he handed me enormous bunches of parsley and coriander in silence, I wasn't surprised. It wasn't like he needed to say anything – I knew what to do – but still, I wondered if anything in particular was responsible for putting him in this mood. More than anything, though, I was relieved he wasn't going on with that 'Pinky' nonsense. Imagine if I called him 'Lanky' – but, no, I'm not that mean.

Paul walked in just on time to break the mopey vibe.

'Kelly, you need to stop going out and drinking every night. You look bloody awful,' he said, shaking his head.

Kelly rolled her eyes and thundered outside, leaving the remainder of the breakfast orders to him.

Paul ignored her behaviour and cooked the rest of the orders with ease.

Fifteen minutes later, Kelly returned much jollier following twenty or so nicotine hits.

I drew a breath and braced myself for the incoming lunchtime madness as dockets came flying in from the waitstaff.

Paul was in head-chef mode and was attending to the orders, as was Martin, while I waited for mine to come in. I busied myself plucking the herbs and sorting them out into containers, which I had labelled with the name of the herb and the date on masking tape. It wasn't long until Kelly, with her sad face on, was sidling up to Paul. Before she even opened her mouth, I knew what she was about to say, and I also knew what Paul's reaction would be. Sure enough, he laughed in response to her asking to go home early and continued flipping a steak in the hot frypan. The butter sizzled as Paul ignored her request and started plating up the smashed potatoes and asparagus for the medium-rare steak order.

Martin called out 'behind' as he walked past Paul and got a tray out for a side of ciabatta. Every side of bread came with virgin olive oil and dukkah.

Paul shook his head at Kelly, who stood staring at him while he plated the steak. 'Kelly, move. You're being ludicrous. We're in the middle of lunch service. Grab your cup, fill it up with icy water, and take a Panadol, for God's sake. Just don't start a drama right now.'

'I feel like I'm going to be sick.' She held her hand over her mouth and ran out the back door.

Paul shook his head in disgust once more, then rang the bell for service.

'Hey, what did I miss? Why's Kel running out again?' Tyren asked as he waddled in.

He was a plump boy with chubby, red cheeks and a face only a mother could love, but judging by his inexplicable confidence, he thought otherwise. He insisted he was a chick magnet.

Paul and Martin were too busy cooking mains to respond to Tyren, so he waddled over to his section and began sharpening his knife.

'Tyren, you're working with Martin today, so anything he needs – you know the drill,' Paul said, not breaking eye contact with the stove.

'Yes, chef, got it,' Tyren replied instantly and gave a nod.

The only dockets coming in were for mains, so I busied myself wiping my bench and fridges. Joel wasn't on until tonight, which resulted in me washing dishes for the whole of lunch service as I didn't have anything else to do. There were no pizza orders, which, come to think of it, was kind of weird.

By half past two, the restaurant was dead, and everyone busied themselves cleaning down their sections.

Paul and Tyren did prep, while Martin left to have a much-needed break.

On my break, Deb called me over to the table at the back of the restaurant under the framed photograph of the Ait Ben Haddou (the Golden-stoned Fortress). I'd never been overseas, but that place in Morocco looked so dreamy, especially during golden hour. I looked down at the table and noticed the hot vanilla latte waiting for me. The subtle hint of vanilla mixed with the strong scent of coffee made my mouth water.

'Oh, you're the best,' I said as I squeezed behind the table to sit and took a sip.

'So, no pizza orders during service?' She raised a surprised brow.

I shook my head and shrugged. 'It's strange, isn't it? Guess no one felt like pizzas today.'

'Everyone was surprised. That hardly ever happens. Usually, your pizzas are bringing in the flocks.' She looked puzzled as she stared at me.

I smiled. 'Yeah. Oh well. Gives me a break, at least.' I tried not to overthink or draw attention to the situation, but underneath, my fingers were crossed, hoping Daniel wouldn't abuse me over it.

'Yeah. So, anywho, I am catching up with a mate tonight after work, so don't wait for me,' Deb said in a casual, sassy tone.

'Alright. Seb is coming over, and we'll probably watch movies again.'

'You're so PG.' She stood, reached for the broom against the orange wall, and began sweeping the floors.

I noticed Daniel peering at me over the coffee machine, so I downed my coffee and walked over to the sink in the kitchen. Once I was through the first load of dishes, I had one final stock pot to do. I bent down and reached for it, and as I was lifting it, I felt a pair of eyes watching me. The hairs on my neck stood up, and as I glanced over my shoulder, I could have sworn Daniel was checking out my arse.

He cocked his eyebrow and leant his long arm on the doorframe. 'Naomi, what did you do all service?' he asked in his condescending tone while eyeing me.

'I did some prep, put away food, and now I'm doing the dishes again.' I lifted the massive pot into the sink and grabbed the sink sprayer. A high-pressure water sound echoed against the stainless-steel pot.

He peered down at the sink and saw that the only thing left in the sink was the pot.

I held my breath, waiting for his response, and hoped I wouldn't cop it hard over the lack of pizza orders.

'I see. Well, as long as you're doing something and not twiddling your thumbs.' His tone was sharp and serious again.

'Of course.' *Oh, piss off, Daniel. As if I'd just stand there doing nothing.*

He turned around in a weird pirouette and paced back to his section behind the drinks area.

Just before night service, Joel arrived and began scrubbing the pots and pans to prepare for dinner. His pug-like face looked red and exhausted, and it jiggled as his hand scrubbed fast with a scourer to get the pots clean. He was a shy fella, so he would often just give an awkward smile unless Daniel or Paul were giving him orders.

Kelly never returned, which surprised no one. We would be okay without her, with the dishy on and Tyren to pick up the slack.

Pizza orders came flying in, unlike during lunch service, as a Swedish waitress with a loose blonde ponytail hung dockets. I was flat-out in my section, running back and forth to the oven with pizzas on boards. The mains came through at a steady but less frantic pace, which was a relief for Paul and Martin, who had been flogged during the lunch rush.

And then, two hours into service, every chef's nightmare came true as an eye fillet was returned. My heart pounded in suspense as I swallowed down a lump in my throat. Was this really happening? Had Paul really stuffed up? *No, this must be a mistake. Paul never buggers up his steaks.*

Daniel stormed into the kitchen, slammed the meat down on the main bench, and called me over with his hand. *Huh, why me? I didn't cook the thing.*

He was staring at my hair and a shiver of fear ran through me as I walked to him. *Oh no*, I thought. *Please not that.*

'Naomi.' His expression was stone-cold. 'This is why we wear hats in the kitchen.' He pinched his thumb and pointer finger together like tweezers and extracted a blonde hair from the smashed potato.

I had no words and felt nothing but total shame until I took a second look at the strand of hair. *Wait a minute.* There were two blonde waitstaff who wore their hair loosely in a ponytail, and yet, of course, Daniel blamed me even though my hair was in a tight bun.

'Don't you think that's a bit short to be mine?' I asked in an innocent voice.

'*Huh?* Are you seriously going to try to deny this while we're this busy? Anything to get out of work,' he said mockingly, then scoffed.

My heart stopped as I just stared at him blankly and swallowed again. This wasn't worth the argument. No matter what I said, he was going to accuse me. That was Daniel. He loved to be right, and it was impossible to defend myself when my only source of income was at stake.

'I'm sorry, Daniel. I will make sure that this won't happen again. I forgot to put on my hat.' I looked down at the floor and nodded.

'Good.' He slid the food into the bin, then walked back out to his area.

This time, I was the one feeling nauseous, except I didn't hold my hand over my mouth and just dealt with it roiling inside my tummy and creeping up my throat. After a few deep breaths, I calmed myself and then faced Paul, who was staring at me with an unreadable expression on his face. He shook his head, grabbed an eye fillet from the container, and placed it in the sizzling pan.

***

On the drive home from work, I instinctually turned to talk to Deb, but she wasn't there. The only thing next to me was an empty seat and the faint smell of cigarettes and her patchouli perfume. God, I missed chatting to that sassy girl after a never-ending Saturday shift. I looked at the time on the dashboard again: 11pm. No wonder my stomach was growling like a feline – I'd forgotten about dinner again. I didn't want seafood from the freezer, and the Greek was shut, so reheated leftover chicken would have to do.

As I pulled into the driveway, I sighed. What an unappealing dinner.

The grey-panelled garage door opened as I clicked the remote on my keys, and I parked my car next to Deb's previously bright red Suzuki Swift. Judging by the last time she used it, she'd need a jump-start to be able to drive it again. It had a thin layer of dust coating it, which made the bright red look murky.

I walked inside and had a hot shower, and as I was drying off, I heard the doorbell ring.

For a moment, I wondered who could be visiting so late, then I remembered I'd told Seb he could come over. Wrapped in my towel, with wet hair dripping down my back, I made my way over to the front of the house and opened the door. Sure enough, there Seb stood.

'Sorry I'm home so late. We were booked out, and I had a ridiculous amount of pizza orders. I should've texted you, but I've been so sidetracked by this kitchen drama that happened tonight. It really threw me,' I said quickly while I pressed my palm to my forehead.

'I only just got here. I texted you saying I was running late. Don't worry about work, babe.' His brows raised as he flashed his pearly whites.

'Oh, I was in the shower and haven't looked at my phone yet.' I folded my arms across my chest and sighed.

'All good.' His eyes ran over me.

I looked down at the paper grocery bag in his hand. *Ooh, what's in there?* My excitement switched to offended as the intrusive memory of the night's kitchen drama entered my head.

'No, seriously, I am really hurt. Daniel told me off tonight for blonde hair being in the food, and I could tell from looking at it, it wasn't my hair. It was short, and you know how long my hair is. God, he frustrates me.' I leaned against the door, sighing again.

'Yeah, bosses can be jackasses. Don't worry about it. You're home now. Sooo ...' He gestured inside, beyond me. 'Can I come in?'

I shook my head, still so preoccupied with work. 'Sorry. Of course.'

He came in and stood looking around the lounge room. 'No Deb tonight? I see the couch is empty.'

'Yes – no Deb. She's out with a friend.' I smiled.

'Oh, Billy is out tonight too. He tried to convince me to stay out with him, but I wanted to come here and see my favourite girl.' He grinned.

'Well, I'm glad because I could use the company.' I could smell something delicious and pointed to the bag in his hand. 'What's in there?'

'I figured you hadn't eaten since brekkie, so I brought you some Thai.'

'Oh my God. You didn't, did you?' Small tears of joy formed in the corners of my eyes as my mouth watered.

'Don't get your hopes up. It's cold, but it'll do the job.' He passed me the bag.

'Yep, that's what microwaves are for.' I laughed, overjoyed at the prospect of eating something other than seafood and reheated barbecue chicken.

He laughed too as I grabbed bowls from the cupboard and placed them on the kitchen counter. I took the takeaway containers out of the bag and put half of the rice in each bowl, then poured red curry over them and topped them with Pad Thai. Once both bowls were in the microwave, I didn't take my eyes off the time countdown until it said zero and there was a *ding*.

We ate the steaming food over the kitchen counter, not even bothering to go to the dining table. I leant across the bench, shovelling the food into my mouth, while Seb sat on the barstool.

'I am so thankful for this, Seb. Really.' I nodded in appreciation.

'No worries, baby. I'm glad you like them mixed like I do.' His face was alight with pleasure at our shared taste.

After we finished eating, I wiped the benches, just like at work, and rinsed and stacked the bowls in the dishwasher. Then we walked down the hallway towards my room. I realised with a jolt I still had only a towel on. *What am I thinking prancing around the house in just a towel?* Clearly, I needed sleep because my mind was in another land.

'Ummm, gosh, I guess I'd better put something on,' I said as I adjusted the towel tighter so that it didn't unravel and reveal my naked body.

'If you want to. You look pretty sexy like that.' He looked me up and down with a thrill in his eyes.

'See you in a minute.' I laughed and headed towards the bathroom.

He grabbed my arm and stopped me.

'What?' I said as I turned to him.

'I want a kiss.' His intense eyes stared into mine as he smirked.

'Can I get dressed first?' I asked with narrowed eyes.

'How long are you going to make me wait to have you?' he let out in a rush of pent-up frustration.

'Seb, it'll happen when I'm ready.' My firm tone matched my expression.

'Naomi, I like you, but, yeah, I get it – you're confused.' His expression turned cold as he looked at the doorframe of my bedroom and sighed.

'Seb, I'm not confused. I'm just not ready for anything sexual just yet. I have to be mentally prepared for that, okay?' I watched as he shoved his hands into his pockets.

He exhaled another deep breath and nodded. 'You're right. I'm sorry.'

I walked to the bathroom, threw on my nightie, and on my return, I noticed there was a small, red, velvet box sitting on my lilac bedsheets. I stared at it for a while, wide-eyed.

I wasn't sure what Seb thought of my reaction, but he leapt awkwardly from the bed, grabbed the box, and snapped it open in front of me. Inside was a blue-and-green-flecked opal necklace that glimmered under the light.

'What's this for?' I asked, mouth agape, as my heart quickened.

'Just something I wanted to give to you. To show you how much you mean to me.' His tone was sincere.

'It's really beautiful.' I stroked my finger against the oval pendant set in gold and swallowed. 'But, Seb, I can't accept this.'

He frowned, and I could see the hurt in the downward turn of his eyes.

'Why? I want you to have this, so whenever we're apart, you can wear it and think of me.'

I began to feel sick. Things were moving faster than I could keep up with, and I still hadn't figured him out.

I smiled so I didn't look rude. 'It's really kind of you, but you really don't have to buy me gifts.'

'It would look so good with your blue eyes and mermaid blonde hair. Come on. At least try it on for me, babe. Please?'

'It's very nice. Oh, okay,' I replied, staring down at it and feeling the pressure to accept it.

'Here. Let me help you with that.' He walked closer to me, took the necklace from the box, moved my wet curly hair to one side, and placed the chain around my neck. It sat high on my chest, and I admired the vivid colours glimmering as I turned to the mirror of my dressing table.

'Come here,' he said as he pulled me down on the bed and gave me a soft kiss on the lips.

'Thank you, Seb. It's really sweet of you.' I looked down at the necklace again and fiddled with it.

'Naomi.'

'Yes?' I lifted my face to his.

'I haven't felt this way since my ex. She was the most amazing girl I'd ever been with, and I didn't tell you this, but she fell pregnant.' He paused for a moment. 'And not to me, but to another man. I would have given her everything. She's so stupid losing me – so, so stupid.' His tone was full of hurt and anger, and his eyes were too.

'Yes, I know people can be awful. Hence why I don't rush into things.' I nodded while staring at him.

'This is *soo* hard to say. So hard ...' He cleared his throat, then spat out, 'Naomi, I love you.' There was a genuine warmth in his eyes but also fear.

What? That's soooo unexpected. He loves me? They're such big words, words I've personally never said, not even to Scott. My heart warmed at the effort he'd been putting in with the breakfast, the necklace, and the 'I love you'.

'You're a cool guy, and I like hanging with you. Thanks for everything you did today, and although I won't say "I love you too" just yet, do know I like you and that I appreciate everything you've done.' I placed my hand on his. 'You have cheered me up a lot and have made me forget about work.'

'That's what I want to do, babe. I want to make you happy and make you forget about the world when you're with me. Man, you're such a challenge – it's mind-boggling. Any other woman would be all over me by now.' He laughed.

'Well, just remember I'm not like just any other woman.' I placed my hand back on the bed and smiled.

7

Pay Day

Deb and I got home just after 9pm. I was flush with the excitement of a wallet full of cash and two days off work. After my shift, Daniel got out his calculator and added up the hours on my timesheet, then handed me cash from the till with his usual sneer.

'Are you looking forward to payday tomorrow?' I asked Deb as I sank into the couch and stretched out my legs. She collapsed onto her usual side, and I couldn't help feeling jealous that her money was being deposited straight into her bank account tomorrow, with her being a full-time employee and all.

'Yeah, bloody oath, I am.' She grabbed a slice of pizza from the box on the coffee table, which was accompanied by her bottle of wine, and closed her eyes as she took a bite. 'Oh my God, Naomi, whatever you do to that dough ... I can't even deal. It's so light and chewy yet crispy on the bottom.' She paused for a moment while she scoffed the rest of the slice. 'Mmm.'

'Thanks, Deb.' I gave her a smile that quickly turned into a frown as I thought about what was really bothering me. 'I wish Daniel would employ me properly. At the time, when I accepted his cash-in-hand offer, I wasn't thinking straight. I was desperate for a job in a restaurant since the last restaurant I worked at closed, and now I feel silly for agreeing to cash. It feels like he just plays games with me.'

With a sigh, I pressed my hands to my face, then knotted them together on my lap.

'It's shit, I know, but that's Daniel. He plays games with everyone.' She sucked her fingers, then wiped them down her work shirt.

'Indeed, but it doesn't make it right, and him treating me like this makes me doubt myself and my abilities ... And as he likes to remind me ... I'm not a "qualified chef". When I was under Dad's wing, that never mattered. None of this title stuff mattered. All that mattered was my ability to cook.'

'You cook better than most chefs I know, Naomi. You're talented. Ridiculously talented, and it's abnormal how well you cook. Like what "cook" can make consommé, seriously? Most chefs even struggle making that.' She grabbed her glass of pinot and chugged it down like it was water on a forty-degree day.

I gave her a weak smile and watched with worried eyes as she refilled her glass.

'You also nail soufflé and béarnaise sauce. You've got nothing to worry about.' She took another gulp. 'I can't cook any of that. My specialty is packet-mix macaroni and cheese, and that's it.'

'Thanks for your support and kind words, Deb. It's just so easy to slip into self-doubt mode when Daniel makes me feel so incompetent. Did I tell you he brought up I'm just a "cook" again tonight?' My eyes flickered with hurt as I sighed again.

'He does that regularly ...' She looked down at her red nails curled around the stem of her glass. 'Hey, why don't you bang Martin? He's clearly got the hots for you. He told me tonight he's mad at you because you got up him for calling you "Pinky". But anyway, what I'm trying to say is whenever I have sex, I feel better and stop overthinking and doubting myself as much.' She turned back to me with raised brows.

I let out an offended laugh. 'Uh, no, I would never sleep with Martin just because he has "the hots" for me. And I don't think he does. He's been ignoring me lately.'

'Duh. Because he feels rejected and you haven't played along. He talks about you all the time.' She rolled her eyes. 'Maybe if his hair wasn't so flat, he'd stand a chance. Poor guy.' She let out a snort as she laughed.

'Mmm. Anyway, what do you want to do tomorrow?' My tone was finally livelier as I thought about my days off.

'I have no idea. We'll figure that out in the morning.' She yawned and stretched her arms, raising her glass to the ceiling.

'Done. So, tell me ... how was last night?' I asked as we both turned to each other at the same time.

Deb grinned. 'It was great, and I mean *really* great.' She smiled to herself as she thought of her night, then took another mouthful of wine. 'Speaking of fun, have you slept with Sebastian yet?' She did the *how-you-doin'* eyebrows.

'Ooh, you're being the secretive one, aren't you? Not going to kiss and tell?'

Deb's face turned crimson. 'I'm sure you're sick of hearing about my stories of men. Now, enough about me. Answer the question. Have you and Sebastian done it yet?'

'No.' I shot her a defensive stare. 'Not yet.'

'Oh, come on. He's bonkers for you. How long are you going to keep him hanging? The poor thing would have the biggest blue balls.'

'I'm not sure. I don't feel ready with him just yet.' I looked into her ebony eyes glinting with mischievousness.

'You're not still hung up on Scott, are you?' Her eyes squinted in interest as she placed her empty glass down.

The word 'Scott' jabbed me in the heart, and that horrible feeling of being rejected returned.

'No, but what he did to me really hurt. I'm thankful he apologised a year later, but before that, he just ignored every one of my texts.'

'Lots of men root and boot, babe,' she said casually while slicking her auburn hair back into a ponytail. 'Just root and boot back. You'll gain power from it. Trust me.'

I shook my head. 'I'm not into sleeping with people to gain power. I'd rather do it when I feel sure and comfortable. I'm still testing the waters with Seb and making sure he's genuine and *truly* wants me.'

'Oh, you're such a typical Cancerian. Ruled by your fragile emotions and cynicism.' She topped up her glass and took another sip. 'Trust me. He's into you, chick. You've got nothing to worry about.'

I smiled. 'He said he loved me and gave me a necklace last night.'

'What? Really? Show me!' Her eyes were almost bulging out of her face as her mouth dropped open.

'Oh, I will soon. Right now, I want to just be a couch potato. I'm so tired. But it was an opal one. It looks so expensive, and I can't believe he gave it to me.'

'You're worth it, babe.' She shoved the last slice of pizza into her sauce-rimmed mouth.

'Thanks, Deb. I really want him to be worth it.'

Gifts were one way to get Deb interested. If you were generous, she instantly valued you. She had been like that since adolescence. I always looked for compatibility and a deeper connection, which was hard to find, but to me, a deep conversation was better than any gift you could buy. And that's not to say that I wanted to date a stinge, of course, but I didn't need to be showered with gifts to fall for someone.

My phone vibrated, and I looked at my text messages – one from Seb, and one from Mum.

The first text I opened was Mum's, which told me how much she and Carlos missed me and asked me over for a roast the next night, which sounded great. I always looked forward to my family catch-ups once a week. We set a time for 6pm, and then I opened Seb's message:

Seb: *Hey babe, can I come over tonight? Xo*

Me: *I am about to go to sleep. We will catch up Tuesday xo.*

Seb: *Why Tuesday? You know I leave Wednesday : (.*

Me: *I'm spending the day with Deb, then I've got dinner at my Mum's house. Anyway, I'm off to bed, night x.*

My phone vibrated again, but I was too tired to read the message.

8

Retail Therapy

We slept in until 11am, then spent until noon getting glammed up. Deb and I decided we'd go to Sunshine Plaza in Maroochydore for some retail therapy. It was the biggest shopping centre on the Sunshine Coast and boasted over three hundred stores. I drove as usual, and when we arrived thirty-five minutes later, I people-watched to see if anyone was leaving the multi-storeyed car park. *Yes!!!* I thought as the blue hatchback began to reverse out of the only spare space in sight.

Once I parked, we strolled side by side towards the shopping centre with grins on our faces, feeling mighty fabulous. My hair was out and blowing in the gentle breeze that swept through the car park, and I wore a black wrap dress with my Doc Martin boots. Deb wore a floral dress that fell just above her knee-high, caramel boots. Her cleavage was on show, jiggling with each step she took. Genetically blessed with great boobs and silky hair. Not fair.

'Naomi, do I look hot or what?' she asked while she twirled to face me. 'I always feel my best in my hooker boots.' She let out a cackle.

'You look great, Deb. I love that dress on you.' I gave her a smile of reassurance.

She looked me up and down. 'I know you can't dress like this for work, but, boy, if Sebastian saw you now, he'd be all over you like a fly to a light. Matte-red lippy was made for your plump lips.'

'Ha. Thanks, sugar, but as I said last night ... I'm still not ready for that yet.' I kept close to the parked cars as Deb walked ahead of me.

She did a double-take to face me. 'Why? I seriously don't get what's taking you so long. He's sooooo good-looking, you know, with his whole bad-boy thing.'

'Yes, he indeed is good-looking and reminds me of that by telling me that any other woman would be with him by now.' I scoffed at that statement and continued to walk.

'Well, it's kind of true. He's *damn* fine.'

'Uh-huh.' *And she wonders why I won't have sex with him straight away. His tactic of telling me any other woman 'would have him by now' isn't something that works for me, clearly. If anything, it plays on my insecurities more. I'll do it when I want to ...*

'Just think about how big he'd be. I reckon he would be massive. He'd make you moan all night.' Deb's voice was sensual and passionate.

I rolled my eyes at her persistence. Did she not get the hint I wasn't ready to sleep with Seb yet? 'Okay, enough graphics, babe. We're in public, and I want to focus on a fun day out together.' I smiled, hoping she'd change the subject.

'Whatever. I know you secretly love it.' She poked her tongue against her cheek, doing the blowjob sign, and moved her fist from side to side.

'Enough now. Just stop.' I laughed and gestured to the sliding doors.

We walked through the doors, went up two escalators, then turned left and kept walking until we reached the glowing lights of Mecca Cosmetica.

As soon as we arrived at the Mecca entrance, their signature smell of Maison Francis Kurkdjian's Baccarat Rogue perfume hit us. Its glorious woody, amber, floral tones made every girl want it, and it sold out like crazy. That perfume was saved to my online 'Mecca Wishlist', and I was undecided whether I wanted to join in on the craze and purchase it. Makeup seemed to give me a better high than fragrance. There was something therapeutic about slathering it on and watching my face transform, and sometimes it was fun just to sit down and play with it all for hours while watching YouTube makeup tutorials when there was nothing better to do. Those beauty influencers sure knew how to make me want every single cosmetic product they were testing. Come to think of it, YouTube tutorials and Mecca were the ones to thank for all of my makeup skills.

A lady with shiny hair and dewy makeup greeted us as we walked onto the off-white, glossy tiles. 'Good afternoon, ladies. Can I help you look for anything?' she asked with a smile.

'No, thanks. We're happy to browse,' I answered for both of us and returned the smile.

We browsed the brightly lit makeup wonderland, and I'm sure we looked like the emoji with heart eyes as we scanned all the aisles of different brands. *Hmm, which section should we visit first? Laura Mercier or Hourglass?*

'Let's look at Too Faced,' Deb said with a casual nod.

'Sure.'

We walked down the aisle at the far left of the store, admiring the cute packaging.

Deb dipped her fingers into the chocolate bar eyeshadow palette and swatched the sparkly, warm brown on her hand. As she tilted the swatch, it glimmered under the fluorescent lights.

One hour, two jumbo eyeshadow palettes, two foundations, and five lipsticks later, Deb and I walked out with bulging pink shopping bags.

We went down an escalator in search of refreshments, took a few sharp turns, and kept walking until we saw San Churros.

'Hey, is it okay if you shout me? My Afterpay account is stacked up,' Deb asked.

'Uh. Yeah, sure.' Feeling put on the spot, I agreed without further thought.

'Cool.' She gave me the thumbs-up.

'Grab a table. What would you like?' I asked Deb as I handed her a menu.

'Churros for two and a Spanish hot chocolate,' she said as her eyes scanned the menu.

'Oh, I'm not having any—'

'So? I still want churros for two,' Deb cut in and smiled.

'Umm, alright. Just two milk chocolate sauces as usual?'

She nodded her reply.

After ordering, we sat at opposite ends, people-watching with my 'healthy' smoothie and Deb's churros and hot chocolate. I was trying my hardest not to eat any treats after the cake I scoffed down at Patrick's birthday. But, damn, Patrick's cake was mighty fine, almost as fine as his lean, sculptured body.

Deb leaned towards me, looking ready for a good gossip session.

We chatted about Kelly's disappearing act last Saturday and her boyfriend with the ugly neck tattoo, who cheated on her. I could tell Deb really wanted to talk about Patrick, though, and waited for her to broach the topic.

'So, I figured out Patrick is a Libra,' Deb said while munching on her churro. Her fingers were covered in speckles of sugar.

'Oh right. He is too. Twenty-eighth of September?' I asked in a casual tone.

She swallowed. 'Yep. I am seriously crushing on him so bad. And I mean sooo bad.'

I tried not to blush as I pictured Patrick's exotic green eyes, long hair, and sculptured face. 'Haha. Every man seems to make it on your hot list lately. I can't keep up. And, yep, he's a super good-looking guy.'

'I have this theory that Libra men are super hard to tie down. I told you John was a Libra, didn't I?' She didn't wait for my response as she could see my mouth was full of smoothie. 'Well, he used to ask for nude pics all the time in high school, but I feel like he never really loved me. I sure loved him, though. I was completely invested in us, but he was just after some fun.'

I swallowed my drink and frowned at her. 'And you think that's got to do with him being a Libra?'

'Yeah, I do actually. I think Libra men are very fussy and hard to please, and they only ever have one true love in their lives.' Her ebony eyes were filled with certainty.

'That's interesting. I don't overly follow star signs to the extent you do, but I think people do act like their signs to some degree.'

'Yes, one hundred percent,' she exclaimed excitedly, her face pink. She always loved rehashing the whole drama with John. 'He is completely whipped on Eden. Like, he takes photos at least once a week posing on a mountain top with her.'

'How unfortunate we aren't Facebook friends. What a pity I miss those enthralling images,' I said dryly as I stared at her pink skin.

'Oh, shut up, you sarcastic *biatch*.' She laughed and swatted my arm with her palm.

I laughed too and shook my head as I watched her swirl two churros in the dipping sauce at the same time before she downed them. I didn't mean to be harsh, but all I could think was: *Another failed relationship.*

Deb grabbed her phone and didn't even need to type further than the letters 'j-o-' because his name was already in her search history. Her mouth dropped and eyes widened as she looked down at her screen.

'What is it?' I asked, intrigued by her facial expression.

'Look for yourself.' She held her phone to my face, and a picture of Eden's bony, long finger had a sparkling engagement ring on it. He obviously didn't know her size because it was two sizes too big.

'Looks very blingy.' I nodded, unsure of what to say about it.

Deb ignored the comment and continued with her rant.

'I can't believe he proposed to her. Like, that's a huge shock considering the way he acted with me. He confused me and just played with my heart. I thought he'd be a player forever and not settle down until his thirties. Oh well, guess he's got his happy ending ...' She sighed. 'I kind of wish we worked out, though. I mean for the reason that he's set for life ... He already pretty much owns his father's construction business, and my dad loved him ... Fuck, John's a dickhead. We were the perfect match, and he was too blind to see it.'

'Guess your first love is always the hardest to get over, hey?' I sighed to sympathise with her and get Scott out of my mind but lost the battle.

I wish I could take back what Scott took from me – my virginity and heart – but I knew that was impossible. I'd spent a whole year crying over him and waiting for him to return my love, but that never happened. Some good came out of the heartbreak, though. It made me stronger and taught me to not be so trusting and giving of myself. It taught me boundaries, and those boundaries were ones Sebastian had to deal with.

The sound of Deb's voice got me out of my reverie. 'Look, he broke my heart, but whatever, really, it's his loss. He never got to feel what it was like to sleep with me.' She put her phone down and smiled. 'And everyone knows Scorpios are the best in bed. I think Eden is a Capricorn, and they're ranked the worst in bed, so she must be doing something right to keep him interested. I wonder what? It's certainly not her dull-brown hair or eyes or her anorexic figure.' She rolled her eyes.

I didn't answer and just blinked at her a couple of times as I didn't completely agree with what she was saying. I'd always found Eden pretty and thought Deb's ranking of sex performance by star sign was ridiculous. There were many Capricorns I knew who were very capable in bed, and Scott was one of them.

'Speaking of sex, do you think Patrick would sleep with me?' Deb asked, her face changing from pink to almost purple with excitement.

My immediate response was a shrug. 'I don't have a clue, sorry. I've only met him once. You know more about him than I do.'

'I have read a lot about him. He owns that restaurant we went to in Hastings Street, one in Sydney, and another in Melbourne. Oh, another interesting thing ... his mother owns a winery on the Mornington Peninsula.' Her eyes were wide with fan-girl desire.

'Oh, of course.' I raised my eyebrows. 'That explains his last name on the champagne bottles on his birthday.'

'I sent him a friend request on Facebook this morning.' She winked at me before scoffing more churros.

'Oh, nice.'

Her face changed as she took another sip of hot chocolate. She looked up at me, serious now. 'You know, sometimes I think I'll end up a spinster. I love men, but I can't see myself ever getting married. I blame John.' She cackled. 'Do you think you'll ever settle down, Naomi?'

I rested my chin on my hands, wrinkling my nose as I thought about weddings and babies. 'I haven't ruled it out, but to be honest, it's not something that crosses my mind much.'

'So, what if Sebastian proposed? Would you say no?' Her eyes widened with curiosity. 'You look so good together. I think he's the one.'

'Well ... obviously. That would be so creepy. We have known each other for three months, remember, and I don't know him well enough.'

She leaned towards me. 'Naomi, do you even like him? When you were with Scott, you couldn't shut up about him, and with Sebastian, you're so reserved.'

Of course, I like him or I would've given him the flick by now, but I just have to be surer. Surer he's genuine and nothing like Scott: a root and boot.

'I definitely have feelings for him, but it's hard to fully feel things when I'm grieving and so afraid of losing someone else in my life.' I exhaled and glanced at the other patrons eating churros. 'And Scott truly ruined my trust for men, and the continual sleazes on Facebook don't do anything to help my opinion either.'

Deb didn't say anything, and I could tell she knew she'd pushed too far with the questions about Sebastian.

'So, anyway, back to Patrick.' Deb checked her Facebook to see if he'd accepted her request. 'He mustn't have seen it yet. Hey, we should try his wine while we're watching Netflix some night this week.'

'I thought you already tried his wine?' I raised a brow.

'Oh, did I?' she said and smacked herself lightly on the forehead. 'Ooh, I've got a better idea anyway. Why don't we book dinner at his restaurant again? We can wear our new lipsticks and talk to him.' She bounced up and down on her chair like a child.

I checked the time on my phone, thinking how nice it would be to get going soon. 'Umm. Yeah ... I guess.'

'Or once he accepts my friend request, we can go over to his house for drinks.'

I fiddled with my nails and avoided her eyes. Deb was getting a little creepy about Patrick. We'd catered one of his parties, not become his new best friends.

Thirty seconds later, I looked back up at her. 'Deb, bear in mind he's thirty-five. Do you really think he wants to hang around with girls like *us* in their twenties?'

'Hell, yes.' She laughed. 'Naomi, sometimes I think you know nothing about men. And I mean, you're only ten years younger than him. It's not even that big a gap. I could tell he really liked us. It was so obvious at the party. Why else did he ask us to stay for cake?'

'You're missing my point. He's a big deal and would hang out with extremely glamorous women and *any* woman he wanted. And I don't know – to be polite, I guess. He runs a restaurant and probably knows what it's like to slave away.'

I looked down at my handbag, pretending to search for my keys. I loved Deb to pieces – she was like a sister to me – but I was realising we had completely different views on things. She was a classic party girl who loved to socialise in large groups, and I was a reclusive cookbook nerd who preferred deep and meaningful one-on-ones.

'God, you're such a cynic, Naomi.' She shook her head at me. 'Anyway, do you want to look at any more shops?' She downed the last of her hot chocolate, licking off the light-brown milk-stache it left behind.

'No, I'm trying to cut back on spending.' I smiled, grateful for the change of subject. 'Well, on makeup, that is. I think if I buy any more, I won't be able to shut my drawers.'

Deb cracked up laughing. 'I think you're right about that. You've got enough makeup to fill a mini shop.'

She shoved her final churro in her mouth, then dipped her finger in the sauce, then into her mouth, and kept doing that until the ramekin was empty.

'Ugh, I know. I kind of got out of control after Dad died.' My heart ached for a moment at the thought.

Deb nodded and reached out for my hand. 'I get it, babe. You've got to numb the pain somehow. Good thing alcohol and churros work so well too.'

I smiled ruefully, suddenly remembering that despite our differences, Deb could be pretty great too. I lifted the pink Mecca bag and grimaced at its weight. 'It does make me feel sick, though. Like, the amount I have bought in the last seven months is obscene, and I can't help but think about how much I could have saved. Mum would be so angry if she knew I was buying so much stuff.'

'Naomi, your dad passed away in March. It's still so raw. Please don't be hard on yourself. Who gives a shit if you blow most of your money on makeup? It makes you look and feel good. That's all that matters.'

'I love my makeup, but I need to buy less and save more, but, God, it's hard.'

'Naomi, lots of people wouldn't have even gone back to work as soon as you did. I know if my dadda died, I wouldn't work for years.' Her eyes were filled with sympathy.

'That's true, but work is such a good distraction, and how else will I earn money? And also cooking makes me feel closer to Dad. Often I replay things he's taught me in my head as I cook. It's so comforting, and it feels like he's there with me.'

'You do what you feel is right, chickie.' She smiled at me warmly, her dimples showing.

I nodded. 'Thanks, Deb.'

She reached for her phone and squealed, her eyes lighting up. 'Oh my God, Naomi. He accepted me. What should I say?'

'Don't ask me. You know I hate starting up conversations.' I let out a laugh.

She rolled her eyes and started tapping away on her phone.

'Deb! What are you messaging him?' I couldn't help but admire her guts.

'I said it was a pleasure working for him and that he and I should catch up for a drink and ... *Oh my God, he just read it!* He's typing a reply now.' She gripped her phone so tight I could see her knuckles turn white.

I checked the time on my phone again. I wanted to get out of there already. 'Hey, Deb, should we grab some groceries at Coles on our way out?'

She nodded. 'Uh-huh.' Her eyes were glued to the screen.

I took a breath, knowing she wouldn't budge until he replied. When his answer finally appeared on her screen, I could tell by the way her shoulders slumped what it said.

'He said "no worries, it was a great night" and to "take care". *What?* He just ignored the question about drinks. What a prick!'

'So, now you hate him?' I frowned in sympathy, preparing for what was coming next.

'He probably thinks he's better than me. Typical hot guy.' She rolled her eyes and put her phone down.

'I wouldn't go that far, Deb. I just think he might be a little weirded out by the random catch-up remark,' I said soothingly.

'Hmm ... whatever ... Do you reckon he thinks I'm fat?' She shifted her eyes back at me.

I tried to hide my annoyance. We'd had this conversation many times already. 'Deb, I don't want to go into this conversation about weight with you again. No, of course, he doesn't think that.'

'What, because I'm a size eighteen, and he's a model, so he thinks he's too good? I'll show him,' her voice was so loud, some diners stopped and looked at her for a moment.

'Deb, cool it. He didn't even say anything wrong. His message was fine,' I assured her in a calming tone.

'Yeah, you're right. I hate how some men make me feel so insecure. I regret eating and drinking this. Now I feel fat.' She blinked, on the verge of tears.

Because we'd had this conversation so many times before, I knew what to say to cheer her up. 'Who gives a crap what he thinks anyway? Or about any guy who makes you feel like you're not enough? I know we're both hard on ourselves sometimes, but no one is perfect, and men who judge you, and especially on your looks, aren't worth your thoughts or your emotions. They clearly don't care about yours ... Honestly, you deserve better than that. You're Debra frickin' Ricci, the sassiest chick I know.' It was my turn to reach my hand out to hers. 'Men who make you feel inadequate aren't worth it. They're nothing but an insignificant waste of time.'

'You're so right, Naomi.' She squeezed my hand. 'Fuck him and every man who has made me feel like shit.'

'Come on. Let's go. And please don't let *men* be the judge of whether you're beautiful or not. You're that judge, no one else.' I smiled at her as I stood.

'You're always so good with your words, Naomi. You just know how to lift me up.'

'That's what best friends are for, and I don't know Patrick, but from what I've seen, he seems like a good guy, though he's clearly rubbed you up the wrong way. Move on. Don't worry about him. For all you know, he has a crazy girlfriend monitoring his messages, plus he is very well-known. He probably doesn't like saying much online.'

'You're right, chickie. You're so damn right. Hey, fuck it. Let's get some ice cream!' She pushed her chair out and stood.

'Alright.' I laughed. 'Then I better have a rest before dinner at Mum's.'

She nodded, feeling revived as we walked to Coles arm in arm.

9

Dinner At Mum's

I smiled as I walked up the orange, paved driveway to Mum's cosy four-bed-room house. The cottage-style exterior was decorated in soft-grey stone, with a pointy grey roof and white double-hung windows. As I reached the pale-green door, I pulled out my keys from my handbag and unlocked it, revealing Mum sitting on her cobalt-blue velvet couch. The Chesterfield couch was a recent gift to herself. Before that, it was a crimson camelback that she'd had for ten years.

'Naomi, you look lovely,' Mum said as she leapt up with her arms wide open.

Her toffee-brown hair was gathered in a stylish bun and golden tassel earrings dangled from her earlobes. I noticed her honey skin was considerably more bronzed than last Monday, which only meant one thing – she'd been gardening all week.

'Have you been shopping again? Is that a new dress?' She looked me up and down with an expression I couldn't quite read.

I looked down at my black T-shirt dress and felt flattered my plain outfit stood out as something new and worth noticing. She looked gorgeous herself with her flowing purple silk dress – material imported from India, of course.

'Uh. No, I haven't.' I stepped onto the travertine floor (arranged in a French pattern) and shut the door behind me while giving my most reassuring smile.

She gave me a quick cuddle and patted my back while I dropped my keys back into my bag.

The house smelled like roast lamb and blooming flowers, and as I stepped further inside, I was almost overwhelmed with nostalgia. A funky orange vase Mum made in her pottery-making days sat on the coffee table. The vase was filled with flowers. Yellows, purples, blues. Every time I saw colourful flowers, I thought of my childhood. For twenty-five years, Mum had bought a fresh bunch every week, along with the groceries.

I turned back to the rest of the room and craned my neck, looking for my brother. 'Where's Carlos?' I raised my eyebrows at Mum.

'He's in his room, playing computer games as usual,' she said with a polite nod and a small smile.

'Oh, *World of Warcraft*, of course. How's he feeling this week?' My eyes filled with sisterly concern and sympathy.

'I believe he's doing a lot better, but I'll let *him* tell you how he's feeling when you see him later.' She gave another small smile as we walked to the dining room, and my eyes widened as I caught sight of the wall.

'Umm, did you repaint the walls? I don't remember the dining-room wall being blue?'

'Yes, just that wall. I wanted it to *pop*, you know, like they say on TV.' She chuckled and took a step back, admiring her handiwork.

Mum was addicted to *My House Rules* or any home renovation show. Creative expression had always been her therapy.

'It looks gorgeous.' I turned to her with an impressed smile.

'Thanks, Naomi. You know I love to mix things up around the house when inspiration strikes.' Her voice was peppered with passion as she beamed, and I could tell I'd made her feel good about her quirky choices.

'Yes, you're always changing things around.' I nodded in agreement. 'By the way, the roast smells amazing.' I breathed in the rosemary, garlic, and lamb scents wafting from the oven.

She blushed. 'I'm glad you said that. I get nervous cooking for you, when you're the star cook of the house.'

I laughed, surprised. Mum had spent years working in Melbourne's most prestigious bakeries.

'Mum, you know I love your meals, but I'm the last person you need to impress, plus you're the dessert queen in this house,' I assured her with a grin.

'I'm glad you say so, Naomi Jean, and, oh, thank you, sweetheart. Most importantly, though, I'm just glad we've got food on the table.'

A pang of guilt ran through me for shopping this afternoon. And Mum being Mum, of course, read my mind by bringing up saving money.

'How is saving going? Are you saving much?' She looked straight into my eyes as she asked those questions.

'Umm ... good,' I lied and nodded casually while looking over her shoulder.

'Naomi, why don't I believe that? Is Daniel paying you properly?' Her tone shifted to concern as she folded her arms.

'Yes, Daniel has been paying me the right amount,' I said as nonchalantly as possible.

'Well, I remember that time he underpaid you by three hundred dollars.' Her blue eyes flickered with anger, but she remained composed. 'I'm glad you caught him out and got the correct pay, but I had to stop myself many times from going in there and talking to him, but, of course, I wouldn't because I respect your privacy and need for independence.'

Mum reminding me of that made my face crumple, and I let out a sigh. Typical Daniel, taking advantage of an overworked staff member who had slaved away for six split shifts in a row. I'd done Tuesday to Sunday with morning starts. He thought he'd get away with underpaying me because it added up to more than he'd realised and must've assumed I wouldn't notice. I was thankful I took a photo of my timesheet and recalculated the hours, or he might have gotten away with it.

'Yeah, thank God, I took that photo of my timesheet.'

Mum nodded, and her face switched to a look of concern again. 'Carlos and I miss having you here.' She reached out to fix a lock of my hair that had fallen out of place. 'Please know the door is open for you any time. I would much rather have you come back home and save for your future than live with Debra. Not that I have anything against Debra, of course. It's just she's not ...', she paused, searching for the right word, '*wise* with money.'

I thought of our pink Mecca shopping bags. 'I know, Mum, but I love living out of home. It's fun, and it gives me freedom.' My words came out a little more rushed than I would have liked.

'Okay, Naomi.' She looked at me closely. 'As long as you're saving and happy – that's the main thing.'

I smiled, hoping I looked believable. 'I am. I promise.'

It was obvious Mum hadn't quite bought my story, but I busied myself setting the dining table, mostly so I could turn my back to her and not lie any further. There was a colourful silk cloth draped over the table and proper linen napkins neatly folded in golden napkin rings. I fetched the polished cutlery – as fancy as the utensils used in any local five-star restaurant – and sat water glasses on agate crystal coasters. The flame from the tealight flickered inside the pewter holder and cast petal-like shapes against the rich silk of the tablecloth.

'Dinner's ready,' Mum called loud enough for the whole house to hear as she began slicing the roast with a carving knife and fork.

Within seconds, Carlos emerged and sat at the head of the table without looking at me. He was wearing Dad's old blue-and-white checked, button-up shirt. In fact, the whole resemblance between those two was uncanny. The same blue eyes, chocolate hair, fair skin, and koala nose. Carlos and I got our wild curls and pearl skin from Dad, and sometimes it was hard to look at him without tearing up. Even his mannerisms were the same as Dad's – the way his lip twitched when he was concentrating or the way he stood with his hand on his hip while stirring something in the frypan.

'Hey, Naomi.' He gave his usual closed-lip smile, and I could tell he was glad to see me.

I smiled at him in a way I hoped was encouraging. 'Hey, Carl. Excited for dinner?'

'You bet.'

'Me too. I always look forward to our family meals.' I pulled out the chair one down from him and sat.

He eyed me suspiciously. 'Well, if you came back home, you could have them every night.'

'I enjoy living out of home, Carl. And now that it's holidays, my shifts are consistent, so I wouldn't be home for dinner anyway. I'm enjoying the steady work; I dread going back to lousy shifts where Daniel has me on call.'

Carlos's brown curls bounced as he nodded. 'Yeah, I get it. Naomi. You don't need to make excuses. I guess Deb's more important now.'

'No, please don't say that. That's not true at all. You and Mum mean everything to me.' My eyes flickered with hurt.

'I reckon your set-up is dumb. You don't earn much and would rather pay Deb's parents money just for *freedom* when you could be here, rent-free and saving. What a waste of money, and I bet you've had to use some of Dad's money to pay the rent.' His forehead creased as his eyes stared deep into mine with a look of betrayal.

Tears formed in my eyes as I tried to swallow back my emotions, but each word he said made me feel guilty. It didn't matter to me who I paid rent to as long as I had my own space. Carlos had been like this ever since Dad passed. He saw me living out of home as abandoning our family, but that's not the way I saw it. I got where he was coming from, though. We only had *one* parent left, and our grandparents on both sides were dead, so I guess he wanted to spend every day with Mum and me while we were all alive. *Was one night a week too little to see your family?* I mean I was only a phone call away, and I regularly contacted them, but I had other commitments like work, and living out of home meant I could have boys over without questions or awkwardness.

'Carl, I don't expect to live rent-free. I don't want Mum to pay for my expenses. I want to be independent and earn my own money. I know it's tough out there, but I feel proud of being a worker.' My tone was calm and honest.

'I'd never leave Mum, Naomi. I don't care about this being independent stuff. I wouldn't be able to live with myself if I moved on with my life and something happened to her. Family is more important to me than anything on this planet.' His blue eyes brimmed with emotion.

'I know, Carlos, and I think you're such a lovely and strong person for doing this. I love our family with all my heart too.' I sighed and fiddled with the tablecloth.

'What a waste of talent.'

I wasn't sure I'd heard him right. 'Huh?' I looked at him with widened eyes.

'You're wasting your talent working there.' His voice was stern, and his eyes were narrowed.

'Why do you say that?' My left brow shot up in interest.

'Come on, Naomi. That Daniel bloke is a user. I mean, you've been working there nearly a year now, and he still hasn't offered you a full-time position. You're the reason for pizzas on his menu. That's Dad's pizza-dough recipe, *remember?*'

There wasn't a day I wasn't reminded of my work situation. Every day it seemed to come up, and, yes, that was Dad's dough recipe, which Paul and I used as the base of the recipes we created together. And, yes, Daniel did take advantage of me, and I'd put up with it for the good paydays, but I knew they'd go back to bad again. My heart quickened at the thought of lean times. Deb was truly lucky she was full-time and that her pay wouldn't be affected when the holidays ended. The only thing making me feel secure money-wise was my inheritance to fall back on, and I was saving that for emergencies.

'Carlos, I get your concerns, and, yes, Daniel is a piece of work, but you know how hard it is to find work on the Coast. I'm just a *cook*, so even if I found somewhere new to work, I would continue to get treated like just a *cook*, which means more casual shifts in a new kitchen with new rules.' I eyed him and watched his facial expression relax at my words.

'Yeah, that's true, but you deserve better than this. Dad would hate to see you in such a poor-paying job.'

I knew I should keep my mouth shut, but the words came bubbling up anyway. I was upset. 'This isn't the way things were supposed to be, you know. Dad and I were going to open a café together, and now he's gone.'

'Yeah, well, time to make other plans now.' His tone was flat.

'Mmmm.'

Carlos's dedication to our small family was admirable, but his unrealistic views on money and careers got to me. Yes, Dad would want us *both* to have high-paying careers, but that wasn't going to happen at the moment.

Mum walked over with a generous serve of roast lamb and gravy, potatoes, pumpkin, and broccoli. She put Carlos's plate down first, then mine, and lastly, hers.

Before Mum had even sat down, Carlos was already wolfing down his dinner. He stopped eating and poured a waterfall of gravy all over his food.

'Woo. Slow down, Carl. Save some for Naomi,' Mum said from the other end of the table as she took her seat. 'Sorry, Mum. I haven't eaten since breakfast.' He looked at her with guilt written all over his face.

I took a mouthful of the lamb. It was so tender and juicy, and the flavour of rosemary and garlic danced on my taste buds.

'Mum, you don't give yourself enough credit. This is amazing,' I said in satisfaction at the well-balanced flavours.

'She's right, Mum. You're a great cook.' His mouth was so full, I was surprised he could even speak.

'Oh, you two. I love roasts, but what I love even more is that we're all together.' Her eyes sparkled as she held back tears.

'Yeah, me too,' I said with a weak smile as my lip wobbled.

We sat quietly, the only sound the scrape of cutlery on plates before Mum broke the silence. 'Naomi, I wish I had a solution for you about work. It really makes me angry that he can pay you so little. Fifteen dollars an hour? Not only is that illegal, but it's an insult to your skills and your upbringing with your father's cooking.' Mum furrowed her brows and sighed. 'But I guess talking about it won't change anything. It's up to you if you want things to continue down this path.'

I took longer swallowing than I needed to before responding. 'I know. You're right. To be honest, sometimes I even question whether I like working in a kitchen anymore.' I paused and thought about the last kitchen I worked in with Dad. It was fun with him being the head chef of the kitchen, but even so, I still couldn't score a full-time position because the owner didn't have enough hours to give. 'The truth is things haven't been great lately, Mum. Would you believe Daniel accused *me* of leaving my hair in someone's meal?' I winced at the memory.

Mum screwed her nose in disgust and stared at me with worried eyes. 'Oh, Naomi. Working in a kitchen is hard work, but you love it and have always wanted to cook ever since you were a little girl. Please don't let Daniel ruin that for you. You're honestly an asset to that kitchen, and your boss is awful.' She sighed. 'There's something certainly off about him, and not to mention, he's patronising as well. It takes a lot of mental and physical strength to last in a job like that. He's very lucky to have you.'

'Thanks, Mum. You always seem to make me feel good at my most vulnerable times.' I smiled weakly.

'Anytime, sweetheart.' Mum stabbed her fork into her potato and plonked it into her mouth as she ate in slow chews.

Carlos said nothing as he took it all in and continued to eat, but his eyes and furrowed brows showed he was hurt.

An intruding thought of Daniel in his annoyingly tight shirt entered my mind as I nibbled on a piece of broccoli. *Thanks, Daniel, for ruining my dinner with an image of your nipples.* Ugh. Everything about him screamed creepy sleazebag.

Minutes later, Carlos finished his dinner before Mum and I were even halfway through ours. He sat there staring at his plate, and I could tell he regretted eating so fast. He finally got up and walked over to the couch to lie down and rested a hand on his bloated belly. It usually took ten minutes for his tummy to settle before he was back to normal. Funny boy. That was a trait he developed all on his own. Dad was a slow eater.

Mum didn't finish her dinner. Her plate still had most of her lamb and potatoes on there. I couldn't tell if she just hadn't much of an appetite or if she was too worried to finish her plate, but I guess not eating much was one of her secrets to keeping so slim. Whenever Daniel and my work situation came up, she always seemed to get distracted. He seemed to have a knack for upsetting everyone, and with the emotions of grief and worry in the room, I wasn't sure how the rest of the evening would pan out.

10

The Devil's Nectar

After dinner, we moved to the lounge room, where Mum had placed huge bags filled with old family photos on the floor. Carlos and I sat at opposite ends of the shaggy, red rug with all the lights on. I rummaged through the photos as delicately as I could, and as I flicked through them, I put the ones I'd looked at into a pile for Carlos. He grabbed a stack of photos and analysed each photo carefully, then placed the seen ones back into the cotton bag. One particular photo of Dad holding a flathead caught Carlos's eye, and he stared at it longer than all the others. He was transfixed by it, his eyes not blinking even once.

'Dad would always say nothing beats cooking and fishing, hey, Carl?' I let out a weak laugh. 'He looks so handsome, doesn't he? Look at his curly hair and blue eyes and the way the sun is shining around him like a golden aura. God, I miss him.' My throat began to burn, and each swallow felt like razors.

Carlos nodded in agreement, then placed the photo on his thigh and looked at me. 'I miss him every second, Naomi, every single second. I don't think I can go back to work like this.'

I nodded in sympathy as my eyes filled with tears. 'I understand, Carl. Take all the time you need. Are you going to start your counselling appointments this week?'

'Yep. Booked in for Thursday.' He cast his eyes back to the photo.

'Maybe we should frame that one. Carl, it's your favourite, isn't it?' Each word I spoke made my throat hurt more, and I used all my mental strength not to break down and bawl my eyes out.

'All good, Naomi. I've already got one in my room of all of us.' He picked up the photo again and stared. 'It's a good photo, though, and I guess looking at it reminds me of the good old days when he took me fishing.'

'You both loved fishing. I remember you'd be out all night and not get back until sunrise.'

He nodded with slumped shoulders. I could see the heaviness in them. It was like a rock was weighing them down.

Mum sat on the Chesterfield lounge, sipping peppermint tea while staring at the orange corner lamp. She didn't utter a word, and I could tell by her eyes she was holding back tears too.

I tried to lighten the mood with a smile but noticed my lip was trembling and so were my hands. My breathing got heavier the more I tried to fight off my emotions. The grief was stronger than me and wrestled me down until I could no longer fight it. The aftermath left me with rapid breaths, a pounding heart, and hot tears streaming down my cheeks. A tear travelled down my lips, leaving a salty taste in my mouth.

Our family was *incomplete* and would always be incomplete without Dad. I was in a state of remembrance of the good and the bad. But the bad was dominating my mind as images of Dad's heavy drinking came flashing back like ambulance lights. It started when I was sixteen – the constant fighting with Mum because he was drunk with no self-control. From then on, that damn wine always got the better of him, possessing him, giving him bloodshot eyes, and filling him with rage. He tried to give it up, and successfully managed to for a year, but on and off, he'd have slip-ups, and the fighting would resume. Mum eventually grew tired of it, and they got divorced five years ago, and then his drinking got its heaviest.

When Dad was drunk, he'd become a stranger. His warm-hearted ways disappeared, and he didn't seem to be fully aware of what he was doing. He even nearly burnt the house down by falling asleep, leaving a fish frying on the stove. I was the one who awoke to the smoke and turned off the dial. That night was his worst; he drank four bottles of wine and smashed all the plates in the cupboard. At the time, I was more frightened than angry, and I was glad he was sleeping because that meant the devil's nectar was wearing off and he'd be him again soon.

'The more I think about it, the more I hate alcohol. It never does any good for anyone. It broke Mum and Dad up and then killed him. I bet if he wasn't such a big drinker, he would've lived until his eighties,' I said in an outburst.

'He drank way too much. It got to the point he was drinking *at least* a bottle a day. I never expected him to go so young. Fifty-four is only half a life lived. It was way too soon,' Carlos said with a sigh into his palm as his elbow dug into his thigh. He put the photo back into the sack.

'It's absolutely devastating. I think what hurts the most is he won't be there for the most important moments in my life.'

'Yep.' He nodded with a blank face.

'Kids, you've got to look after your body and not abuse it. You've only got one body in this life, and it should be treated like a temple,' Mum added as she looked at us both with tears in her eyes.

Carlos and I agreed. It was scary how often people abused their bodies with substances to mask the pain. I couldn't talk – I abused my bank account by shopping for makeup and skincare. Doctors always seemed to blame it on stress. I wasn't sure. All I really knew for sure was that alcohol had gotten the better of my dad, and the ironic part was he died with a bottle of shiraz in his hand. That was the last thing he touched while he was still alive. Not *us* – damn devil's nectar.

Mum stood and wandered over to her laptop, which was sitting on the lowline unit beside the television. She crouched down and searched the web for music. After some contemplation, she decided on a seventies music channel to lighten the melancholy in the room. Once the music was on, she unravelled her bun so her hair was out.

She wiped her eyes, then stood to face us. 'Your father loved you both so much, and he was very proud.' Her voice was breaking. 'I know both of you get upset that we didn't stay as one happy family, but that's life, and your father's drinking was out of control. He was a good man, but he chose a different path.'

Carlos excused himself and went to the bathroom, holding his blank face as he walked out. I nodded in agreement with Mum, distracted by a vision of Dad. As I closed my eyes, I saw Dad and me, working side-by-side again, but this time, running our lavish dream café. We planned to serve plump quiches, sweet pies, pizzas, gourmet sandwiches (all made with our dough and pastry, of course), vibrant salads – oh, and coffees. *But what would it really have been like? Would he still have died, leaving me alone to run the business?* Just the thought made me shudder. Things were tough, but a part of me felt like maybe not getting the café had turned out for the best.

I opened my eyes. 'Yes, I know. The alcohol was the worst thing to happen to Dad. It got a strong grip on him and dragged him down and made everything worse for him. You know it makes me so mad when I see people constantly glamorising alcohol like it's such a wonderful experience, so euphoric. It's just commercialised bullshit, and I drink it sparingly.' I stood and took a seat next to her on the couch. The soft velvet pressed against my legs.

'You've always been so strong-willed and sensible, Naomi; you show great maturity for your age.' She slid towards me on the couch.

'Thanks, Mum. I've been through a lot – we all have – and it has changed me. I can't help but look at things differently.'

Mum nodded. 'It takes a powerful mind to filter through those experiences and gain strength and humbleness like you have.' I could see a flurry of tears forming again in her sparkly eyes.

'Oh, Mum, stop. You're going to make me cry again.'

I wrapped my arms around her waist and rested my cheek on her shoulder as she cuddled me back. There was nothing more comforting than a mother-daughter cuddle. Her maternal warmth sent my heart thumping and made me feel like a duckling, tucked under a mother duck's wing, protected by her love, and then I recognised this is what *true* love is. An unbreakable bond between a mother and a daughter. No games, just pure loyalty.

She took a deep breath and moved to sit back up, tucking her hair behind her ears. Always her shorthand for *'okay, back to business'*.

'So, tell me what's been happening in your life this past week?'

I let go of her. 'Oh, same old. Work and hanging out with Deb.'

'Is that all?' Her damp eyes stared into mine with brows raised.

'Yes, afraid so, and what about you?'

Mum grinned. 'Actually, I've been working on a new painting! I think it will be done in the next few weeks.'

'Can't I see it now?' I asked, thrilled to see Mum so passionate about something.

'Hmmm, I would rather surprise you when it's finished.'

I looked around the white lounge-room walls (Mum called them her blank canvas waiting to be decorated) and noticed she had swapped her tulip painting for a rainbow leopard. She certainly had unique taste. Dad taught me how to combine flavours, but Mum was also responsible for the creativity I loved in my cooking. One time I was asked to make a dessert pizza for a Valentine's gift, and I created a heart-shaped pizza, with a biscuit base, filled with vanilla custard, topped with heart-shaped strawberries, and finished with a swirl of raspberry puree. That customer made an appearance in Mon Amour every fortnight after that.

I pointed to the picture on the wall. 'I love your rainbow leopard so much. It's beautiful. Look at its eyes.' I stood and walked closer to it so I could get a better look. Flecks of smooth paint gave a three-dimensional effect to the painting. The orange-yellow eyes were truly hypnotic.

'I finished it yesterday. I am really happy with it.' She beamed as she stood beside me.

'Well, you should be. You're immensely talented. Why aren't you selling these?' I raised my brows and turned back to her.

'Oh, I couldn't. I love my paintings too much.' You could see the attachment to them in her facial expression.

I imagined Mum's art in a gallery and envisioned all the viewers' mouths open with awe. Just the thought of it made my heart quicken with excitement.

'I think people would pay *big* money for art like yours. It is so colourful and exuberant.'

Mum squinted her eyes with her finger on her lip, and I could tell she was considering it. Moments later, she headed back to the kitchen, probably to start the dishes. I was about to follow her when my phone buzzed. *Debra?*

Carlos returned and busied himself with tidying the photo bags.

I slipped the phone from my pocket and looked at the screen. *Nope, Seb.*

Seb: *Babe, how's your family dinner going? I can't stop thinking about you. What should we do tomorrow? Xo.*

Me: *Dinner was great, it's so lovely to spend time with my family. What do you feel like doing?*

Seb: *Something special. Are you wearing your necklace?*

Oh, the necklace. I thought about it sitting in its box on my dressing table and felt a sudden twinge of guilt for not wearing it, but then again, if I had, Mum would have just questioned me more about shopping. And come on – it's not like opals are cheap, and if I told her I hadn't bought it, she would ask where I got it from, and I sure wasn't in the mood for that conversation.

Me: *Yes, I am, it's lovely, thank you again. See you tomorrow x*

After I followed Mum into the kitchen, she insisted I just relax and hang with Carlos as she didn't need any help washing up, but I shot back that I knew what a pain those trays were to clean. After a bit of our usual kitchen banter, we compromised. She did the washing, and I dried and put away the dishes.

It took just over an hour to comfort Carlos, and once I knew he was okay, I left and drove back home. As I walked inside, I noticed the lights were off and Deb wasn't on the red couch. The only trace of her was the silhouette of two wine bottles neatly lined up on the coffee table. *Hmm.* Did she have an early night? It was only nine o'clock. I walked to her bedroom and knocked on the door. No answer. *Weird.* I walked into my room with my phone in hand and logged onto Facebook to see if anything was happening in the land of social media. As expected, there were just countless news stories about all the horrific things happening around the world that I have no control over. *Sigh*.

Just as I was about to log off, I noticed I had a pending friend request. *Oh God, please don't be another annoying sleaze that wants to have cybersex.* I'd had too many of those creeps lately. But to my surprise, it was not a sleaze. It was Patrick ... Patrick frickin' Vitello. *Wait ... why is he adding me? Did Deb say something to him? No, surely not – she was upset over his rejection, and I doubt she said anything further to him after that. So why would he add me?* I only catered for his party one time and had only met him that once. *Weird.*

I clicked *'Confirm'* and hoped to God that Deb was fast asleep and not browsing Facebook so she wouldn't notice I was now friends with him. The last thing I needed was another drama over Patrick.

Curiosity got the better of me, so I decided to look at Patrick's profile and noticed his relationship status was hidden. *Hmmm. He is a private man, indeed.* I scrolled through his pictures, which were mostly of just him, or him with his Mum, food, wine, or his restaurants. Then I clicked on his profile pic. His sculptured face, alluring green eyes, and charming smile filled the screen and gave me a weird butterfly sensation in my tummy. I shoved the sensation away, signed off Facebook, and lay staring at the spinning ceiling fan above my bed. My heart was racing, and I suddenly felt overheated.

A Date With Sebastian

There was no better feeling than sleeping in until 11am. Peace and quiet filled my mind, and the house too. The air conditioner was set to twenty-two degrees, blowing cool air across my face and arms while the rest of me was cocooned under the blankets. *I really could just lie here all day,* I thought, *and ignore the sweltering heat outside.* Just as I was about to close my eyes again and sink my head back into the pillow, I heard the doorbell ring. *Postman? Oh, I hope so.* I'd ordered this new organic skincare online I was dying to try. *It should be due now – it has been over a week.*

I wrapped my dressing gown around myself and made my way to the front door. As I opened the door, I saw there wasn't one parcel but two in the postman's hands.

'Howdy. Just need a signature for those, love,' he said while beads of sweat trickled from his bald head down to his neck rolls. I couldn't wait for him to go so I could shut the door and enjoy the air conditioning again.

He handed me the pen and leant the digital signature pad in my direction. I signed *'N. Clarke'* and smiled.

'Have a good day, miss,' he said as he handed me the parcels.

'You too.' I gave a warm smile.

I closed the door, carried the parcels to the dining table, and opened the first one, which was obviously the skincare. Its baby-pink parcel bag and the logo, Plump Cherry Organics, were a dead giveaway. *Oh yes*, I thought as I unpacked the products that were wrapped in pink tissue paper. I'd ordered a cream cleanser, an exfoliating scrub, moisturiser, and facial oil. Let's hope the rave reviews online were right … It cost a lot, being organic and all. Mum's words at dinner about saving money echoed briefly in my ears, but I shook my head to banish them and moved on to the next parcel.

What could it be? Sometimes I ordered so much online I lost track, but I had been *trying* to be good lately and buy less.

As I pulled out the black tissue-papered package from the padded bag, I noticed there was a black cardboard letter slipped under a twirled red ribbon. The message was printed in gold cursive writing.

It's our last day together before I fly out, so I wanted to make sure we had a great night together. I think this red lingerie would suit your sexy blonde hair. Stay gorgeous, baby. Seb xo.

Hmmm. My curious fingers unravelled the package, and, of course, it had to be the raunchiest joke of a lingerie set I'd ever seen. *Really, Seb? I thought we were making progress here.* Red lingerie was the cliché gift you'd give your lover for Valentine's Day if you hadn't much of an imagination. When Scott was playing 'nice guy', he gave me a pair of red lacey knickers on V-day, which made me nervous considering we hadn't had sex at the time. Was this Seb's way of hinting he wanted to have sex tonight? I knew it was what Scott was alluding to because he told me to wear those knickers the day I lost my virginity to him.

I held the see-through bra to my chest and examined the ant-sized black-felt hearts that were apparently meant to cover my nipples. They'd cover half a nipple if that, I concluded as I touched the material. Who designed this? It certainly wasn't 'sexy'. If he insisted on buying me lingerie, couldn't it have been tasteful like Eres Paris or something? And more importantly, how did he know my size? *I bet he got the wrong one*, I thought as I checked the labels. Nope, it was correct – 12-C bra and size 12 knickers. *Lucky guess?*

Why did I keep attracting sleazy men? First Scott, then cybersex men, and now Seb. I pressed my face into my hands and sighed. This was a kind gesture that should have made my heart flutter, not stir up my emotions and distasteful memories. Was this a vicious cycle, and would Seb have sex with me and just leave?

My train of thought was interrupted by the doorbell again, so I dropped the lingerie onto the table, and as I opened the door, I saw Sebastian standing there. He was wearing a plain white shirt with black denim shorts frayed at the knees, paired with navy Vans shoes. Simple, but he looked good. *Dammit.* Why was he so attractive?

'Soooo, did you like your present?' he asked, his face beaming.

'It was a kind gesture, Seb, but I don't wear lingerie. I'm more of a comfort kind of girl. Also, how did you know my size?' My brow shot up as I waited for his response.

His bronzed face turned beetroot red. 'Babe. This stuff is super sexy on, and Deb told me.'

I frowned at his mention of Deb and glanced over my shoulder into the living room. She should have been out of bed by now. It was unlike her not to be up at this time, puffing on a cigarette with a coffee in hand.

I turned back to Seb. 'Oh … Deb … of course, she did. And how do you know how sexy it is? Did you try it on?' I said in a playful tone dripping in sarcasm.

'No!' He frowned and crossed his arms. 'Deb thought you'd like the set.' He uncrossed his arms and shrugged.

'Oh, did she now?' My brows raised. 'Seb, I think it is very sweet you took the trouble to post me a gift, but I want to set something straight. I don't wear that kind of stuff, so if you feel the need to get me a present, please keep it simple, like flowers, and remember you don't have to woo me like this.'

'Wow. I thought you'd love it. It was one of the more expensive ones in the shop.' He swallowed hard, his eyes full of disappointment.

He looked genuinely hurt, and for a moment, I felt bad about setting him straight, but if I didn't tell him how I felt, then I'd just be pretending to like it to keep him happy, and that wouldn't benefit our developing bond.

'I think it's very kind. I do. Look, I am sorry to hurt your feelings. I am just being honest.'

He exhaled. 'My ex always loved stuff like this, and it brought us closer together.'

I leant against the door jamb and sighed, reminded of Scott again. Seb meant well and was only being himself, and I knew he was trying ultra-hard to prove himself to me, but he had no idea who *I* was. If his ex was into that lingerie, good for her, but I wasn't her.

'Naomi, you're driving me nuts. I feel like nothing I do makes you happy. I buy you a necklace, and you don't want to accept it. I buy you lingerie, and you don't like it. You only see me when it's convenient for you, and you hate me paying for things!' He looked down at his Vans before continuing. 'I'm out of ideas on how to win you over.' There was a series of squeaks as he dragged one foot across the tiles in sweeping motions.

'Seb, I know you're trying your best. I get that, and you're following a formula that worked in the past, but that formula isn't working for me. I don't mean to be complicated or challenging. I just have different tastes and a different personality to some of your exes.'

'Naomi ... Can't you see I want to be that lucky guy who gets you?' He stepped closer to me and placed his hands on my shoulders. 'I want you all to myself.'

'That's sweet, Sebastian.' I looked down at the floor, copying his earlier motion but with a shoeless foot, unable to maintain eye contact.

Part of me liked Sebastian's dedication – I wasn't exactly a believer in 'real love' like the kind in cheesy romance novels, but his persistence did make me feel special. *Maybe he's as good as it gets?* Everyone has flaws and different personality traits, and maybe we'd learn to accept each other's differences. And maybe my fear of being hurt again was all in my head. *Is Deb right? Is he the 'one'? And will I see that in time?*

'I really love you, Naomi, and it drives me mad that you don't show me much affection. What has a bloke got to do to get your full attention?' He let his hands fall by his side.

I took a deep breath and raised my eyes to meet his. 'I don't even know what to say, Seb, because the truth is ... I'm so numb and emotionally wounded, and I can't reciprocate the love you give to me just yet, but I'm working on it.'

'I know what it's like to feel numb.' He sighed. 'I just want to help you feel better.'

'I really appreciate all your effort, Seb. Thanks for sticking by me while I'm grieving and figuring things out.' I looked into his russet eyes, which were filled with emotion.

'I'll do whatever it takes to prove to you that I'm serious, Naomi.' He took a step back. 'Whatever it takes,' he insisted.

I let out a little laugh and gave him a smile. His efforts to prove he cared were admirable.

I nodded. 'I better get changed.'

As I got dressed in the bathroom, I found myself putting in the same effort I did on our very first date, and even wore the same aqua bodycon dress and French pear and freesia perfume. I did my makeup natural with a bold red lip and placed his opal necklace around my neck. I noticed my heart was racing. The final step was doing my hair, which seemed like the longest part of getting ready.

'Everything okay in there, cutie?' Seb called out and rapped on the door.

'Yes.' I swung open the door and glanced at his curls gelled back.

His eyes admired me from head to toe as he flashed his pearly white teeth.

'Shit, Naomi, you're going to kill me dressing like that. How did you get so bloody sexy? You have the hips of a goddess.'

As soon as he complimented me, my cheeks bloomed red. 'Thanks, Seb. Thought I'd dress up for old times' sake.'

'You never disappoint, do you? Your legs are fucking killer. You should wear more tight dresses like that.' His face was enchanted as he admired the contours of my body.

'Do you remember when I wore this on our first date?' I smoothed my dress down. 'We went to that all-you-can-eat Turkish restaurant, and you took those photos of me under those colourful lanterns. And remember that waiter who got cranky, and his responses were grunts every time you changed your order. You were really testing his patience. He looked like he was going to explode.' My head fell back with laughter.

'Yeah, the angry prick. I remember the first night I met you. It was in May, and Billy and I were having a few beers in Mon Amour, and we ordered a ham-and-pineapple pizza and those spicy chips, and I swear after eating your pizza, it was love at first bite. It was the best pizza I'd ever had.'

I laughed again, thinking about that night. 'When you came into the kitchen to meet me, I was shocked. I've had a few people want to meet me for my pizzas but not ever for ham-and-pineapple.'

'Well, you can actually cook properly. Some people put too many ingredients on and it becomes soggy, and some people use tinned pineapple. You can always tell the difference between tinned and fresh. Baby, you treat your pizza like it's a masterpiece with respect and ...' He paused and squeezed his eyes shut thinking of the right word. 'And, uh ... balance.' He opened them and stared at me, smiling.

'I'd never use tinned pineapple ever. That's just a shortcut, and thanks, Seb.'

'Now, speaking of food, should we get lunch or something?' His head nodded eagerly as he awaited my reply.

As soon as he mentioned lunch, my stomach reacted with a grumble before my mind could think anything.

My eyes widened. 'Yes, I'm starving.'

He let out a laugh. 'Awesome.'

***

We decided to grab fish and chips with a side of salad and ate it along Noosa River in one of the wooden gazebos. Jet skis and boats whizzed past, making the calm water rock and splash. The water was bluer than usual and so clear you could identify each fish swimming by. Sunshine shone on our skin as we stuffed battered fish and multiple chips down our mouths. My plan was to have the salad, one piece of fish, and a handful of chips, but I gave in to the chips' delicious greasiness and ate far more than I intended to. *Why can I never just have a handful of chips and be satisfied? Oh, those crispy things are lethal. So much for healthy eating. Ugh.*

An hour later, as the wind picked up and the crowds did too, we went home.

'Hey, kids,' Deb said as we walked in. She was sitting on the couch drinking a glass of water. She was still in yesterday's floral dress, and the bags under her eyes screamed, '*Hello, I'm hungover.*' Her puffy 'sex hair' was a dead giveaway she'd done more than drink last night.

'Wow, Deb, did you get hit by a truck? You look half-dead,' Seb asked with amusement plastered on his face.

'Oh, gee, thanks.' She crossed her arms and looked down at the floor, blushing. Her freckles peeked through her splotchy foundation.

He shrugged. 'Sorry, but what happened? Rough night?'

'I went out last night and had too many drinks – you know, the usual. Anyway, I haven't slept yet, so I'm going to hit the hay. You two love birds enjoy yourself, hey,' she answered with an emotionless smile and no eye contact. I couldn't tell if she was pissed off about what Seb said or whether she was hiding something. My gut told me it was both, but I couldn't be sure.

She walked to her bedroom.

When Deb was out of sight, Seb said, 'She looks like a hooker. I've never seen her look so bad before.' He laughed at his own joke and hit his thigh.

'Seb, that's uncalled for. It's clear she's had a rough night, and don't call her that. She's my best friend, and this is *her* house, remember.' I looked at him with narrowed eyes.

'Stop sulking. I'm just having a joke.' He snarled his lip in defence.

'To be honest, I'm pretty worried about her.'

'Why? What's been going on?'

'Well, she used to drink only with friends a few times a week, but now drinking seems to be an every-single-day occurrence, and her smoking has increased too. She even sits on the toilet in her room and smokes when she can't be bothered going outside.'

'All that's telling me is she's laaazy.'

I shook my head. 'Her habits are only getting stronger, and I'm not sure what's causing that. Either her addictions have gotten the better of her or she's depressed, but something has definitely changed in her over the years, and especially *now* – she isn't the same Deb anymore, and it worries me. I'm so scared of losing the old her.' I let out a heavy breath. 'I keep hoping it's just a phase and she'll snap out of it, but something is definitely not right today. I can feel it in the pit of my stomach.' I pressed my finger against my lip and squinted my eyes, trying to think of what could be upsetting her and making her drink more and more. Nothing came to mind.

'Aren't all women feisty?'

I rolled my eyes. 'If provoked.'

'Well, I better not provoke you then.' He poked his finger into my arm and stuck out his tongue. I flinched away from him and shook my head, half-grinning. 'So, baby, what do you feel like doing?' He looked right into my eyes.

'Well, after the early departure at the river, I am tired now. So, I'm thinking a movie day.' I reached out and stretched my arms.

'I'm sick of movies. Do you want to just chat in your bedroom?' His voice had an edginess to it.

'If you want.'

'Cool. Let's do that.'

We walked into my room, shut the door, and sat on the side of the bed. Then we turned to face each other.

'I want to know more about you.' He placed his hand on mine and tickled it with his fingers.

'What do you wanna know?' I twirled a loose lock of hair around my index finger.

'What does it take for you to fall in love with a man?' His words came out in a rush.

'Umm ... I don't know. Compatibility, I guess.' I let the lock fall back into place.

'Sooo ... do you think we're compatible?' His brows raised in suspense as he waited for my answer.

I could tell he needed reassurance after our earlier conversation. 'If I didn't, then you wouldn't be on my bed right now.' I brushed my foot against his leg and watched as goosebumps speckled his flesh.

'You sound sexy when you say *bed* like that. Say it again.'

'Bed,' I said in a soft, playful tone.

'Your voice is so sultry right now. Fuck, you drive me crazy.' He ran his hands through his gelled curls and eyed me sideways.

I let out a playful giggle.

He gave me that intense stare of his, and I just couldn't stop myself from moving closer to him. I looked at his bronzed muscly arms, then at his toned thighs, then back at his face. His pupils were dilated, and there was a stray curl dangling down his forehead. As I moved close enough so that our skin touched, I felt his warmth. Something in me gave way as soon as his warmth touched my skin, and I wanted to feel his body on top of mine. Deep down, I was still unsure about Seb, but what I was feeling right now had very little to do with love.

He placed his hand on my thigh and moved his wet lips in to kiss mine. Our soft kisses soon turned to French kisses as his hand stroked my thigh.

'Can I finally taste you?' he asked with a devilish grin.

I nodded as my heart quickened.

He spread my legs apart with his hands, got down on his knees, pushed up my dress, and then took off my underwear with his teeth. It took a few attempts and a few nips on my skin, but once my underwear was out of the way, he placed both of his hands on my thighs for support and looked up at me lustfully with another grin. I jolted as I felt his warm tongue glide up and down between my thighs and scrunched the sheets under my hands. As his movements got more intense, I sank my teeth into the back of my hand and tilted my head towards the ceiling. My eyes watered as soft moans escaped my lips, and I moved my hands to his head to massage it back. The massages grew aggressive, and I messed up his curls as I climaxed into his mouth.

Afterwards, he wiped his face on his T-shirt, popped a peppermint from his pocket into his mouth, and then lay on top of me, his tanned strong arms holding mine down.

'Did you like that, Naomi? I don't do that often, but I could do that to you every day. You're so sweet and silky.' He smiled devilishly.

I nodded, unable to speak or maintain eye contact.

He peeled off his shirt, and before I knew it, all of our clothes were on the floor, he was slipping on a condom, and we were having sex. My arms were pinned against the bedhead, flexing as he went deeper inside me. The bed squeaked more loudly the faster he moved, and my eyes watered some more. All the pent-up tension in my body dissipated, and I dug my hands into his back as I felt the rush of euphoria that only sex could bring.

A few minutes later, Seb got off me. The room felt hot and sweaty, and the thickness of Sebastian's breath covered his words.

'You were amazing, Naomi. You have no idea how long I've wanted to do that,' he said, resting on his side as he regained his breath.

I faced him, smiled, and watched the rise and fall of his chest. 'It felt right. I felt like doing it. Now I think I should flick the air con on,' I said as I fanned my face and clicked the remote.

'I love you, and I mean that. You're bloody amazing.'

I smiled and kissed his lips again. 'You weren't bad yourself, Seb.' I gave a quick wink and dabbed my forehead with my palm.

I wanted to do it again. I didn't know if it was the lack of sex I'd been having or whether my feelings were becoming stronger, but he was definitely growing on me. And it felt empowering to have slept with someone else since Scott.

Was I falling in love with Sebastian? Or was it lust? Only time would tell. My stomach sank as I thought about him going back to work for two weeks. Of course, I had to get attached to him when he was about to leave. *Great move, Naomi. Real smart.*

12

Goodbye, Mon Amour

Once I'd farewelled Seb before his morning flight, I slumped on the couch next to Deb and stretched my feet on the grey, shaggy rug. She took small sips of her instant coffee and stared blankly ahead. After studying her body language, my senses alerted me that she was burdened with something she was yet to share. Or would she even share it at all?

'You look a lot fresher than yesterday.' I turned to her and looked at her makeup-free face and hair slicked into a ponytail. 'How are you feeling?'

'Yeah, I'm okay.' She looked down at the rug. 'How was your night with Seb?' She slipped her red nails in her hair and scratched her scalp.

'It was really lovely, and guess what?'

'What?' She turned to face me.

'We did it.'

Her mouth dropped, and her blank face shifted into a smile of surprise. 'What!'

'Yeah, I know. I thought I wouldn't do it for ages, but I just gave in, and it felt really nice.'

'Go, girl!' She waggled her eyebrows at me. 'So, was he as big as I thought?' Her ebony eyes glinted with mischievousness.

'Oh, shut up, Deb.' I blushed and hit her with the red cushion. A splash of coffee flicked up on her pyjama top. She stared at the spillage for a moment, then ignored it like it never happened. Her face went blank again as she swallowed hard and stared at the ground before speaking.

'Na-o-mi?' Her voice wavered.

'Yes?'

'You're my best friend, and I don't want to lose you, okay?'

'Of course. You're mine too,' I assured her.

'Okay, good.'

She sucked in a sharp breath and turned to me as if she was about to say something, but she just looked at me. It was as if the words were stuck in her throat, so lodged in there I'd need tweezers to pull them out. Her face was pained as she swallowed down the words, and I felt a sick feeling slice through my gut.

Whatever happened was obviously bad enough for her to act really strangely for days and bad enough for her to fear losing me. *What on earth was going on?*

'Is everything okay, Deb?' I reached out and placed my hand on her shoulder for comfort.

'Yeah, all good.' She nodded. 'I'm going to have a smoke. I need to clear my head.' She half-smiled and stood.

'Okay. Just remember you can tell me anything.'

'Yeah.' She nodded again and slipped a cigarette from her bra, then pinched it between her lips, heading for the back door.

That sick feeling returned as she left the room, and I let out a long sigh. The deeper I thought, the more I was certain the new guy she was seeing was the cause of her strange behaviour. And what about this guy made her so silent? She, without a doubt, would always brag about every lucky man she'd been shagging and all the sexual activities they'd been up to. What had this guy done?

I checked the time on my phone and realised with a jolt if I didn't get a move on, I'd be late for work. I'd been too worried about Deb to keep track.

***

As I walked into Mon Amour, Daniel blocked me from walking into the kitchen with his hands spread-eagled as his six-foot-something body towered over mine. There was no way I'd be able to get past him unless I ducked and crawled through. His muscles were tensed as his veiny hands gripped the doorframe. And I could have sworn he was either wearing a tighter shirt or it had shrunk because his nipples were a whole lot bigger. *Weird.*

His wide hazel eyes studied my face closely, with a look that made me instantly uncomfortable.

'Naomi, we need to have a *chat* after your shift, okay?' he said with a sharpness in his voice and his chin lifted high.

'Uh. Is everything okay?' I asked in my syrupiest way as my heart jumped into my throat.

What is he going to chat to me about? Oh my God. This is so unnerving. Deb was acting weird and now Daniel wants to 'chat'. This was too much for one day. A bead of sweat trickled down my neck, and I swallowed hard, so hard Daniel eyed me with amusement as he tilted his head.

My first day back at work for the week was definitely getting off to a rocky start. There's no way I'd be able to focus. I looked at his smarmy face and eyebrows and noticed his left one had a slit of hair missing. My thoughts raced as I waited for answers to put my panic-stricken mind at ease.

'Talk later.' His tone was blunt as he dropped his arms and folded them. He made a sharp turn and headed towards the coffee machine. An overpowering smell of plum and fig perfume mixed with a sharp reek of perspiration hit my nose.

'Okay,' I said quietly. My heart was pounding in my chest, and my gut was sinking by the second.

The rapid flow of pizza orders and desserts kept me running around the kitchen like I was competing in a marathon. My continually racing heart must've done wonders for my metabolism. But no matter how many orders came flying in, nothing could take my mind away from what Daniel was going to say to me.

***

After my shift, Daniel called me over with a hand for 'that chat', once everyone had left. My heart pounded some more as I walked to the table at the back of the restaurant where Deb and I usually sat for a latte. I took a seat next to him and swallowed as I observed his serious expression and stiffened shoulders. His usual slicked-back hair had a loose dangling strand that fell on his forehead.

'Naomi, you aren't as good as you think, you know,' Daniel said, looking down at me, his chin lifted high as he tried to give off that superior vibe.

'Huh?' My head turned, perplexed.

'I'm sick of your slackness in the kitchen. You need to work faster, woman.'

'Are you joking?' I spat out and felt a sense of pride in saying that to him. 'You've got to be kidding me. I worked extremely hard tonight and managed every single one of those pizza orders on my own, and not to mention, I did the desserts and dishes too.'

My forehead was perspiring from close-down, and my heart was still pounding at an unsettling rate, though I'm sure the latter was from Daniel asking to chat to me in private and being extra douchey.

He held his long finger to his lips to indicate for me to be quiet and looked me up and down. A filthy smile spread across his thin lips, and he leant back into a more comfortable position with his legs spread. I couldn't help but notice the flake of skin on the bottom of his lip. It was so distracting, and just when I thought he couldn't get any more disgusting, he licked his lips and made them moist. A quiver of repulsion ran through my body as he moved in his seat, shifting his leg over until it touched mine. He placed a hand on my thigh and stroked my inner thigh up and down while leaning in to sniff my hair. The sound of his sniff blew through my left ear, and I instantly flinched away from him until I was almost crawling back into my seat.

He tutted. 'Naomi, you *know* I don't appreciate employees, especially women, talking back at me. It's disrespectful. I run a fine business and have eyes in the back of my head. I see everything that goes on in the kitchen. You're hopeless.' He licked his palm and slicked the loose strand of hair back into place.

'Huh. Hopeless? You can't be serious, Daniel.' Tears formed in my eyes, and my throat began to burn as I thought about all the hard work I put in every single shift. Why was he lying, and why was I letting it affect me so much?

'You're so fucking weak, Naomi. You don't have what it takes to be a chef; that's why you're just a *cook*.'

He looked more amused with each insult he threw at me and stared down at my breasts.

'It's clear to me that you never bothered to read my resume, and you haven't the faintest clue who I am because if you did, you'd know that I'm not "just a cook".' I used air quotes to emphasise how insulting I found his wording. 'I hold a Cert Two in hospitality, I'm a qualified barista, and I have my RSA.' I took a deep breath and blinked back the tears threatening to spill down my face. There's no way I would let Daniel see me cry. 'Daniel, I've worked in kitchens since I was sixteen. I'm—'

He scoffed. 'Get over yourself, woman. Listen to you try and defend yourself. It's highly amusing, I must confess … But please remember in that blonde head of yours that you're *pathetic*, and you'll never get anywhere in life. That's why you've got to work for me because you're *desperate* for money and no one else will hire you. *You need me.*' He pointed his finger in my face as flecks of spit hit my cheek.

I shook my head in disbelief, hardly believing what I was hearing.

'Daniel, all workers depend on someone else's money to survive.' What I really wanted to say was, *'State the frickin' obvious, you prick,'* but I didn't dare go that far. Yet. Instead, I replied, 'You're so wrong about me, Daniel, so wrong.' I felt the anger rising. *Uh oh. Here it comes.* 'You know what?' I stood up. 'I don't have to put up with this. I'm sick of you looking over my shoulder every minute, and I'm sick of working for pretty much nothing. I deserve a pay rise, and consistent shifts. Otherwise, I'm *out.*'

He began to laugh hysterically and stood as he clapped his hands.

'You need a good fuck – that's what you need,' he muttered under his breath.

'Excuse me? What did you just say to me?' I raised my eyebrows in horror.

'Nothing.' He smirked. 'I'm *never* going to give you a pay rise, Naomi. You're comical. You make a joke out of yourself every day. What makes *you* think *I'd ever* give *you* more money?' He cackled some more, sounding highly amused, but I could tell by the way he stood so close to me, he was turned on. He could barely take his eyes off my chest, and he looked like any moment now he'd start licking his lips like the Big Bad Wolf. *What a sick prick*, I thought to myself. *He's getting off on the power he thinks he has over me.*

I flashed back to all the moments over the months I'd caught him looking at me. I'd thought it was just him monitoring my work, but now I knew better. He was checking out my arse all those times I glanced over my shoulder and saw him staring at me. *Creep.* I continually brushed it off, over and over, but now it was evident this had been his plan all along. He wanted to make me feel worthless and needy, so I begged for my job and gave in to him. That prick really believed I'd fall for his ploy and not speak up for myself and let him get away with his abuse like I did every other shift.

I stepped backwards to a safer distance, while I shook with rage, and something else too. Strength. Unfortunately for Daniel, I'd seen manipulation before, and I wasn't going to stand for it again.

'You sicken me,' I said, my voice trembling, and a rush of tears fell down my hot cheeks. Rage tears. I clenched my nails into my hand until it hurt and took a deep breath to steady myself.

'Go on. Walk out, you slack bitch. You will come running back in the morning. How else will you make money?' The bulge in his pants was unmistakable as he took a seat and leant back into his chair with his legs spread. I knew he wanted me to see it.

'You're wrong, Daniel, so wrong. I'm out for good, and you're bloody sick, you know that? I know what you're up to, and I would never sleep with a pathetic man like you. Go screw yourself.'

I turned away from him and marched out of the restaurant and didn't stop walking until I reached my car. Deb was leaning on the passenger's side, inhaling her cigarette deeply. She looked a tear-stained mess, just like me, her face streaked with mascara as she stared blankly at the car park.

She seemed to wake up as she heard me approach. 'Finally! I was going to walk in there and see what was happening—' She broke off as she saw my face. 'What happened? Why are you crying?'

'Daniel fired me. Can we just get out of here?' I slipped out my keys and unlocked the door. I'd been well aware of how angry I'd felt, but I didn't realise how *scared* I'd been as well until I climbed inside and locked the door. My hands shook as I inserted the keys into the ignition, but I breathed deeply and counted to ten until my hands were steady enough to drive. Somehow, Deb knew not to question me. I just wanted to leave. Daniel gave me the creeps so bad, and the last thing I wanted was for him to sneak up behind my shoulder. The thought alone made me shudder.

Deb continued to sit beside me in silence as I drove out of the car park. A quick glance at her told me all I needed to know. Shock and frustration were spelled out clearly across her face. I could tell she was in shock about me being fired and frustrated about something she was yet to tell me.

I glanced in the rear-view mirror as the restaurant disappeared from view behind us and thought to myself, *I am never going back there ever again.*

13

The Dalliance

Deb collapsed onto the couch and let her flats fall with a slap to the ground as she kicked them off her feet. Tears flooded down her cheeks as her limp body shivered and she drew in laborious breaths. I'd never seen her so distraught in my life. I was utterly shaken by what had happened earlier, but I shoved it down deep as I sat beside her in silence. She needed me more than ever now. Daniel must have upset her too, but what did he say to push her so far?

I held her hand and let her cry it out, so she wasn't catching for breath when we finally spoke.

'Deb, what's wrong? Did Daniel have a go at you as well?'

'Yep.' Her voice broke. 'He ... sacked me.'

I nodded in sympathy, not surprised considering his nauseating behaviour tonight. 'What did he say to you?'

Deb sucked in a huge breath and pointed her gaze at the sliding door that led to the garage. 'I fucked up, Naomi.' She was almost whispering.

'It's okay, Deb. You can tell me.' I reached out to take her hand again, but she moved it away.

'You're going to judge me so bad for this. It's all my fault. I'm such an idiot.' She turned her face towards me just enough for me to see that tears had started falling down her cheeks again. She wiped her hand under her nose and let out a pained sigh.

'Deb, just tell me. You know I wouldn't judge you.' I gave her a look of sympathy.

'I ... I've been fucking Daniel.' She was facing me now, though her glassy, reddened eyes stared at the floor.

My heart dropped at her words and so did my mouth. 'No, Deb, no. You didn't, did you? You're kidding me.'

'I'm dead serious.' She began to cry harder again, her breath coming in sobs.

'But he's married?'

She buried her face in her hands. 'I've been going to his house the past few nights while his wife was away.'

So that's who she'd been shagging and why she didn't brag about him. I was aghast, but I tried to hide it. The last thing Deb needed right now was for me to make her feel any worse. I took a breath to steady myself and sat closer so I could rub her back while she continued to sob. 'I was wondering where you'd been disappearing to.'

She lifted her head and ran both hands through her greasy hair. 'I feel terrible.' Her words were choked. 'I am so stupid, and now I have made us both lose our jobs.'

'Does his wife know? I thought he had a kid.'

She sat up and reached for a tissue from the box on the coffee table. 'Yeah, she found out – well, caught us out by coming home early. Daniel, the twit, got the dates of her return mixed up, and she walked in and caught him banging me on their bed. And I soon learned they were her favourite sheets too. She was so angry, Naomi. She pulled him off me, then slapped him multiple times and chucked her suitcase at him. She kept calling him a lying cheating piece of trash, and I really thought she was going to kill both of us.'

I sat beside her in silence, trying to figure out what to say next.

Deb blew her nose and turned to me. 'You hate me now, don't you?'

I could tell by the look on her face how important my next words were.

I put my arm around her shoulder. 'Of course not, Deb.'

She sighed with relief. 'Thank God. I've been so scared to tell you.' She gave me a crumpled smile. 'Look, I got us into this. I will go to my parents tomorrow and tell Mum we got sacked. She won't care. She'll help us out with money until we find new jobs.'

'No, I don't expect you to do that, Deb. I don't want your mum to help us out. She has nothing to do with this.'

'Naomi, I am doing this for us. This is all my fault.'

I looked at her with what I hoped was a reassuring smile. 'Deb, this is Daniel's fault. Not yours. He should know better than to cheat on his wife with a younger woman, and to be honest, I don't even care that much about getting sacked. I was pretty close to leaving anyway. He was *never* going to give me a pay rise, and deep down, I knew it. I guess this just snapped me back into reality.'

'How did him firing you even happen? What did he say?' She raised a worried yet quizzical brow.

'Uh. He said I was just a "cook", and I was pathetic and slow. He pretty much implied I was an incompetent fool and tried his hardest to make me feel worthless.' I let out a sickened sigh.

'What the fuck, Naomi. No way. That's such bullshit.' She shook her head. 'Do you understand how many compliments you get when your food goes out? Dozens. Nearly *every* customer raves about your food. You are the reason we get so many tips. That's not even an exaggeration, and Paul too, of course. But seriously, Naomi, don't listen to him. He just said that because he's angry at me. He's such an arsehole.'

I nodded in vigorous agreement. 'I think he's had it in for me since the day I started. I genuinely think he doesn't like women.'

'Yeah, you're right.' She looked ashamed.

'And what about you? How did he fire you?' I asked in concern.

'Mine wasn't as abusive as yours. He took me out the back near the bins and said, "You're finished, Debra. I can't have you working for me anymore. You've ruined my marriage and basically fucked my life. You're a troublemaker, and you seduced me. All of this is your fault."'

I frowned, unsure of how to respond, and cleared my throat. 'You don't have to answer this, but is that true? Did you seduce him?'

He wasn't the first older man she'd slept with, so her seducing him wouldn't have been a surprise, but I didn't know for sure.

'No! It was one hundred percent a mutual agreement. We both were attracted to each other, and he was lonely …' She trailed off, smiling to herself. 'And I loved the thrill of it.'

The thought of her sleeping with a married man didn't sit well in my gut and made it churn, but I nodded and waited for her to say more.

'His main concern was keeping us a secret. He didn't want anyone to find out we ever slept together. When he was talking to me out the back, he was looking around a lot, with his voice lowered. He looked really paranoid. I think I made him lose the plot tonight. I probably shouldn't have even come in.'

Her usual sass had come back into her voice. *Thank God.*

I wanted to offer her more words of comfort, but I was just as exhausted as she was. 'Well, anyway, it's over now. It'll be okay. We all bugger up from time to time. Just learn from this experience.'

She nodded. 'Thanks so much, Naomi. I'm so relieved I've told you everything now.' She smiled weakly, her eyes crinkling with tiredness. 'Anyway, I'm going to hit the hay. I can't think, and I just want to cry some more in bed – let it all out.'

'Okay, take care, Deb. Goodnight.'

'Love you, chicka.' She leant in and kissed me on the cheek, and I stood up to give her a big hug. Then she walked to the fridge, grabbed her bottle of wine, and cradled it all the way to her room.

With more than a little relief, I made my way into my own bed. I crawled under the doona, sank my head into the pillow, and checked my phone. One text from Sebastian, and another from … my heart started pounding as I saw the name *'Daniel (Boss)'* on the screen. I opened Daniel's text first.

Daniel (Boss): *Naomi, I was just playing around, you know this, right? It was a tough night and I was angry. See you tomorrow at eleven. Sleep well, Dan.*

I shuddered at the casualness of his text message and didn't reply. *Was this man on drugs? What an absolute weirdo.*

I opened Seb's text in hopes of something sweet and comforting but was presented with a picture of his erect penis under fluorescent lights and a toilet behind him. How flattering. Underneath the image were the words: *Miss you, you make me so hard, baby. Can't wait to nail that silky pussy again.*

What the hell, Seb? We have sex, and now you're acting like the ultimate sleazebag, and instead of asking me how my day was, you present me with a picture of your penis and sex talk? Cheers. That's just what I need right now. My head tossed and turned on my pillow as I tried to get into a comfortable position but couldn't. The pillow felt deflated and uncomfortable; it fell to the floor as I sat up in haste to sigh and stretch out my arms to the ceiling. I reached for the pillow and chucked it back into place while I let everything from tonight sink in.

What an awful, awful night. Was all of this my fault? Did I somehow just attract rubbish behaviour from people? I was punctual every shift and did everything that Daniel asked of me. Without fail, I did what he asked, and maybe that was my problem? I was being too nice, and my niceness was being used against me. The same could apply to Seb.

I had sex with him, and now he thinks it's okay to send penis pictures and jump straight into sex talk. I guess that quote 'Give an inch and they'll take a mile' is utterly true, and that's what is happening to me right now.

Usually, Deb and I spilled all our secrets to each other, but I couldn't tell her what Daniel said to me earlier that night because I didn't want to believe it to be true. His words repeated in my head: *You need a good fuck – that's what you need.* I felt the disgust rising again and sank my fingernails into my palms for the second time tonight. Why do men always think that's the answer to everything? As much as I hated to admit it to myself, my fears about sleeping with Seb had come true, and I regretted it. I shouldn't have given in like that. The boundaries I had set were just thrown away like they didn't matter, when they did. I rolled over and pictured my life as a knotted ball of string I hadn't the first clue how to untangle, then before I could stop it, a little voice inside my head whispered:

Maybe Daniel's right after all, and you're just a jobless little fool. I gritted my teeth, angry with myself. *No. I will not let that poisonous effwit inside my head.*

As empowering as it was to walk out on Daniel, working for him did pay my bills, and now I was jobless, which meant I'd have to live off my inheritance with no wage to replace what I spent. *Oh no.* I was going to go backwards. I felt my stomach sink as my mind raced in a marathon of panic. It was so hard to find a job, and I sure didn't want to be a dishy.

Once I had calmed myself enough to shut my eyes and attempt sleep, my phone dinged, and with weary eyes, I glimpsed at the screen. My heart started booming as I saw a Facebook message from Patrick Vitello. *What else could possibly happen today?*

Patrick Vitello: *Hello, Naomi, how are you? This might be a bit unexpected, but would you like to get a coffee?*

What? This has to be some kind of joke. Am I on Punk'd right now? Why would Patrick Vitello, of all people, want to have coffee with me? I shook my head at the thought. *That's Daniel, inside my head, after all.* Patrick had seemed like a nice guy. Not like the others.

Before I could contemplate it more deeply, in my half-asleep state, I responded: *Hi Patrick, I'm well, thanks. Nice to hear from you, coffee sounds good.*

He opened the message almost instantly, and I watched as the replying dots jumped up and down as he typed his answer.

Patrick Vitello: *Glad to hear things are going well, I might have to order one of those sublime pizzas again. Everyone has been raving about them and now I feel my pizzas are inadequate lol.*

I smiled at his response. He'd even used a couple of winky faces in there. Cute.

Me: *Well, since you mentioned it, I quit Mon Amour tonight, so I won't be able to make you a pizza there. I guess I'll have to let you know where I'm working next and you can come try my food then.*

Patrick Vitello: *Well, I'm curious to hear more about that, how about coffee tomorrow morning, say 8?*

I thought about responding: *Wow, bit of an early bird, are we?* But instead, I wrote: *Sounds good. Where?*

Patrick Vitello: *Gerardo's on the beach in Hastings Street.*

Me: *See you then. Night.*

Patrick Vitello: *Goodnight Naomi.*

Life was hilarious. Just when I thought everything had gone wrong in my life, an unexpected nice thing happened. *I can't believe I'm going to see Patrick again. Patrick Vitello. Out of all the people in the world to get a message from! I could do with a mature friend right now, and he well and truly has his life together. Fuck you, Daniel. I am Naomi Clarke, and I don't take shit from anyone, and I wake up early. Yes, I am the queen of early mornings.*

14

The Opportunity

Sunlight pierced the gap between the linen curtains and shone right onto my face. A light breeze made the curtains billow and swept cool air across the room, for a moment. Magpies out in nearby trees sang their cheerful tunes while other birds rudely interrupted with their chirps. And as much as I wanted to shut the window and close the curtains, I convinced myself: *You're an early bird now, Naomi. Come on. Up you get*. I rubbed my eyes and let out a long yawn. Change was in the air – I could feel it – and even the sunshine and birds appeared to agree, having woken me long before my alarm was set to go off.

As sleep faded, my mind turned to last night. It was appalling the way Daniel treated me and had treated me the whole time I worked there. All my hours slaving away for a measly wage were not worth the mental abuse I received. And what an obnoxious, in-denial fool to text me afterwards as if last night was some kind of joke and his behaviour was excused because he was angry and it was a tough night. *How so, Daniel? How was it such a hard night to make a few coffees and pour some wines while the rest of your staff actually ran the restaurant and served food?* Arrogance at its finest.

I felt for Deb but couldn't help but think Daniel was not the first older man she'd slept with. She lost her virginity to a forty-year-old, smartly dressed banker with a bald, shiny head on her eighteenth birthday, leaving me at the club by myself. Anytime a man was powerful 'money-wise' she got instantly lured in by them and would do anything for their attention. I hated to admit it, but both Daniel and Deb were at fault for what happened. They were both adults who made their own life choices. Daniel was the one I was furious at, though. You marry someone, have a kid, and then when they go away, you sleaze onto someone younger, and an employee, for that matter. *Do you enjoy what you created for yourself? I hope you go broke. No, actually, I don't even care. I just never want to see you again.*

Once the rant was out of my system, I checked my phone: 6:50am. *Hmm, should I tell Deb I'm going to coffee with Patrick? Or will that only make her more upset? Best to let her sleep in and tell her about it later.*

I showered, then stood in front of the large bathroom mirror and inspected my face. My eye colour looked greyer, and my hair was a frizzy mess. I sighed and spent what felt like hours brushing my hair and disposing of the loose bits in the bin. Nothing a bit of argan serum can't fix, I thought as I crouched and grabbed the brown-tinted bottle from the cupboard and squeezed some into my palm.

After my hair was smoothish, I decided I'd let my curls down for the day and watched as the blonde locks fell to my waist. I felt an influx of nervous butterflies invade my stomach and noticed my cheeks were flushed, and so was my throat. My heart was racing so fast I could hear it in my ears. Why am I so damn nervous around this man? *He's gorgeous, yes, but he's nice. My God. Get a hold of yourself, Naomi.*

A few minutes later, after many deep breaths, I leaned into the mirror too close, and my mouth fogged my view. I wiped the smear with my clammy palm. I applied my makeup with a shaky hand, and dropped a few utensils in the process, but did a good job, considering. The end result was a natural, glowing look with a pinky-nude lip and coral cheeks.

Feeling quite pleased with how I scrubbed up, I went to the wardrobe and hunted through my clothes in search of the perfect dress. Usually, I'd throw on a T-shirt dress and Doc Martins and be done with it, but today was different. Today, I would be having coffee with one of the most successful restaurateurs in Australia, and I wanted to look my best.

I got changed into the prettiest-coloured dress in my closet. It was a cotton dress the colour of pink fairy floss that was tightly fitted around the bust and had white buttons all the way to the bottom. I smoothed the Peter Pan collars, then turned side to side in my dressing table mirror and admired how the belt cinched in my waist. The fabric was soft against my skin and fell just above my knees. *My goodness, going all out this morning*, I thought as I put pink rose earrings in and spritzed Chloe perfume on my décolletage and wrists. Nude sandals and my pink crossbody clutch finished the ensemble. My neck was still red with nerves and my hands were ridiculously clammy as I walked to the garage.

I took big breaths through my nose and exhaled through my mouth in hopes of steadying my heart rate and butterflies, then hopped into the car and reversed out of the garage with my cat-eyed sunglasses on. Elvis Presley, who'd always been Dad's favourite, sang through the speakers as I navigated the moderate Thursday traffic, passing modern houses as I drove.

Thankfully, there was only the occasional twit on the road, the worst being the creep who slammed on his brakes in the middle of Gympie Terrace while looking for a park. I get it – Noosa River is great, but you could have at least indicated. *Ugh*. Despite that, I wasn't running late for coffee with Patrick. It was going to be a good day, even though I had no job ... but I'd deal with that later.

The luxurious beachside buildings came into view as I reached Hastings Street. The heart of Noosa Heads. Tanned surfer dudes strolled the footpaths, with boards on top of their noggins as they walked barefoot and crossed the road towards the beach. For a moment, I envisioned Seb, shirtless, walking beside them with his board, but the thought quickly vanished as I caught sight of the families dressed in beach attire, strolling in huddles while their kids ran excitedly ahead with Boost Juice smoothies in hand. I could only imagine how eager they all were to press their feet into the smooth sand and leap into that refreshing sea. Nothing beats Noosa Beach.

I drove past the taxi rank to the main roundabout, flicked on my left indicator, and gave way to the influx of traffic coming from all entries. A speedy man wearing a helmet zigzagged on his moped in and out of the traffic and whizzed on ahead. Judging by his black pants and chef jacket, he worked in one of the kitchens.

The whole street was lined with cars – nearly every second building was a first-class restaurant, each with its own cuisine, and breakfast menus were always popular with the tourist crowd. The buildings that weren't restaurants were a mix of boutiques, gift shops, beachfront resorts, bars, and galleries. I resisted the urge to slam on the brakes myself, now that it was my turn to look for a park down the six-hundred-metre street. The patrons who weren't going to the beach, dressed stylishly in bright colours, strolled the streets with recyclable coffee cups.

I kept driving to the end of the main street until I passed Patrick's enormous restaurant: Casa di Vitello. A cleaner was wiping the already spotless windows while another one swept the expansive timber deck. The exterior of the restaurant exuded a relaxed, inviting feel with its wooden structure and stone walls. Patrick even had a cherub wishing fountain on the left side of the deck, where people could throw coins.

My car snailed behind the vehicles in front as I scanned for a vacant park. All full.

Just as I was about to give up and try further down towards Noosa Spit, a lady in a silver Range Rover began to reverse out. I flicked on my indicator and slithered into the vacant spot. What a score.

Feeling immensely satisfied with myself for scoring such a good park, I crossed the road smiling and strolled along the footpath. A trio of women in pink bikinis and cowboy hats scuffed their sandals along the cement as they passed me. They smelt of coconut body lotion and giggled as they chatted amongst themselves.

I sucked in deep breaths with each step as I got closer to Gerado's and gave way to a lizard running across the path heading towards a nearby garden. During the walk, I passed the fairy-light-wrapped trees and a stressed-out chef who was sucking on a cigarette with his phone in hand. Clearly, someone had messed up their restaurant's delivery as I heard him yell: 'How the hell could you forget twenty punnets of tomatoes when that's the main ingredient we need? It's on you if we're down on sales because we run out of chutney.' He drew in another drag of cigarette to calm his frustration.

The man's voice faded as I walked on. *I can't believe I'm meeting with Patrick for coffee. What a strange twenty-four hours.*

The staircase before the restaurant was sprinkled with sand, which made a gritty sound beneath my shoes as I climbed the steps. I was almost at Gerado's clear glass doors when a gusty ocean breeze flapped my dress above my thighs. Thank God no one was behind me, or I'm sure the poor bugger would have seen my underwear wedged up my arse.

I held my dress down with one hand and pulled open the door with the other. As I stepped inside, I absorbed the white walls decorated with seashell-framed art, the seashell chandeliers, and ginormous bar. Gerado's was half the size of Casa di Vitello but could fit at least two hundred and fifty diners and was very chic indeed.

As I removed my sunglasses, a waiter who looked more like a model greeted me behind the guest desk with a warm smile, 'Hello, miss. Can I help you?'

'Oh, umm ... I am meeting someone here. I'm not quite sure whether I have a reservation ...' I trailed off, hoping I didn't look as out of place as I felt. This place was fancier than I'd expected.

'So, you don't have a reservation under your name?' he asked with an arched eyebrow.

'No. It might be under Vitello, though?'

The man let out a sarcastic snort that I probably wasn't meant to hear. 'Oh, one of those girls, hey,' he muttered under his breath.

One of those girls? What is that supposed to mean?

I looked at my phone – 8:10am – and tried to ignore a rising surge of panic. *What on earth am I doing here?* I fought the urge to leave as I looked around for Patrick and caught sight of the panoramic beach views. The restaurant was buzzing with coffee snobs and mimosa drinkers who gave off laidback holiday vibes as they sat unfazed in their seats, waiting for their breakfasts. *Where was he? Oh, please don't tell me he's a no-show.*

I swallowed hard and turned back to the waiter. 'Yes, can you check, please?' I said, not quite making eye contact.

'Mr Vitello is on the list, but he only booked for *one*.' This time, his face was almost territorial.

'We were just planning to have a coffee. He, uh, invited me last night.'

'That's what they all say.' He sniffed, which was at least a slight improvement over his snort.

The door swung back open and in walked Patrick, just in time to save me from my embarrassment. He was wearing a white linen shirt with the first two buttons undone and caramel-coloured shorts folded at the knees, paired with tasselled loafers. His leathery scent drifted in the air, mixed with a hint of ocean breeze. *My God, his body's good.* There wasn't an ounce of fat on him – he was just tall and lean. At least six feet.

'Mr Vitello. Good morning, sir,' the waiter said, almost bowing.

'*Ciao*, Simon. Is my table ready for *two*?' He held up two fingers.

'Yes, right this way.' The waiter grabbed two leather-bound menus from behind the service desk and walked us past the bar. He kept walking until he stopped at a table set in linen with polished cutlery, completed with beige rattan dining chairs. At the heart of the table was a flickering tealight candle in a stylish glass. Our spot had the best views of the sparkling ocean through the windows. The waiter pulled out Patrick's chair and placed a linen napkin on his lap, then did the same for me.

'The usual, Mr Vitello?' the man asked.

'*Si.*' He nodded.

The waiter ran over to the bar without asking me for my order.

Patrick raised his hand and waved for the man to come back over.

'Yes?' He came running back so quickly it was almost laughable.

'You didn't get my friend Naomi's order.' He gestured his hand over to me.

'Oh, my apologies, Mr Vitello.'

'What can I get for you, miss?' he quickly asked as Patrick watched him.

'I'll get a vanilla latte, please.' I smiled.

'Of course.'

He didn't bother to write down my order and dashed back over to the bar. I listened as the coffee beans were being ground.

Patrick turned his green eyes back to me, and I felt my stomach flutter. 'How are you, Naomi? That colour really suits you, by the way.' He peered down at my dress.

'Oh, really?' I adjusted the top of my pink dress so that my boobs bulged slightly less. 'If I am perfectly honest, I feel really awkward.'

'Don't worry about him. He's always strange.' He smoothed his dark, tousled hair with his palm and gave a warm smile.

'Do people always address you so formally, Patrick? I'm not really used to this. I kind of feel like I'm in a business meeting or something.' I felt my neck go red again and placed my hand on the spot to cover the evidence of my obvious nerves.

Patrick laughed. 'That's adorable. Unfortunately, yes, they do, but it helps with business, so I play along.' He flashed his perfectly white, straight teeth.

His honesty was refreshing, and I relaxed as the conversation began to flow effortlessly, as if we were close friends.

'So, what's the usual that you order here?' I asked.

'A double-shot espresso.'

'Oh, nice. Do you usually order breakfast too?'

He shook his head. 'Not usually. Why? Do you want something?'

'Oh, no ... I'm actually not much of a breakfast person.' I laughed and shifted my sandals under the table, causing a scuffing sound.

'Sure. So, it's up to you if you want to tell me, but I'd love to hear why you left Mon Amour?' His green eyes glinted with curiosity.

'Oh, umm—'

Our conversation was interrupted by the waiter placing our coffees down on the table. The strong aroma instantly wafted up to my nose. *Mmm.* A delicate leaf pattern was embossed on top of the foam, and Patrick nodded his approval as the waiter left us alone again.

Morning sunlight cast across the table, warming our hands, and frothy waves crashed the shoreline. Fresh ocean breezes swept in every now and then, calming me. Just sitting there and soaking in the environment was enough to lift a bit of my leftover misery from last night. Maybe all I needed was some fresh air and stunning scenery to clear my mind so I could search for jobs more revived.

I looked around the restaurant as Patrick took his first sip of coffee. I could hear soft chatter from other patrons, and I could see every second person was eating either eggs Benedict with salmon or smashed avocado on toast. They would take a bite of their food and wash it down with either a mimosa or coffee.

The clink of a coffee cup on the saucer caught my attention, and I looked back at my dining partner. He smiled at me and tucked a loose strand behind his ear, revealing his golden hoop earring. 'We were interrupted. You were about to tell me why you left Mon Amour?'

'It's embarrassing, really.' I looked at his eyes – the sclera was as white as the linen tablecloth and showed no signs of stress. *His diet must be ultra clean, or he has good eyedrops.*

After I recounted the events of the previous night (except for the sleaze part – I left that out), Patrick looked aghast.

'I knew Daniel was rude, but I didn't think he was that bad, and you're very talented for an unqualified chef.' He glanced over his shoulder, then back at me, smirking. 'I will tell you a little secret. I only hired him for my birthday because he tracked me down. I didn't even know him, but he kept calling my restaurant, and he said, *"You have to come try our food."* So, I gave him the benefit of the doubt. It was good food, but I think that's because he wasn't cooking it. Am I right?'

I laughed and nodded my agreement, instantly feeling better about being insulted by Daniel. 'You're right about that. God, he's a demanding man.' I shook my head at the thought.

'It was worth it in the end. I got to meet you.' He grinned and took a sip of his coffee. I studied his hands; he wore a gold ring on his middle finger with the leaning Tower of Pisa imprinted into the metal and the same ruby ring from his birthday. *How sweet that he wears a little piece of Italy on him.* Not often did I see a man in jewellery, but Patrick pulled it off so well. *Oh boy, did he ever pull it off. What a well-dressed male.*

I swallowed a mouthful of my latte, a bit nervous about what I was going to say next. 'That waiter, Simon, or whatever his name is, acted strangely when I said I was having coffee with you. Like, he said *"one of those girls"*. What was that about?' I whispered in case the waiter was listening.

I could have sworn he blushed before replying, 'Oh, it's nothing. Sometimes women come in and say they have a reservation with me because they get to know my table and what time I come in, and he knows that ninety-nine percent of the time, they're lying. I almost always come in here alone.'

Of course, women chased him. He was gorgeous, so that was no surprise at all.

'Well, I guess it's good you have someone to look out for you.' I winked, suddenly feeling more confident.

He let out a hearty laugh and nodded in agreement.

'So, while I have you here, I may as well ask you – would you like to come in for a trial? Say, tomorrow?' he asked as his eyes stared into mine.

'In your restaurant?' My eyes grew with surprise.

'*Si.*' He nodded.

What? Could things get any better? Was Patrick seriously asking me to come in for a trial at one of the most prestigious restaurants in Australia? Play it cool, Naomi.

'Okay, sure. What time?'

'Let's make it eleven, and we'll work out the rest from there. I will warn you, though, it's *extremely* fast-paced due to the constant influx of customers. We're fully booked every night. That's why I'm trialling you at lunch service because it's less busy.'

'I'm good at adapting. I'll definitely give it a go. Thank you for this opportunity, Patrick. I appreciate it.' I smiled, nodding.

'My pleasure. Naomi.' The corners of his eyes crinkled as he smiled at me broadly.

'I'll see you tomorrow at eleven?'

I nodded again, squealing with delight on the inside, and returned a smile I hoped was just as charming, then finished my latte and placed it back on the saucer.

'Also, I've been meaning to ask you ... Who taught you that pizza-dough recipe?' He shot an eyebrow up.

'Oh, my dad did.' I smiled as I thought of Dad teaching me the perfect ratios of his secret pizza-dough recipe.

'Daniel was sure lucky to have that dough in his restaurant.' He looked down at his blue-and-gold Rolex watch, then looked up at me. 'Well, it looks like it's time for me to go, but it was truly lovely seeing you.'

'Thanks, Patrick.' I twisted the silver clasp on my clutch and pulled out my wallet.

Patrick shook his head. 'It's all covered, Naomi.' He finished the rest of his coffee, then stood up from the table.

I stood, and he ushered me out of the restaurant with his hand on my lower back and escorted me to my car. He was very old-fashioned, which felt nice for a change. *Thanks, Deb*, I thought to myself. She was the one who convinced Daniel to hire me as a waitress for Patrick's function. Now I could have the job of a lifetime. *Fingers crossed.*

15

Another Favour

As I walked through the garage door into the lounge room, I noticed Deb sitting in her usual spot drinking a glass of pinot grigio. She wore a black mini dress that covered half her thighs and matching sandals. Her foundation was thick enough to cover her freckles, and her lips were burgundy. The ceiling fan whooshed above her, and the air con was set to at least twenty degrees as the room was freezing compared to the humid garage. My stomach sank with sadness seeing her morning coffee being replaced with wine, and an image of my dad came into my mind. I shook my head to banish the thought of him dead with a wine bottle in hand and forced myself to focus on the good news of today.

'Woot-woo, look at you.' Her ebony eyes widened as she looked me up and down. 'Seb would be jealous. Where have you been? You seriously look incredible.'

'I've got news,' I announced as I walked towards her and padded across the shaggy rug.

'Good, I hope?' She gave a pained face.

'Yes, good at last.' I let out a sigh of relief and smiled as I took a seat beside her and sank into the couch.

'Well, come on. Spit it out.' She faced me, grinning over the rim of her lipstick-stained wineglass.

'I have a job trial at Patrick Vitello's restaurant.' I pulled my phone from my bag and rested it on the arm of the chair, ready in case anyone was to text me.

'What?' Her eyes widened, and her face displayed a look of disbelief.

'He messaged me to have coffee this morning and asked if I wanted to come in for a trial, and how could I resist?' I smiled and ran my hand through my hair.

'He *messaged* you? Or did you message him?' Her eyes narrowed.

'No, he randomly messaged me last night. It was so out of the blue.' I lifted my hand and rested it under my chin and used my thigh to support my elbow.

Deb's mouth dropped open.

'Are you joking? Naomi, please don't fuck around right now.' She drew her brows together, causing her forehead to wrinkle with annoyance.

'No, of course not,' I assured her with a shake of my head.

'Well, I hope all goes well for you.' She glanced at me and poured chilled wine down her throat.

'Thanks.' I held my hands together in my lap and gave her a slight nod.

I could sense she was annoyed at me for getting a job trial before her and could tell she was still upset about Patrick rejecting her drinks offer, but there was no way I was bringing that up again. She'd be hysterical, and we'd get into an unnecessary fight. The air suddenly felt dense, and I noticed Deb had stiffened and was looking at the floor, deeply ruminating about something. I looked away and hoped she wouldn't bring up that drink rejection or the fact that she was the reason for me getting the trial.

Today was certainly my lucky day as Deb didn't mention it again and instead said, 'So, anyway, Kelly from work messaged me this morning. Woke me up, actually.'

'Oh really? What did she say? Did she ask why we both left?' It was strange – working at Mon Amour was already beginning to feel like a distant memory. *Shows what distraction does, but I'm sure that'll change once I slip back into negative thoughts of Daniel.*

'Oh yeah. I explained Daniel went psycho, and you're not going to believe this, chicka.' Her eyes were serious now.

'Oh, God, it's something else to do with Daniel, isn't it?' I couldn't help but roll my eyes at his name.

'Yep, you guessed it. So, Kelly also said she had an argument with Daniel a few weeks back, and guess what it was regarding?'

'I don't know.' I shrugged. 'Money?'

'Cha-ching! Yep. So, apparently, Daniel has been paying Martin ten thousand dollars more than Kelly per year, yet she does more hours. Go figure.'

My mouth dropped at the same time as my stomach, and all I could think was: *You sexist prick.* I shook my head in disgust.

As if on cue, my phone started ringing and vibrating against the couch as *'Daniel (Boss)'* appeared on the screen.

'Oh my God, Daniel is calling me right now. Can you believe it?' *Speak of the frickin' devil.*

She rolled her eyes so far back into her head that just the whites showed. 'Do you want me to answer it?'

I shook my head. 'It's just funny he can say all of those false things to me last night, yet he is calling today like it never happened. Now who's desperate?' I let the phone ring out and smirked with satisfaction.

'Yeah, he's such an arse. We'll show him.' She took another sip of wine and looked deep in thought.

'We sure will. I won't ever go back to that again. I'm not putting up with abuse from *anyone.* Employer or not, everyone deserves to be treated fairly, and I'm not letting myself get used again.'

She came out of her thoughts. 'Go, girl.' She paused. 'So, I need to ask a favour.'

'Alright, what is it?'

'I've had a few drinks this morning, and I slept terribly last night. Any chance you could drop me at my mum's house so I can milk her for some money?'

I sighed, trying not to show my frustration. 'I'm pretty low on fuel at the moment, Deb, and I was just going to rest today.'

'Oh, come on. You can get some on the way. Don't neg out, babe. I'm going through a rough time, and the last thing I want to do is drive.' She pressed her hand into her forehead.

See, this is what I mean. I just said I didn't want to get used anymore, and now I feel obliged to drive Deb to her parents' house because they're owners of the house I'm living in, and I don't want her drink-driving. It breaks my heart because I want to help Deb out and be there for her, but her constantly asking for money and for me to drive her everywhere is draining. I'd rather do heartfelt things because I want to, not because I'm constantly asked to. My mum was right – with my shopping and shouting Deb, it's impossible to save.

What I wanted to say was 'I'm tired and going to rest – maybe catch a cab?' But what I ended up saying was 'Let's leave now, though.'

She nodded with her thumb up.

I waited five minutes for her to scull the rest of her wine and smoke a cigarette before we journeyed to her parents' house.

16

Ice-cream And Tears

I was in the midst of a comfortable evening with my feet up, eating mushroom risotto and watching season three of *Gossip Girl*, when I got a hysterical phone call from Deb asking for me to pick her up. The fact that fuel was nearly $2.50 a litre made my dinner churn in my stomach, and I let out a sigh. *On my way, Deb. Naomi to the rescue,* I thought as I kicked off my slippers, grabbed my clutch, and walked into the garage. A chuckle escaped my lips as I looked down at my lilac nightie and pink dressing gown, and without further thought, I hopped in the car and drove seven minutes down the road to Deb's parents' elaborate two-storey house. It was pure white with a massive balcony overlooking her mother's flower garden. My headlights revealed Deb sitting on the driveway with her arms wrapped around her knees, sobbing. An ache ripped through my gut as I sighed.

As soon as she noticed my car, she leapt up and ran straight to the passenger's side and hopped in with a quick slam of the door.

Her parents' lights were on, and I could see a shadowy figure standing in the window looking down at us. An awkward feeling crept over me, and I could tell by the sobs Deb was making she wanted to get out of there pronto, so I put the transmission stick into reverse and checked both ways before backing out.

'What's going on, Deb? Are you fighting with your parents again?' I asked with sympathy in my voice.

'Yes. Mum and Dad are so angry at me for losing my job. They are so angry like you wouldn't believe. They both told me to grow up and that I'm ... a failure.' Her sobs intensified, and I reached out with one hand and quickly rubbed her arm. She cleared her throat. 'They both told me to start acting my age and to stop asking them for money. Then Dad gave me a lecture about being in the wrong job. He said I should own my own house by now and that I should've listened to him and worked in business.'

Her sobs increased some more, and she sniffed loudly.

'Oh, Deb. Did you tell them about Daniel? And I've got tissues in the glovebox.'

She opened the glovebox, grabbed a tissue, and blew her nose so loud my ears almost rang.

'Are you kidding me, Naomi? Of course not. You know what my dad's like – he would kill him.' Her miserable voice had some sass back mixed with agitation.

I thought back to the time her dad lost his temper at her for coming home too late. He yelled for hours, and loud enough for the whole street and sleeping dogs to hear. A few dogs in the street actually barked at the volume of his thunderous voice. He accused her of sleeping around, and she denied it, but her puffy hair, smudged lipstick, and reek of Lynx deodorant said otherwise. His ice-blue eyes looked straight into mine as he asked me, 'Was there a male between her legs tonight?' His eyebrows raised and the vein on his head grew with frustration. We both lied and looked at the floor and told him 'no' in our sulkiest, most innocent voices. He didn't believe us for a second and kept yelling.

She was daddy's little princess, and no boy was ever good enough for her, except John, but all the rest he labelled scum that thought only with their dicks, and if they didn't have money, they weren't worth his or Deb's time. 'They needed to be hard working and pay their way,' he'd say. They were his top priorities, and every time he said that all I could think was, *Realistically, how many adolescent boys are on high wages and aren't checkout workers or dishies?* No wonder Deb went for rich older guys; it was ingrained in her brain.

All throughout high school, Deb's dad demanded to meet her boyfriends and his ice-blue eyes would stare deep into theirs and scrutinise them as he asked what their parents did for work.

'Yeah, I forgot how bad his temper is.' I kept my eyes on the road as we passed through her modern neighbourhood.

'I can't take this anymore, Naomi. I need to get out of here,' she let out in a pained rush.

I didn't say anything for a moment. The only thing in my life that felt secure was my living arrangement, and it sounded like that soon could change too. There were so many changes happening in my life that I was having trouble keeping up with them all.

I glanced at her, my hands gripped tight on the steering wheel. 'You're kidding, right?'

'No, dead serious. I have to get out of this town. I can't stand it here any longer. There's nothing here for me. Nothing at all.' Her face shifted into self-pity, and she dug her heel into the car mat.

'So, what are you going to do? Move back to Brisbane again?' I shot up a questioning brow. 'And it'll go back to how it used to be when you only talked to me sometimes? Us moving in together was your way of making up for all the lost time we had when you were gone.'

'I'm going to have to. I need work, Naomi.'

'Okay, well, I guess you have to do what is best for you. I'll probably move back to Mum's and look for a job in one of the kitchens here.'

She looked down at her hands, knotted tightly together on her lap. 'You don't have to leave. You can stay put.'

'Uh, no. I am not paying all of that rent on my *own*.'

'It wouldn't make that much of a difference, considering you pretty much cover most of it anyway. You're such a good friend, chicka. Always helping me out.'

I glanced at her again, this time with a weak smile, then turned my eyes back to the road.

'Can we stop somewhere and get chocolate, please? I just want to veg out on the couch and eat chocolate and ice cream.' Her voice was filled with hope.

'Yes, sure. I need fuel anyway.' I looked at the fuel meter and noticed it was nearly on empty.

'Uh. One problem.'

'Mmm ... and what's that?'

'Mum didn't give me money so could you, pretty please, pay, and I'll make it up to you?'

I clutched my forehead with a hand and let out a deep breath. 'Uh ... yeah, sure, but just remember I'm out of work too.'

'I know, chick, but desperate times call for desperate measures. I'm so glad I have you as a best friend. Seriously, you always save my head from the chopping block.'

She hit my soft spot, and I thought, *May as well shout her as it could be my last time with her if she moves back to Brisbane.*

'I'll fill up the car and will give you the money, but can you go in and pay for it and get whatever you need?'

'Why can't you come in too?'

'Because look how I'm dressed!' I pointed to my pyjamas and laughed.

Deb rolled her eyes. 'Fine.' She shook her head and let out a giggle.

***

After stopping at a BP, we arrived home with a full tank of petrol, Ben & Jerry's ice cream, a block of chocolate and, of course, Deb's cigarettes.

We had the air con pumping, cooling us from the early October heat. Deb sat on her side of the couch with her feet up. She was holding the TV remote in one hand and the container of ice cream in the other. Within minutes, she was through at least five huge scoops of chocolate chip cookie dough. An ad came on the screen showing a happy family at the beach, which must have gotten to her because she started crying again and dropped the remote in favour of the chocolate block. She broke off a huge piece and dropped it into her mouth. This wasn't the first time she'd pigged out like this. The last time she fought with her parents over money, she ate a whole loaf of bread and a block of cheese in one sitting. I wondered if this fight might be the final straw or if they'd make up, like they usually did. Their relationship was rocky at times, but she was their only child and they loved her to bits.

The biggest problem always seemed to be money. Deb was a terrible budgeter. Almost all her pay went on cigarettes, booze, makeup, and takeout, so whenever she ran out, she'd ask her folks for help, or me. Her parents were trying to enjoy retirement and save their money, but Deb was adamant she needed money, and what were they supposed to do?

'I can't believe you have a job trial tomorrow,' Deb said through a mouthful of ice cream. Her cheeks were wet still, but her tears had slowed down. She began waving her hand in a fan motion on her lips. 'Brain freeze!' She squinted her eyes.

I looked down at her ice cream, then at the block of chocolate resting on the arm of the chair. God, healthy eating was tough. That chocolate was calling my name; just looking at it made my mouth water.

'Slow down, then. You've eaten, like, half a tub. You'll hate yourself in the morning.'

'Oh, shut up, Naomi. It's better than doing drugs.' She sniggered. 'What are you anyway, the health police?'

'Oh, good one. Smooth.' I laughed.

'So, anyway, how come Patrick messaged you? Like, that's really weird. Can you show me what he said?' She grabbed the phone out of my hand and opened the Messenger app. My impulse was to snatch it off her, but then I thought, *I've got nothing to hide.* It still annoyed me, considering most of the time she'd have her phone hidden and I wouldn't ask to see her texts.

She clicked on Patrick's messages and scrolled from the bottom. Ice cream dripped from her spoon onto her dress. She furrowed her eyebrows, then widened her eyes as she got closer to the top.

'Okay, yeah, he must really like your food. No surprise there.' She handed me back my iPhone.

I put the phone on the arm of the chair. 'I'm excited but really nervous. There's so much pressure to perform well tomorrow.'

Deb shifted her eyes my way and let out a long breath. 'When *don't* you perform well?'

'Well, most of the time I try to, but, you know, everyone has off days, and I'm just hoping tomorrow isn't one of those days where I make a fool out of myself.'

'You'll be fine, and since you aren't eating any chocolate, I will have it all.' This time, instead of breaking off a piece, she bit into the side of it, leaving a bite mark behind.

'Oh, Deb, you're hilarious, and you're right. I don't want any chocolate. I think I might have a mango later or more risotto.' *Thanks for making it easier to resist.*

'Healthyyyy.'

'Oh, I forgot to tell you.' I got into a more comfortable position with my left leg crossed over the right.

'What?' Her tears had dried. I suspected the food must have helped numb her pain.

'Daniel messaged me and tried to call me two more times today. He sent a text asking where the hell I was and told me I was ruining his business.'

Deb's mouth dropped open, and she moved her head back in disbelief. 'What? He's become a nutjob. Do you reckon he's mental or something? He clearly fired us, and now he's asking why you didn't come in?' She paused for a moment, frowning. 'Did he ask anything about me?'

I nodded in agreement, glad to see Deb showing signs of life again. 'He's gone truly crazy. Poor guy. I'd hate to be him. Not only is he a sexist control freak but he's clearly a miserable bastard.' I looked down at my sparkly silver toes and wiggled the one supporting my other leg into the shaggy rug. 'Oh, and no, he didn't mention you in the texts.'

The sound of Deb biting into the chocolate caught my attention, and I looked at the bite mark on the other side of the block.

'I feel like the biggest fool admitting this,' she said through a full mouth. 'But the reason I slept with him was because I kind of had a crush on him, and I wanted to be naughty.' She shrugged her shoulders. 'You know I love my bad boys. The forbidden fruit of the dating world.'

'Oh, ew, Deb. This particular fruit was forbidden with good reason: not only is he a disgusting pig, but he's also *married*. I'm still really surprised, to be honest. You always used to pay him out and told me numerous times he did your head in.'

'Yeah, but that happens. Look how you treated Sebastian. You made him wait for ages before sleeping with him, and I guess I'm a sucker for the whole "treat 'em mean, keep 'em keen" bullshit.' She shrugged again.

'No, that's a completely different situation. Seb and I are both single and had genuine feelings for each other.' Her bringing up Seb made me think of that dick picture he sent, and a wave of annoyance came over me.

'Whatever.' Deb looked down at her ice cream and realised it was starting to melt, so she got out of her comfy crevice and walked to the freezer. 'Can I tempt you with anything while I'm here?' I heard the sound of the freezer door being pulled open.

'No, I'm fine.' I stared at the chocolate block again, now half-eaten, resting on the arm of her chair.

She returned with a glass of pinot grigio in her hand and sat back down. 'Now, what should we watch?' She picked up the remote again.

I thought about *Gossip Girl*, episode ten, and how I'd only gotten five minutes into the episode when Deb rang. Not that it mattered that I didn't get to finish watching it because I had watched the whole series five times before. Come to think of it ... Deb's situation with Daniel was like Serena van der Woodsen and Tripp van der Bilt's dalliance. He was a forbidden fruit, being married and all, and Serena knew this and still pursued him. Deb and Serena had a lot in common with their flirtatious natures.

The sound of chocolate getting bitten into broke my train of thought for the second time, and I looked down at my phone. Nothing. No action tonight. *That's a relief.*

The light from the corner lamp shone a warm glow across the room as Deb scrolled through Netflix categories and let out a sigh of frustration. 'Definitely not watching a romance. Barf,' she said.

'I love romcoms. They're always so light and fun to watch.'

'So, there's a hidden romantic in you somewhere, hey?' She nudged her elbow into my arm. 'Hey, hey?' Her brows waggled.

'Probably buried deep down, but I still don't believe in *"true love".'* I used air quotes, hoping they showed the disdain I felt.

Deb smiled ruefully. 'I think my parents are the definition of true love.'

'That's lovely, Deb. I'm glad you can speak so well of them even though you're fighting with them. I can't say the same about mine, but back when we were all together, it was great.' I thought back to our family dinners when Dad and I made bread rolls, Mum made the salad, and Carlos handled the seafood. The memories became less pleasant, however, when I thought of his shiraz. It was like as soon as the booze started flowing, a switch flicked in Dad, and he changed, like a shark smelling blood. The slightest irritation enraged him, and he'd pick fights with Mum that pushed her to breaking point. It was devastating to watch but also eye-opening in the long run. Things were different when we were on our own. I loved the one-on-one times with Dad – listening to Elvis, cooking, and mucking around. Those were good memories. The more time that passed, the more I realised that both of them had shaped me and Carlos into the people we were. I looked up to see Deb watching me.

'You're a really strong girl, Naomi. I mean that. I can't even imagine what it feels like to lose a parent so young, but you're amazing. I've been thinking about moving to the city so much, but then I think about being away from you again, and I feel so sad. I think that's what's been stopping me, to be honest.'

I have to admit, I was moved by her words. I hated how tense things had been with Deb the last few days. 'Aww, that's so sweet. I'd hate for you to move away again.'

'You just get me. You understand me more than anyone else.'

I replied, 'You too.' But I felt like a liar. Us reconnecting had been nice, but the truth was that, more and more, all I could see were our differences. It appeared that the older we got, the less we had in common, and Daniel seemed to be the main topic that we did have in common. I'd always love Deb, and often tried to push our differences aside, but something in my gut told me we were slowly drifting apart again.

'You know what? I can't figure out what to watch, and I feel sick from eating all of this, so I think I'll just go to bed.'

I nodded, a little relieved. 'Okay. Goodnight, Deb.'

'Night, chickadee.'

She switched off the TV, grabbed her half-eaten block of chocolate, and swigged the rest of her wine.

Once she'd disappeared into her room, I got back into my own bed, pulled the sheets over myself, and closed my eyes. Then as if on cue, my phone vibrated. It was Seb.

Seb: *Baby ... why haven't you answered my pic? Don't keep me hanging, I miss you like crazy.*

Me: *One of my pet hates are dick pics. They aren't my thing and disgust me.*

Seb: *Huh? How can you say this to me after we had sex? What type of person are you? I 'disgust' you? Guess I was wrong about you. Have fun sleeping with other guys while I'm away. Cya.*

What? Is he a child? I blinked a couple of times to let his text sink in and to make sure I read it correctly. *Yep, read it correctly. Bit of an overreaction, if you ask me. All I was trying to do was tell him how I felt about a matter, and now he's blown it out of proportion. What was with the flighty relationships in my life?* Daniel, Seb, and now even Deb these days. Daniel had me wrong and foolishly abused me, and now Seb was getting me wrong too. I rubbed the corners of my eyes and exhaled as his suggestion that I'd sleep around really sank in.

Me: *Uh, no, Seb. I will not be sleeping around while you're gone, and if you'd bothered to ask how I was, like a proper lover, you'd know that I lost my job and have had other things going on in my life right now. Grow up.*

Seb: *Shit, I'm bloody sorry baby : (I just get jealous and I hate the thought of you getting with anyone else. I was being serious when I said you were the best I've had. What are your bank details? I'll send you some money to live off while you're in this shit run.*

My heart warmed at the fact he offered to give me money to live off during my unemployment debacle, but that feeling was soon quashed by his sulky paranoia about me getting with someone else. *He should drop that idea because it's not going to happen.*

Me: *My bank account's fine. I have my inheritance to live off if worst comes to worst, but I don't think that will happen because I have a job trial tomorrow and I plan on finding a job asap. Anyway, it's been a long day. I'm going to sleep now.*

Seb: *Really? Deb said you didn't have much money because you buy so much makeup, and she never mentioned your inheritance to me. She told me that your hours were all over the place.*

I sighed and pressed my hand into my face. Why did things always have to be so damn complicated? And why did they both have to know exactly what I had in my bank account? I never asked anyone for money or how much they had. Ever.

Me: *It appears you and Deb talk a lot about me ... Look, I'm not in the mood for this conversation about my financial situation, I'm not destitute, I will be okay. I'm a worker and I always find a way to pay my bills. I don't need handouts from anyone, but thanks for your concern.*

Seb: *I know that, Naomi, you're a rare sort. I just miss you like crazy. Can you please send me a pic?*

I replied with a picture of the ceiling and wrote: *Goodnight, Sebastian.*

Seb: *Awww not fair : (*

Just as I was about to shut my eyes for the second time to get some sleep before my big day, my phone buzzed yet again. *Oh my God, go away, Seb.* Nope, this time it wasn't him. It was Kelly.

Kelly: *It was so crap tonight without you. Everyone in the kitchen is missing you bad, especially Martin. He hasn't shut up about you. Tyren's pizzas are okay, but they aren't like yours. He tried making your dough recipe, but his turned out too moist so when he cooked the bases they sagged at the tip. Please don't tell anyone I told you, also Tyren had lots of pizzas returned and I overheard customers saying the pizzas are soggy amateurly made and lack flavour.*

I rolled my eyes. *I'm gone one night, and everything was already turning to shit?* I felt bad for Kelly, but I couldn't help but smile a little thinking of Daniel's reputation suffering. And also, was I actually that good at pizza? Sounds like I sure was an asset to that kitchen, after all. *Hmm, Daniel's loss, not mine. Guess he really is the desperate one now.* I felt my confidence boost as I thought about tomorrow's trial. Great timing.

Me: *Thanks for your message, Kelly, hang in there, hopefully things will get better. I'll miss all the kitchen crew, but it's time I move on and look for work someplace else.*

17

The Trial

As Casa di Vitello came into view, I took a deep breath and pinched my arm to make sure that this was real. Just last week, I was at Patrick's house serving him food from Mon Amour for his birthday, and now I was standing out the front of his restaurant about to walk in for a job trial. My heart raced, and all I could do was think about how proud my dad would have been that I was getting an opportunity like this – all thanks to his dough recipe. He would have hugged me and given me the kind of high-five that made your hand sting for minutes afterwards, just like he did when we aced a new dish together.

I smoothed my shirt before heading for the front entrance. *You can do this, Naomi. You can*, I repeated like a mantra in my head as I walked up three short steps and stepped onto the expansive wooden deck. There wasn't a leaf in sight, and the deck looked freshly polished. The sound of cascading water caught my attention, and I turned to the white cherub wishing fountain. I reached into my pocket for a coin and tossed it in for good luck.

When I turned around, I noticed an exotic woman with glowing skin in her mid-twenties standing behind the outdoor service desk. She was examining the guestbook and bobbing her head to the classic Italian restaurant music coming from inside. I imagined the music was like something you'd hear in a restaurant in Rome. Her dark curly hair was twisted into a bun high upon her head, and a pen was balanced behind her ear. *'Casa di Vitello'* was emblazoned in white letters across the chest of her silver apron, and the leather straps were duck-egg blue. Her simple uniform of a tailored white shirt and black pants gave her an air of casual sophistication.

'Hi. How can I help you?' She looked up with a curious glint in her eyes as she observed my black T-shirt and checked pants. After inspecting me, she looked into my eyes and gave me a warm smile.

'I'm here for the job trial. Patrick asked me.' I returned the smile.

'Oh, yes, of course.' She looked down at her silver watch. 'You're early.'

'Yes. I'm Naomi. Pleased to meet you.' I held out my hand.

She shook my hand. 'I'm Clara. Come this way.' She gestured for me to follow. I noticed the leather straps of her apron sat criss-crossed on her back. She began walking through the enormous restaurant that could sit over five hundred diners.

I followed her inside, reflecting on the differences I could already see between here and Mon Amour. On my first shift in Daniel's restaurant, I got told to only ever come through the back and *never* through the front. He gave very specific instructions in a text message, and would scream at any chef if they walked in through the front – that was a big no-no. It was like he was embarrassed of his kitchen staff. They weren't classy enough for the patrons to view – no, they had to come in by the back entrance. The ironic part was the chefs were the real stars, being the ones who cooked the fabulous food.

Casa di Vitello was modern and decked out with crystal chandeliers, which added a warm, ambient glow. Each dining table had a perfectly positioned white linen tablecloth, shiny cutlery, velvet duck-egg-blue chairs, wine glasses, and a small white vase of pink roses. The flowers added a pop of colour in contrast to the lighter colour scheme of silver and white walls.

The bar was long and elegant with its white marble surface and duck-egg-blue padded barstools. A bartender dressed smartly in a white shirt and silver tie stood in front of the rows of gleaming, top-shelf liquor bottles, his face a mask of concentration as he shook a cocktail for a woman at the bar. He was a bit of a spunk with his hair styled in a quiff, and his white shirt truly complemented his olive skin. I watched him pour the yellow foamy liquid into a grande glass and instantly recognised it was a pina colada. He sprayed whipped coconut cream on top, which smelt citrusy, like limes, then garnished the drink with a maraschino cherry.

A waft of Italian cuisine greeted me the closer we got to the kitchen. *Oh yum. That's definitely pesto sauce.* I could recognise the basil and pine nuts a mile away.

Clara must have noticed me breathing in the aromas, as she did the same, and said, 'Everything is made fresh daily. Patrick owns a private farm from where he gets most of his produce.'

'He has his own farm?' I shook my head in appreciation. *What doesn't this guy have?* 'That's so cool. I bet it's organic too.'

'Yes, it sure is. He doesn't use any pesticides on his produce. Everything is grown and made with love.' She gave me a quick look up and down before continuing. 'And congratulations for getting this trial, by the way. There were over one hundred other candidates eager for this position.'

I swallowed hard and tried to soak in what she just said. *One hundred?* I hoped Clara couldn't tell how nervous I was, but to me, it felt like I was just about to cook for the Queen of England. 'So, I'm the only one being trialled today?' I raised a brow.

She nodded. 'Yes, as far as I'm aware. You must have impressed him. He's a very hard man to please.'

Knowing this did not help quiet the butterflies in my stomach, which were now flapping uncontrollably. As we stepped into the kitchen, I looked around with awe; it was the biggest, most pristine preparation area I'd ever seen in my life. With shiny worktables, and so many staff! I counted at least twelve chefs prepping and preparing for the service ahead, filling every section of the kitchen. We stopped at the first workbench, which was mounted to the wall near the doorway. It had fridges underneath the tabletop just like Mon Amour, and I noticed further down the kitchen there was a massive cold room for produce.

Clara craned her neck as if looking for someone. 'Naomi, just wait here, and I'll get our head chef.'

I stood and looked around, trying to absorb as much as I could, then closed my eyes and inhaled the aroma of Italian food – fresh and mouth-watering.

Clara walked over with a woman dressed in a white chef's coat, tall hat, and black pants. I was instantly reminded of Paul – black chef's pants equal authority at Mon Amour – though she was fair-skinned and blue-eyed with red cheeks and a pointy nose. She grabbed a paper towel from her pocket and dabbed sweat from her forehead, and as she lifted her hat off, I noticed curly strawberry-blonde hair tucked up in a bun. She rolled up her sleeve, then put out her hand to shake mine. 'Hi, Naomi. I'm Trisha. Nice to meet you, and thank you for being early. Punctuality goes a long way in this kitchen.' She fanned her face with her hat.

'It's an honour to meet you! I'm so thrilled to have this opportunity.' I smiled, hoping she hadn't noticed my hand trembling. 'Should I call you Trisha or Chef?'

'Trisha, or Trish is fine.'

'Sure.' I smiled. She seemed nice so far.

'Well, I'll get back to front-of-house. Was nice meeting you, Naomi,' Clara said as she darted out the door before I had the chance to say anything back.

Trish turned her full attention to me. 'So, I will warn you – this isn't like most restaurants where you get occasionally quiet days. It is extremely fast-paced, and all the time.'

I nodded. 'Patrick warned me.'

'Good. Patrick informed me you're *very* experienced in pizza and bread-making, which is exactly what we need.' She placed her hat back onto her head.

'Yes, my dad trained me, and I previously worked at Mon Amour, which was Moroccan-inspired, despite the name—' I rolled my eyes slightly, hoping she wouldn't be put off by me putting my former employer down, but I didn't want her to think I thought Mon Amour was a good name for a Moroccan restaurant. 'They do a lot of modern food, and I ran the pizza section.'

'Oh, I know that place. Been there once. Is Paul still head chef?' She rose a thin, sculptured brow.

'Yes, he is.'

'He's a top bloke. I have known him for years.'

I relaxed a little at her casual language. 'Oh, did you work together?'

'We worked in the same restaurant in Melbourne.'

'Patrick's?' My eyes widened.

'No, one before that. So, anyway, back to this kitchen ...' She paused and chuckled. 'See this section behind you?' She pointed over my head. 'That is the pizza section, and over there is the pizza oven you'll be using.'

'I have never used an oven like that before. What's it made from? Brick?' As soon as the words were out of my mouth, I wondered if I should have pretended to have cooked in something similar before. I swallowed hard, hoping I hadn't blown it already.

'Yes, it's a brick oven. That's how they traditionally cook pizza in Naples.'

Trish appeared unperturbed by my comment, and I relaxed. 'Oh, wow. I can't wait to try it.'

She walked me over to the dome-shaped oven, and I instantly felt its heat against my face. The outside tiles were glossy and red.

'What is the surface inside made out of?' I eyed the grey-speckled stone curiously.

'It's volcanic stone, and it only takes ninety seconds to cook a pizza in here. We set the temperature to four hundred degrees.'

'Sounds like a superior pizza oven.' I grinned, excited to try it out.

'It sure is. So, Patrick will be in very soon. He'll be working with you on the pizzas today.'

'Oh.' My eyes widened in surprise. 'I thought he just took care of front-of-house?'

'He usually does, but he said he wanted to train you today.' She shrugged and half-smiled.

I frowned. *If he thinks I need supervision, why give me this trial?* 'Does he always train his pizza staff?'

'No, never. I think you might be the first actually.' She thought about it for a moment before continuing. 'I usually get one of the kitchen crew to teach someone, but we don't often get new people in. We are all about quality here, and sadly, most hopefuls who come in for trials don't make the cut.'

'Oh, okay,' I said, my voice going higher than I would have liked on the last syllable. I cleared my throat and nodded to show I understood what she was saying, but inside, my guts clenched tighter and tighter.

'I don't think you have anything to worry about, Naomi. Patrick has talked favourably of your pizzas.' She gave me a gentle smile. 'Keep your chin up, and don't let nerves get in the way.'

'Thanks.' I smiled back, kicking myself at the realisation I mustn't have hidden my nerves from her, after all. The pressure was on now.

My heart skipped a beat when I saw Patrick enter the kitchen in his relaxed way. His dark hair was pulled back into a ponytail, and he had a white chef's jacket on and black pants! Casa di Vitello was similar to Mon Amour in terms of the kitchen dress code, with just the head chef wearing black pants and the other chefs wearing checked, but today, there were two head chefs. Double authority. As he moved in further, one of his gold hoop earrings caught the fluorescent light.

'Hello, Trish. Hello, Naomi.' He nodded at both of us and stood next to me, setting off a distinct tingle all over my skin as my neck began to burn again. I frowned at the sensation and immediately swore to myself I would absolutely not develop a crush on this man. *No way.*

'Morning, boss,' Trish said, beaming. Her cheeks flushed and her blue eyes sparkled that extra bit brighter than they had while she was talking to me.

Patrick sure was dangerous to be around, I reflected. I bet most women he's met have fantasised about him at least once in their lives. My God, even his jaw structure was ethereal, lethal even.

'Alright, let's get started, Naomi.' He clapped his hands enthusiastically. 'I will walk you through each pizza to make, and then you can give them a go.' He gave me a smile, and I could've sworn his eyes lit up when they caught mine.

I nodded. *God, I'm so nervous. Get it together, Naomi.* I turned around to see Trish back in full head-chef mode, monitoring the kitchen to make sure everything was going smoothly.

'Didn't anyone show you where to put your bag?' he asked with eyes squinted.

I shook my head and peered down at my brown bucket bag, tucked snuggly under my arm.

'Come with me. I'll give you a quick tour.' He gestured with his hand for me to follow.

'But isn't service about to start?' I looked around at all of the chefs chopping away and stirring things on the stoves.

'Trish has got it covered.' He winked his reassurance.

'Sure.'

Patrick walked past the pizza oven and continued until we reached the back door, which was next to the main sink. The dishy looked exhausted as he sprayed and scrubbed the pots and pans with a speedy hand. They were stacked up in the biggest pile of dishes I'd ever seen in my life. Poor guy.

'Uh. Is the dishy okay? There is a lot there.' I gave the dishy a sympathetic look, but he was too busy to notice.

'He's fine. We call him "Rocket" because he's so quick.'

Patrick opened the door and turned left into a room lined with lockers. I unzipped my bag and quickly put on my stripy apron and hat.

'I'll just put your bag in the spare locker for the time being,' he said as I passed him my brown bucket bag.

'Thanks, Patrick.' I smiled in appreciation.

He secured my bag inside the locker and turned back to me. His eyes twinkled. 'I think we'll have fun during service. But I must warn you, we're fully booked.'

'Well, I guess that's to be expected with your reputation.' I blushed and wanted to put my hand over my mouth to muffle my words, but it was too late. *Dammit.*

'Been reading about me, hey?' He smiled, and his eyes revealed a spark of interest.

'No, Deb told me all about your restaurants, and I'm going to shut up now.' I instantly regretted blurting that out. *What is wrong with me this morning?*

He laughed and held open the door, and we walked back over to the pizza section. I noticed the dishy was indeed a rocket as the stack had visibly decreased in the few minutes we were outside.

Why did this trial feel so overwhelming?

The words Patrick said at Gerado's ran through my mind: *We're fully booked every night. That's why I'm trialling you at lunch service because it's less busy.*

Uh, yeah, sure, Patrick, less busy ... It's peak hour, and you're fully booked. Oh God. I sucked in a deep breath as he crouched down and pulled the dough balls from the fridge underneath the bench.

As the service bell rang nonstop, waitstaff paced in and out of the kitchen, balancing plates on each forearm and palm. The pasta dishes seemed to be the favourites as I caught a glimpse of the seafood linguini and beef ragu.

Patrick sprinkled flour across the bench, then flattened a dough ball with his palm. He dipped the dough into a coating of flour, then put it back on the bench. I couldn't help but notice the way his perfectly arched brows drew together in a frown of concentration as he dimpled the dough in the middle, making sure it stayed flat while the outer edge was slightly raised.

'Is this how you do it, Naomi?' He flipped the pizza back and forth on his hands, and I watched as it stretched out into a perfectly round pizza base.

I cleared my throat. *Focus.* 'No, I usually just flatten the dough and round it with my hands, then roll it out with a rolling pin.'

He nodded. 'Well, this is how we do it here because it's the traditional way. Did you notice how I'm not flattening the outer edge? That's because you get a lot of natural bubbles from the fermentation.'

I nodded and watched him closely. *Got it.*

'Another tip is when you're making a Vitello Margherita pizza, don't overdo the cheese. The sauce is the main hero. Do you think you can manage what I just showed you?'

I swallowed hard, picked up a dough ball, and began manoeuvring it while thinking about what he had just shown me. His teaching was playing in my mind like a movie as I worked with the dough. I glanced behind me to check if he was watching me. He wasn't. *Phew.* He had grabbed a pizza rack from the slots and was busying himself preparing another base.

After a few minutes – albeit more time than it had taken Patrick – I had my first ever traditionally made pizza base ready.

'See, you're a natural.' He grinned at me with an approving nod.

My stomach melted at the look in his kindhearted eyes. He was almost *too* nice and encouraging. I looked back at my base and noticed with a frown it was slightly uneven in parts, and I was about to point it out but stopped myself. *If Patrick Vitello of all people approves, I must be doing something right, and I guess you could say it looks rustic?*

As the orders continued to fly in, Patrick made the pizzas while I watched him carefully. My duty was to turn the pizzas in the oven and cut them, while he sprinkled them with the perfect portion of toppings.

I flashed back for a moment to all those afternoons making pizzas with Dad. He always chuckled at how Australians wanted their pizzas pre-sliced. 'Not like in Italy,' he used to say. As I watched Patrick pull out the pizza cutter and deftly slice his pizzas, I realised he didn't exactly follow *every* tradition after all.

After watching Patrick do at least three Margheritas, I felt confident enough to try one myself. I spread the napoli sauce in the centre, then placed ten balls of fresh mozzarella around it before tearing the basil leaves and sprinkling them on top. Once the ingredients were on, I seasoned it with salt and pepper, then slid it into the oven.

Within seconds, the sauce began to bubble, and I felt my excitement rise along with the crust as I watched the cheese melt. When the edge closest to the flames was nicely charred, I rotated the pizza for a perfect, even cook. The leoparding was my favourite part to watch form.

I reached for the paddle, gently lifted the pizza from the oven, carried it to the workbench, drizzled it with olive oil, and then began slicing it with the pizza cutter.

'So, is this pizza going out to a customer?' I asked.

'No, you and I will eat it.'

I looked up at him and blinked. *Was he joking?* 'Really? Do we have time?'

'*Sì.*' He didn't break eye contact with me as he reached for a slice of the pizza I'd just prepared. His stare was so intense, I felt a bead of sweat slip down the side of my forehead. Before he could take a bite, I turned away. I felt weak for doing it, but I couldn't face his rejection after attempting one of his own recipes. He knew exactly how it should taste, and how all the components should marry together in perfect harmony for the tastebuds.

Out of the corner of my eye, I saw him wipe his mouth with a napkin.

He let out a hearty laugh. 'You can look at me now, Naomi.'

I swallowed and raised my eyes to meet his. *This is it.*

'I'm impressed. You know Margherita pizzas are one of the pizzas that get judged by critics because of the simplicity of their ingredients, but sometimes the simplest recipes are the hardest to execute, and ...' He paused for emphasis. 'This is great. I'd proudly serve this in my restaurant.'

I smiled so wide my cheeks hurt, and to my horror, I found myself on the verge of tears. A montage of the last twelve months flashed before my eyes – losing Dad, and then my job. What a toll it had all taken. But now, on this day, Patrick Vitello giving my pizza the thumbs-up finally felt like a real turning point.

'Go on. Try a piece for yourself before we get more orders.' He gestured to the pizza.

I nodded and grabbed a slice, grateful for the opportunity to not talk. He was right. It was good. Although, I thought to myself, it was hard to go wrong with his exceptional produce; everything in this kitchen was sourced, grown, and made with so much passion and love. It was my turn to wipe my mouth with a paper towel, and as I reached for a roll on the counter, I took the opportunity to sneak a glimpse at Patrick. He had gone back for another slice, which I took as a good sign. *Maybe I really can do a great job in this kitchen. I'm in my element here, just like Patrick.* We both cooked from our hearts.

By the end of lunch service, I had learned how to cook five of Casa di Vitello's pizzas off by heart: Margherita, Capricciosa, Funghi, Prosciutto, and Seafood. My Margherita and Seafood pizzas had the honour of being tested by a customer and, to my delight, were received with a flurry of joyful comments.

Just after three o'clock, Patrick took me out the back of the restaurant. I knew he'd want to discuss how my trial had gone, and despite his positive feedback and the rave reviews from diners, I couldn't help feeling nervous.

'Naomi, I knew you'd be great, and I'm thrilled to have found you.' He looked into my eyes with sincerity.

Relief flooded my body. 'Patrick, I'm honoured you even offered me this trial, and I'm so glad you're not disappointed. Thank you so much.' *Wow, that was quite eloquent. Not bad, Naomi.* I smiled at him.

'Well, I think my kitchen would greatly benefit from having you work here.' He paused for a moment, his eyes staring at the lockers. 'So, I'd like to offer you a full-time position.'

Naturally, my mouth dropped open at his words. *A full-time position? How is this even possible?* People never got full-time positions handed to them so easily. It always took at least a year of hard work and being an on-call casual. *This couldn't be real – no way. This is a dream. Does Patrick think I'm cute or something? No, surely not. Look at him. He's perfect. And just a nice guy.*

I wasn't entirely confident in my ability to form a sentence, but I managed to sputter, 'A full-time position?'

'*Si*, I like to build a connection with my staff, and you fit in perfectly. It also helps that your pizzas do not disappoint.' He winked at me. 'You'd be doing my Noosa business a favour.'

I exhaled, and before I could stop myself, I hugged him. 'Thank you. Thank you sooo much.' My lip began to wobble, and then that's when it finally happened. The dam burst, and I began to sob. 'You have no idea how much this means to me.'

He wrapped his arms around me and patted my back with his palm in a soothing manner. Despite my joy at being offered a job and the whirlwind of emotions rushing through my mind, I was instantly distracted by his body heat and toned chest. Still shaking slightly, I was about to repeat how grateful I was when the door behind us swung open. We both turned around at the same time to see Trisha staring at us. Patrick and I let go of each other instantly, and he gave her a smile.

She frowned slightly before arranging her face back into a smile and cleared her throat. 'Great work today, Naomi. The waitstaff told me your pizzas received a lot of praise. I guess congratulations are in order.' She looked at Patrick, who nodded. 'Welcome to the House of Vitello.' She shook my hand again.

'Thank you again, both of you, for this opportunity.'

'You earned it. Patrick has always had a knack for picking the right person.' She raised her strawberry-blonde eyebrows at Patrick and gave a closed-lip smile.

I nodded my thank you to her.

'Alright, well, I'll let you sort out your shifts, and I'll see you in the next few days.'

'Okay. See you then.' I lifted my hand in an awkward wave.

She nodded and shut the door.

As I turned around to face Patrick, my heart fluttered, and my neck went hot as our eyes met. He stared at me for a moment, then flashed his white teeth. I smiled a goofy smile back and hoped I didn't look like too much of a dork, while my mind visualised what it would be like to kiss him against the lockers, hard and passionately, as his sculptured body pressed into mine. *No, Naomi, he's your boss and your source of income. Get those foolish thoughts out of your head.*

'So, were you wanting to do the same shifts as at Mon Amour?' Patrick asked in his relaxed manner.

'Oh, yes, sounds great.' I let my words out too fast and felt my cheeks burning red.

What the hell is wrong with me today?

He let out a laugh and eyed me curiously. 'And what days were those?'

'Wednesday to Sunday.'

'Perfect. I'll get the paperwork for you.' He brushed past me as he walked inside, leaving me with goosebumps.

18

Disagreements

I walked inside the house with a smile as big as a crescent moon etched on my face, but it quickly vanished when I caught sight of Victor, the French waiter from Mon Amour. *He's the last person I expected to see.* Deb sat beside him with a wine glass the size of a fishbowl in her hand. Indie music blasted through her portable Bluetooth speakers while she bobbed her head and waved her arms with her eyes shut. She looked like she was at a rave instead of sitting in our living room. Two bottles of sauvignon blanc sat on the coffee table, one empty, one half-empty. *Sauvignon blanc? Oh, of course. Victor's favourite.*

'Naomi, you're home,' Deb said as she caught sight of me and waved me over to join them.

'Hey, guys,' I said with a smile. A potent ashtray scent drifted from their clothing.

'*Bonjour*, Naomi,' Victor said in his thick French accent while flashing his chipped-tooth smile.

'When shit hits the fan, you drink booze. Booze is my one true love,' Deb said as she took a sip from her humungous glass. She cried with laughter for a few minutes, then wiped the tears from her eyes.

'Guess what, Naomi? We've been practising Aussie slang, haven't we, mate?' Deb nudged Victor's arm. 'Victor's brilliant. You've got to hear him.'

'That's right, mate,' Victor replied in a deep Australian voice, and I couldn't help but chuckle.

'That was great. Anything else?' I asked, eager to hear more.

He shook his head.

'I'm having such a good day, thanks to this bad boy.' Deb pointed to her glass and grinned.

'*Oui,*' agreed Victor.

'Work was honestly driving me off my rocker.' She laughed. 'So, tell me, mate – how did your job trial go?' Deb asked as she crossed her legs and got comfortable.

'Incredible! I can't believe a restaurant like that even exists. I'm seriously so overwhelmed I even got the chance to work there.' I flashed another huge smile.

'What happened? Do they want you to come back, or will they call you?' She narrowed her eyes.

I took a deep breath, not sure what kind of reaction to expect from Deb. 'You're not going to believe this, but ... Patrick offered me a full-time position.'

'Bullshit.' Deb looked taken aback. 'No, Naomi. Don't fuck with me.'

Her shift in energy was like a slice to the heart.

'I'm dead serious. I have the papers in my bag.' I dug for them and raised them to show her.

'I don't understand. It's so hard to get a job at Patrick's restaurant. Like, it's one of the most sought-after restaurants to work at in Australia.' She narrowed her eyes again and frowned.

'I guess I did something right.' I shrugged, put the papers back, and pulled off my boots. I wasn't surprised by Deb's reaction – I didn't quite understand what had happened myself this afternoon.

'Naomi, this isn't normal. You know that, right? This is seriously a big deal, and you have no idea how many people would kill for that job.'

'I know. When I walked in, Clara, the waitress, said one hundred other people applied for the position.'

'So, they aren't even going to test anyone else out?' She raised her brows with annoyance as her skin flamed red.

'I'm not sure.' I shrugged.

'Hmm.' She stared at me, a strange look on her face. 'I think he's got the hots for you.'

'Oh, shut up. That's the most ridiculous thing you've ever said to me.'

'Well, think about it. Why else would he hire you so quickly? It's weird. Like, I know you're talented, but so are many other people who happen to also be *qualified* chefs, and if you couldn't make it at Mon Amour, what makes you think you can make it at Patrick's restaurant?'

'Are you serious, Deb? What, you can't be happy for me and have to bring up the one label I hate and remind me I'm just a *cook* and not a *qualified chef*? Why are you criticising me right now? You sound like frickin' Daniel.'

No wonder I always doubted my skills when the line of being just a cook got shoved in my face constantly.

Victor snuck outside with a cigarette in his mouth to avoid the tension building in the room.

'I'm happy for you, but that's just bullshit, and, yes, I reckon he's got the hots for you. Why else would he add you on Facebook and message you for a coffee? He's clearly just another arsehole who wants to bang a young blonde. I bet he'll end up being just like Daniel and abuse you too.' She rolled her eyes and crossed her arms.

I turned away from Deb, my heart beating faster with anger, and took a deep breath to steady myself. After a few seconds, I swirled back around to face her and blurted out the first thing that came to mind. 'No, Deb, he's nothing like Daniel. He is a decent person who has manners.'

She sat back so hard on the couch, one of the cushions fell to the floor. 'You don't even know him. You're stupid, Naomi, absolutely stupid. Get the hell out of my face.'

My jaw clenched as I stormed off to the bathroom. Inside, it was killing me how our friendship was deteriorating, and I didn't have the faintest clue how to patch it up. *Maybe I'm the one who should move. Would that save our friendship?*

Hmm. I don't know what to do. Why does Deb have to be so scornful right now? If it was her that got the job, I'd be ecstatic for her.

After I undressed, I stepped into the shower and turned on the taps until they could no longer twist. Water came pelting out and fell hard on my chest, making it hurt more than it already did. Then the tears came gushing, and I just let myself cry until my throat stung and I couldn't cry any longer.

Nothing in life was ever smooth sailing, was it? It was a vicious cycle of gain followed by loss or a struggle, and no matter what, those elements balanced each other out like salt did with sickly sweet caramel.

I chucked on my nightie after my shower and went straight to bed, sandwiching my head in the pillow to block out Deb's music. Remembering her words about Patrick having the hots for me made my skin go funny again. *Could it be? Does a thirty-five-year-old, sexy-as-hell restaurateur really have the hots for me?* I knew older guys liked to sleep with younger women, but for real, I wasn't exactly a model. I was only five foot five with short legs and small boobs. He could have anyone, truly anyone, *so why would he even look at me that way?*

My thoughts were interrupted by a knock on the door.

'What?' I groaned. *Why didn't I lock the door?*

'Naomi, it's me. I'm so sorry. I know I got carried away. I'm just drunk and jobless. Please don't be mad at me. I'm your best friend. Come have a few drinks and loosen up. Let's celebrate your new job.' Her voice was laced with sadness.

I felt a tiny bit of my anger start to melt, and I lifted my head from the pillow. 'It's unlocked.'

Deb swung open the door, sat on the end of the bed, and tickled my feet.

'I'm sorry, Naomi. I really am. I know you're going through a rough time. It's just I am hurting so bad at the moment. What do I even have to look forward to when I wake up in the morning? A ciggie and drink? Is that all I've got?' Deb said with a frown.

'Deb, you've got so much more to look forward to than just smokes and drinks, and you know it. Plus, you having a house all to yourself is pretty great, isn't it? Lots of people would kill to have a house to themselves.' I sat up and moved beside her, ready to offer my emotional support.

'It's okay. Could be bigger.' Her face was full of sorrow.

'Deb, don't be silly. It's a five-bedroom house, and there's only two of us here.'

'I guess.' She sighed. 'Naomi, it's not even the Daniel thing that's getting me down. I'm so ugly. Look at me. Older men seem to be all I can get.'

'No, Deb. You know that's not true, and you're far from ugly. We've had this conversation hundreds of times. Look at how silky your hair is, and look at your naturally big breasts. Come on. People pay thousands to have features like that.'

She blushed and gave me a smile. 'Yeah, I guess. Thanks, chicka.'

'Cheer up, buttercup. I need my sassy and confident Deb back. Stop being so hard on yourself. Life's too short.' I did her signature move and pinched her left cheek.

She smiled for a brief second, and then her face fell again. 'Is it all my fault that we both lost our jobs?'

'Oh ... Deb ... do we have to talk about this right now?' I looked over at my paperwork waiting for me on the nightstand and sighed.

'Yes. Yes, we do.' There was an eagerness in her voice.

'Look, you like older men, and that's okay, but you needed to think about his wife and the consequences of sleeping with a married man. He had no choice but to fire you. What did you think would happen?' I raised my brow and knotted my hands in my lap.

'I didn't think I'd get fired – that's for sure.' She looked at the floor with sadness in her eyes. 'I hate to admit this, but I thought maybe he'd keep screwing me, and we could do it in hotels when his wife came back. Oh, did I end up telling you why his nipples are so big? He uses a nipple pump; he thinks it makes them more tingly. Every time I sucked on them, he got the biggest hard-on.' Her voice was unnervingly passionate.

Before I could answer and process the image, she started speaking again.

'He called me today and told me his wife wants a divorce.'

My stomach dropped as I thought about how his poor wife must be feeling. She'd be destroyed.

'Deb, that's to be expected. He cheated on her. With you.' I noticed my voice was stern and hoped it wouldn't ignite another fight.

She put her hands over her face. 'I know, I know. It was fun at the time, and the sex was great, and you should've seen his dick.' She spread her pointer fingers to demonstrate the size of it. 'Don't worry. I hate him now.'

I couldn't feel any more uncomfortable at her demonstration as I was reminded of his hard nipples, the bulge in his pants, and loud sniff in my ear.

'My life is fucked. I'm so over everything. I can't believe you've got a full-time job, and I'm jobless. It's not even fair.' Deb looked down at the floor and sighed in frustration. 'Do I have bad luck or something? I'm supposed to be the successful one, remember? My dad's right. I should own my own home by now.'

'Deb, that is highly unrealistic. You would have to be on at least one hundred grand a year to be able to pay off a mortgage, and, no, of course not – you make your own luck and you can change this situation. Why don't you apply for places tomorrow? I can come with you.' I turned to her with a hopeful smile.

'I'm capable of looking for work on my own.' Her eyes flickered with annoyance.

'Well, I hope you feel better soon, and let me know if I can help you in any way.' I patted her on the shoulder.

She pulled away from me. 'Nothing feels better than sex and booze.'

'Yes, you say this a lot.'

'Shut up, Naomi. What's your suggestion to numb the pain?' She turned to me, her ebony eyes questioning me.

'Look, it's hard to offer advice when you blow up. I feel pain too, and I'm no saint. I've spent thousands of dollars on makeup, so that's my way of numbing the pain, but it never lasts. I don't think anything really gets rid of the pain altogether; the pain is always there, and you get so used to it. It becomes a part of you, and you slowly forget how painful it is because something else painful will happen to distract you from the previous pain.'

Deb's face changed to a look of shock, and she swallowed hard. 'Shit, I never thought of it like that, and you're right. You've just lost your dad, and I'm talking about my problems constantly. I'm sorry, chick.'

'I don't want to fight anymore, Deb. I hate it.' I put my hand out for her to grab and felt her small hand slot into mine.

She nodded in remorse. 'I love you, chicka.' She wrapped her arms around me and rested her cheek on my shoulder.

Our moment was interrupted by blasting Indie music and Victor's off-key singing as he appeared at my bedroom door, Bluetooth speaker in hand. He didn't know a word of the song, and me and Deb both started giggling to the point of tears at his terrible attempt at singing along. It was a relief to be laughing with Deb again.

'Hey, where my party girls at?' he said in his lilting French accent while waving his other hand in the air.

Deb sighed as her laughter trailed off. 'I just told Naomi about Daniel getting a divorce.'

His eyes widened, and he said, 'Rough.' He bounced his head along to the rhythm of the music. 'I'll let you two talk about that. I think the wine is calling me.'

'I'll be out in a minute, Vic,' Deb said.

'*Oui,*' he said and pouted his lips.

'*Oui, oui, oui,*' Deb said back as her head fell back with laughter.

It was obvious Victor was after a good time and wasn't going to offer Deb any emotional support. I barely knew him, but even I could tell that wasn't his style.

Victor walked away dancing.

'So, what do you want to do, Deb?' I asked as concern filled my voice.

She rested her head back on my shoulder. 'Well, eventually, I'll look for a job, but right now, drinking and numbing it all feels great. I might just keep pestering Mum for money and drinking until I feel ready to work again.'

'I don't think it's right to ask your parents to pay for *your* drinking addiction while you're sad. Have you thought about getting counselling? Carlos got counselling, and I'm going to call Mum later and see how it went.'

'Counselling?' She screwed her nose at the suggestion. 'What are you trying to say, Naomi? That I've got issues I can't sort myself?'

I shook my head and looked at my wardrobe door for inspiration on what to say next. 'No. What I'm trying to say is, if you're having trouble sorting out your issues yourself, maybe you should seek professional help, as drinking is just a quick fix and not a long-term one.'

'I hate that you're so right about everything. Maybe you should be a counsellor yourself.'

I thought about Sebastian and Scott and sighed. 'I can assure you, I'm not right about everything.'

'Anyways.' Deb sat up and ran her hands through her sleek, auburn hair. 'I was thinking about maybe staying at Versace on the Gold Coast for my birthday. It's just a suggestion. Nothing is set in stone or anything. I just need fresh scenery. A few nights away in luxury away from this shithole.'

I thought about my new roster, which was probably being created as we spoke. 'What day does your birthday fall on?'

'On a Friday.'

Could I ask for time off so soon? 'Well, my shifts are the same as at Mon Amour, so I only have Mondays and Tuesdays off.'

She stuck out her bottom lip. 'But it's my birthday on the Friday, and I need my best girl there.'

'Deb, this is my first full-time job, ever, and you know this. I have always been casual. I'm a dedicated worker and don't want to make a bad impression. I don't think I should ask for days off so soon, but I'll make it up to you. I'll take you to dinner somewhere.' *Please don't let us start fighting again.*

'So, you're saying that I have to celebrate my birthday on a Monday or a Tuesday because you can't make it on that day?' she asked with a raised voice.

'No, not at all. What I'm saying is we can do something together on the Monday and celebrate just us two.' I smiled and hoped that would make her happy.

She shook her head. 'No, you either come to my birthday on the Friday or don't bother coming at all.'

My God. Even the simplest things in life seem to turn into one complicated calamity. 'Look, I'll ask Patrick if I can swap a shift. Will that make you happy?'

She turned to me with a pleased-with-oneself smile. 'Yes, there's my girl. I want you to drink lots of booze with me.' She clapped her hands with excitement and bounced on the bed.

'How will we get to Gold Coast?'

'Drive, silly.' She rolled her eyes.

'So, you're going to drive to the Gold Coast?' I arched my eyebrow.

'No. Of course not. Why would I drive there on my *own* birthday?' She shot a defensive stare.

'I don't know. It's your idea, so fill me in.' I shrugged and felt like I needed to hold my tongue so I wouldn't say anything else wrong.

'Well, if we go, I was hoping you could drive. It's only just over two and a half hours to get there.' She smiled and gave me an innocent look.

'Yes, I can do that. But who will pay for the Versace hotel?'

She rolled her eyes again. 'Mum and Dad will pay, of course.'

'Uh. Have you asked them this?'

'Not yet, but I will.'

'Have you even spoken to them since last night?' I asked with genuine concern.

'No. Wow.' Deb's voice started rising again. 'What's with the fifty questions about my parents? Look, if worst comes to worst, I'll throw a party here or go out to a bar or something.'

'Mmm. Alright.' I really didn't have the energy to start fighting again.

'Just make sure you get the twenty-sixth off, okay? It's not fucking hard.' She lifted her hands in the air to emphasise her annoyance.

I nodded as my mind slipped back to my birthday in July and how Deb's biggest effort for me was a card and a Woolworth's mud cake. Come to think of it, I had to remind her that morning it was my birthday and drove her to the shops so she could run in.

'Good girl. Anyway, duty calls. My booze is getting warm, so we'll sort out dinner later.' She blew a kiss.

'Sure. Let me know when you want it.' I smiled, relieved to be able to relax again.

Deb instantly switched back into party mode as she leapt off the bed and shimmied her body as she shut the door. Indie music and the shimmy – interesting mix.

As soon as she left, I locked the door and then sank my head into the pillow. Five minutes passed, but the music was too loud for me to drift off, so I figured I might as well get started on the employment paperwork Patrick had given me.

After I finished filling it in, I dialled Mum, excited to hear her reaction to my news.

'Naomi Jean, how are you, darling? How did your job trial go?' Her voice was warm and curious.

'It went so well, Mum. He offered me a full-time position! I just finished filling in the paperwork.' I looked down at the paperwork on my nightstand and flashed a smile of accomplishment.

'Oh, Naomi, this is so good to hear. I'm ecstatic for you! Your first full-time job!'

I could hear the joy in her voice, and I felt proud to have made her so happy but wished I could've heard Dad's voice too. 'Well, it only took twenty-five years, but, hey, I've finally received my pay rise.' I frowned slightly. *I just couldn't help getting a slight dig in at myself, could I?*

'Don't be so hard on yourself. I've seen all the effort you've put in! You deserve this, darling. I'm so proud of you. I knew you'd do well.'

'Thanks, Mum. Your reassurance this morning made me feel so much more confident.' I got into a more comfortable position by lying on my stomach, with lifted legs and ankles crossed, while my palm and elbow supported the weight of my chin.

'I'm glad. Is Deb really excited for you too?'

'Err, yes and no. You know how I told you that she lost her job too? Well, yeah, she's not taking it so well.' I sighed.

'Why did Deb get fired too anyway? You never did tell me the rest of the story.'

I lowered my voice and cupped a hand over the phone. 'Oh, Mum, I'm home at the moment. Deb's here, and I don't want her to overhear me telling you about it. She would flip.'

'Okay, darling. Just promise me you're still happy living at Deb's?'

'I am, Mum.' I kicked my feet in the air.

She paused for a moment. 'Mmm. Well, I better get going. Carlos and I are making grilled fish and salad for dinner. You'll be pleased to know he went fishing this morning, and he's feeling much better since having a few counselling sessions.'

'Oh, Mum, that's great. I'm glad you brought up that because I was meaning to ask you how it went. You don't understand how wonderful it is to hear things are finally turning around for everyone. I love you both very much.'

'We love you too, Naomi Jean. Goodnight, sweetheart.'

'Bye, Mum.'

After I hung up, I got thinking. *Why was I so damn tough on myself? And what would I do if I didn't have Mum's constant support?* The thought of ever losing her made my heart stop. Life was so fragile, so damn fragile. Dad had taught me that. And I knew I deserved happiness – if others did, why didn't I? I thought of all those affirmations I'd seen people post online, and figured, what the hell? Worth a shot, right? I took a deep breath and moved to the mirror, where I stood, facing myself, and spoke the words, 'You are worth it. You deserve this job, and you won't let anyone make you feel otherwise. You've absolutely got this, you goddamn pizza queen.'

19

The Breakup

My mind wandered back to yesterday's shift. It was knock-off time, and Patrick stood in the doorway watching with a facial expression I couldn't read as I cleaned down my section. He was dressed in a tailored white shirt and black pants, with a silver vest, duck-egg-blue tie and black tasselled loafers. His warm, spicy, leathery scent drifted off his skin and smelt as strong as it did in the morning. After I finished wiping the bench, I turned to him with a curious smile.

'Did you need to speak to me?' I asked as I caught sight of his alluring green eyes.

He folded his arms, and I glanced at his rings as they glinted in the fluorescent lights above.

'You're a remarkable lady, Naomi. I must say, you've caught onto every recipe quicker than any previous pizza chef.' He eyed me curiously.

'Thank you.' I gave him a proud smile and watched as he walked closer to me. *Oh no, don't come too close.* Too late. He stood only inches away and leant one hand on the stainless-steel benchtop for support. My cheeks and neck began to burn, and I tried my best to swallow away the feeling.

'You've impressed me more than most qualified pizza chefs. It seems that talent plays a bigger part than qualifications.'

'I guess so. I've cooked since I was a kid.' I shrugged. 'Actually, I've noticed our dough recipes are quite similar, and maybe that's why I've got the knack for your pizzas so quickly.' I eyed him and watched his facial expression transition into a look of intrigue and a huge grin.

'Is that so? Do share.' He raised his brows, eager for me to elaborate, and gestured a hand towards me.

'Well, my dad's recipe is quite simple. It's just all-purpose flour, salt, olive oil, water, and dried yeast. I think pizza dough is simple, really, and ratios are the biggest mistake people make.' I thought of Kelly's text about Tyren's stuff-up and wondered if he concocted his own ratios.

He nodded.

'Anyway, the only difference between our dough is you use triple-zero flour and fresh yeast. It's fascinating how potent dry yeast is in comparison to fresh – you don't need much dried.' My eyes were alight with passion with every word I spoke.

'See, and this is why you impress me, Naomi. You understand ratios and dough as if you invented them. It's an honour to have you work in this kitchen.' He crossed one leg over the other as he leaned against the bench and gave me the face that you give someone you're very proud of. It warmed my heart instantly.

I was already blushing like a mad woman from how close he was standing but felt my cheeks burn even more after he said those words.

'Well, over the years, I've learnt not to take shortcuts when it comes to cooking. Slow and steady well and truly wins the race when it comes to flavours and texture. Every time I see someone use warm water instead of cold in their dough to quicken the process, I have a mild anxiety attack because it's like witnessing a murder. If you be patient and wait for a slow rise, the crust becomes airy, crispier, and more delicious.'

'*Sì.*' He nodded his approval once more.

I let out a laugh, and we continued talking about pizza until it was time to close the restaurant.

***

I can't believe it's the twenty-second of October already, I thought as I stared at my sunset-picture wall calendar. It had been almost three weeks since I first stepped foot in Casa di Vitello's kitchen, and since then, the pizza section had become as familiar to me as Mon Amour's. I knew Patrick's kitchen well and the pizzas even better, and I felt as though I'd cooked in the oven forever. Looking at the calendar with its sunsets from all over the world was my way of visiting places without physically going, since I'd never been overseas.

***

Seb arrived on the eighteenth for a two-week break and would be attending Deb's birthday party whatever she decided to do. We still hadn't caught up because I'd been busy with work and he'd been on a pokies spree, pub-hopping with Billy. They both spent big. Sometimes they'd punt five-hundred-plus dollars a day; they only deemed a win worthy if it was over the one-thousand-dollar mark. Billy had rich parents, so the Uber driving money was just extra pocket money on top of his weekly allowance. So, the miner and the Uber boy lived it up every chance they got. Their motto: *'Punt up 'til I die.'* I'd rolled my eyes more than once at that one.

Speak of the devil, I thought as my phone vibrated against my nightstand.

Seb: *How's my baby going? I'm super horny. Hehe. Are you keen for a tumble in the sheets? ;)*

Me: *I was just about to go shopping and find Deb a birthday present, and no, it's that time of the month.*

Seb: *So? It's just a bit of blood. I've done it before and don't care.*

Here we go ... Bringing up past things he's done with other women, like that means it should be the same with me. I shook my head and pressed my hand to my face. *Why is it so hard for him to treat me as an individual? Some women are into that, and that's perfectly fine, but I'm not.*

Seb: *Babe????*

Me: *I'm not into that.*

Seb: *Whatever, Naomi, whateverrrrr. It's just a bit of extra lube.*

Oh, wow, how did I get so lucky with this man? I stared at the eye-roll emoji he'd stuck at the end of his last comment as rage bubbled in my throat. *God, I really know how to pick them, don't I?* At least we weren't in an official relationship or anything, but what is it that made me still want to pursue him? Ever since we had sex, his sleaziness has been out of control. *Perhaps he feels entitled to act that way since he's had me? He uses his looks to his advantage and thinks he can get away with this behaviour, but frankly, it's getting too much, and it's hindering my feelings from growing further. But then a part of me believes there is hope for us and maybe we'll work things out.*

Without replying, I dressed in a baby-blue shirt dress and Docs to go to the plaza, solo, because I didn't want Deb to see what I was buying for her. She was staked out on the couch with her fishbowl glass in hand and squished cigarette packet on her chest. I tried not to shake my head on my way out at the empty pinot grigio bottle on the wooden coffee table. There were also coffee ring stains from whoever forgot to use a coaster.

'Never too early for a beverage, and hangovers can fuck right off,' Deb said, stopping me in my tracks.

'I'm going out. I'll see you later.' I swivelled to face her and noticed she was still in her pyjamas, which consisted of a black T-shirt (her ex-work one) and yellow polka-dot underpants. Her hair was unbrushed, and I could tell her teeth were too. Yellow marks stained her fingers from all the smoking, and one of her fake nails had snapped off.

'Where are you heading?'

'Plaza quickly. Got to run some errands.' I gave a weak smile as I tried to fight off the nausea from seeing her like this.

She did the captain sign with her hand and sank into the couch, squeezing her eyes shut. Her pale skin and the bags under her eyes were undeniable.

***

Hopefully, I'll find her such a great present today, it will make things like they used to be, I thought to myself as I drove to the shopping centre.

Ninety minutes later, I was back in the car, smiling at the memory of a pleasant afternoon. I'd window-shopped, with a vanilla latte, and admired pretty things but surprised myself by not buying anything for me. *Mum would be proud*. Deb's present from Mecca had been my only purchase. It took a lot of restraint to wander the aisles of that makeup wonderland and only buy for her.

I felt proud of myself for not caving in and self-indulging as I made my way back home. It took the usual thirty-five minutes to get back and park the car. The sound of the sliding door to the garage caught Deb's attention as I walked through.

'Hey, chick,' Deb said as she got off the couch and headed to the fridge.

I walked over and moved past her into the kitchen, glad that her present fit into my bag so I could sneak it in without her noticing. 'Hey, Deb. How are you feeling?' I squirted some soap onto my hands and washed them in the sink, then patted them dry with a tea towel.

'Oh, same old, same old.' She sighed and opened the fridge door to get a chilled bottle of wine. She glanced at my arms, empty of any shopping bags. 'Didn't you buy anything?'

I shook my head. 'No, nothing that I wanted.' I smiled a self-satisfied smile. Just as I was about to walk away, I noticed toast crumbs sprinkled all over the kitchen counter. Without thinking twice, I had the multipurpose spray and sponge in hand and was wiping away the crumbs into the bin.

'Bummer. So, are you going to get kinky with Seb tonight or what?' She waggled her eyebrows. 'It's weird how you haven't been hanging as much. He was all over you like a rash. What happened?'

'Nope, it's that time of the month, so I plan to gush in peace. And I've been at work all week, and this is my first day off.' I paused for emphasis, groaning a little. 'And he's also on a pokies spree with Billy.' I chucked the sponge back into the sink and walked closer to Deb as I leant against the kitchen wall.

'Pokies, hey?' Her reddened eyes lit up. 'Oh, and men don't care about period blood, honestly ...'

I didn't reply to her comment. *Why did everyone always try to talk me into doing things I didn't want to do?* I grasped at a topic to change the subject. 'How's job hunting going?' I asked.

'Non-existent.' She flashed me the peace sign. 'I'm enjoying the slack life.' I noticed she hadn't bothered to get her wine glass. She was just slugging it straight from the bottle with her head tilted towards the ceiling. I frowned with concern. Concern for her and also concern that I was about to piss her off again. 'You used to love working, though,' I said, crossing my fingers for a reasonable response.

She lowered the bottle from her mouth. 'I need a break, okay? I'm super stressed about what happened, so get off my case.' Her ebony eyes flickered with annoyance as she ran her free hand through her greasy, unbrushed hair.

'Okay.' *Shit. Not this again.* 'Sorry, but your drinking is becoming over the top. It's so hard to see you like this all the time. You know where my dad ended up because of this recklessness.'

She sighed. 'As I said, I'm stressed. Anyway, did you get my text about picking me up some ciggies? I've run out.'

'Do you have any money?' My brow shot up in curiosity.

'Mum transferred me two hundred dollars today, so I'm sweet.' She stuck her thumb up. 'She gave into me and is going to pay for me until I find a job.'

I nodded my okay, but inside, I couldn't help but think of how little Deb paid her own way. Even the car she never used was bought for her. It seemed that her dependency on others to pay for her was only getting worse.

'Can you pick up my ciggies from the servo, please?' she asked without even a suck-up smile; it was just a blatant order.

'I was just out, Deb.' I glimpsed at her polka-dot undies wedged up her bum as she reached into the fridge to grab a piece of banana bread from her special plate filled with slices she had pre-lathered with butter.

She spun around with her mouth full. 'Naomi? What the fuck? Please. I'm super stressed out and can't drive.'

What I wanted to say was 'no'. But what I ended up saying was 'fine'. Because I knew she would just keep pestering me until I gave in.

***

Deb sank into the couch, unpeeled the plastic slip off her Winfield Blue packet, and slipped out a smoke. I knew the day would come when she thought it'd be okay to light up a cigarette in the lounge room, considering she did it in her bathroom. She slipped out a zippo lighter from her bra and sparked up her smoke, then sucked in a deep drag; I watched the ash form on the tip. She held the smoke in her lungs for a few seconds, then let out a puff.

She was still in her black shirt but thankfully had put some jeans on. Her hips were muffining over, and she had to keep doing the zip up, which she did with a grunt. She didn't smell like her usual jasmine and patchouli; she smelt like sweat, tobacco, and depression. Vibrant Deb was dead, and the only thing she cared about was her cigarettes, bread, booze, and Indie music.

I walked away, unable to stand there and watch her like that. It was too much. Seeing her succumb to depression in that way was breaking my heart, and I had no say in the matter. She would just flick off my opinions like an ash on her cigarette. In truth, I was at a loss for what to say or do to help her.

After I tucked her present away in the cupboard, I sank my head into the pillow and thought about work again and how badly I wished it was Wednesday. It wasn't fun living here anymore. Deb and I didn't hang out like we used to. We'd stopped telling each other secrets, shopping, and laughing endlessly about silly things. At this rate, she could be out of work for months, and I'd be coming home to a house that stank of stale cigarette smoke because she was too lazy to open the windows. As annoyed and worried about her as I was, the truth was, I just really missed my friend.

I grabbed a cookbook about Italian cuisine from my side table to distract myself and read about pasta until the words were blurry. My plan had been to have an afternoon nap, but between Deb's music and all the worry, I was wide awake.

Minutes later, my phone vibrated – it was Seb again. *Hmm, wonder what he's up to now.*

Seb: *Hey baby, what's doing? Want to chill? x*

I thought about it for a moment and considered my options: I could read more later, watch Netflix on my own, or I could have Seb join me. Why not? I couldn't get to sleep anyway, and he'd been away for two weeks. He could entertain me with his recent antics and get my mind off Deb. And, as much as I hated to admit it, I found him very nice to look at with his bronzed skin, muscly body, and russet eyes, which I'm sure he knew all too well. A small fragment of me was attracted to his cockiness, even though most of me hated it, and I did miss the feeling of a warm body pressed against my back, cuddling me. Complicated thoughts and relationships seemed to be the story of my life.

Me: *Come over, if you'd like.*

He arrived ridiculously quickly, and I mean within minutes. I suspected he was in the neighbourhood or might've been out the front texting me. He strolled in with a grin fixed on his face, wearing a black T-shirt, a leather jacket, and faded denim jeans. *How he manages to wear jackets all the time in this heat is beyond me. Style over comfort, I suppose.* His jacket even looked about a size too small – to emphasise his guns, most likely.

'How's my babe going?' He maintained his grin as he slid into bed next to me.

His hair was gelled back, and his eyes were bloodshot, and I nearly gagged as I caught a whiff of beer breath.

'Do you want a breath mint or something? I have some in the drawer,' I said politely, my eyes pointing in the direction of the nightstand drawer.

'Are you saying I stink?' His eyes flickered with hurt.

'Your breath just smells potent with beer.'

'Oh, loosen up, hot stuff.' His tone was laced with agitation.

I burst out laughing at 'hot stuff'. I'd always loathed that phrase, probably because I'd heard so many bogans use it as a pick-up line in pubs.

He rummaged through the drawer until he found the mints and tipped three into his clammy palm – the remaining mints jingled as they slid back to the bottom of the tin. He closed the lid and placed the tin on the table.

'Is it hot in here or what?' he asked while chewing loudly. His sweaty forehead answered the question for him.

'Maybe take off your jacket?' I arched my brow at the problem.

'Yeah, that might help.' He sat up, slipped his arms from the jacket, and chucked it onto the floor, then reached over me and picked up the book, which still lay by my side. 'Cookbooks, eh? I never understood how people read these for entertainment. So boring. Hey, maybe you could cook dinner for me sometime soon? Show off your wife-material skills.'

I ignored his question, bristling slightly at the putdown of my reading choices. 'Do you cook much?'

'Never. I can't cook to save my life.' He let out a happy-go-lucky laugh.

So that explains why we always get takeaway or eat out. 'It's not that hard if you follow a recipe. I could teach you if you want?'

'Nah, I don't have the patience for that shit.' He shook his head as if it were some absurd thing to suggest.

'Right.' I nodded, unsure of what to say next. God, this was more awkward than I expected.

He moved closer to me and stared at me with that ridiculously intense gaze of his, then grabbed my breast.

I pushed his hand away and furrowed my brows. 'Ow. They're tender,' I said.

He let out a dramatically frustrated sigh. 'Oh right, I forgot you were on your rag. You should have reminded me over text. If you won't have sex, can you at least give me a headie?' He began to pull down his pants in expectation of a positive answer.

As soon as he said those words, I regretted inviting him over and wished I'd chosen to stay in bed alone with my cookbook. I seemed to have a knack for making wrong decisions.

'No, I'm not in the mood for that. I just want to relax. I thought we could chat and catch up on things.' My voice was hopeful our conversation could go down that path.

'All my exes would do this for me. They loved that they could still get me off when they were on their period. Come on, babe. Just a few sucks.' He nodded to his blue great-white-shark underwear.

I cringed at his 'get me off' comment. Like women were lining up just to please him.

'No, I'm tired. Look this was a bad idea. I thought we'd catch up and have a laugh, but now you're starting to annoy me. Maybe you should go.'

'Are you fucking kidding me, Naomi?' He stood up and used his hands to express his annoyance. 'I haven't seen you for two fucking weeks.'

'I don't think this is working, Seb.' As soon as I said those words, his upper lip snarled and he shot me a pissed-off look.

'You haven't even given us a proper go. You fuck everything with all these restrictions. I get you're upset about your dad, but I'm a top bloke. You're making a big mistake giving me the boot.' He shook his head.

'I've been thinking about it, and the truth is I don't think we're that compatible. Maybe we're better off as friends.' I rested my chin on my palm for support while I lay on my side.

'*Pffftttt.* Friends that fuck, hey? Good luck doing better.' He narrowed his russet eyes.

'Goodbye, Sebastian.' I gestured my free hand to the door and rolled my eyes.

'If that's what you want, then fine.' He bent down and reached for his jacket on the floor, then flung open the door. 'See ya later, you straight-edged sook.'

I didn't bother replying as I got out of bed to lock my bedroom door.

As much as I was attracted to Seb, his personality, I wasn't. I thought it was the right decision to end things with him. He wasn't treating me as an individual or considering my feelings and tried to dominate mine. We couldn't even have a proper conversation, and I wasn't in love with him the way he wanted. Maybe friends were all we should be. I walked over to the dressing table, grabbed the opal necklace, and stared at the blue-and-green flecks dancing under the light. *It would be wrong of me to keep this. I'll call him tomorrow to tell him to collect it.*

Once I'd cleared my head, I opened my bedroom door and walked to the fridge to grab a water bottle but was distracted by chatting in the lounge room. *Wait a minute. That voice is … Sebs's. I thought he left.* The last thing I expected was for him to still be there.

I walked into the lounge room and saw Seb and Deb sitting on the three-seater couch. Seb crossed his arms and frowned as soon as our eyes met, and Deb gave me a smile.

'Hey, what are you guys doing?' I asked with confusion written all over my face.

'Hanging out,' Deb interjected with another smile.

'I was just leaving actually,' Seb said as he stood and avoided eye contact with me.

'You really hurt him, Naomi,' Deb added.

'Deb, that's between me and Seb. Things just weren't working out.' I let out a long sigh and was the one folding my arms this time. They were ready to shield me and defend my honour.

'I happen to think you and him are a great mix and that you're making a huge mistake splitting up. There's not that many great options, you know, and Seb is a great guy and is nothing like Scott.' She fixed me with her ebony eyes. 'You and him are like the Brangelina of Noosa.'

I couldn't help but think of the time Seb called her a hooker behind her back but was glad they had formed a connection since.

'We weren't really together to begin with,' I said in haste, then instantly felt bad. *Is Seb really that bad? He's gorgeous-looking, and the sleaziness is the most off-putting thing about him. Maybe Deb's right, and Seb is genuine, and all he needs is some guidance and a deep conversation because conversation skills are where he's failing.*

'Ouch,' Deb replied.

Seb walked towards me and looked into my eyes. His eyes were all puppy-dog sad and his strong body looked defeated.

'You're my weakness, Naomi. I don't think I can get over you as quick as you seem to be able to get over me. Can we chat about this in your room?' He looked at the floor, afraid of my answer.

Him wanting to talk about it and not storming out of the house showed me another side to his character and utterly surprised me.

'Yeah, okay.' I nodded.

We walked into my room and sat on the edge of the bed.

He turned his head to an angle so our eyes aligned, then said, 'I don't want things to end between us, baby. I love you and want things to go back to how they were the night when we first had sex.'

'Yes, the sex was good, Seb, but I just get over the sleaze talk and you comparing me to other women. And more than anything, I just wish we could have more proper conversations and, I don't know, some laughs.'

'Babe. I promise to stop that. Can you please just give me another chance? I'll try and change for you.' His voice sounded sincere and his eyes looked it too.

I took a moment to respond and thought about whether I should or not. His arm muscles were tensed, and I caught myself admiring the definition. *Hmm. I guess it's always good to give people the benefit of the doubt and give them a second chance. Maybe this needed to happen in order for him to listen and change.*

'Okay, but you have to *promise* to stop with the sleaze talk.' I looked at him with dead-serious eyes.

'Deal, babe.' He put out his finger, and we shook pinkies.

20

Happy Birthday, Deb

Before I knew it, it was 26 October and Deb's twenty-fourth birthday. I set my alarm for 7.30am and cooked Deb her favourite breakfast of eggs Benedict on a bed of spinach with smoked salmon and ciabatta toast. She ate her breakfast in bed with her eyes closed as she revelled in all the flavours. Warm sunshine flooded the room through her east-facing window.

'Thanks, chicka. You're honestly the best human.' She smiled with deep satisfaction as she finished her last bite, then licked her plate. 'Your hollandaise is always on point. What is your secret? Kelly is a breakfast master, and even she's fucked up hollandaise multiple times and made it split, but no, not yours – yours is just bloody flawless.'

I let out a hearty laugh and clutched my chest. 'It's all about pacing. So, I make sure I have a steady hand when I slowly pour the melted butter into the mixture, bit by bit, and whisk it in. That's the secret.'

She nodded. 'And what's that you got there?' She eyed my hand tucked behind my back.

'Happy birthday, Deb.' I beamed as I passed her a sparkly red envelope with silver ribbons twirled around it.

She tore into the paper and opened it; her face lit up when she saw the sleek black Mecca gift card, which would buy her one hundred dollars' worth of goodies.

'Oh my God, Naomi, trust you to do this! Guess this calls for a shopping trip. Thanks, my girl.' Her eyes were wide and happy.

My heart warmed at her facial expression and hoped it would stay that way for the day. 'No worries. I truly hope your day is fabulous.'

'Yeah, thanks for actually getting the day off.' She nodded in appreciation and placed her gift card on her nightstand.

'Well, Patrick is a ridiculously lenient boss, so you've got him to thank.' I winked.

'Mmm. Well, I guess he would've let you take more than one night off to go to the Versace hotel if I decided I wanted to do that.'

I was more than relieved that she changed her mind about that idea; a drinking binge in a luxurious hotel for a few nights was the last thing I'd want to be around.

I nodded my reply and glanced at the sunlight spilling through her window.

*****

The evening was when her real party began. Deb's mum had paid for an unlimited bar tab at the same restaurant we'd been at when my toilet paper incident occurred. *Oh, memories.* We even had the same table as last time too. Deb, Victor, me, Kelly, Martin, and Seb sat on the barstools with champagne buckets and bottles of pinot grigio spread across the table, while weighted, metallic-red helium balloons bobbed about at both ends of the table.

Deb, Victor, and Martin sat on one side, while me, Seb, and Kelly sat on the other side. Seb was situated behind the balloons with his chin on his palm, elbow on the table, and half-drunk beer in front of him while he tapped away at his phone. He seemed to be more interested in Facebook memes than socialising.

I couldn't help but notice how close we were to Mon Amour and wondered why Deb had chosen this restaurant, of all places, for her birthday. Was she secretly hoping to run into Daniel?

'Chyeahhhh boyyy,' Deb said with the biggest smile I'd seen in weeks plastered on her face as she clinked her glass with Victor's. She had her makeup done at Mecca that afternoon and looked gorgeous with her glowing skin and vampy red lipstick, and she smelt like her old patchouli and jasmine. I smiled as I observed her outfit of a V-neck black dress, which could barely contain her breasts, and her knee-high caramel boots. It was good to see Deb out of her pyjamas and back to her stylish self again.

'Let's all booze up. It's my birthday, motherfuckers.' Deb chugged her glass of wine. Some of the liquid missed her mouth and dripped down into her cleavage, and I watched as Victor licked it off and stuck out his tongue afterwards like he was at a rave in Ibiza instead of at an upscale bistro in Noosa. I blushed and looked around at the other diners, but thankfully no one seemed to be looking at our table.

No one reacted to Victor's behaviour; they were too distracted by the drinks on the table. So distracted that most of them were drunk already after an hour and a half and were reaching for wine after wine. Martin was hammered. He was having gin on the rocks and sat there staring off into space, looking as though his head was spinning. Just the sight of him made me dizzy.

'Happy birthday, Debra Ricci,' everyone chanted in harmony and held up their glasses, except Martin, who did a Kelly and stumbled outside with his hand over his mouth. No one paid attention to his disappearance or even asked where he was.

'Now, should we do presents or what?' Deb asked, cackling with laughter while looking around at everyone. Her face was pink with excitement, and her pupils were enlarged and unfocused.

'Yeah, why not,' Kelly said with a nod as she passed Deb something wrapped in a crinkled paper bag.

Deb grabbed the package and tore into it. 'Oooh, pretty. Thanks, darling.' She blew a kiss and slipped on the silver bangle.

'Sorry about the paper, dude. I didn't have time to find anything nice.' She ran her hand through her blue hair.

'No worries, chick.' She winked as she scrunched up the paper and plonked it onto the table.

Deb drum-rolled on the benchtop with her fingers, then turned to Victor. 'Get me anything, sexy?' She shimmied as her auburn hair swished, and as she stopped moving, I noticed her upper lip was damp with sweat.

'Ah, yes, my presence.' He grinned and pointed his finger towards himself.

She elbowed him in the arm and laughed, then waved her hands in the air to the jazz music playing in the background. 'Wooooo,' she yelled as she dropped her hands in favour of the wine bottle and pressed it to her lips.

Victor chanted 'scull, scull, scull' and clapped his hands while his chipped-tooth smile spread across his face.

Deb obliged and began draining the liquid from the half-full bottle and didn't stop until it was empty.

I sipped on my soda water and lime, highly grateful I was sober. The wine bottles all over the table made me think of my dad, and as soon as his crinkly eyes and checked shirt came into my mind, I felt my heart sink. I clutched my chest and sighed, imagining being someplace else. Somewhere calm and not so chaotic and loud, where my heart heavy with grief could heal. After I did my breathing exercises, I told myself, *It's Deb's birthday. Be happy for her sake.* My grief and anger disagreed with this, but I tried to distract myself for the time being before I became overwhelmed.

As I observed everyone around the table, I noticed Seb was still on his phone, Kelly looked tipsy, Victor and Deb were on the verge of being smashed, and Martin was still missing. It seemed glaringly obvious to me that Victor was there for free drinks. I had my eye on him ever since the first night he came over and drank wine with Deb in the lounge room. Once he left the following morning, Deb told me she shouted the wines and cigarettes, and he hadn't chipped in a cent. He did a signature Deb move to her. He said he didn't have any money and asked her to pay, and, oh boy, did she bitch about it.

I looked back at Deb to see her smiling at everyone around the table. Her eyes were bloodshot, and her lip was sweating like crazy. 'Booze hard or go home, motherfuckers,' she yelled with an embarrassing loudness as diners behind us stopped eating their dinner and stared at her with their cutlery mid-air. She noticed them and howled with laughter as she stuck up the finger. 'Fuck off, you old pricks. So sick of people trying to kill my vibe.' Her words had started to slur so 'trying' sounded like 'vying'.

Their expressions were shocked as they turned away quickly and continued eating their gnocchi.

'I'm sooooo glad you all came to party with me.' She leant her chin onto her palm and squeezed her eyes shut as her head swayed to the music.

My mind drifted back over the past few weeks. If I was honest with myself, I'd been thinking more and more that maybe it was time I moved back into Mum's. The environment these days at Deb's really wasn't my scene, with the binge eating, the excessive drinking, and the constant smoking inside, not to mention Victor coming over several nights a week for sex and free drinks. He was just using her; it was so obvious. I wished Deb could hurry up and see it as well.

The sound of Deb clearing her throat caught my attention, so I looked at her again and sighed, trying to ignore the feeling in my chest and the nausea in my stomach. She turned to Victor, talking nonsense and laughing, which gave me a chance to talk to Seb, who'd been sitting in silence the whole night. Things felt awkward between us still, but I was trying to put that aside and see what could come of us.

'Hey, is everything okay?' I asked him and placed my hand on his shoulder.

He lifted his head from his phone. 'Yeah, just feel bloody zonked.' He let out a yawn, which made his eyes water.

'Me too, and it's hard to watch everyone get drunk like that,' I said in a low voice so that only he could hear.

His voice was loud in response. 'Why? Just have a few like you did last time we were here.'

Oh yes, when I walked around with toilet paper dangling from my pants and spewed out a car window. No thanks.

'This kind of drinking reminds me of my dad, and it's difficult to watch. I feel really bad I'm not enjoying myself right now, but to be honest, I feel on the verge of tears, and I just really miss him and would do anything to have him back, and staring at the alcohol makes me angry.' My eyes were glassy, and that familiar burning feeling in my throat returned.

'Naomi, if you're getting triggered by this drinking, maybe we should bail?' He arched his perfect brow.

'I can't do that to Deb. She'd be devastated.' I sighed, feeling stuck.

'But she's got other mates here, babe. Come on. Can we please go?' He nodded towards the door.

Deb overheard Seb and shot him a death stare, and, boy, if looks could kill, Seb would be dead right now. 'Hey, hey, hey. Vhat's going on, kids? Party shas just begun. Can't leave yet!!'

I didn't overthink Seb's eagerness to leave and just went with it because I didn't want to have a breakdown in front of all Deb's guests and ruin the night. It was her birthday, and I wanted her to have fun. I didn't need to steal her attention with my tears and have to explain why. And maybe Seb could finally prove himself and comfort me like a 'real' boyfriend would. Show me he wasn't just a sleaze but a man who was capable of nurturing a woman's feelings. The woman he supposedly loved.

'I'm sorry, Deb. I've got to go,' I said as I held the tears back.

'Vhateverrrr.' She grabbed the neck of the bottle and began to chug more wine down. She didn't say anything, but her eyes showed she was furious and completely drunk.

As we walked outside, my emotions were soon overtaken by the thought of where Martin might be. He had vanished, and no one bothered to look for him. Two athletic blokes, dressed in business attire, walked past, and I smelt their 1 Million cologne as the wind drifted in my direction. I overhead them laugh and caught their words about seeing a guy passed out in the bush across the road.

My immediate reaction was to go to the convenience store and buy a bottle of water, and so I did that, while Seb stalked off to the car. I raced across the road and found Martin instantly. He was lying on his side, covered in bark and weeping next to a pool of gin. I crouched down and placed my hand on Martin's back, comforting him with nurturing pats.

'Hi, Martin. It's Naomi. I'm going to call you a cab, okay?' I passed him the bottle of cold water, and he clutched it in his hand before cradling it to his chest.

He nodded with half-open eyes as he drooled and cried some more.

I dialled the cab and waited for it come, which took only six minutes, then escorted him with help from the taxi driver as he stumbled into the back seat. Martin leant his head against the window and weakly took small sips of water, then waved to me as the taxi took off. I waved too, then headed to my car parked behind the restaurant.

As Seb and I hopped into my car, I couldn't help but feel guilty for leaving Deb's birthday party, especially since I'd taken a shift off work so I could be there. Maybe the truth was my friendship with Deb was coming to an end. I just wasn't enjoying myself like I used to. She had changed since drinking became her number one priority. My emotions were a complicated vortex, and each one would fight the other about what the right thing to do was. But even though I was grief-stricken and taking care of myself, a part of me felt as though I should've stayed for Deb's sake. I'd broken our treaty to always be there for one another and couldn't help but feel like the ditcher she was to me on her eighteenth birthday, when she left me in the club alone. At least she wasn't alone, though, and I was only trying to protect my heart.

'Seb, am I a bad friend leaving her like that?' I yanked at a thread dangling from the bottom of my dress. It fell on the floor, and I let out a sigh.

'No, you wanted to go. What's the harm in that?' His voice was nonchalant.

'Well, would you leave Billy if it was his birthday party?' I felt my stomach crumble with guilt.

'Nope, I wouldn't.' He shook his head.

'Exactly my point.' I swallowed down my guilt.

He shrugged and looked out onto the street.

'I feel horrible, but it's becoming too much. She's a raging alcoholic, and you're right – it just triggers me too much. It gives me high anxiety thinking about if something were to happen to her, you know? What if she got liver poisoning and got really sick? I'd hate to see that happen, and I have no say in this. She doesn't listen to me about it, and I've told her many times what I think about binge drinking and the effects I've seen it have on friends in the past.'

'Hey, ease up. I sink bottles too.'

'That much?' I arched a worried brow.

'I like to have a couple of drinks a day.'

'Mmm, well, your drinking isn't in my face every day for it to affect me.' I looked at his brown eyes.

'Anyway, babe, is it alright if I go out with Billy and have a boys' night tonight? Please? He texted me, and I feel like chugging a few beers and playing pool.'

'So, that's the real reason you wanted to leave? Because you wanted to have a *boys'* night?' My eyes widened with shock.

He didn't say anything and fiddled with his seatbelt.

'Are you serious?' I asked as my sad eyes were now filled with annoyance.

'Look, I'll stay with you if you want.' He looked out the window to the other cars in the car park.

'Seb, I want you to *want* to stay with me. This has to be a mutual decision.'

He turned to me. 'Babe, I'll make it up to you tomorrow. Billy needs me. He has some stuff going on.'

I didn't buy his line about Billy having some stuff going on, but I didn't want to question him. If he wanted to leave, then he could leave. There was no use arguing about it.

'Yeah, alright. I'll drop you at home, then he can pick you up. I've got work tomorrow anyway.' My voice was casual, and my face was too. Him leaving should have hurt me, but it didn't.

'You're the best, Naomi.' He leant in and kissed me on the cheek.

21

Midnight Drives

The only noises I could hear were the whirring fan above my bed, the crickets chirping outside, and the fluttering of bat wings flying through the night sky. It was just past 11pm, and Deb still wasn't home, but I wasn't worried. It was still early, and I didn't expect her back until well after 2am.

After another hour of browsing sales on fashion websites and makeup on Mecca and enjoying the rare peace and quiet, my phone vibrated in my hand. A Facebook message from Patrick appeared on top of the screen. I exited out of Mecca and opened his message.

Patrick Vitello: *How was the party? I saw Debra stumbling along Hastings St as I was driving home from work. I hope you've had a good evening.*

Me: *Oh haha. Typical Deb. I'm in bed relaxing. I tapped out early, so don't worry, I won't be hungover for work tomorrow. I stuck to soda water.*

Patrick Vitello: *Sounds like you should have come into work after all ... It wasn't the same without you on, everyone missed you. Hey, I'm wide awake from the buzz of work. Do you want to come over?*

Patrick and I had formed a good friendship over the last couple of weeks. We often chatted after our shifts, but he'd never invited me over so late before. The last time I was at his house was his birthday. *Hmm. I wonder what's going on with him? I hope he isn't after a quickie.*

Me: *Yeah, sure. I can hang out for a bit. Is everything okay?*

Patrick Vitello: *Everything is fine. I just feel like one of our chats. What's your address? I can pick you up?*

I was startled by his offer to pick me up; no one ever offered to pick me up. I was always the one who had to drive.

Me: *Yeah, sure. 16 Blossom Court, Tewantin.*

I ran into the bathroom and checked the mirror to see mascara smudged beneath my eyes. *Oh God, please don't tell me I looked like this all night.* What was with that restaurant and me coming home with racoon eyes?

After washing my face with oil cleanser and patting it dry, I got out my new glow oil that had arrived in the mail earlier that day and added a few drops to my face, hoping it would make me look semi-refreshed, before reapplying my mascara and berry-tinted lip balm to accentuate my features. My cheeks were already flushed so there was no need for blush. *Fabulous*, I thought as I took a step back and looked at my dewy skin, although my face did feel rather itchy. *Oh well, no time to waste. Got to get dressed.* I changed into a white shirt-dress, pulled on my Doc boots, and spritzed myself with Chloe perfume, and then waited on the driveway for him.

Patrick arrived fifteen minutes later in his purring white Jaguar convertible. The roof was down, and he was listening to a mix of eighties music. As I got closer, I noticed red-and-black leather seats.

'Hello,' he said, smiling. 'Hop in.' He patted the vacant seat beside him.

'Wow. Nice ride.' I opened the car door and shut it in the gentlest way possible, then buckled myself in.

He turned to me and smiled again. 'Ready?' His hands were gripped on the steering wheel, and his foot was pressed on the brake.

I couldn't help but notice the way the red-and-black seats set off his olive skin. *Gorgeous man.* I nodded and smiled back.

He pulled out from the side of my street, the car making typical V8 sounds of vrooms, pops, and crackles. I looked up at the dark sky speckled with thousands of stars as the wind whipped through my hair and realised it was the first time in months I'd taken the time to look at the stars. They were beautiful.

'So, tell me. How was the birthday?' Patrick asked in a playful tone.

I scoffed. 'A bit boring, to be honest. I just don't find it fun sitting at a bar getting blind drunk anymore. I guess I used to like that when I was younger, but now I just see the consequences of overindulging and how it ruins people. I just can't seem to be able to escape it.' I sighed and thought of my dad's alcoholic ways and how Deb was going down that path.

'Mmm. I agree. Moderation is key.' He nodded to himself, eyes on the road. 'I don't see any harm in a wine here and there to complement a gorgeous meal but drinking to oblivion isn't my style either.'

'I guess that's the Aussie culture. We're surrounded by messages about how much fun it is to drink.' I sat back in the seat, picturing my dad out on the patio sculling his shiraz with one of his friends while Elvis was playing through the stereo. They were laughing, playing card games, and I was jealous I couldn't drink too, being thirteen at the time with no understanding of the consequences. 'Some people don't understand the concept of moderation.'

'*Si.*'

'And I don't know ... maybe I blame alcohol for ruining parts of my childhood.'

'What do you mean?' He glanced at me before turning his attention back to the road, which was illuminated by his car lights. Toads skittered into the gutters to escape the rolling wheels.

'Oh, my parents broke up over Dad's drinking, and he ... well ... Dad passed away earlier this year, and I can't get this haunting image out of my mind of him dead with a wine bottle in his hand. It just upsets me so much even to think about it.' I turned my face to the window, hoping Patrick wouldn't see the tears forming in my eyes.

'Oh, Naomi, I had no idea. I'm deeply sorry for your loss.' He swallowed hard. 'I lost my papa too, to a stroke. I know how hard it is. And you want to put the blame on something for taking them away.' His voice was full of hurt, and then he whispered, 'I miss my pa every day.' He exhaled a shaky breath, which made my stomach sink, and told me he'd been battling hard with grief too.

I nodded, not quite trusting my voice.

He must have realised I didn't want to reply because he continued. 'One good thing, though, is that it makes us realise what's important in life, and that's family and friends. You have to always cherish your family because you never know when it'll be the last time you see them.'

I cleared my throat and took a breath before responding. 'Very true.'

He took one hand off the wheel and reached out to squeeze my hand. 'Things will get easier, Naomi. I promise. You'll always feel like a piece of you is missing, but you'll learn to cope.'

The warmth of his hand on mine felt wonderful. 'I do try to be strong.'

'I can see your strength. You show your capability every time you get up and work in the kitchen. Losing a parent is … gut-wrenching. When I lost my papa, I found it extremely difficult to keep motivated, and I felt lethargic every day, but … exercise, food, and making people happy is what makes me happy, so I found peace in doing what I loved.'

I smiled my broadest smile in weeks. It felt so nice to be with someone who understood and was on the same page as me. 'Me too. I just kept cooking because it made me feel closer to my dad, and it helped take my mind off the pain. A little, anyway.'

'The pain will always be there deep down, but every experience has shaped you into the person you are now.' His green eyes glanced at me.

I beamed at him. 'I guess, if anything, it's helped me become more mature.'

'Your honesty is refreshing, Naomi. It's a rare quality.'

It felt strange to have such a deep conversation with a man about my emotions, death, and family. Conversations with Seb were mostly shallow, and Deb was the main person I got deep with, which is what made the idea of moving out so hard. She was my rock. When things got out of hand, we'd always have each other's backs. She was the one person there for me during my parents' divorce, when I needed someone more than ever. But did I need to make my mental health suffer to be a good friend? There was no way she was going to change her drinking habit, and I wasn't happy, so was the answer to put myself first and move out?

Patrick was the most mature and understanding man I'd ever met. He was so generous, and not to mention beautiful, I admitted to myself as I admired his profile. *Uh oh, I cannot fall in love with my boss. This is dangerous.*

As we pulled into his spacious garage, I turned to Patrick.

'Are you okay?' he asked in a sincere tone.

'Yes, I feel much better after our chat.' I nodded with a relaxed smile.

'No, I mean your skin. It's bright red.'

Oh no. I slipped the compact mirror from my handbag and stared at my red, blotchy skin. *The glow oil.* I stammered with embarrassment, 'Uh, I guess this new skincare's rave reviews were deceptive.' I swallowed. 'No glowing skin for me, just an allergic reaction.'

'Well, you're certainly glowing!' He must have seen the look on my face because he quickly added, 'It looks painful. Does it sting?'

'No, it's okay. I think I should rinse it off, though.' I unbuckled my belt, ready to go to the bathroom.

'I'd say so.'

We hopped out of the car, and Patrick escorted me down his lengthy hallway to his opulent bathroom, then closed the door, leaving me to clean myself up. His bathroom was tiled with travertine, floor to wall. The tall ceiling was a gloss white, and a crystal chandelier hung from the centre of the room.

I walked past the white spa bath adorned with gold taps and past the shower big enough for three people and made my way over to the double-basin vanity. The basins weren't regular ones but were large, white clamshells made with some kind of porcelain. Golden highlights decorated the textured lines of the outer shells, which were adorned with more gold taps. I admired the ornate chandelier wall lamps on the outsides of the humungous mirror. They gave a soft, romantic glow to the setting, and the imitation wicks flickered slowly, looking identical to real candlelight.

After splashing water over my face in one of his double basins and patting myself dry with a fluffy, white handtowel, I stared in the mirror and examined my face. My mascara had run down my cheeks, along with the oil. *Great.* I looked super attractive with more racoon eyes and irritated red skin.

I made a mental note to never buy skincare online before trying it again – rave reviews be damned!

Thanks to the help of more water and cotton tips, I managed to wipe the smudges away but was still left with irritated, burning eyes. *This is as good as it's going to get,* I thought as I walked out of the bathroom and searched for Patrick in his huge, immaculate home.

During my search, I stumbled across an oil-painted family portrait encased in a baroque-style golden frame. It was positioned perfectly straight on his hallway wall. My heart stopped as I caught sight of his tall, handsome father, whose life had been robbed by a stroke. He had kind, golden-brown eyes, deep-olive skin, and a receding hairline. Next to the father stood Patrick's mother with her hair backcombed and her dusty-pink lips pursed. In the bottom row stood Caterina in the middle, Patrick to her left, and a man who I assumed to be his older brother on the right. His brother had a larger build than Patrick and was taller too. He had his father's golden-brown eyes, deep-olive skin, and the look on his audacious face showed he was the naughty one in the family. He also gave off an alpha-male vibe with his arms crossed while all the others had their hands knotted neatly together. They all looked young; I guessed Patrick and his siblings were in their late teens at the time of the painting.

'Patrick, where are you?' I called as I continued to search for him.

'Just in the kitchen, Naomi,' his soothing voice echoed down the hallway.

As I walked into the stainless-steel and marbled kitchen, I was presented with an antipasto platter on a round wooden board. There was a ramekin of olives in the centre, cherry tomatoes garnished with basil, folded salami, strips of prosciutto, a huge bunch of red grapes, a cup of breadsticks, and cubes of Camembert. *Yum.*

'Who's that for?' I asked, looking at the platter, suddenly feeling embarrassed about my face.

'Us, silly.' He laughed. 'Us Italians love a late-night meal.' He winked. 'How did you go with your rash?'

My body relaxed at the kindness in his voice.

'Oh, it feels a bit better. I think the cold water helped take away some of the redness.'

'I've got some aloe vera gel from my farm if you'd like to use some?'

'That would be lovely, thanks.' I gave a warm smile and watched as he walked off down the hallway.

He returned minutes later, and I was expecting to apply the gel myself, but he did it for me with his caring hands as he patted it into my skin with the precision of a dermatologist. The butterflies inside my stomach flapped to the rhythm of his hands.

'Thanks for that.' I nodded with another smile. The gel felt sticky and cool against my skin.

'My pleasure.' He placed the aloe on the table next to the platter, bringing my attention back to the food.

'Geez, that's sure one elaborate-looking antipasto.' My eyes widened at the meticulousness he put into presenting the food as if it were going out to a king.

'It's just a throw-together from the fridge.' He gestured with his hand to confirm it was no hassle.

He was so thoughtful. How could anyone be this hospitable at this time of night?

'Now, I know you don't like drinking, and you can say no if you want to, but I'd love you to have a taste of this wine,' he said as he placed two glasses down on the glossy bench and a bottle of wine.

'Uh. Okay, but only a sip.'

He twisted off the cap and poured some Vitello Sauvignon Blanc into my glass, half filling it and sliding it towards me.

'Give it a swirl, then have a taste. This is one of our bestsellers.' His eyes were full of family pride.

After giving it a swirl, I closed my eyes and took a small sip. A fruitful, crisp flavour swirled on my tastebuds. It was the perfect combination of sweet and dry, and, my God, it was delicious.

'Did you like it?' he asked, eager for my verdict.

'Yes, I love it, and I think you may have changed my mind about wine if it tastes this good.' I held my glass out to him.

'*Grazie.*' We clinked glasses.

'That means *thank you* in Italian, right?' I raised a brow.

'*Si. Corretto.*' He nodded with his charming smile plastered on his face, and I glimpsed at his long, toned neck, which was in perfect proportion to the rest of his lean body.

'Oh, Patrick, is this an Italian lesson now?' I laughed, unable to contain my smile.

'No, just having some fun.' He chuckled, grabbed a prosciutto strip, and wrapped it around a breadstick.

'So, do you bring all your staff over for late-night chats?' I placed my glass on the counter, detached a small vine of grapes from the bunch, dangled them into my mouth, and bit one off, glancing at him sideways.

'No, just the naughty ones that don't come into work.' He took a bite of his breadstick.

'Guess I'll have to take work off more often, then.' I cast him a playful wink. *Was I seriously flirting with Patrick Vitello in his kitchen in the middle of the night?*

'Ha. Don't get any bad ideas. We need you in that kitchen.' He finished his breadstick.

'Well, that's reassuring. Daniel sure thought otherwise.' I wanted to kick myself for bringing him up.

'Daniel is a fool. Don't let him ruin one more day of your life. You're out of his hands now.' His green eyes were serious yet passionate.

'And into yours.' I winced at how romantic that sounded. *Shit, I hope he doesn't think I'm cracking on to him.*

He didn't say anything and took a sip of his wine while looking at me curiously over his glass.

'So, not to sound like a creep or anything, but are you single?' I asked. 'And I'm just asking out of curiosity.'

He nodded. 'I am.'

My mouth dropped slightly. 'Oh, I thought you were taken for sure.'

'And why's that?' His pupils enlarged with interest.

'I don't need to state the obvious, do I?' I raised my eyebrow.

'Enlighten me.' He gestured towards me with his hand.

'No, because then I *will* sound like a creep.' I crossed my arms with the grapes secured in my fist.

'I don't think you're a creep, Naomi.' He tucked a fallen strand of his tousled hair behind his ear.

'Alright.' I sighed and tried my hardest not to sound like I was fawning over him. 'Well, you pretty much have it all, and I guess a lot of women would want a guy like you.'

'But do they want me for *me* or for my stuff?' He waved his hand around at the stainless-steel appliances and marble benchtop. 'I'm not making that same mistake again with a woman. My ex, Stephanie, was one of those women who wanted me for my stuff, and I fell for it because she got me at my weakest, when my papa died.' He pressed his fingers to his temples and exhaled.

'I'm sorry. I shouldn't have even asked.' *Stupid move, Naomi.* 'Now I've put a dampener on the night.' Why was I being so nosy? It was none of my business whether he was single or not. *Oh my God, I am acting like Deb.*

'No, please don't feel bad. I'm not upset you asked. It's just been really hard to get over, but I'm happy to talk about it. I shouldn't keep it bottled up.' His tone was reassuring as he placed his glass on the bench next to mine.

Thank God he didn't seem scared off. 'Were you together long?' I unfolded my fist and plopped more grapes into my mouth.

'Three years too long. To be honest, she ripped my heart apart.' He let out a painful sigh and looked down at the marble floor.

After I finished chewing, I replied, 'Oh, no. You don't have to tell me about it if you'd rather not, but if you do want to get it off your chest, I'm happy to listen.'

'She ... wasn't just my ex ... but my fiancée.' His eyes squeezed shut for a moment as she haunted his mind. 'She loved playing mind games and drove me crazy trying to make me jealous. One night, she took it too far.' He cleared his throat and looked at me. 'She slept with my older brother, Marco.'

'Oh, my goodness, Patrick. I'm so sorry to hear that. How could your fiancée and your brother do that to you?' I struggled for the words to express my horror. 'That's the lowest thing they could do.' I leant over the counter and placed my hand over his in a way I hoped made him feel understood.

'I gave her every part of me and bought her anything that she wanted, and you know what it taught me?' He moved his hands away and folded them on the bench.

I shrugged, not wanting to say the wrong thing. 'I don't know. Umm. Not to trust women?'

'No, not at all.' He shook his head. 'I'm not bitter. I understand that it was just her, and that not *all* women are like that. What it did teach me was that material items don't prove love, and that love is much deeper than that. If someone truly loves you, it's not about how many gifts you give each other, but the deep connection you share. That's where she and I failed; we got swept up in a pretend romance driven by material objects. It was like we were putting on a performance to the world and showing off our false, perfect life. We were addicted to people's reactions.'

My heart melted at the words he was saying. I could see how true it all was, how heartfelt. 'So, I guess you'll be extra careful about the next woman you pick, then, hey?'

'Sure will.' He smiled.

'So, what kind of woman are you looking for?' My skin did that stupid thing it does when I'm nervous around him, and I was thankful for the cooling gel or I would've looked like a beetroot for sure. *Am I being too forward and crossing over to the more-than-friends territory?*

'One that is dedicated to me, *honest*, and shares the same passion for cooking as I do.'

'Mmm, loyalty is a must.' I nodded in complete agreement. 'Sounds like the perfect woman.'

'Sure does.' He smiled. 'But what frightens me, Naomi, is everyone knows me and knows I have money. How can I find someone that just loves me for me, and not for what I have?' His face held a look of uncertainty.

'You will find someone.' I gave him a warm smile. 'I know you will.'

'Thanks, Naomi. So, enough about me. Tell me about you. Do you have a boyfriend?' He raised an eager eyebrow.

'Uh. Yeah, sort of, but nothing serious.'

'So, you're not in love, then?' He looked into my eyes with curiosity.

'Not in love, no.' I reached for my wine glass on the bench. 'I'm not sure how I feel about Sebastian, to be honest.'

'Ah, complicated.' He nodded. 'Something I avoid.'

I nodded and took a small sip from my glass. 'I think I agree. I'm not sure how compatible he and I are anyway. He's just been so persistent and made me feel special, but I'm confused, and I don't know how to feel. I don't think he gets where I'm coming from, and my emotions are so mixed up from losing my dad. Some days, I'm an emotional wreck, and other days, I feel numb and lonely ... and angry too.' I shook my head in surprise at how comfortable I felt opening up like this to Patrick. He was my boss, after all, not to mention a significantly older guy.

'I understand.'

I grabbed a piece of cheese from the antipasto platter and began to nibble it. 'I really enjoyed this chat and the food. Thank you.'

'My pleasure. I'm glad you came.'

I smiled, and he smiled back.

We took the platter outside onto the patio and stared out at the moonlight glimmering along the water. A fresh, salty breeze filled my lungs and rocked the speedboats stationed near the docks. The mansions along the water were mostly lit up, providing a stream of warm light over the darkened river. Patrick looked up at the almost full moon.

'Did you see last night's full moon?' he asked as his linen shirt billowed in the wind.

'No, I missed it.' I frowned, disappointed that I hadn't been paying attention to the moon and the stars.

'Something as beautiful as that is hard to miss. I can't get enough of nature. Every spare moment I get, I am out here enjoying the sunshine or the moon.' He smiled as his eyes lingered on the sky.

It was a magical night. For the first time in a long time, I felt like I could be myself and let my guard down, even more so than if I was talking to Deb or Mum. *Hmm? Why does it seem so effortless with Patrick? I can only dream of being with someone like him. Whoever ends up with Patrick Vitello will be one lucky girl.*

22

Broken Friendships

'I screamed at Daniel last night,' Deb said as she pulled out a cigarette and chucked the packet on the kitchen bench next to her box of Nurofen. The silver packet of capsules had three lines missing and was squished. 'He's a fucking idiot, and I can't stand him. I'm not taking the blame for his marriage breakup. He *chose* to sleep with me.' She sparked up her smoke and sucked in a deep drag. Her eyes were the reddest I'd seen, and her face still had last night's makeup on it, but her outfit was different. It consisted of a black, lacy G-string and a singlet that just covered her stomach.

Before I could get a word in, she started speaking again.

'Oh, and thanks for ditching me on my birthday. That was bloody nice of you.' She blew out the smoke and let out a cough. A waft of her perspiration mixed with tobacco and a hint of perfume flew my way, making my nose crinkle.

'I'm sorry, Deb. I was so upset about my dad, and you know I don't enjoy drinking.' I thought about last night, having one glass of wine with Patrick, and instantly felt guilty. Maybe drinking with the wrong people was really what I didn't like.

'Yeah. I know.' She rolled her eyes. 'I got home at three-thirty, and you weren't here, so explain to me what you were doing.' She took in another drag.

'I went to Mum's.' I stepped back and waved my hand in my face to try to avoid breathing in the smoke.

'Don't lie to me. You left your car here, and I can't see your mum picking you up late at night when you're perfectly capable of driving. You weren't even drinking last night, so tell the truth.' She stood in front of me with one hand on her hip as her ebony eyes looked at me questioningly.

'I'm so sorry for leaving, Deb, but as I said, I was sad about my dad and didn't want to have a breakdown in front of your guests and steal the attention away from you. Plus, it's not like you haven't left me before, like on your eighteenth, and at least you had people around you. I was all on my own that night.' I folded my arms defensively because, in the pit of my stomach, I could feel things were going to get nasty.

Deb was clearly caught off guard and didn't say anything. She finished the rest of her cigarette, then flicked it into the sink. The ash sizzled as it landed in the residue of water.

'True, true, but that's in the past, and that guy was hot, and he managed a bank … Look, whatever. Stop avoiding the question. Just tell me the truth.' Her defiant attitude weakened for a moment.

'I was visiting a friend … And I don't question *you* about who you're seeing.'

'Seeing?' She raised a curious eyebrow.

'You know what I mean. Hanging out with,' I quickly corrected myself.

'But you never hang out with people, so who would be so important to see?' Her eyes squinted with interest.

I didn't answer her question because I didn't want her to know. Instead, I looked over her shoulder, hoping she would drop it so I could relax before I got ready for work.

'We made a promise we would tell each other anything and everything. Does our friendship mean nothing to you anymore?' Her nose flared with fury.

'It does, Deb. I'm just tired, and I've got to go to work soon.' I let out a yawn.

'Dodging the question, hey, just like a bloody politician.' She rolled her eyes again. 'Oh, and if you're sleeping around on Seb, you're so fucking low.'

I could feel my face redden with anger and my heart rate speed up as soon as she said those words.

'I haven't TOUCHED another man, and I can't believe you're accusing me of that.' I shook my head at the absurdity of her accusation. 'Are you really accusing me of sleeping around? Sounds like you lost most of your brain cells last night. Is this seriously our friendship? It's turned to crap. Let's stop pretending we're amazing friends and everything is okay, because it's really not. We're two different people and aren't in high school anymore.' *What was I saying? Did I really want to end my friendship with Deb? Too late now ...* The words had left my mouth, and I could tell by the look on Deb's face she was livid.

She scoffed and eyed me up and down. 'And, what, you think you're perfect? What, just because you've lost some weight, don't drink or smoke, and have a job at Patrick's restaurant, that makes you so fucking fantastic, does it? You know you wouldn't have even gotten that job if it wasn't for me. I got you that catering job. Remember that.' She clenched her fists.

'I know that, and I thank you for convincing me to do it, but Patrick liked the food. It was all about the food ... I cooked that, not you or Daniel, just me and Paul.' I could feel myself losing my patience and getting more and more frustrated by each word she spoke.

'I'm done with you. I'm so done with you and this whole pathetic friendship. I think it's time for you to move the fuck out. You're a vibe-killer.' She pointed her finger at me as her reddened eyes narrowed.

'Fine by me,' I said with an attitude that was out of character for me.

'I hope you feel guilty. You're the shit friend that ditched their best friend at her birthday party. Oh, and by the way, I saw Seb last night, and a hot chick was dancing on his lap.' She smirked as her eyes flickered with bitchiness.

My stomach dropped, then tightened as thoughts rushed through my head, tumbling over each other. *I can't stand this any longer. I refuse to cop abuse from Deb and be made to feel guilty for being myself, and I don't know if that's true about Seb, but if it is, it doesn't surprise me. She's never driven me anywhere in her life and acts as though I'm the worst friend in the world. I sure as hell don't feel guilty for not wanting to drink. And sure as hell don't feel guilty about getting a full-time job.*

I swallowed and managed to catch my breath before responding. 'You're lying, Deb. You're just trying to hurt me.'

'He's clearly lost interest in you, Naomi. Just get over yourself. Everyone can see you think you're better than us because you work for Patrick.' She sounded like a nasty schoolgirl, and she looked as though she'd burst out in laughter any second.

Everyone? Who's everyone? It was the first time in my life I was glad I was awake at 8am because I had time to pack my belongings and move into Mum's before work. Lucky for me, my belongings were simple things like books, makeup, skincare, clothes, shoes, and doona sets.

'I'm out, Deb. I'm moving back to Mum's. Have a nice life.' I shook my head at her and could barely look at her face without feeling angry.

'Good. Go run off, you dickhead. I'm *officially* done.' She gesticulated with her hands to emphasise her anger.

I stormed out of the kitchen, went straight into my room, and locked the door. No time for folding, I thought as I pulled all my clothes off hangers and shoved them into a suitcase while hot tears brimmed my eyes. Deb didn't appreciate me one bit. I was so done trying to be a good friend to her and offer guidance.

Five jumbo suitcases later, I was ready to officially move out. I cracked open the door and heard nothing, so I dragged my first suitcase into the living room. Deb was nowhere to be seen. She was probably smoking in her bathroom or drinking another bottle of wine. *Oh well, not my problem anymore*, I told myself, shaking my head and forcing back more tears.

***

I drove back to Mum's house, and as I reached the orange driveway, I felt a sense of relief that I didn't own any furniture at Deb's house. The process of leaving was so quick; it happened in a flash. All my paraphernalia was shoved into suitcases, and then, *bam*, I was out the door. I pulled a suitcase from the boot and wheeled it up the driveway, then pulled the rest out piece by piece. The moment I opened the front door, I felt a surge of comfort. I'd missed the French patterned floors and the blue dining-room wall, the flowers, Mum's art, the Chesterfield couch, and that aroma that just smelled like home.

'Naomi, what are you doing here?' Mum asked as she placed her herbal tea on a coaster on the coffee table and paced over to me. She expressed a motherly look of concern.

'Deb and I had a huge fight, and I'm moving out.' My eyes were still glassy, but I took in a deep breath to steady myself.

'Oh, sweetheart. I kind of suspected this would happen. Debra has always been trouble. But, aside from that, I'm just so glad you came home.' She gave a concerned smile and placed her dry-paint-speckled hands on my shoulders.

'Mmm.' I nodded, unsure of how to feel about what had just happened. *Did I seriously just move out of Deb's house?*

'We've really missed you.' She looked deep into my eyes with a sincerity that made my heart melt.

'I've missed you both too.' I thought briefly of my shopping trips with Deb before shaking my head to shut out the memory. 'Oh well, it was fun while it lasted, I guess.'

'Here, let me help you.' She grabbed the suitcase and rolled it inside. 'I'll bring all these into your room, and you go get ready for work.'

'No, I'll do that.' I shook my head. 'I still have an hour before I have to leave.'

'You look so worn out, though, darling. Did you have a late night?'

'Yeah, kind of.' I looked down at the floor and sighed.

Mum let go of the suitcase handle and wrapped her arms around me, giving me a warm, motherly hug. Just what I needed. I rested my chin on her shoulder while I breathed in her faint scent of lavender oil. She must have had a headache this morning – lavender oil was her go-to headache remedy. As I looked over her shoulder, I noticed her rainbow leopard painting had been replaced by a new one – an Amalfi Coast scene of sweeping town views overlooking the Tyrrhenian Sea. The painting was breathtaking with its boats whizzing by on blue water and depicted exactly the kind of beauty I'd seen on Google Images. Springtime must have been her inspiration because the vibrant bougainvillea flowers were in full bloom.

How peculiar that she has been working on a painting of Italy, and now I'm working in an Italian restaurant. My heart warmed as I thought about my journey and how I ended up the pizza girl at one of the most prestigious restaurants in Australia. Even though life was filled with many obstacles, everything felt worth it now I had found my dream job, and that's where all my focus wanted to be.

23

The Confrontation

As soon as I finished my ridiculously busy shift and stepped out of the vicinity of Casa di Vitello, I checked my iPhone for any text messages. There was one from Kelly and one from Seb, but none from Deb. *Guess our friendship really is over.*

Seb: *Deb told me you moved out? I wanted to see you this morning before you went to work. We need to talk. Message me when you finish.*

The text message made my stomach lurch, and all I could think of was some girl grinding all over his lap while he sat down with his legs spread. Was that even true, though, or was Deb just trying to take Seb from me and sabotage our relationship? But what would be the point in that?

Me: *I'm finished now, so you can meet me on the boardwalk outside of the Noosa Surf Club for a chat.*

Seb: *See you in ten.*

I drove to the Surf Club car park a few minutes down the road and parked under a tree, then opened Kelly's message.

Kelly: *Hey Naomi, I hate to tell you this, but I just had to. Deb was paying you out all night as soon as you left and told everyone you were a really bad friend and that she was going to kick you out. Anyway, she and I had a massive fight because I saw her corner your man, Seb, and she tried to kiss him and grabbed his pecker. I loathe cheaters!!! I know this will shock you, but I'm just looking out for you. You've always been really nice to me and I feel sick Deb did that to you. Oh, and is it true she banged Daniel?*

I blinked multiple times and stared at the tree branches swaying in the wind as I allowed that information to sink in. *WOW!* Maybe Deb was the girl grinding all over Seb, and maybe she said it was another girl because she felt guilty and wanted to pin it on someone else, the bloody liar. She did ask me about the size of his dick quite a bit too – guess her hand got the answer to that.

My work shirt suddenly felt too tight, and my car felt as though it was deprived of oxygen, so I flung open the door and stepped out onto the bitumen to suck in a deep breath. There were no cars parked beside me, and all around me felt empty – it wasn't the usual buzzing Hastings Street. My head started drowning in all of the information, and my heart pounded to keep up with my colliding thoughts. Nausea thrashed around in my stomach like crashing waves, and my throat felt narrow, making it impossible to breathe. I gasped for air and looked up at the sky glittering with stars, hoping it would clear my mind and take away some of this shock. *What the fuck.*

Seb must have slithered up without me realising as when I looked around after calming my breathing and taking multiple gulps of water, he was already on the boardwalk. He stood under a lamppost, wearing a black shirt, knee-length jeans, and his Vans shoes. I paced over to him and felt my heart quicken with anger with each step I took.

'Hey, gorgeous,' he said and stepped close to me so he could kiss my lips.

'Uh, no thanks.' I held up my hand to block his kiss and took a step back.

'Woah. What's up with you?' His eyes were wide with shock.

'Read this, idiot.' I held up a screenshot of the message from Kelly, with her name cut out, to his face.

I watched as his eyes read the message and waited until he looked back at me. 'I can explain.'

I crossed my arms and exhaled. My legs and feet were aching, and all I wanted to do was have a hot shower, a glass of juice, and a nap, but, no, I had to have this chat with Seb because I needed to know the truth. I needed to hear it from his mouth – the-man-who-supposedly-loved-me's mouth.

The only thing that was comforting me right now was the warmth coming from my handbag and the container of beef ragu Patrick had given me to try. He wanted me to come over after work, but I told him I needed to clear my head. He understood. He always understood.

'Hurry up and explain then, Seb.' I crossed my arms tighter.

'Get a grip, Naomi. Are you really going to say you've never made a mistake?' He looked at me with cold, dark eyes, his mouth turned up in a sneer. *Who was this person?* 'If you weren't such a neg, you would have stayed out and kept drinking like a normal person.'

Huh? I couldn't believe what I was hearing. 'You told me you were bored and were going to have a boys' night! And a neg? What, because I don't enjoy drinking as much as you do? Maybe you and I are just not compatible if you think not getting drunk makes me a "neg". And what mistake are you talking about? Huh? Go on. Tell me, you coward.' It took a lot of strength to resist pushing him off the boardwalk. A part of me wanted to see him land face-first in the sand.

He shoved his hands into his pockets, exhaled, and then looked out at the beach. The frothy waves crashed on the shoreline as he slid his foot around on the sandy path making annoying scuffing sounds, like a child.

'Here we go with the compatible crap again.' He sighed. 'There's no easy way to say this, Naomi, but we aren't exclusive or anything ... So, it's not like I cheated—'

'*What? Cheated?*' I spat out the word, feeling my blood boil.

'Look, there was a hell of a lot of alcohol involved, and some coke too. I was horny, and this really amazing blonde chick was grinding on me, and, well, what do you expect me to do? I'm a hot-blooded male with the sex drive of a god.' He looked down at the path. 'So, I ended up going back to her house, and we fucked.' He looked up with that flatness back in his expression and shrugged. 'To be honest, I don't even feel guilty. You and I aren't exclusive, and I'm sick of waiting around for you to properly commit.'

'Commit? I've been committed to you this whole time. We just never put a label on us. You said you loved me. Is that what love is to you? Is that how you treat someone you love? It sounds to me like you don't know what love is, because you'd never treat someone you love like that.' I paused for a moment to catch my breath, then continued, 'And let's be real here. You slept with someone else because I wouldn't have sex with you the other night.' I exhaled a breath of anger. 'If you *really* loved me, you wouldn't have even thought about touching another woman. Your feelings are as fake as your personality.'

He didn't say anything. He just kept looking out at the dark ocean illuminated by the moon.

'And did you really kiss Deb?' I braced myself for his answer. Funnily enough, this hurt more than knowing he'd had sex with someone else.

'Foul. No way. I pushed that fat trollop away.' He shot me a look of pure disgust.

I felt a tiny sense of relief, but it was crushed like a sandcastle in a crashing wave by the knowledge I'd lost my best friend and lover in the one day. Two deep stabs. I was too angry to cry, and I knew there was no point arguing if there was nothing to gain, so I turned away to walk back to my car. Seb called my name once, but I could tell it was just for show. He'd gotten what he wanted out of me. I was just some amusement for him when he was home from the mines. Someone whose challenging personality bolstered his ego. I was just the mouse to his messed-up cat-and-mouse game, and nothing more.

If this was the way people carried on in life, then I wanted no part of it. I didn't need friends – one way or another, they were bound to hurt you. They always did. I didn't need anyone.

***

Once I was back in my cosy, lilac-walled room at Mum's, my head wouldn't stop spinning with images of Deb trying to kiss Seb and her groping his crotch. I was grateful when my thoughts were interrupted by a knock on the door.

'Come in,' I called out as my legs dangled over the side of my bed.

'Are you okay?' Mum asked, standing by my door in blue silk pyjamas. Her hair was up in a bun, and her face was dewy with moisturiser. I could smell her face cream from across the room, and I felt comforted for a moment, remembering sitting beside her at her vanity as a child. I'd missed being there for her night-time routine.

'Hi, Mum. I'm fine.' I tried to smile but could tell from Mum's expression I was doing a bad job at faking it.

'You don't look fine. Did something else happen today? I hope it's not your job?' Her voice raised in concern as she said the word 'job'.

'No, work is great. I'm just upset about this guy I was seeing. Tonight, he told me he slept with someone else, and I just feel sick.' I shook my head at the thought.

Mum sighed. 'And you've broken up with him, I hope?'

'Of course. Straight away. What's he going to do to fix it? He's already done the damage, and there's no way that type of damage can be undone.' I pulled off my boots and let them clunk to the floor.

She nodded in agreement. 'Good. Most of the time, cheaters never change.'

'Yep, so they say.' A part of me felt satisfied I'd never truly committed to Seb. Most couples had photos together plastered all over their social media accounts, which they painfully had to delete, but Seb and I had zilch. The one benefit of it was I never gave every part of me to him in the way I did to Scott. So, I must be making some progress in the land of relationships.

'He's just a boy, Naomi. Another one will come along,' Mum assured me.

'Yeah, no thanks. I'm done with men.' I grabbed my feet and stretched out my calves to relieve the pain from standing on my feet for twelve hours.

Mum let out a laugh and said, 'Well, you know what I think about relationships. They aren't always worth it, in my opinion. They're too much work.'

'I think they're unpredictable, which can be exciting, but also really exhausting and, in my case … disappointing.' I let my legs dangle back over the bed and put my hands on the mattress for support.

'Mmm. So, what did Deb do?' Mum came and sat next to me on my bed. 'What pushed you to leave?' She raised her brows, and I could tell she was very interested in what I would say in response.

'It was a combination of things. We just weren't getting along like we used to, and she was drinking every day and even accused me of sleeping around, and then she tried to seduce Seb, the guy I was seeing. It hurt like hell because all I did was try to be a good friend to her and was treated like the villain for being myself. She's changed, and maybe we've just grown apart.' I was silent for a moment, nodding. 'Yeah, maybe that's what it is. We've grown apart and aren't in high school anymore. We just want different things in life.'

'Hmm, it gets to a point where you realise people you think are your friends actually aren't, and you just stay together for old times' sake. People grow apart all the time and want different things. That's just a part of life and a part of growing up.' She reached out to stroke my hair.

'Yeah, I couldn't do that to myself anymore. I don't hate Deb. I still want peace between us. We're just not suited to living together anymore, and the trust is definitely gone.'

'It's good you walked away, Naomi. It takes guts to walk away. You're showing Deb and this guy they can't treat you like that. You're showing them your worth. In the end, it will be their loss, and they'll both miss you.'

I thought about it for a moment. 'Yeah, you're right.'

'I'm sure it's a hidden blessing, Naomi, and now you can learn and grow from these situations. Each situation we face in life either makes or breaks us, so you be the decider of that outcome.' She spoke with years of wisdom, and her tone was soothing.

'I know.' I nodded as I looked down at my lilac socks. 'It's just hard to finally say goodbye to Deb after all these years. She's been my best friend since high school, and we've mostly been inseparable, and Seb, the cheater, was, well ... I don't even care about him. We were together for a few months. But what hurts is he played with my head and convinced me he loved me and even bought me presents too. No wonder people have trust issues. How can he say those words with sincerity and buy me things and then sleep around?' I shook my head at the absurdity of it.

'Not everyone is good-natured like you, Naomi. Some people have hidden agendas. At least you know now, rather than further down the track.' She sighed. 'Put it this way, at least you weren't married to him.'

I could tell Mum was about to go on a tangent about women in marriages being cheated on, but she stopped herself. I breathed out a sigh of relief. 'Oh God, no. I would never marry Sebastian.' My body cringed in reaction to the thought. 'I'm more upset about Deb. I never thought she'd do this to me.'

'Maybe it was time for those people to leave your life.'

'Yeah, you're right. It's not like I have time for friends anyway. I'm too busy with my full-time job.' I smiled a smile so bright, for a moment I forgot I was upset.

'And Debra and this Sebastian can't take that away from you. You got that all on your own.' She patted me on the shoulder.

I nodded and smiled once more. There was no point dwelling over failed relationships. I had tried my best to be a good friend to Deb, and a good worker to Daniel, and give the most of me I could to Seb, and none of it seemed to be enough for any of them.

Things didn't work out, and there was nothing I could do but focus on the things I could do.

'You're strong, Naomi. You remind me of your father when I first met him. He was such a strong-willed man with high morals and, oh, was he talented. He could cook anything I wanted with ease.' She smiled at the thought and looked as though she was lost in her memories. 'You just need to believe in yourself.' She placed both her hands neatly on her lap.

My heart melted at her words. I felt so proud to be the daughter of such a talented chef and was glad his legacy could live on through my cooking. 'Thanks, Mum. Thanks for everything, honestly. I'm so lucky to have you in my life.'

'I'm just so glad you decided to come back home. It's not the same when you're gone. You're a breath of fresh air.' She tucked a loose strand of hair behind my ear and kissed my forehead.

'Thanks, Mum. I'm glad to be home. I missed this cosy cottage.' I smiled.

'I love you, Naomi. Now, go take a shower, you smelly thing,' she said, laughing as she opened the door and left the room.

'Haha. That's the plan. Love you too, Mum.'

Despite an awful day, it was ending pretty wonderfully, I thought. A hot shower followed by Patrick's beef ragu sounded perfect.

24

Crepes And History

My cat-eyed sunglasses tried their best to shield me from the Monday morning sun as I drove to Patrick's house. We both had the day off, and I couldn't say no when he'd offered to cook breakfast for me; the memory of his delicious beef ragu still made my mouth water. People were obsessed with quality in life, and Patrick's restaurant was the definition of quality. Every day, he received compliments on the food, décor, drinks, and service, and I couldn't be more honoured to work there.

As I pulled up out the front, the electric gate slid open, revealing a smiling Patrick standing on his cobblestone driveway. He must have been waiting for me, a realisation that made me happier than I cared to admit. His outfit consisted of a white linen shirt, navy blue shorts, and black, tasselled loafers. *Mmm, very him.* As I got closer to him, the gentle breeze wafted his cologne my way, and, *my heavens,* I thought, *this man never disappoints.*

'Good morning. *Luce del sole,*' he said as I pushed my sunglasses onto my head, smoothing my wild curls from my face.

'*Luce del sole?* That's a new one. What's that mean?' I eyed him curiously with a small smile.

'Sunshine.'

'Cute.' I smiled and held out a coffee I'd stopped to buy for him on the way. I already knew what he liked – double-shot espresso, of course.

'Oh, you didn't have to do that.' He grabbed the coffee and shook his head, then took a sip while staring at me over the top of the cup. 'But *grazie*. Nice dress. Sunflowers suit you.' His ridiculously green eyes creased as he smiled.

'Oh, thanks. I found it in my closet at Mum's. I haven't worn this in so long. It's been probably a year or so, and I was surprised it still fit actually.' I cringed a little at the over-share. *What was it about him that made me gush so much?*

He let out a hearty laugh and gestured for me to come inside.

We walked inside, and instantly the panoramic view of the alluring blue water greeted me. That was certainly a view I'd never be bored of. I'd never been to his house in broad daylight before and was mesmerised by the sunlight sparkling on the river. It looked like fairy dust, the way it glimmered. Two speedboats whizzed past, creating little waves, which rattled his jetty, and a flock of seagulls flew about squawking and carrying on while they searched for food.

'So, what's for breakfast?' I asked, looking around the kitchen and noticing a silver bowl filled with a creamy batter.

'Well.' He grinned. 'I'm having a cheat day, so crepes with lemon and sugar.' He began whisking the mixture lightly as his eyes looked down at the swirling whisk.

'Sounds delicious. Surprisingly, I haven't had that combination before.'

'It's one of my favourite treats of all time.' He kissed his fingers in that traditional Italian chef way. It was dorky and cute, and I giggled watching him do it.

'I must say, I'm rather traditional with maple syrup and bacon on pancakes.' I lifted my brows and spoke in a serious tone sprinkled with playfulness.

'How very Canadian of you.' He laughed.

He walked over to the induction cooktop and brushed melted butter in a crepe pan –much like a normal frypan but with lower edges. Once the temperature was perfect, he poured a quarter cup of batter into the pan, and I listened as the butter sizzled. He tilted the pan with meticulousness, creating a thin, even layer and watched it cook. I'd seen people use a wooden crepe tool before on cooking shows, but Patrick didn't need one – he was that precise.

'Bit of a crepe expert, are we?' I asked with a grin as I leant my elbow on the cold marble and rested my chin on my palm.

'I do get passionate about my crepes, I must admit.' He flipped the crepe over after about fifty seconds, then waited for the other side to become golden. Once the crepe was cooked, he put it on a large plate and then continued cooking until all twenty crepes were ready.

My eyes widened at the height of the stack. 'Uh. I hope we aren't eating ten each. I usually can only fit in three.'

He laughed. 'Eat as much as you want. I'm feeling quite crepeish today.'

I let out a little laugh in response to his. 'Alright. Thank you.' I flashed a warm smile.

He carried the stack of crepes over to the main bench, then grabbed out two plates and placed them down. 'So, three for you?' he asked.

'Perfect.' I nodded.

He carefully separated them, then placed pre-cut cubes of butter onto each crepe and topped them with freshly squeezed lemon juice and sprinkles of sugar. 'Okay, there's plenty more if you get hungry again later.' He gave me a little wink.

Does he mean anything by that? I blushed a little, cursing my overactive imagination, and watched as he finished filling them with lemon juice and sugar, smiling at the precision of his crepe folding.

'Do you mind grabbing the cutlery and opening the gate for me, please?' he asked as he carried both plates out onto the terrace.

I swooped up the fancy silver flatware, stacked both coffees on one another, balancing them under my chin for support, and opened the gate. We walked down three wooden steps and turned right onto a small deck with a white umbrella over a round table and cane chairs. He put my plate down first, then his, and pulled out a chair for me.

'Why, thank you,' I said as I sat down in the padded chair and placed the coffees and cutlery beside each plate. The stone tabletop was warm from the sunshine against my arms. I leant back, breathed in the fresh air, and felt my muscles relax.

'*Bon appetit,*' he said in his best French accent as he grinned at me.

'Okay, French boy,' I joked, grabbing my knife and fork.

'Italian, actually,' he corrected and winked.

As I sliced into the crepe, my stomach rumbled at the sight of it. *Oh, my goodness, yummm,* I thought as I took a bite of the light, fluffy, very thin pancake. The combination of the crunchy sugar, the zesty lemon, and the creamy butter danced on my tastebuds. It was so good, I had to close my eyes to truly appreciate the artistry. Patrick seemed to master the technique of simple flavours.

I licked the sugar off my lips and opened my eyes. I noticed Patrick was already onto his last crepe. It was surprising to see such a well-proportioned male eat so fast.

'Thank you for introducing me to this wonderful combination,' I said. 'It was delicious, and I'm officially converted.'

'No problem, *luce del sole,*' he said, this time in a Spanish accent.

'You and your accents.' I laughed and rolled my eyes. 'You must have travelled a lot, I assume?'

'You could say that. And you?' He raised his brows as he waited for my response.

'I've never been overseas, but funnily, I've always wanted to visit Italy.' My cheeks blushed but, thankfully, my neck didn't.

'It's a scenic country.'

'I bet.'

I liked how playful he was being. We were at a stage where our friendship was becoming more comfortable. *And he keeps calling me sunshine – that's sweet. What could I call him? Hmm. Fabio sounds too cliché. Maybe I'll just call him Pat.*

'So, Pat, thanks again for this wonderful meal,' I said as I placed the last bite of my crepe into my mouth.

His face twisted a little, and he half-smiled. 'I hate the name Pat. Stephanie used to call me that.' He looked out over the rippling water.

Crap! Trust me to say something that ruins our perfect morning by reminding him of his ex.

'I'm sorry.' I frowned and looked down at my sugar-speckled plate.

'Oh, no need to worry about it.' He waved his hand in reassurance. 'I don't want to think of her. I just hate that nickname.' He shone a bright smile at me, making me feel better instantly. 'Feel free to call me Patrizio, like my mama does.'

'Patrizio, it is then.' I smiled with relief. 'Do you have a middle name?'

His face lit up as if he was about to tell me something he was very proud of. 'Joseph.' He smiled and looked lost in thought. Moments later, he said, 'It was my papa's name.'

My heart melted at the fact Patrick's father's memory lived on in his middle name. 'Oh, that's so sweet. My middle name is Jean, which was my mum's mother's name.'

He flashed a warm smile. 'It suits you. Naomi Jean. I like that.' His expression changed from thoughtful to playful again. 'So, tell me, *luce del sole*, what's the craziest thing you've ever done?'

'Oh,' I said, taken aback. *Where was he going with this? Quick, think of something cool!* 'The craziest? Uh, let me think about that.' I pressed my finger to my lips, then took a sip of coffee to buy some time. 'My dad and I cooked a three-course meal for a private function of one hundred people once, just us two.'

'Impressive.' His eyes were wide with amazement. 'It sounds like your pa was an impressive chef.'

'He sure was. He was a very talented man and taught me everything I know.' I nodded and smiled. 'Now, what's your story, hey?' I flashed a mischievous smile his way.

'The only thing coming to mind is this time ...' He pressed his manicured nail to his lip, copying my motion from before. 'Well, it's not really worth telling because it's not exactly *crazy*.'

'Oh, come on. Any story will do,' I said encouragingly.

'Well, okay, here goes. Marco, my older brother ... You might remember him. I mentioned him the other night,' he said with a quick roll of his eyes before continuing. 'He took me out on an adventure on our olive farm in the pitch dark to find Babau. Babau is a legendary bogeyman in Italy, and Papa used to scare us by saying if we didn't come inside for dinner, Babau would get us. So, Marco, the crazy kid, wanted to prove that Babau was real. He took me on an expedition looking for him. As it turns out, of course ...' He held his hands out, palms facing up. 'Babau wasn't real, and when we got caught, we were made to do chores all weekend.'

'That's a fascinating tale, but you're right, not very crazy. So, you grew up on an olive farm?' A smile spread across my face as I imagined hundreds of rows of olive trees flourishing on rolling green acreage.

'Yes, Ma and Pa ran an olive farm in Tuscany. My uncle took it over, but we still earn revenue from it, and I use the oil in my restaurants.' He took a sip of coffee from his cup.

'Oh, is that why the food tastes so good? Secret olive oil from Tuscany, hey?' I lifted my brows and decided to take a sip of coffee too.

He nodded eagerly. 'A lot of effort went into crafting those recipes. It's my whole life's work.'

We chatted about his family history and how his father's mother taught Patrick to cook in her restaurant from a young age. The first dish he learnt to cook was gnocchi during his apprenticeship, and he spent hours perfecting the recipe. When his grandmother passed, the Vitellos sold their Naples restaurant and moved to Australia to take over Patrick's mother's parents' winery on the Mornington Peninsula. His mother, Elizabeth, was holidaying solo in Italy when she first met Joseph, and it was love at first sight. She was Italian-obsessed and always wished to be one, so she couldn't resist Joseph's charm, good looks, or caring nature. They did everything together and travelled the whole of Italy – studied every ruin, tasted every wine, learned about Parmesan, browsed every museum – and found they had an unbreakable bond and got married after a month of knowing each other.

After hearing about his history in Naples, I found myself wanting to know more about how the famous House of Vitello was created.

'So, when did you open your own restaurants?' I asked with curiosity in my eyes.

'At twenty-six, I opened the one in Melbourne.' He paused and looked like he was thinking back to old memories. 'It was hard at first because I only knew how to cook and not how to run a business, so it was trial and error, but the long hours paid off, and I had consistent clientele who loved my authentic Italian food.'

'Did you run it on your own?'

'I had to. My family was too busy with the winery, and Marco was trying out his fitness career, and Caterina, my sister, was studying interior design. So, just me and my staff.'

I thought back to meeting Patrick's sister at his birthday and assuming she was his Italian girlfriend. Her chic Valentino outfit was still imprinted in my mind, and so was her flawless olive skin. She was the doppelganger of Monica Bellucci.

I gazed at him and took small sips of coffee while he shared his history. I'd always been a sucker for tales of family history and learning about the ones who paved the way before us. It was fascinating how we both were taught to cook by someone dear in our family we'd both lost, rather than a stranger. The way we both cooked was deeply rooted in us from generations of knowledge. How nice that Patrick left gorgeous Italy and journeyed his way over to Australia to open his restaurants. His story truly was as amazing as he was.

'Caterina helped me decorate the restaurant, though,' he added and took another sip of coffee.

'Is your sister a model? She is very pretty.' As soon I asked that, I wanted to sink into the chair with embarrassment. God, I hate it when I do that – make a big deal about someone's beauty. Who cares if she's a model or not?

'Ha. *Si*, she did some modelling for a bit, but now she's running the Melbourne restaurant while Marco runs the Sydney one.' He chuckled.

'So, she turned from being a model to a designer to a restaurateur?' *I just couldn't help myself, could I?* I moved forward in my chair and placed my elbow on the table so I could rest my chin on my palm as I waited for his reply.

'After Marco and Caterina saw how much money I was earning, they soon became passionate restaurateurs.' He laughed again and shook his head at the thought.

Oh, typical. Of course, people want to be involved in your business as soon as they see how much money you're earning.

Patrick lowered his voice and looked around before speaking. 'Keep this between us, but Caterina pulled out of modelling because she's got extreme anxiety. She struggles on and off with an eating disorder, and there are times she doesn't eat for days. It's very sad. She's obsessed with being beautiful.'

'Aww. Sorry to hear. I wouldn't have guessed that at all. She's so well-kept, and well-spoken, and doesn't look bony but in perfect proportion. Actually, this is funny, but when she opened the door at your birthday, I assumed she was your girlfriend.' I let out an embarrassed chortle.

'I love her dearly.' He sighed with worry. 'One of our big family secrets is that Caterina gets weekly therapy. She doesn't like anyone to know it, though, because of her obsession with being beautiful and being perceived as someone who has her act together and can solve her own problems. But her image obsession is dangerous because she's ashamed of needing help. She thinks that makes her weak and gets paranoid people will judge her for that. Mama is partly to blame for this obsession.' He sighed again, and I could tell he felt guilty for saying that. 'Mama always told us image is very important in life and image is power.'

I just listened to him intently and didn't utter a word.

'We all have problems. You're mad if you think otherwise. That's one thing that irritates me – people having preconceived ideas about families with money.' He frowned. 'Yes, life is more comfortable – I can't deny the privilege that comes with wealth – but we still have problems like any other family.'

I looked around at his mansion and sparkling river views. 'I'm not one to judge someone's personality on their level of wealth. That's ridiculous. We're all individuals, but I know what you mean. Even I thought Caterina had the perfect life just by looking at her.'

'Mmm. We're all far from perfect. I think all of my family feel pressure to act a certain way for the public eye. Being a Vitello is tiring and demanding work, and everyone thinks they know us *so* well. But it's refreshing to be able to talk to you about this. It's not a topic I talk about enough.' He paused for a moment and smiled before continuing, 'You just know how to make me feel comfortable, and I feel like I can be myself around you. It's strange ... I feel like I've known you for years.'

Uh oh. My cheeks and neck did that ridiculous burning thing again, and a warm, loving feeling rushed inside me.

My mind wandered back to the first time I had coffee with Patrick on the beach and how that waiter addressed him so formally. He was such a big deal, and I thought about how his life must be much like a celebrity's, with people constantly looking at him and judging. It would be high pressure to look gorgeous all of the time and act in a certain way that pleases the public. *The way he is right now must be the real him, a man who is soft-hearted and open with his feelings. He's frickin' beautiful.*

'I'm glad you feel comfortable talking to me about this and that you can be yourself around me.' I gave him a big smile and could feel my cheeks were still blushing, but my neck had settled. 'So, was Marco at your birthday?'

'We're civil now, but, no, he didn't come. He said he didn't want to leave the restaurant.' A flicker of anger flamed in his eyes, and I could tell he hadn't fully forgiven him. 'I'm grateful Ma and Cat always make the effort to see me. They've never missed a birthday, whereas Marco – he has missed a few of mine over the years.'

'Oh, that's good you're civil now. It must be really hard to speak to him after what he did.' I gave him a look of sympathy.

'Sure is.' He let out a quick breath.

He suddenly shook his head as if coming out of a reverie. 'I hope I'm not boring you with all this talk about my family. You haven't spoken much about yours.'

'Well, we're pretty dull compared to yours,' I said, blushing again. 'My mum, Savannah, is a retired baker, now an artist, and my brother, Carlos, works for a seafood market.' I shrugged. 'I don't know. We're just a quiet little family trying to get through life.'

'Quiet.' He nodded. 'I like that.'

I smiled ruefully. 'It's relatively peaceful, at least.'

He sat forward as if remembering something he'd been meaning to tell me. 'Oh, by the way, Deb has been posting some strange things on Facebook.'

'I haven't looked today. What's she been posting?'

'She created a GoFundMe page to support her while she gets back on her feet.'

He raised an eyebrow at me. 'Apparently, she can't pay her rent.'

My mouth dropped open. 'What?'

'Is she okay?' He gave a look of genuine concern.

'Well, she lives in one of her parents' houses, and they would be covering all her expenses until she finds work. I guess she's feeling it since I've left and stopped giving her money.' I looked out at the rippling water.

'Did you give her a lot of money?'

I turned my attention back to him. 'Yeah, I always helped her out and paid more, but that's okay. It's all the past, and I don't regret anything.'

'Have you spoken since your fight?'

'No. We haven't.' I looked down at the plate and frowned.

'Probably best not to for the time being.' He leant over the table and looked as though he was going to grab my hand but fiddled with his cutlery instead.

I nodded. The last thing I needed was for us to argue again. That would break my heart.

'When you told me about you both getting fired, you never told me why she did?' His eyebrows raised with curiosity.

'Oh, it's embarrassing really.'

Even though Deb and I weren't on talking terms, a part of me still loved her and felt bad for telling Patrick about her. But then the other part of me felt deeply hurt and betrayed by her.

'Are you going to tell me or is it a secret?' he asked as the sunlight shone into his green eyes, making him squint.

'She slept with Daniel,' I blurted and pressed my hands to my lips.

Patrick expressed a look of pure disgust. 'He didn't ever try to sleep with you, did he?'

I was taken aback a little by his question, and by the memory of Daniel's words flashing through my head: *You need a good fuck – that's what you need.* Should I tell Patrick? I wasn't sure I was ready to open up quite that far. 'No, he didn't, thank God.' I hoped Patrick wasn't as good at reading minds as he was at cooking.

'Good.' He glanced out at the water, then scooped up the plates from the table. I grabbed the cutlery and coffee cups. As we stood to walk back inside, I noticed a new tension in his shoulders. *Was it something I said?*

My heart started to beat a little faster. 'Is everything okay? You seem annoyed. Did I say something wrong?' We walked back to the kitchen and placed the tableware on the bench.

'No, not at all. Just irritated by Daniel sleeping with Debra. He's a married man ...' He shook his head and sighed. 'Loyalty seems to be a rare thing these days ... You're really lovely, Naomi, and you deserve to be treated with the utmost respect. Sorry you've dealt with all this drama. Must be a relief to be away from it all.' He filled up the sink with hot water and dishwashing liquid and began to scrub the dishes.

'Yeah, Daniel is disgusting, but don't worry about me. I'm used to the way people carry on. If anything, it's just given me a tougher skin,' I assured him, distracted by the fact he was doing dishes by hand instead of using his dishwasher.

'Have you sorted out your complicated situation with this Sebastian?' He paused with a plate in his hand.

'Oh yes. We're officially over, alright.' I rolled my eyes in repulsion. 'He slept with another woman on the night of Deb's party.'

Patrick's eyebrows raised. 'That's a surprise. Sorry that happened to you, *luce del sole*. It's not a good feeling.' A glob of foamy water dropped from his hand into the sink.

'Yep, I'm officially done with men for the time being. Well, him.'

'So, your main focus is just on work?' A strand of dark tousled hair fell down his cheek, and I felt a strange desire to move it away for him but decided against it.

'Sure is.' I grinned. 'I'll be one dedicated pizza girl. I officially have no extra baggage.'

'What if you met the right person? Would you consider dating again then?' he asked while looking down at the plate he was scrubbing.

'Depends on who the man is.' I smiled as for a brief second I wondered if Patrick could have a tiny crush on me. 'Do you need any help with those dishes? I thought you would just put them in the dishwasher.'

He shook his head. 'It's good exercise to do them by hand, and there's only a few here. I use the dishwasher for messy meals, and, no, relax, Naomi. You're my guest.'

'Oh, don't worry about that. I'm more than happy to help.'

He ignored my response and asked, 'Do you just date men your age?' He looked up, directed his gaze into mine, and maintained a casualness to his face.

His question took me by surprise – I hope he didn't think I was like Deb and slept around with older men. I searched for a quick response that wouldn't give him the wrong idea. 'I haven't dated that many men, but, no, Sebastian was thirty, so age isn't really a priority when I'm looking for someone. I just look for compatibility, which is so hard to find these days.'

Oh my God, why is he asking these questions? Is there actually a chance he could like me as more than a friend?

'Interesting.' He nodded, smiling to himself.

I smiled and decided to try not to think about Daniel, Seb, or Deb for the rest of the day. I just wanted to enjoy my time with Patrick.

We spent the rest of the day chatting and laughing, and I stayed for dinner – homemade rosemary focaccia, Caprese salad, meatballs and fresh Mooloolaba prawns – which we ate back out on the terrace, enjoying the river breeze. The food was sensational, of course, and we ended the night eating organic macadamia nuts coated in white chocolate while watching *La La Land* in his home cinema room.

His theatre was incredible, with its midnight-blue walls and ceiling fitted with mini-lights that imitated a starry night sky. The floors were fitted with plush black carpet, which black leather reclining chairs rested on, and a massive screen was built into the wall that a projector at the back shone onto.

It was ironic that in the movie we decided to watch, the main character just so happened to be called Sebastian too. Funny that.

When I turned to look at Patrick, I noticed our hands were only inches apart on our armrests. More than anything, I wanted to reach out and touch his hand, but I was too afraid to make the first move. What if he rejected me? I looked at him and waited to capture his attention. He turned to me and smiled, then looked down at his hand and noticed how close it was, and instead of touching my hand, he moved his away and stretched his arms out, reminding me that we were nothing more than friends. Maybe Deb was right that Libra men did only have 'one true love', and clearly, that wasn't me.

25

Love Confession

I thought back to that morning's hairdressing appointment at Colour n Cuts, where I was booked in for a regrowth retouch. As I stared into the long salon mirror, all I could do was think of Seb's words to me about my blonde hair: *Your blonde hair just turns me on.* His words tormented my mind and made my jaw clench. I was on the verge of tears, and before Sandy could mix up the dye, I said to her, 'I've changed my mind. I don't want to be blonde anymore. Can you show me the brown colour chart?' My tone was certain, and I spoke decisively.

Sandy gave me a surprised look, followed by a smile, and handed me the chart. I tried my hardest to focus on the hair colours and not my memories of Deb, but it was impossible not to think of her, when she usually sat in the chair next to me getting a recoat of auburn. She'd drink her caramel latte and flick through *Cosmopolitan* until she landed on the horoscope page, then she'd recite our horoscopes aloud. And to remind me of Deb some more, Sandy asked, 'Where's your friend today?' Her platinum-blonde fringe was smooth like satin, and her skin was as fair as porcelain.

'She's ... she ... is busy,' I stammered.

She nodded and instantly picked up the vibe I didn't want to talk about it and instead busied herself with her equipment.

After analysing the chart for a few minutes, I decided on the toffee-brown.

Back in my bedroom, I studied my straightened and trimmed brown hair in the mirror. It fell just below my breasts, smelt like a tropical island, and was the silkiest I'd ever seen it. The brown made my eyes look bright blue, not grey, and my face appeared slimmer. *Hmm, not bad.*

It only took a few seconds before Seb crept back into my mind, and I imagined the sleazy things he'd say to me if he saw me. I shuddered and got mad that he wasn't as easy to brush off as I thought. He had meant something to me, and I believed he loved me. How stupid of me.

My mind took me back to the movie last night. Maybe *La La Land* hadn't been the best choice because hearing the name Sebastian made me want to cry with humiliation. It was difficult to sit there with my eyes glued to the humongous screen, taking in the storyline, while I was distracted by Seb and his lying ways.

Patrick alternated between sipping his red wine and munching chocolate-coated nuts. He was utterly engaged with every facet of the movie – the colour, the passion, the singing; in fact, he was so involved, he thankfully didn't notice I was bothered.

It seemed that no matter what I did or where I was, I was reminded of Daniel, Seb, and Debra. You'd think being next to someone as charming as Patrick would make me forget about them, and most of the time I did, but without fail, they crept back into my mind. And I guess everything would've hurt even more if Patrick hadn't come into my life. I was so thankful I had met him.

I think what bothered me the most was how the movie exposed what a lie my relationship with Seb had been. Mia and Sebastian's relationship failed in *La La Land*, but before the failure, there was love. Seb and I weren't love – we were a lie, a pathetic lie that did nothing to change my opinion of 'true love'.

If Seb and I were a movie, people would be glad I had the strength to walk away from an awful man. They'd be cheering me and anticipating me getting my happy-ever-after with someone else, but this was the real world, and sometimes you didn't ride off into a fairy tale at the end. Sometimes, you kissed many toads, and the toads just kept jumping right into your lap.

At this rate, I mused, I might stay single forever, considering I seemed to only attract sleazebags.

I knew it was probably a bad idea, but as I sat on my bed, I grabbed my iPhone and opened Deb's page on Facebook to check out her GoFundMe for myself. I couldn't find it – *hmm, has she deleted it?* All I could see was selfie after selfie after selfie. I closed Facebook and went to Messenger: nothing. What a disappointment that my high school best friend and ex-lover still hadn't apologised to me even after three days.

And as if on cue, a message notification from Deb popped on the screen.

Deb: *Naomi, I am soooo sorry, and I mean, so sorry for what happened. Anyway, I have some good news! I'm moving back to Brisbane, and I found a job! AND, you're not going to believe this, but you know how everyone always thinks I look older? Well, that sure as shit has paid off because I scored a manager's position in an Italian restaurant. The sassy bitch is back. Miss you, chicka.*

What? A manager's position? But how will she pull that off with just her waitressing experience? I shook my head and half-smiled imagining the lies she would've told to score that position. When she wanted to be, she was a great talker.

Me: *I'm still hurt by our fight and you accusing me of sleeping around when you know I'm not like that, if anything, I'm the opposite, and I can't believe you tried to kiss Seb and grope him. Drunk or not ... that's the lowest thing you've ever done to me. I'm supposed to be your best friend.*

Deb: *OMG, Naomi. I was so upset you ditched me on my birthday, like, you have no idea how much it hurt. I get it, you don't drink anymore, but I do! I love to drink, and that'll probably never change. I made a mistake trying to kiss Sebastian, but he's a disgusting pig anyway and you can do better.*

I laughed aloud about her comment saying 'I could do better' when only last week she was convincing me to stay with him because he was 'such a great guy'. *Hmm, so calling Seb a disgusting pig justifies her actions and makes it okay for her to kiss and grope the guy I'm seeing?* Okay, yes, she was right. He was a pig, but still ... *Ugh. You do your thing, Deb, sleep around with whoever you please, but don't touch your best friend's man or married people.*

Me: *I want to be civil, and I'm happy you found a job and are moving, that's great, but I don't think we can go back to what we were. You hurt me real bad. And I've had enough of you using me to drive you everywhere and not appreciating me as a person.*

Deb: *Look, I know I was wrong. I stuffed up and acted like a shitty friend I was just in a dark place. I was upset and hurt, okay.*

There was no point discussing anything further with Deb. Too much had been said and done, and there was no changing that. All I could do was forgive her and move on and hope she learnt some valuable lessons from this experience. Deb and I weren't ever going to be roommates or best friends again. The trust was broken, and I didn't see how it could ever be recovered.

Me: *Take care, Deb, and good luck with everything.*

Deb: *You too, chick, all the best.*

I lifted my legs onto the bed and sank my head into the pillow as I looked around my lilac-painted room. I stopped when I caught sight of my oakwood bookshelf filled with hundreds of cookbooks. My attention was grabbed by the vibration of my phone in my palm, and as I lifted the screen to my face, my stomach dropped as I saw Seb's name flash on the screen.

Seb: *Miss you.*

Arghhh. Is that all you've got to say, Seb? 'Miss you' with a bloody dot? Not 'I'm sorry' or anything?

A surge of anger streamed through my veins, and that message was the final straw. I didn't want to play his game any longer and didn't want to be reminded of him ever again. My feet swung off the bed, and I walked to my dressing table. I grabbed the opal necklace and shoved it in my sock drawer where I put his raunchy lingerie (which I'd sell on eBay or Facebook sometime this week). He'd blown his chance of me giving those items back to him.

With a smug grin on my face, I blocked his number, his Facebook, and Instagram account and felt nothing but pleasure. *There, that'll show him. I'm gone, and I'm never, ever coming back, Seb. You blew it, baby.*

I swung open my door and walked to the kitchen to fix myself an instant coffee and a banana from the fruit bowl. Seventies music was coming down the hall from Mum's bedroom, and I couldn't help but smile. God, it's peaceful at home. And Carlos, the night owl, was either asleep or playing his computer games.

As I slumped into the dining-room chair, I looked down at the steam rising from my coffee. After letting out a long exhale, I pressed my face into my hands and was mad that I couldn't look at instant coffee without thinking of Deb. I attempted a sip but couldn't stomach it, so I tipped it down the sink and put the banana back into the fruit bowl. *Guess cookbooks in bed it is for the day.*

On my return, my mind played guessing games on who was calling as my phone began to chime. It's weird how you don't hear from people for ages, then you hear from them all at once. Funny that.

The biggest smile spread across my face as I saw Patrick's name on my phone screen, and my heart quickened as I lifted the phone to my ear.

'Hello. Is everything okay?' I asked. I thought he'd be at work as it was eleven o'clock in the morning.

'I decided to take another day off, and since you've got the day off too, why don't you come over?' His voice sounded flat, and he didn't seem his usual relaxed self.

He's taking another day off from his buzzing restaurant and wants to hang with me? My heart galloped, and I felt my whole body go warm and tingly, and, of course, my cheeks and neck were burning up again. This man was more addictive than makeup.

'Sure, sounds good. What time?' I said, trying to sound as unflustered as possible, while inside, I squealed.

'Now?'

'See you soon.'

'Great. *Ciao.*'

He hung up.

Right. Better get dressed. T-shirt dress, it is. Plain and simple, I thought as I rummaged through the neatly folded clothes on my corner stool that were waiting to be put away.

***

During the drive to Patrick's, all I could do was think about how close his hand was to mine when we were watching *La La Land* and wondered why he moved it away before touching mine. Was he actually interested in me as more than a friend? All the signs showed me he liked me, but then I second-guessed myself because he was so good-looking and also my boss. And if he had feelings for me, wouldn't he have just grabbed my hand and tried to kiss me? My heart clenched as I thought of how hard I'd been trying to fight off the feelings I was forming for him. His green eyes and charming smile were always in the back of my mind, and I craved seeing him like lemon and butter craved sugar on crepes. He was the missing ingredient in my life.

As I pulled up on his driveway, the gates opened, but there was no Patrick smiling and waiting for me on the cobblestones. I got out of the car and walked through the wide-open door into Patrick's house. He was leaning against his kitchen bench, dressed in black silk pyjamas, and there were dark rings under his eyes.

We hadn't paid great attention to our clothing choices this morning.

'Is everything okay?' I asked. I stepped closer until we were only inches apart.

'Stephanie called after you left last night. She wants to get back together.' He closed his eyes, reached his hands around the back of his neck, and rubbed it like he'd twisted it during the night. 'I didn't sleep very well after that.'

I swallowed hard and felt my heart crumble a little. 'And are you going to go back to her?'

'No!' He shook his head vigorously. 'Of course not. I don't want anything to do with her.'

'Speaking of relationship woes, I blocked Sebastian from everything this morning.' I gave a satisfied grin.

'Did you?' His eyes widened.

I nodded. 'I liked doing it; it felt empowering. I love the fact that he never gets to contact me again.' I ran my hand through my hair, hoping to draw attention to it considering Patrick hadn't even said anything.

'Hmmm.' Patrick raised his eyebrows. 'I think I might do the same.' He pulled his iPhone from his shirt pocket, tapped a few buttons, and then put it down, smiling. 'I should have done this a long time ago, and your hair! You look so *bella*.' He reached to touch it and twirled a finger in it.

'Oh, you think? I just wanted a change back to my natural colour.'

'Natural looks wonderful. You're such a *bellezza*.' He moved his hand away and put it back beside his body.

I let out a giggle. 'I love how you throw Italian into your sentences. Is it hard not to speak fluent Italian all of the time?'

'I know both English and Italian equally well, so it's fun to mix the two.' He cleared his throat, looking suddenly nervous. 'Naomi, I want to tell you something, but I don't want to scare you.'

My stomach dropped and I had the feeling of being too close to the edge of a cliff with slippery feet.

'What is it?' The words flew from my mouth.

He exhaled, then looked down at the floor. 'Naomi, you're like sunshine in my life and ...' He trailed off.

I swallowed hard. 'And what?'

'I feel guilty. I feel so guilty I'm going to break your trust.' His eyes remained on the floor, and I watched his throat move as he swallowed hard too.

I felt tears burning behind my eyes. *Please, not Patrick too.*

'Please, just say it. It hurts more that you're holding it in.' My voice was sharp and abrupt. The natural defence mechanisms inside my body were hard at work as they shielded my heart from a suspected bullet that was about to hit.

He looked at me with his ridiculously green eyes, and I felt my knees go weak. It was as though the floor was butter and I was going to slip over any minute.

'Naomi, I have feelings for you ... and I know you said you didn't want another man in your life, but I can't help it. Your energy is addictive.' He turned his back to me for a moment and faced the water views, and I could've sworn he was crying. He took a deep breath and faced me again with dry eyes. 'I know I'm going to scare you off and you won't want to spend time with me anymore.' He sighed and looked down at the marble floor again.

Patrick Vitello has feelings for me? Patrick Vitello? You've got to be kidding me. 'Come again?' I asked and blinked a couple of times to make sure this was reality and not some hallucinogenic dream I was having.

He laughed, then said, 'I've fallen in love with you, Naomi.'

'I ... I don't know what to say.'

'Don't say anything. I just thought it was something you should know.' He flashed a warm but weary smile.

I couldn't breathe. Patrick was my boss. Working in his restaurant was my livelihood, not to mention the opportunity of a lifetime. Granted, he was nothing like Daniel, but still ... I always thought that we were just good friends, that I was the one with the crush and was reading into his motives too much, but hearing the words from his own mouth ... *Oh my God.*

'Patrick, I'm shocked ...' I stood there and blinked at him for a little while.

'The last thing I want to do is push you away.' His eyes were full of sincerity, which made my heart melt some more.

A little voice niggled in my ear: *Do you want to end up like Deb and get fired for sleeping with your boss?* But then I thought to myself, *Well, Daniel was married, and Patrick isn't, and oh my God, what am I getting myself into?* I took a deep breath. Deep down, I wanted this too. 'I appreciate the honesty, Patrick.'

He nodded and waited for my next words.

'I don't want to lose this friendship, ever. You're the one person that I can be completely myself with,' I said with worry-filled eyes.

'Me too, Naomi. I can't help it. Ever since I met you on my birthday, all I wanted was to know more about you. You are the most down-to-earth woman I've ever met, and I love how connected you are to your heritage in the way you cook. We connect on so many levels, and that's what I'm looking for. You're what I'm looking for.'

I thought of Dad, Scott, Deb, Seb, and even Daniel. 'You don't understand how afraid I am to lose another person in my life. It petrifies me.' I let out an exhale of anxiety and noticed my hands were shaking.

'I never want to hurt you.' He frowned, searching for his next words. 'We can stop spending time together if it makes it too difficult.'

'I don't want to lose this, though. I love hanging out with you.' I looked at his golden hoop earrings, his sculptured olive face, and dark tousled hair, and felt frightened by the thought we could stop hanging out.

'Me too.' He nodded as he stared at the floor.

Truth be told, I could see myself slotting into Patrick's life. We had so much in common, our conversations flowed like wine. Part of me felt like he was the missing piece, the Libran male to balance out my fragile Cancerian emotions, but I was scared of being hurt again. So scared. But I knew if I let fear control my life, I would never be happy, and I would hate to miss out on an opportunity to be truly happy with someone. We'd both been hurt, and a part of me knew I'd never meet anyone like him again. He was so rare.

'Patrick, you're the most incredible man I've ever met, and I feel like you came into my life at the most perfect moment.'

He smiled and looked deep into my eyes. His stare was so intense, goosebumps spread over my skin as desire rushed through my body and we instinctually moved closer to each other like two magnets. He cupped his hands around my neck and kissed my forehead. It was a light, gentle kiss, but my skin tingled as if it was my first. I wrapped my arms around his waist and rested my head on his chest, breathing in his faint spicy, leathery scent. Tears formed in my eyes, and my emotions rushed about as though caught in a cyclone. He lifted my chin, looked deep into my eyes again, and then kissed me, gently massaging my tongue with his.

Patrick took my hand and led me up the staircase toward his ornate Art Deco bedroom. I felt as though I was in a daze. *Was this really happening?*

'Do you want this, Naomi? Do you want it as much as I do?' His voice gave me chills at how sexy he sounded.

I nodded. 'Yes, more than anything.' We walked across his plush carpet, and I hopped onto his silky king-sized bed, my eyes not breaking contact with his.

He climbed on top of me, pressed his hands into the mattress, and kissed my neck, then worked his way down to my belly before stopping and looking into my eyes again. *God, he was beautiful.* I sat up, pulled off my dress, and chucked it onto the floor, revealing just my bra and underwear. He looked down at my breasts and gently squeezed them, cupping them in his hands, then stroked my nipples with his thumbs, which sent tingles all the way down my thighs. I'd never felt so much lust in my life; my whole body craved him.

'You're so beautiful, Naomi. Your body is like a Botticelli painting.' He ran his finger down my abdomen and began kissing me just above my underwear.

I didn't say anything. I just stared into his eyes and grabbed his face, leading his lips back to mine for a kiss. The kiss was warm and passionate and made the goosebumps return all over my skin.

He pulled off his shirt, and I couldn't help staring at his smoothly muscled torso. I wanted to tell him he looked like a Michelangelo sculpture, but I was having trouble forming words. His shoulders were in perfect proportion to his body – not too wide and not too narrow. Just right. He reached over to the drawer in his nightstand and slipped on a condom, and I felt an instant warmth between my thighs.

Finally, the rest of our clothes were on the floor, and we were naked in his bed, limbs intertwined. I let out a soft moan as I felt him enter me and looked up at his skylight dappled in sunlight while my eyes watered with pleasure. My hands dug into his toned back as his spearmint breath mixed with the intoxicating vanilla scent of his room drifted my way.

'You really are a goddess, Naomi.' He let out a soft pant as he thrust deep into me and lifted my hand from his back to kiss each finger. 'Your skin's softer than flower petals.'

We had sex on and off all afternoon until we were left breathless and staring into each other's eyes.

'I wish we could do this every day,' he said, his chin resting on his hand as he lay beside me in the rumpled sheets.

'Me too. I would do anything to feel like that every moment of the day.' I laughed.

He rolled onto his back and stretched luxuriously. 'We should have a spa, then go to dinner. Where do you want to go?'

'A spa sounds good.' I winked at him. 'But I'm not really dressed for dinner.'

'True.' He smiled. 'It would be nice to not have to put our clothes back on for a while.' He stood and walked to his ensuite. I admired his naked rump before he disappeared out of sight, and a moment later, I heard running water. 'You joining me?' he called.

'Oh, yes.' I quickly wrapped the crinkled sheet around me and walked into the bathroom, my legs weak from all the exertion, and watched as the huge spa filled with warm water and bubbles. The bathroom window looked straight onto the water. It reminded me of a picture I'd seen on Instagram of a posh Amalfi Coast bathroom overlooking the Tyrrhenian Sea. The only difference was his window outlooked the Noosa canals. I dipped my toes into the water to check the temperature. *Perfect*.

Patrick hopped in first and held out his hand for me to join him. I let the sheet drop to the floor and stood with my arms folded over my breasts, then quickly hopped in.

'You know what would make this perfect?' he asked with a 'genius-idea' look plastered on his face.

'I can't imagine anything being more perfect than this, Patrick.'

He smiled broadly. 'How about champagne and strawberries? One sec. I'll be right back.'

He stood, water running down his sculptured back, and I just stared at the beauty of his body. He was a walking Adonis. After he left the room, I sank my head into the bubbling spa. *How did I get so lucky?*

Upon his return, he handed me a champagne flute and a red, ripe strawberry. As I took a sip and closed my eyes, I felt more relaxed than I ever had, and all my worries seemed to dissipate and drain out of me. *I'd love to feel like this every day of the week.*

'How's the champagne?' he asked while looking into my eyes.

I stared right back at him and raised a suggestive eyebrow. 'Really nice.'

He smiled, then took a sip from his glass.

'Where shall we go for dinner?' he asked as his green eyes caught the light of the pink and orange sunset painted across the sky.

'Oh, let's just stay in.' I put my champagne glass down and stood, moving across the spa towards him.

He put his glass down too and grinned as I slid down onto his lap. 'Sounds good to me.' He lifted my hand up and kissed it.

26

Mother Vitello

They often say time flies when you're having fun, and in my case, when you're utterly in love. In the four and a bit weeks since Patrick and I spent our first night together, time had well and truly sped up, and it was already December. It felt like just yesterday that Patrick confessed his feelings to me. Things had gotten serious between us, and in those four and a bit weeks, I really did become the queen of early mornings. We often got up before sunrise, sat on his terrace with coffees and homemade croissants, and watched as the sun rose behind the mansions, filling the pale blue sky with its warm rays the higher it climbed.

I thought back to the discussion we'd had about whether to tell anyone at work about our relationship as I brushed my hair in Patrick's ensuite mirror.

'Should we tell anyone at work about us? I mean we keep talking out the back alone, and we always go in together. Is it becoming obvious?' I asked Patrick as I sat on the black silk sheets on his bed big enough to sleep four adults.

'Naomi, it's up to you. I have nothing to hide,' he said with a nonchalance in his tone while he stared down at me.

'Won't it change how people treat us, though? And I'm ten years younger than you.' I folded my arms, suddenly overwhelmed with fear.

He shook his head. 'I'm not worried about that, *mio luce del sole*. I'm not just the manager. I'm the owner too, remember.' He flashed his smile that showed he wasn't afraid of what people thought and that he took me seriously.

'Alright. Whatever you're comfortable with.' His smile made me fall into a bubble of happiness, and I felt light and tingly.

After that conversation, Patrick made it clear to everyone at work we were a couple and didn't shy away from hugging me at the end of our busy shifts. And as he predicted, no one treated him differently.

I put down my paddle brush on the bathroom basin and washed my face with his fluffy face washer as the morning light came shining in. For once I felt secure and in love – *yes, I was in love* – to the point my heart ached when we spent a night apart. *Go figure, Naomi Jean Clarke. You are really in love. You've finally let your walls down and trusted a man!*

A pang of nerves coursed through my stomach. I was about to meet the prestigious Elizabeth Vitello – *the* Elizabeth who criticised Patrick for not wearing a tie on his birthday. I swallowed hard as our conversation the first time we had crepes replayed in my head: *Mama always told us image is very important in life and image is power.* My stomach sank. *What if she disapproved of me?!* He called her at least once a day, and they chatted about business, and sometimes I'd overhear him talking about me. Even after the dozen times he told me not to worry and that she'd love me, I still couldn't help feeling anxious. How would a coastal girl like me stack up to Patrick's glamourous exes? I'd seen photos of Stephanie on her Instagram; she was the most beauty-obsessed person I'd ever laid eyes on. She had a big following too, which only made her more intimidating. Seventeen frickin' thousand people fangirling over her wardrobe and makeup posts compared to my paltry four hundred and something who seemed to, at best, vaguely enjoy my pics of food and the occasional rainbow.

Stephanie was a platinum blonde with silicon breasts and bee-stung lips, and I had none of those things. I was brunette, small-breasted, and had average-sized lips. The photos of the two of them together were what made my heart twist. They genuinely looked happy and were picture-perfect, and Patrick had a softness in his eyes when he was next to her. A softness that showed me he was deeply in love and would've done anything to please her. She would have fit Elizabeth's 'image is power' motto perfectly.

I guess these nerves were to be expected – I was meeting Elizabeth Vitello for frick sakes. It wasn't even just that she was Patrick's mother. She was also the incredibly sophisticated woman responsible for that amazing wine that seemed to sell out nearly as fast as Kylie Jenner's lip kits. Well, maybe not that quick, but it was in high demand nonetheless.

Elizabeth will compare me to Stephanie as soon as she sees me, won't she? What if she thinks I'm plain and not up to their standards? *Oh God, why am I doing this to myself?*

'Are you ready?' Patrick called from the bedroom as he buttoned up his silver vest over a white shirt. I could see him getting dressed for work in the mirror's reflection, but that was the plan: meet his mother, then go straight to Casa di Vitello for the lunch rush.

'Think so.' I sucked in a deep breath and examined my pale mint-and-peach V-neck maxi-gown in the mirror for any spots or loose threads. The floral organic cotton was soft and floaty, complementing the thin brown belt around my waist. Very bohemian luxe of me, I thought with approval. I was saving this dress for a special day, and today felt special enough to debut it.

One thing I knew for sure: I was the opposite of Stephanie. Come to think of it, since being with Patrick, my shopping habit had simmered down to the point I even threw out makeup. Can you believe it? Trust me – it was a really tough decision, but by the same token, why did I need thirty foundations when only two were my holy grails? Some girls loved buying makeup as a hobby, and that was fine, but I always knew deep down the reasons for my shopping sprees were much darker – I'd been treating shopping for makeup like it was pain medication.

The doorbell rang, and a wave of nausea rolled through me like the surf at Noosa Beach.

'You truly are a goddess, Naomi,' Patrick said as he eyed me from head to toe before disappearing down the staircase.

I sat down on the bed unable to move for a moment. The air went thick, and I was struggling to catch a breath. I sucked in some air, but each breath I took didn't feel deep enough. They were too shallow. *Oh my God, am I going to faint? How embarrassing.*

The sound of an elegant though very excited mother's voice said, 'Oh, Patrizio, my darling son. How I've missed your handsome face.' This was followed by the sound of kisses being exchanged.

'Naomi?' Patrick called. 'Are you coming down? Mama's here.'

I managed to choke out the words 'just a second'. Then I swung my feet off the bed to stand on wobbly legs, went into the bathroom, spritzed some Chloe perfume on my chest, and sucked in a massive breath. *Okay, Naomi, you've got this. It's just his mother. What could go wrong?*

After I finally got my breathing in a steady rhythm, I walked down the stairs and caught sight of Elizabeth's flamboyant aqua-and-pink kaftan that looked designer label. Camilla, no doubt. Expensive stuff. As I clutched onto the wooden handrail, I noticed they were both looking up at me. Patrick was smiling, but I couldn't quite read his mother's expression. And then, in possibly the most embarrassing moment of my life, I tripped on my dress, landed on my bum, and slid down four steps. My worst nightmare. *What a grand entrance, Naomi. Now she'll think you're some incompetent fool. And my bum hurts. Ow.*

Patrick rushed to me and held out his hand to help me up. His eyes twinkled at me in reassurance.

'My goodness. Are you okay, dear?' Elizabeth walked to the stairs and placed a delicate hand on my shoulder.

Huh? She wasn't going to laugh at me? Maybe all my ideas of what she'd be like were just anxiety all along. I wondered if she could sense my surprise at the warmth and kindness in her voice, the tone that sounded so much like Patrick's. As I looked up at her, I noticed her eyes were like his too – she was beautiful with her backcombed hair and a delicate yet structured face.

'I'm alright,' I said as I regained my balance and smiled, ignoring my aching rear end.

And to further my shock, she opened her arms and embraced me in a big motherly cuddle, kissing me cheek to cheek.

I blushed and looked over at Patrick's happy expression with raised brows as if to say, *She approves of me, hurrah!!!* Could he read my thoughts?

'Now, I want to hear all about you, Naomi, but first, I need to get settled in my room.' Behind her were two Louis Vuitton roller bags, and she had her velvet pink-rose bag looped on her wrist.

'Of course, Mama. Here, I've got your bags.' Patrick grabbed her luggage and led her upstairs to the guestroom.

How could I be so silly and so quick to judge? His mother was lovely, and she wanted to hear all about me. So what if she was obsessed with image? That didn't mean she was judgmental. She was just a woman of great taste.

***

After Elizabeth was settled into her room, she came back downstairs in a cloud of Chanel No. 5.

'Come, let's sit at the table,' she said, waving to me and Patrick to join her at the luxe sandalwood dining table big enough to seat twenty people. 'So, I've heard you've created quite a bit of talk about the pizzas in Noosa,' she said to me as she sat down on the cushioned chair.

Patrick and I sat on opposite sides in the next seats over from her.

'Oh, really?' I smiled at how impressed she looked as she spoke to me.

'Yes, it sounds like Sydney and Melbourne could do with your magic touch.' She nodded as her emerald eyes stared at me with intrigue.

I smiled again and laughed, having no idea how to respond to such an incredible compliment.

'It's nice Patrick has found a woman that can cook. He's always wanted a woman he could share his passion with, someone equipped for his busy lifestyle.' She lowered her voice and cupped her hand before saying the next line. 'His ex was a hopeless cook.' She let out a laugh. 'Oh!' She snapped her fingers as if suddenly remembering something important. She turned to Patrick, then said, 'You wouldn't believe it. Marco and Stephanie have started canoodling again.'

I observed as his face changed and watched his throat as he swallowed hard. 'Has this been an ongoing thing?'

'Stephanie seems to have many boyfriends, just as Marco has girlfriends. They're both as bad as each other.' She shook her head and let out a chuckle.

'Well, I hold deep regret for ever proposing to her, but it sounds like she's the perfect fit for Marco.' His eyes flamed with hurt.

As soon as she looked into his eyes, she realised she was being insensitive. 'I shouldn't have laughed at such a sensitive matter. I'm sorry, Patrizio.' She placed her manicured hand on his.

'It's okay, Mama. I'm used to your light-hearted nature.' He smiled.

She nodded and smiled too, and just by analysing that moment, I realised Elizabeth loved her children equally as much and that it would have been so hard for Patrick to make peace with Marco.

'Anyway, I thought I'd let you know that Marco was still carrying on, but I must say, he's doing a good job of running the Sydney restaurant.' Her high-arched eyebrows raised in approval.

He nodded in agreement. 'I've been checking the figures, and all looks well in that regard.' He stood and walked over to the kitchen. 'Does anyone want a cup of tea?'

'I'd love one,' Elizabeth said with a warm smile.

'Naomi?' he asked while looking directly at me.

'Just a mineral water, please.'

'Mama, I've got Earl Grey or green tea. Which one would you like?' He got out his wooden teabag organiser and stared at them.

'Earl Grey, with one sugar and a dash of milk, dear.'

'You haven't changed a bit.' He smiled as he flicked on his matte-black electric kettle.

She returned the smile, then turned her attention back to me. 'So, Naomi, are you excited for Christmas?'

'Yes, I love Christmas time.' I nodded with a grin.

'When Patrizio was a little boy, he always liked to put the star on top of the tree, so that's been our tradition every year.' Her pink lips spread out into a smile.

'I can't believe how quickly December has come around. How's it the first already?' I gulped, a little embarrassed at my lame small talk.

'Mmm. It's come around very fast indeed.'

Minutes later, Patrick came over with the drinks, and put his mother's cup of tea down on a coaster, then placed my sparkling mineral water on one too. He was so precise with his movements; everything was done just so, as if he was at the restaurant. The mint leaves and lime wedge were even muddled at the bottom of my glass. One of my favourite things to do was watch him in his element as he created gorgeous food and drinks.

I took a sip of my mineral water, admiring his face as he looked down at his Rolex watch.

'We better get going, Naomi. It's ten thirty.' His voice was in work mode.

I finished my drink in two quick gulps. 'It was lovely meeting you, Elizabeth,' I said as I stood to leave the table.

'You too, dear.' Her pink, manicured nails were curled around the Mediterranean-printed teacup handle as she sipped her tea.

'I'm sure you'll find something to entertain yourself with, Mama. Love you.' He kissed her on the cheek.

'I've got plenty to do, Patrizio. Don't worry about that,' she assured him with a beaming smile.

I made my way upstairs to quickly change into my uniform before leaving.

27

Workplace Rumours

It was flat out in the restaurant; we were completely booked out, and Trish was in a foul mood, swearing at everyone in her vicinity. Whenever she was in a bad mood, her nostrils would flare and she'd point at you. Not a fun experience.

Trish stormed over to me with a kilo's worth of onions and dumped them on my station.

'Peel and dice these, and make it bloody quick.' She banged her hand on the bench, signalling for me to get moving.

It was my least favourite task in the world – chopping onions always made me cry, no matter what trick I tried to avoid it – but I obeyed and cut a slit in the bag with my knife to pull the onions from because the job had to be done.

Once I'd finished the onions and placed them in a large silver bowl, I positioned them on Trish's workbench in the middle of the kitchen and ran back to my section to prepare for the pizza orders.

Lots of orders flew in, and I lost count of how many pizzas I prepared and cooked, but my arms ached enough to tell me it was a lot. Today's shift was go, go, and go some more, and it left me feeling as though I had stood in a sauna with heavy weights all day. And even though I received multiple compliments, Trish's attention seemed to be targeted more on what I was doing rather than cooking her mains. She kept walking over to my station, watching over my shoulder, and saying things like: *work quicker, too much sauce, not enough cheese, too much herbs, not enough seasoning.* Trish was picking on me for ridiculous things that no one else in the kitchen or dining area seemed to have a problem with, and to be honest, it was annoying and grated on my nerves. If she wasn't the head chef, I would've barked back, but I maintained placid and copped it.

After the afternoon shift was done, I exhaled a massive sigh of relief and watched Trish call Patrick outside to talk. A feeling in my stomach warned me something was wrong because, despite the swearing and nit-picking, she was usually pretty even-tempered. Why was she so angry and snippy at me? What was her problem? God forbid I was in the firing line for another strand-of-hair drama. Was there something I had done that I hadn't been notified about?

Five minutes later, the back door swung open and Trish walked in with teary eyes. *Oh shit.* She stalked in my direction and stared at me for a moment with her nostrils flared. *What have I done?*

'I caught up with Paul and heard about the shenanigans that happened at Mon Amour.' She shook her head and sneered her nose in disgust at me. My stomach plummeted like I was on Dreamworld's Giant Drop ride. 'I should have called Daniel before rushing into hiring you.'

'I'm not sure what you're talking about?' I asked with an eyebrow raised.

'I just told Patrick about what happened, and you've made him sick.' Her voice was filled with repulsion.

'*Excuse me?* What supposedly happened? Where is Patrick?' I had to grip the bench for balance as my head spun in confusion.

'Just leave him be. Look, I think you should do yourself a favour and leave this restaurant before you make this mess of yours even worse. He needs a *woman,*' – she almost spat the word at me – 'not a little girl impersonating one.'

'I'm not a little girl. I'm twenty-five, and I have no idea what Paul or Daniel has told you, but I assure you, I haven't done anything wrong.' I could hear my voice shaking. *Why was this happening?* I thought I'd closed the chapter on Mon Amour, and now I was back in the firing line for something.

Trish scoffed and took a step closer to me with her finger pointed. 'You and your little mate Debra both slept with Daniel and had a threesome, which broke up his marriage. Patrick doesn't need a homewrecker working in his kitchen. We're run with dignity, which seems to be something you lack.'

'What?' I was surprised at how loud my voice was in reply. 'I never, ever slept with Daniel. I have no idea who told you that, but that's the biggest lie I've ever heard.'

She screwed up her nose and folded her arms. We both turned as we saw Patrick come back into the prep area.

'Naomi,' he said with hurt in his voice that made my heart crumble to pieces, like an apple pie gone wrong.

'Yes?' My voice was steady, and I was ready to hear what he was going to say.

'Did you sleep with Daniel?' His green eyes looked straight into mine.

'No, of course not.' *I've already told you this.*

Trish scoffed again. 'Oh, as if she's going to admit it, Patrick. She's lying. Look how guilty she looks.'

'I'm not guilty!' I fought the urge to reach out and hit her. 'I'd never sleep with *Daniel*, and, Patrick, if you believe that, then I'm more than happy to go.'

'Maybe it's best if you take the rest of your shift off, Naomi. I need time to think, and the last thing I need is lies. I'll talk to you tonight,' he said in a serious tone, one that made my heart stop. It was a tone I'd never heard him speak to me in before.

I couldn't believe it. He was actually doubting me. I couldn't hide my shock, or my disappointment. 'Okay, Patrick, you believe what you want, but I *did not* sleep with *Daniel*.'

And just like that, I'd gone from being Patrick's loving, trusted girlfriend to being called a liar. *How could he believe this? Didn't he know me better by now?*

A numb feeling came over me as I walked out of the kitchen to grab my bag from the locker. I left the restaurant and kept walking down paths, weaving through crowds of people, until I reached the taxi rank and hailed down a cab.

I hopped in, and the whole drive home, I felt empty and sick. Did this mean I was going to lose my job? And my relationship? *Everything was going so well, and I've just met his mother. What will she think? I guess she'll think I'm just like Stephanie – a lying sleep-around.* My God, things could change in a snap of the fingers.

The taxi pulled up at Mum's house. I paid the driver and hopped out, feeling wobbly as I walked up the orange driveway. I was in love with Patrick Vitello, *so in love*, and now, I might have lost him forever because of some nauseating gossip. *It's actually utter nonsense he told me to go home instead of talking to me like he usually does. I didn't think our relationship was so weak. Why would he even believe Trish over me?*

'Naomi? What are you doing home so early?' Mum asked as I swung open the front door. I walked inside and stopped behind the couch. This feeling was way too familiar – another failed relationship in my life.

'Patrick told me to go home; Daniel told the head chef I slept with him, and I think Patrick believes it.' I burst out crying. Mum walked towards me with her arms out and swooped me into her arms like a mother goose. She rubbed my back with soothing pats.

'Patrick doesn't believe that, does he? He should know you better than that by now,' she spoke into my hair.

I let go of her and took a step back with my arms folded.

'We've only been together for just over a month, and his ex-girlfriend cheated on him. He's got his own trust issues, and he previously asked me if Daniel tried to sleep with me, and I told him no, and now he probably thinks I'm lying.' I let out a sigh and dabbed my fingers under my eyes. 'And you're right. He should know me better than that.' An image invaded my mind of me and Deb having a threesome with Daniel, and I felt acid reflux fizz up my throat as I quickly dismissed the thought. *Yuck, never.*

'Look, don't worry about it, sweetheart.' She reached out to brush the loose hair from my face. 'You didn't do anything wrong, and you have nothing to feel guilty about. He will come to his senses.'

It seemed like every day I was reminded of my past and the people from my past. No matter how hard I tried to escape from it, and them, I couldn't. They were inescapable.

'I hope so, Mum. I really do, because ...' I thought of the way Patrick looked at me every morning when we woke up together and started to choke up. 'Sorry, Mum. I'm just going to clean myself up in the bathroom.' I didn't wait for her response as I headed down the hall.

Once I was alone in the bathroom, I grabbed my phone and texted Daniel.

Me: *If you don't message Patrick the truth, I will tell everyone what you said to me and that you were touching my thigh inappropriately and were erect, you sick pig.*

I never told Patrick about Daniel telling me I needed a good fuck because then I'd have to go into the full extent of what happened and how I used to catch him staring at my bum but ignored it, all so I could earn some money and be independent. The truth was his behaviour made me feel weak for staying there and putting up with his abuse, and I wanted Patrick to see me as strong and as a girl who didn't put up with that behaviour. I loved the way Patrick saw me and didn't want anything to jeopardise that.

A shiver ran down my spine as I remembered Daniel perving at my breasts. I couldn't believe he had the guts to actually stroke my thigh with his hand while he spat abuse in my face. And what was the most disgusting thing of all was he was turned on by abusing me; it made his penis hard. What an absolute pig.

Daniel (Ex-Boss): *And what supposedly have I lied about?*

Me: *What the hell is wrong with you? You're a repulsive liar. Not that you care, but you may have just cost me my job and my boyfriend. You're so immature making up that Debra and I had a threesome with you. God you've got some sick fantasies running through your head.*

Daniel (Ex-Boss): *I cost you, your job? Listen here woman, you ruined my pizzas walking out like that. I had to pull pizzas from the menu because everyone is incompetent twats who can't make pizza dough. I'm done-zo with Noosa anyway, I'm moving. So, deal with your petty shit yourself, woman. And nice to hear you finally filled your hole with something other than a dildo. Catcha.*

I didn't bother messaging him back or getting upset over his vulgar language – it was a waste of time. I knew what I had to do, and I wouldn't get it done by wasting any more energy on Daniel.

28

Christmas Wonderland

I checked my phone for the twentieth time. Nothing. It was 11pm, and I still hadn't heard one word from Patrick. I felt sick to my stomach, so much so that I couldn't eat Mum's famous Greek salad at dinnertime four hours ago. My body remained limp, slumped on the Chesterfield couch as I wept into the velvet. When I finally gained some strength, I walked outside onto a patch of damp grass and looked up at the sky to clear my head. Even the charcoal sky seemed heavy with sadness as thick clouds floated by, covering the twinkling stars.

A loud sigh escaped my lips. I looked at the grass, ready to make my way back inside, as a bolt of lightning flashed in the sky, illuminating the backyard in an electric purple. Rain began falling from the sky and hit my skin like bullets. I ran for shelter and went back into the lounge room. I sank back into the couch and sat there staring at the floor. As I looked up, Mum's Amalfi Coast painting caught my eye, and that magical feeling of my love for Patrick came rushing back into my heart along with anger. *I will not let lies dictate my life. No way,* I thought as a surge of rage flowed through my body, fuelling my energy.

Once I was dressed again, I called a taxi, and as I sat in the backseat staring at the rain-spotted window, I felt angrier and angrier. *I've done nothing wrong. In fact, I've done all the right things: I've been honest, I've been faithful, and I've been myself. I deserve this love – I do – and I won't let anything, or anyone, sabotage that. Daniel has no control over me or my life.*

A taxi dropped me out the front of Casa di Vitello, and as I ran up the steps to reach shelter from the drizzling rain, I saw Patrick sitting with Trish on the barstools. They were inches apart having an Aperol spritz, and her hand was on his. *Was she trying to seduce him?*

Once I was within earshot, I cleared my throat loudly, then said, 'Why is your hand on my *boyfriend's?*'

She moved her hand away and blushed. 'Relax. We were just chatting.' She tucked her hair behind her ears and grew redder the longer I stared at her.

Oh God, she was in that giddy mode again, and I could tell she was utterly mesmerised by Patrick. So mesmerised that she had applied red lipstick and dangling earrings, and was that Chloe perfume that I smelled? That was one bad thing about dating a gorgeous man – nearly every woman checked him out and craved his attention.

'Naomi,' Patrick said as he stood up. He looked exhausted, and all I wanted to do was kiss him, lay my head on his chest, and cuddle up to him.

I shook my head – *I should be angry right now.* 'What's going on here? You both look super friendly. Too friendly,' I said as my boots squeaked across the floor.

'Trish, can you give me some time with Naomi,' Patrick said with a drop of annoyance in his voice.

'Yep. I'm going home anyway.' She got up, avoiding eye contact with me, and headed out the front entrance.

'I didn't sleep with Daniel.' My words came out in a rush as I walked closer to him.

'I know, Naomi. I shouldn't have doubted you like that. I let my fears get the best of me, and I didn't know what to believe as Trish has never lied to me before. She's been my trusted head chef for many years.' He nodded and faced his stool in my direction, then sat back down. 'After thinking about it long and hard, I realised that isn't who you are, and I was meaning to message you, but work got chaotically busy.'

'I was just surprised you didn't talk to me about it in private when you asked me earlier today. My heart hurt so bad when you told me to leave. All I could do was worry about what you thought of me and whether this would break us up.' My eyes drooped with sadness.

His eyes flickered with hurt, and he nodded in shame. 'I'm so sorry I made you feel that way. Trust issues are something I'm working on. I promise not to do that to you again. I was put under a lot of pressure because Trish threatened to quit ... I knocked some sense into her, so don't worry. She's staying put, but what an eventful day.' He sighed, then continued. 'Once I reassured myself that you weren't like that, I had to convince Trish also. When she has an opinion about someone, it's not easily shifted. She used to work at my Melbourne restaurant, and she relocated to Noosa for a change.'

Oh, this was all too obvious. How could Patrick be so gullible? Trish was in love with him. Why else would she follow him all the way to Noosa? I was torn for a moment about whether to say this to Patrick, but I decided to keep my mouth shut for the moment. 'I'm so glad you believe me now.' My eyes filled with happy tears.

'I love you. You're the *amore* of my life, the queen of my heart, and the queen of the pizzas too.' He chuckled.

I smiled at his words as my eyes widened. 'I love you too, and that's what's scary. I'm becoming jealous and feeling things I've never felt before, and I don't like it.' I let out a sigh, then ran my hand through my damp hair.

'You always get me with your honesty, Naomi. I've probably told you this a hundred times, but it's so refreshing.' His voice was sincere and made my stomach melt like warm honey.

His reassurance was all I needed to hear and that made me crave him more than I ever had, but then I wondered if I would be in this predicament at all had I been one hundred percent honest in the first place. 'I like hearing you say that,

Patrick. You can tell me this any day. I actually don't think I could get sick of you saying it, to be honest.'

It was so easy and natural to slip into love mode with Patrick and just numb myself to everything else, but deep down, I knew I had to face my demons and address the real problem at hand. After a deep breath escaped from my lips, I looked into Patrick's green eyes and contemplated whether I should tell him exactly what Daniel had done. A part of me wanted to keep it concealed, but another part wanted to tell him everything. *I should. I should just tell him. He's my boyfriend, my actual boyfriend, and after what happened tonight, why not tell him how bad Daniel really is?*

His eyes were full of questions as he stared into mine.

'What's the matter, Naomi?' He brushed my cheek with his thumb, resulting in tingles down my neck.

'I should have told you all of this to begin with, but I was extremely embarrassed.' My already fair skin turned whiter.

'About what?' A concerned look appeared on his face.

I sucked in a deep breath. 'Well, the night I left Mon Amour, Daniel told me I needed a good fuck, and he was acting inappropriately and perving on me and … it got so bad to the point that he put his hand on my thigh and was aroused while he was abusing me.' I gulped and shuddered before continuing. 'And before that night, I used to catch him staring at my arse and ignored it, because the truth was, I was desperate for an income and my own independence, and now thinking about what I put up with makes me feel sick.'

Patrick didn't say anything, but I could tell he was hurt by the slump of his shoulders and the shock in his eyes.

'The reason I never told you any of this was because I didn't want you to see me differently and think I was weak or something. I love the way you look at me and the respect you have for me. I never want to lose that ever.'

'Come here.' He wrapped his arms around me, with his legs spread, and I just stared into his eyes as I stood between his warm thighs. His eyes had a way of pulling me in and making me get lost in them. Every time he looked deep into mine, my knees went wobbly.

'Naomi, what Daniel did to you was ...' He paused for a moment, searching for the right word, before continuing. 'Immoral, and they were *his* actions, not yours. What he did would never make me think less of you or change my mind about how I feel. You did nothing wrong. And please know you can tell me anything.'

I nodded. 'Thanks, Patrick. You scared me tonight. I was so scared I was going to lose you.'

'You will *never* lose me,' he assured me. He moved his warm hands up to my cheeks and pulled me in for a kiss. It was our most passionate kiss to date, and I didn't want the moment to end. My cheeky mind wandered off to the bedroom and envisioned our makeup sex that would absolutely happen later tonight. 'And not to be highly inappropriate or anything, but you can't blame the man for staring at such a perfectly round bottom.' He chuckled with mischievousness.

I swatted his arm and giggled too. 'Well, it's all yours now.'

'Sure is, *mio luce del sole.*'

***

After we closed the restaurant, we went out the back to his car, and my thoughts returned to Trisha. I couldn't help myself. 'Patrick, why did Trisha have her hand over yours?' I asked while I buckled myself in.

'Because she told me she was in love with me ... but I made it very clear I was dedicated to you, and that we were serious.' He cast a look my way and smiled.

I knew it! She was in love with him. It was all I needed to hear to reassure myself I wasn't losing my mind. And just hearing him say he was dedicated to me made my heart melt. I'd never had a man say that to me before. Usually my relationships just ended in heartbreak, but this was different. He was smart, sensible, frickin' incredible, and *all mine.*

'Let's go home, my *bellezza,*' he said with another smile as he drove the car onto the main street.

I smiled and leant back in my seat, feeling warm and happy as we passed the trees wound in twinkling fairy lights that lined the strip of Hastings Street. Gentle rain fell from the sky onto his windshield as his wipers moved side to side. The rain eased to a stop just before we got back into his garage.

As we walked inside, I did a double-take in disbelief at what I was seeing. It was a Christmas wonderland. Forest-green garlands were weaved up the staircase railing, and the further we walked in, the more we were engulfed in Christmas delight. In the lounge room, there was a huge snow-frosted tree decked out with pinecones, colourful flashing lights, red baubles, candy canes, and tinsel. It was decorated so perfectly, it looked as though a professional was hired for the task. There was even a green-and-red train looping around a track underneath the tree. Did Elizabeth do all of this while we were at work?

Christmas carols hummed on a state-of-the-art sound system, and stockings were strung across the eight-foot fireplace. I could see the names embroidered on the fabric from where I stood: Patrizio, Marco, Caterina, Naomi, Carlos, and Savannah. *Oh, my goodness, how sweet of her to include me, Carlos, and my mum in this. This Italian family sure knew how to make you feel included.*

'This is amazing,' I said, awestruck.

'It is, isn't it?' He smiled with pride.

'Do you always decorate your house like this? It's magical.' The lights from the trees reflected in my eyes.

'Yes. We go all out for Christmas. It's Mama's favourite holiday.' He grinned and placed his arm around me.

As I got closer to the tree, I noticed there was something missing: a star. 'There's no star on the tree.'

Patrick dropped his arm, looked around the lounge room, and noticed a gold star sitting on the coffee table. He picked it up, then looked at me with another smile.

'She left it for me. Do you want to put it on top?' he asked with shining eyes.

'No, that's your tradition. Maybe next year.' I smiled shyly.

He raised his eyebrows at me. 'Next year, huh?' He seemed pleased as he stood on his toes to place the star on top.

A pad of footsteps caught my attention. *Was Elizabeth awake?*

Patrick turned around to face the lounge-room entrance. 'Mama, what are you doing up?' he asked as Elizabeth appeared. She had her hair twirled into a bun and was wearing an emerald silk dressing gown. As she got closer, the smell of musk body lotion drifted from her skin.

'Oh, I needed to see your face, darling,' she said while looking around the room. 'Do you like the decorations?'

'How could we not?' Patrick answered. 'They're stunning.'

'I can't wait for us all to be together again. It will be so lovely.' She adjusted a drooping bauble.

I could see in Elizabeth's eyes how fatigued she was and felt touched by the realisation that she'd stayed up to do all this out of passion for her family and Christmas.

'Did you do all of the decorating yourself?' Patrick asked with a raised brow and a grin.

'No, of course not.' She laughed. 'I hired someone.'

'Well, they did an exceptional job,' I added.

Elizabeth looked at me and smiled warmly. 'Oh yes, they did, didn't they?'

I nodded and couldn't wipe the smile off my face; I felt so content, and the twinkling lights warmed any lingering cold spots on my body.

'Typical Mama,' Patrick said, smiling. 'You spend so much money just to make us happy.'

'There's no EFTPOS in heaven,' she shot back with a wry look on her face.

'Touché, Mama.' He nodded while maintaining his smile.

Elizabeth turned to me under the glow of the Christmas lights. 'You're very pretty, Naomi, much like an old-fashioned beauty. Actually, you remind me of a girl painted from the Renaissance period.' She stroked her thumb across my cheek, and I felt fluttery with affection. 'Fair like one, too.'

'Thank you, Elizabeth. Patrick has said this to me also.' I beamed. 'You're very beautiful yourself.'

'You've got youth on your side, dear. I'm glad Patrizio has found someone natural for once. You suit each other.' She let her hand fall back to her side.

'I do feel rather lucky,' Patrick added and wrapped his arm around my back, warming me even more. I felt like a melting marshmallow.

Elizabeth yawned, tapping her hand over her mouth, then said, 'I think I might go to bed. Well, you both enjoy this. Goodnight.'

'Night, Mama.' Patrick kissed her on the cheek.

'Goodnight, Elizabeth. Have a restful sleep.' I smiled.

'Feel free to call me Lizzie, Naomi.' She patted me on the shoulder.

We watched as she climbed the stairs. Once she was out of sight, Patrick spun me to face him and looked into my eyes. He wrapped his arms around my neck and kissed my forehead. *Yes, please keep kissing me like that. It makes me feel tingly.* He looked down and smiled, then let out a little laugh.

'I never thought you'd go for me, Naomi. I thought you would get scared off and say no to me.'

'Are you kidding? There's probably ten other women just at your restaurant who'd fight me to be with you. You liking me was the biggest shock of my life.' My eyes widened with amazement at what he was saying.

'But none of those women are you, so I'm not interested.' He grinned. 'I'll never forget the day we first went out for coffee. You looked like a glowing angel dressed in that little pink dress with buttons. That's when I first noticed your goddess figure.' He smiled to himself at the thought. 'To me, you were the most attractive woman in that room.'

I smiled and never felt more desirable in my life. It was crazy how simple words like those could make me feel so special.

Patrick grabbed my hands and began swaying with me to the soft Christmas tunes playing in the background. I wasn't a dancer – I'd always been a bit un-coordinated outside of the kitchen – but I could manage this gentle side-to-side motion. As I nuzzled my head into his chest, I breathed in the scent of his skin. He smelt just like the first time I met him, and a million memories flooded my mind. I still couldn't believe how much had happened over the past couple of months – if you'd asked me in June if this was what I'd envisioned by early December, I would have laughed. This was all so unexpected, but I guess the best things in life often are.

29

Christmas Eve

The sunlight poured through the skylight above Patrick's bed, awakening me. I squinted, then rolled over to pick up my phone from the sleek black nightstand on my side. The nightstand had golden drawer pulls, which was fitting, with his blue wallpaper decorated in golden arch shapes. His room exuded an Art Deco vibe. As I checked my phone for messages, I got distracted by the background photo of Dad and our flour-covered faces. *Love you, Dad. Hope you're having fun cooking up a storm and singing with Elvis in heaven.* A happy tear slipped down my cheek. Mum had told me a dozen times how proud he'd be of me, and it hurt like hell I'd never see him again in this life, but I was grateful for technology keeping happy moments alive through snapshots. I had zero messages as of yet, but that didn't matter because my phone reminded me it was: December 24. Christmas Eve.

As my head hit the plump pillow again, I thought back to everything that had happened this month: Patrick and I had spent every night together, and we went into work together each shift. He handled front-of-house, and I remained queen of the pizza section and even had the honour of putting a coriander and basil pesto chicken pizza on the Noosa menu. The words he said to me when he tried my creation still make my cheeks blush: *'This is incredible, Naomi. Everything you make has a magic touch.'* Trish also raved about it and said it was one of the best-constructed pizzas she'd had. It was a big deal putting anything new on the menu, and everyone in the kitchen had to agree on it or it wouldn't make the cut.

Trish had been ridiculously nice since the whole Daniel drama to the point she got me cold drinks every shift and even asked for my opinion on food she'd cooked. It was bizarre and flattering that, all of a sudden, she treated me with the same level of respect she did Patrick.

Daniel sold his restaurant to Paul and moved to Cairns for a fresh start, and there were rumours he'd bought an adult entertainment shop. The change in Mon Amour under Paul's leadership was incredible: this time, it wasn't just Moroccan-inspired – it was delicious, authentic Moroccan.

Deb messaged me every so often, bragging about her job and how much money she was earning, and she posted dozens of selfies on Instagram. It was nice to hear from her and see her doing well. I appreciated the good memories and did miss our extravagant shopping trips to Mecca. We'd never be close again, but I would always wish her well.

Looking back, I can say with honesty I never expected to fall in love with Patrick Vitello. *Love was just a fairy tale*, or so I'd always told myself; love was something that led to disappointment or failure. It was safer to keep my heart tucked in my chest. Scott and Sebastian were fine examples of why, but life with Patrick had proved me wrong and altered my mind. Being with Patrick felt dreamlike and effortless. I'd even vaguely entertained the idea of what our wedding might look like, later down the track, and sometimes looked at diamond rings in jewellery boutiques. Oh, how quickly things can change. Just like that, one person walks into your life and makes you rethink everything, and *boom* – you're in love.

'Good morning, *mio luce del sole*,' Patrick said as he walked up the steps and into the bedroom. He leapt effortlessly onto the bed like a panther, then leant down to kiss me, bringing me back to my current life.

'Good morning,' I whispered back as I stared at his black linen shirt and oat-coloured cotton pants. He was already dressed and smelled divine.

'I've got a surprise planned for you today,' he said as happiness twinkled in his eyes.

'Really?' I smiled. 'What is it?'

'It's a *surprise*.' He flashed his perfect white teeth. 'All I'll say is … No, you can wait.'

I wasn't used to surprises on Christmas Eve; that was more a Christmas Day thing.

'Just wear your sunflower dress.' He winked at me.

I nodded, got out of bed, and padded over to my suitcase in his humungous walk-in wardrobe. As I got dressed, I admired the shelves lined with designer suits and linen shirts and glimpsed his red velvet drawer filled with men's jewellery. The jewellery was protected with a spotless glass lid. His closet was like something you'd see in a Hollywood mansion. Very suave.

Once I was dressed, I walked over to him and twirled around in my dress with a big grin on my face.

'I could never be bored of that dress on you,' he said as his smiley eyes crinkled.

'It definitely holds some good memories.' I smiled again.

He nodded while I stared at the sunlight on his olive skin. His hair was loosely tied back, revealing his golden hooped earrings, and he was propped up against the black leather headboard, one leg over the other, with both hands behind his head. He exuded a regal yet casual vibe no matter what his body was doing.

I fought off the urge to climb on his lap, sit there, and kiss him but knew I'd better save that for later.

He stood and said, 'Now time for your surprise. Close your eyes, and I'll walk you downstairs.' His warm hand grabbed mine, and just that feeling alone warmed my entire body.

'Okay.' I squeezed my eyes shut, and a flutter of excitement ran through my tummy as we hit the first step on the staircase. *I wonder what my surprise is.*

It was scary walking down the steps with no vision; my feet did all the work, and my heart raced with nervous excitement. I sure didn't want to fall over again, but I had full trust in Patrick's hands.

A surge of relief came over me as my feet hit the marble floor at the bottom of the staircase. He kept walking me for a little more, then stopped.

'Open,' he said with a smile.

My face lit up as I looked at the bouquet of sunflowers arranged in a red vase on the kitchen counter. It was the biggest bouquet I'd ever seen – there were at least fifty flowers in there. You could tell they were chosen with such precision because not one petal was wilted or marked.

'Oh, my goodness, Patrick. They're beautiful.' I reached out and stroked one of the petals. It felt silky under my fingers.

'Not quite as soft as your skin, but close, hey?' He winked and shoved his hand into his pocket. 'I was going to wait to give you this tomorrow morning, but today seemed more fitting.'

He slipped out a green velvet box and snapped it open, revealing a golden sunflower pendant on a delicate chain.

I grabbed the box and stared at it in awe. 'This is so gorgeous. Thank you, Patrick.' On closer examination, I noticed the split in the middle of the sunflower and curiously parted it with my fingers, and as I did, a round silver pendant appeared inside with the words *'Mio Luce Del Sole'* etched into it. My heart melted as I admired the unique, heartfelt gift. It was so beautiful the way the sunflower opened like wings – I'd never seen anything like it.

'You discovered that quickly.' He flashed an impressed smile my way. 'Turn around.' His pointer finger motioned the 'turn around' signal. 'I'll put it on for you.'

I turned around so that I was facing the wall and passed him the box so that he could place the necklace around my neck.

Once it was on, he said, 'That's not all. Put on your sunglasses and meet me on my dock.'

'Oh, you're so full of surprises this morning.' I nodded with a grin. 'See you in a second.' *How fun.*

Once I had my sunglasses on, I ran outside onto the dock and lifted my cat-eyed sunnies to look for Patrick, but I couldn't see him. *Where was he?*

'Patrick?' I called out as I searched for him on the water while one hand shielded my face from the sun. 'Patrick, where are you?' For a moment, I thought he was the tanned man in the canoe wearing black speedos, but surely that wasn't him, was it? He wasn't the type to wear speedos, and gosh, that man had one hell of a hairy chest. Definitely not Patrick.

To my shock, my eyes suddenly found him. He was sitting on a gondola, while a man dressed in a shirt the colours of the Italian flag stood at the back steering. The man wore a traditional straw boater hat, the kind I'd seen in travel pamphlets. My heart thrilled with excitement; I'd never been on a gondola before. The driver parked the boat at the jetty and lifted the hatch of the roof so I could climb in. Patrick stood up and reached for my hand as he pulled me safely onboard, and I sat against the padded leather seat. The seat was black with red cushions.

On the table in front of us lay an antipasto platter just like the one I had the first night I visited his house. And of course, a bottle of Vitello champagne, a bowl of chocolate-coated strawberries, and macadamia nuts. I truly didn't think my life could get any better than it was, but Patrick always seemed to outdo himself.

'Merry Christmas Eve,' he said while he draped his arm across the top of the seat and his other passed me a champagne glass.

'Merry Christmas Eve, Patrick.' I smiled back, and we clinked our champagne glasses together.

As I sipped the delicious champagne, I was glad to reflect that the occasional glass of wine no longer carried such negative connotations.

The boat began moving, and splashes of water flicked up and left droplets on our arms and legs. The wind whipped our hair to the point I wished I'd tied my hair back, but the smell of sea salt and refreshing summer breezes were too good not to enjoy. God, Noosa was heavenly.

We travelled through the canals and watched the ducks swimming behind us, quacking and playfully ducking their heads in the water. There were also a few pelicans to our left floating along the river, soaking up the sunshine and dipping their heads in the water, hunting for fish.

Along the waterside were mansions like Patrick's, all with glorious glass doors that led out to the river. I craned my neck so I was looking at Patrick's stunning profile. 'Thanks for taking me on this. I really didn't expect it.'

'That's the thing with you, Naomi. You don't expect anything, and it's the most refreshing thing I've ever experienced.'

'I guess you give me all the things I require, and I don't need anything else.' I flashed him a smile.

'And what are those things?' His brow raised with curiosity.

'Security, dedication, honesty, and love.'

'You're the most beautiful woman I've ever met. Just your mind and heart are everything a person could want.' He reached out to stroke his thumb across my cheek.

I blushed and tried not to feel overwhelmed by his comment, but I couldn't help it. It was so hard to accept those nice remarks and believe them to be true. But I guess that's what self-love is, knowing your value and believing you're worth it, and I was getting better at it every day as my self-doubt began to slip away.

'Thanks, Patrick.' I grabbed his hand and admired the rippling water views.

He moved my hand to his lips and kissed it gently while staring into my eyes.

'You make me so happy. You make me the happiest I could ever be.' He gave me a look that only someone very much in love could.

'You too.' I returned the look and leant in to kiss him.

I rested my head on Patrick's shoulder and just enjoyed the boat, the sunshine, and his warmth. The whole afternoon I smiled until I could no longer because my cheeks hurt. That's what Patrick did to me – he made my insides hurt because I was so damn happy. He made me forget about the hard times and reminded me of what there was to look forward to every day.

Two hours later, the gondolier dropped us off at Patrick's jetty. We hopped off and walked back inside. I always loved walking into Patrick's house; I wasn't sure if it was the beauty all around or because I was so besotted with him. I think it was probably both – I could never get sick of either him or his house.

'Well, that wasn't Venice, but Noosa's pretty nice,' Patrick said with a stretch of his arms to untangle his stiffened muscles.

'It was amazing. So why a gondola, anyway?' I eyed him curiously.

'You said you always wanted to go to Italy, so I thought I'd bring Italy to you.' He let his arms fall back down and smiled.

As soon as he said those words, the whole morning made sense – the sunflowers, the gondola, the antipasto platter, the champagne. It was true I'd never been to Italy, but being with Patrick brought me to Italy every day. Today was just extra special with the gondola ride.

'Aww, you're too sweet.' I beamed.

'I'll have to take you to the real place one day, though.' He smiled to himself. 'It's winter there now.' He looked back at me.

'One day, but I can barely imagine it being better than today.'

As the day went on, we drank mineral water and wrapped presents together in the middle of the lounge-room floor because the dining table had been taken over with luxurious tableware and festive decorations. I loved the smell of wrapping paper. There was something about Christmas paper – it smelt like sweet wood and pine trees. Every time I wrapped presents, the smell and silky feel of the paper transported me back in time. Christmas was always my favourite time of year because it was a time of giving, sharing, and reconnecting. And it felt like everyone's birthday.

It was exciting but nerve-wracking imagining the Vitellos and Clarkes together for Christmas, but meeting Elizabeth had cast any remaining doubts from my mind. She was so thoughtful; I still couldn't believe she'd had stockings hung for my family members too.

After hours of wrapping presents, Patrick stole my attention away from the purple and pink sunset with his Christmas carols on the piano. I stared down at his strong yet delicate hands and watched as they pressed down onto the keys. Warm sunlight poured through the crystal-clear windows and streamed across his hands. He began to sing but soon stopped himself after hitting a few off-key notes. Both our heads fell back with laughter at his bad singing. I took over, placing my hands on his shoulders, and sang as I listened to him play.

'I didn't know you were such a bad singer.' I squeezed his shoulders gently. 'So, you do have flaws, after all.'

He laughed and looked up at me. 'Everyone is riddled with flaws. Just sometimes it's better to focus on the good traits and not the bad ones.'

I nodded my head in agreement. 'You're right about that. I can definitely say since I met you, my self-doubt has diminished.'

'I'm glad.'

I sat between his thighs with my back pressed into his firm chest, and we watched the sun sink behind the waterfront mansions while our hands remained threaded. He pecked me gently on the nape of my neck, then rested his chin on my shoulder.

***

Later that night, after passionate sex, we lay cuddled up in Patrick's gigantic bed – my arms wrapped around his neck, and his arms around my waist. I listened to the sound of his steady breath and relished the tickle of his eyelashes on my cheek while our heads nuzzled together. I was so happy that it brought tears to my eyes; my heart had never felt so warm and whole.

He kissed my forehead. 'Imagine if we died like this together,' he said in a soft romantic voice as his hand locked with mine.

I laughed. 'One day, we might.'

About the Author

Coral A. Ward lives in Noosa, Australia, with her family and pet staffie that resembles Winnie the Pooh. Her bedroom walls are pink, and she has a penchant for collecting French-styled lamps. One of her favourite things to do in her downtime from studying Law or working as an administration officer, is snuggling on the couch while watching a rom-com movie. Coral put her degree in Creative Writing to good use by writing her debut contemporary-romance novel: A *Slice of You,* and plans to write many more heartfelt romance books with a hint of comedy.

To learn more, follow Coral on Instagram and Facebook: @coralawardauthor